Trees for the Forest

Denise Siegel

Published by

Wyrd Sisters

Dedicated to:

Arthur Jerome Siegel
&
Murel Dean Phillips

ONE

A solar flare six months earlier had caused a new wave of the Skeleton Plague. For some reason, Ira and I were immune - maybe it was good genetics, or a vigilant use of our UV suits, or maybe the black-market vitamin supplements Ira wrangled had helped. I hated driving through the streets of D.C. during high alerts, watching the walking skeletons being marched to some hidden medical facility.

The government said Skeleton Plague was communicable, but I knew better; it was an autoimmune disease. The scientific community was still debating its genesis and treatability, but that was it. We knew something was turning white blood cells into cannibalistic machines, whether it was UV-B or UV-A rays or some other solar radiation mixed with pollution.

The drive to Digibio was slow. The streets were blocked. Traffic was detoured to provide plague victims with some privacy. Even still, I'd catch a band of them marching in the gaps between buildings, or at the end of blocked streets, and it was hard not to stare. They looked like death. Pale and so emaciated even the sockets of their eyes protruded through their thin skin. They were reminders of the great nothing at the end of suffering.

I refocused. Thinking about all the ills of the world did no good. I had no power. I was small and the world had far too many problems for me to begin to tackle. All anyone could do was try and enjoy this life and focus on the here and now. The earth had survived a lot of things. We had somehow managed to get through dark periods in human history. Someday there would be a cure for Skeleton Plague. The world would balance. Europe, Asia, Africa, Central and South America would come back to life and flourish. I had to believe that somehow we'd prevail. We always did.

TWO

For three months I had worked at Digibio Technologies, but each day the security guard double-checked my ID badge, ran a series of computer checks and called my supervisor, Geraldine Shumaker. Today was no exception. A line of cars was forming behind me at the gate. It was embarrassing.

I gave the guard my name, again. "Psyche Hershenbaum."

After a brief conversation with my supervisor, the guard nodded and started, "You'll be parking in..."

"Space 1133," I said. He glared with awe, as if I were a voodoo queen. I chuckled at the thought of having any vexing paranormal power, as if there were anything more than routine going on. But in the past 20 years the world had changed from rational to reactionary to hysterically religious, overrun with True Believers who saw the hand of God in each and every mundane transaction. Some "pilgrims" had even trekked into the shattered ghost cities - despite contamination warnings issued from scientists -- to see the Virgin Mary on the side of broken-down buildings, at the behest of the national church, The Wrath of God Inc., run by Jessie and Sandy Applegate. Later, of course, these pilgrims died of plague or UV exposure. To me, there was nothing more evil than the Applegates' fanatical right-wing church. They prodded their terrified flock into the slaughterhouse in the name of salvation.

Being a newbie at Digibio, it was a long walk to the elevators and even further through the bowels of the sub-city where I worked in the chlorophyll research lab. There were thirty-five cameras I had spotted so far. Heaven knew how many more were too hidden to see.

The building itself wasn't much to look at, inside or out. Cold industrial steel bones, concrete flesh and mirrored glass with eyes always watching from the side you couldn't see.

Through the labyrinth of hallways I contemplated the heavy security. Most of my research had been in and for universities. I hadn't worked in the corporate sector much, but I had worked briefly for two other companies, and their security was nothing like Digibio's -- a gate, a few security personnel and a couple of cameras mounted in the parking structure.

Digibio made no sense. Information was not shared between departments or scientists. This was the most peculiar facet of the work and the company itself. It went against all ordinary scientific protocol, with the potential side effect of slowing down or quashing advancement. Why isolate each sector with different department heads and keep researchers on micro-projects for years without any idea of what or why they were researching?

I was limited to the reproduction of chlorophyll in genetically altered plants. At first, my suspicion was that Digibio was trying to produce seeds and rhizomes strong enough to stay mutation-free. After the great floods in the Midwest, farmers couldn't produce edible corn or wheat because the loss of ozone resulted in high levels of radiation. A hearty, edible plant could be extremely valuable as a staple food if it were UV-resistant. And if Digibio had total control, it would reap all the financial rewards. But this line of logic quickly broke down. The population was rapidly decreasing and it made no sense to be so clandestine and elaborate when there was little or no competition.

I finally got to the bio-sector iris scan and put my chin on the rest. The beam stung. I hated those things. There were fingerprint scans and so many other ways to do the same thing without causing pain. Scans were even installed at the food court, the only common area, where they were completely redundant. It bordered on sadistic.

Ira had started calling me Sleeping Beauty because of my project ignorance. It was a clumsy metaphor. The sleeping part, maybe, but I had no illusions of being a beauty. I was made acutely aware of this as far back as I could remember. Some insults haunted me into adulthood -- hooknose, horsey face, sack of bones and, of course, the universal favorite, kike. With a name like Psyche Hershenbaum, there was no hiding Jewish roots.

I clocked in as Geraldine walked by and nodded at me. It was eight in the morning and back to the grind, repeating the same experiment on the manufacturing of chlorophyll in Digibio's patented rapid-growth Planimal. A hybrid engineered by splicing cactus, cockroach and rat genes, it was vital that the cells stood up to intense ultraviolet rays, and so far my research had yielded mixed results. I suspected the ratio of genetic ingredients needed to be tweaked and had filed a report with Geraldine about this opinion, but there had been no acknowledgment of my findings thus far.

Later that day, just after getting back from lunch, Geraldine tapped my shoulder. "Follow me," she said.

For such a tiny woman, Geraldine's clip was hard for me to keep up with. When we reached the digi-block, Geraldine put a hand in front of the scanner, telling the computer, "Meeting with Paul Lamont, section 5-a, special privileges extended to Psyche Hershenbaum, code number 771133."

"Iris scan indicated," the computer responded, and we put our faces to its lens.

The tension in my neck squirmed into knots. We took the elevator to corporate headquarters in the main building. Few employees had ever seen the inside of the above-ground building -- only those with special clearance, heads of departments and corporate-business types. Geraldine was fidgeting and didn't say a word. It made me nervous.

An armed guard met us outside the elevator and took us to the boardroom. A plaque outside read Trilateral Room. This was it. *The* it. The place where all company decisions were made. Where careers ended, lives were ruined or made. I took a deep breath.

The guard keyed the wall. It opened.

Lamont, the head scientist, smiled and extended his hand. I let out a breath when my palm met his. And even though he said, "Good to meet you, Psyche. Geraldine has nothing but praise for your work," with a twinkle and charm that should have made me feel as though I were at a dinner party, I felt very uneasy.

Paul was uncannily handsome -- a tall man with a full head of silver-streaked hair, sharp features and wolf-like sky blue eyes with a disarmingly warm smile. As I studied his face, my eyes wandered to a spot of dried blood on his chin from what looked like a shaving accident.

"Nice to meet you, too, Mr. Lamont," I returned. He smiled again and turned to shake Geraldine's hand. They exchanged small talk and his smile faded for a moment before he pointed us to our seats at the boardroom table.

He punched some numbers into his wristcom and, reading the screen, said to me, "Graduated six years into school with your doctorate. Something of a prodigy, aren't you?"

"No, not really, I just took an extra course load, worked hard and finished a few years early."

"Modest." He winked. "We like that in our researchers. What were you, twenty four?"

"Yes, sir."

"So you're thirty now?"

I nodded. He looked at his wristcom again.

"My data shows your age among company scientists ranks in the fifteen percent group and your company seniority, ha, is so low it hasn't even been entered."

I smiled. "That explains why the guard at the gate never knows I'm an employee."

Lamont lifted his wristcom and spoke into it, "Computer upload Psyche Hershenbaum's system files into the main frame." Paul turned back to me and said, "All taken care of."

The wall opened. Several men walked in tandem, huddled closely around someone I couldn't see until he sat down.

I gasped. It was the president. The current reigning President of the United States of America, Reginald Strauch, and to his right, his wife, Camille Pamela. My heart raced as it fell into my stomach.

They had the queer magnetism of power and an air of entitlement only a child born into a political dynasty could embody. It was as physical and real as gravity. Reginald's father, grandfather, paternal great-grandfather and great-great-grandfather had been Republican presidents – before FDR they'd been involved in politics as Southern Democrats. Some Democrats and Republicans argued for campaign finance reforms because the office had become nepotistic. People voted for names they had heard of. An ordinary candidate couldn't compete with the money an ancient dynasty had or could raise. Republicans made similar arguments against the Democratic family dynasty, the Blakes. Some far left of Washington's political center had gone as far as accusing these dynasties of cultivating a plutocratic oligarchy akin to the Caesars of ancient Rome. People argued America resembled feudal Europe, with corporations playing the role of the church during the Dark Ages by using their power to manipulate the president, who was now nothing more than a pawn of industry. This was not the America the forefathers had envisioned; changes were needed to preserve the spirit of our democracy, or the concept of America would blow away in the gust of corruption like a seed on the wind.

By the turn of the century, Americans were a dying peasant class drowning in debt. They had lost the plot and were mislead by advertising, double-talk and corporate/political naiveté. Ten years after the third Strauch was elected, there was talk of legislation to disqualify presidential candidates whose family history included political leaders, though of course this was knocked down -- not just because the Strauchs were again in power, but because most of Washington had familial roots in politics.

The faces around the boardroom table were a blur. All the lead scientists of the various departments, including Geraldine, were present, but I didn't know any of them. The only people I recognized were the Strauchs and Lamont.

Lamont was the founder and CEO of Digibio. He led the meeting. Publicly he was seen as an uncomfortable mix of scientist and businessman. He had first come to the media's attention when I was a child, for manufacturing organs to be used exclusively for wealthy people in need of transplants. His face decorated every major magazine and the ethics of such transplants sent a chill around the world. But despite an onslaught of criticism from nearly every religious leader in the world, his work continued to be funded by unspecified sources. In D.C., rumors of Strauch-dynasty support abounded but were largely dismissed because of the Strauchs' close connection to, and financial support of, The Wrath of God Inc.

After the obligatory introductions, President Strauch told the hovering swarm of Secret Service agents, "Take a hike. Go guard the corridor."

Lamont called the meeting to order. "There have been significant findings in the development of ultraviolet resistance in the patented Planimal Cell. Miss Psyche Hershenbaum has found variable mutations and, according to her paper, she estimates stability at ten years unless there is 'a significant restructuring of DNA.' We've brought Psyche here to explain her findings and illuminate us with her proposed solution. Which, I might add, looks very promising. Psyche, I turn the floor over to you."

"Thank you, sir." I wasn't prepared for a presentation, but my research had been hard-wired into my brain through repetition. I tried to steady my voice. "What I've seen in the experiments are multiple results from exposure. In some instances, the cells have shown little to no effect from increased ultraviolet light. In others, they've completely mutated. The range of change is so varied from one cell to the next that I think there is a very minute code problem in the non-coding RNA genes, which may be causing the mutations. But further study is needed."

Lamont interjected. "Please keep this simple, Psyche – layman's terms, please."

I nodded. "Right. Basically, I took it upon myself to isolate those cells which performed best under ultraviolet conditions. I was given permission from Mrs. Shumaker to deep-freeze the specimens for later study, and if everything checks out, I believe we can clone those cells and fix the problem."

"Well, that's a relief," President Strauch said. He glared at Lamont and with a wave of his hand said, "What are you waitin' for? Get your people on this right away."

Lamont smiled. "Yes, sir."

"OK, this meetin' is over," the President said, getting up from the table with his wife. "Well, boys, I've got some big fish to fry. I'll check in with you later." In seconds he disappeared in a swarm of suited men down the hallway.

The scientists were exiting when Lamont pulled me aside. "Excellent job. Thank you."

I wondered why there had been no warning about the meeting, but all I said was, "You're welcome, sir."

"Keep up the good work." He clicked through his teeth and walked out, leaving me alone with Geraldine.

The guards escorted us to the elevator. A sea of Strauch's Secret Service agents parted for Lamont and the two walked toward his office. The elevator doors shut.

What the hell was going on?

Why did the President of the United States of America care about my research or Digibio's production of the Planimal? The elevator felt uncomfortably silent. I tried to break the tension by saying to Geraldine, "That was a great honor, meeting President Strauch."

Geraldine's eyes met mine with a queer look I couldn't read. After a long, uncomfortable walk back to the lab, Geraldine said, "Very well done, Psyche. Go ahead and catalog the frozen samples then put them in the fridge for study tomorrow."

So that was it?

The rest of my day was devoted to freezing Planimal RNA. It had been a strange morning. Everything had taken a 180. I had to reevaluate my research and reorganize how my project was going to be handled, from catalogue samples to designing a new series of experiments.

There was one advantage to the fresh set of problems -- Geraldine let me go home early. When I arrived, Ira was sitting on the couch in his boxer shorts and dress socks, watching the news with a bale of rice treats. It looked as if he'd been there all day. Chi, our Himalayan, was draped over Ira's legs, belly up and fighting something in his dreams.

"Shouldn't you wake Chi? It looks like he's having a nightmare," I said.

"No, he's fine. It'll just confuse him," Ira said, turning up the screen's volume.

I scooped up Chi and sat next to Ira to watch the news.

"New York City has been devastated by this unforeseen monster. Shouldn't the NWS have warned of this killer hurricane?" anchorman/actor Bill Surnow queried. Shaky video footage from surveillance cameras around the city ran behind him. Buildings swayed in the high winds, and when water suddenly crashed through the streets, the camera went blue. "More after we take a break," a disembodied voice said.

I grabbed the cordless phone and dialed my mother, simultaneously asking Ira, "What's going on?"

"Didn't anyone tell you?"

I shook my head. "There's a busy signal."

"Yeah, I've been trying all day. They say the lines are down."

I dialed my mother's cell and waited as it endlessly rang.

Ira's voice cracked. "I've already tried that number, too."

The heroic New York that had survived terrorist attacks, plagues and earthquakes was now being washed out to sea. The images were gruesome and horrifying. I couldn't stop thinking about my mother's short white hair. Her hunched, feeble body and the familiar smell of her sandalwood oil, drowning.

The fear Mom had to have experienced, seeing the ocean pitched like a tray of water; the sound of bricks breaking, mortar splintering, glass shattering and people screaming.

Mom alone. Trapped in the brownstone.

Warren Street bursting with salt water, busting down the cobbled street, exploding 200-year-old row houses into broken brick walls with rocking chairs and baby cribs, sofas and teddy bears, pouring out of holes – everything taken by the water - men, women and children struggling to grab anything floating by to keep themselves steady in the raging flood. The water infested with rats and trash. The tide crashing hard against each new building it sought to destroy.

My home.

My mother.

I was outside myself.

It wasn't like me to cry. Even now the hot tightening in the deep of my throat was in a tunnel far away. I was frozen. Emotionally paralyzed. "I spoke to her yesterday. She's all right. Right? She's OK, isn't she?"

Ira moved gently across the sparse room and caught my hand in his. Its warmth momentarily penetrated my numbness.

The commercial break ended. A grim Surnow stood at the anchor desk to announce, "Early estimates for Hurricane Xavier include hundreds of thousands dead and many more missing. One source reported most of Brooklyn and Long Island shore entirely decimated. There is little hope the area will ever recover."

Surnow cut to a local reporter who was standing in the middle of an ER in Queens. "The hospitals are inundated with the injured. In Manhattan, F5 winds cracked and shattered windows, glass shards sharp as daggers hurtled in every direction. The scene is more gruesome than words can describe."

I dialed my mother, Miriam, again. Again, nothing. Mom's cell phone: "All circuits are busy." The university where she worked: "Your call cannot go through. Please hang up and dial again." I went through lists of friends and relatives, but to no avail.

I bottled up the urge to throw the phone across the room and instead demanded of Ira, "When?"

"Around noon the Weather Service started to see signs of a hurricane gathering..."

"But how?" I asked him.

"The conditions were just right off the coast of North Carolina..."

"But why? Nothing..." I stopped myself because my voice was starting to quiver. It was as if my cranium had cracked like the polar ice caps and they were melting so fast the water was drowning me. I raised my voice at Ira. "It's impossible. Nothing like this has ever happened, not so big, so fast."

Ira, who had arrived at my side to give comfort, retreated. "Take it easy, Psyche, everything is going to be alright." He said this with all the skill and assurance of a man who had never had to utter such words.

"Don't tell me to take it easy. And it's not going to be OK. My mother is missing. She's probably dead, and you have no answers. No one has answers." I grabbed my coat and headed toward the front door. Ira followed after me.

"Where are you going?"

"I need to think."

"You can't go out, it's dark and late."

But I darted past him and left. The storm that had hit New York was coming into town and it was cool and misty. Ira burst out the front door and ran after me. "It's dangerous."

"I need to be by myself." He tried to grab me, but I shook him off. "Please. Just leave me alone."

"When will you be back?" He pleaded. He looked concerned and confounded. In eight years I had never raised my voice or shed the smallest tear in front of him.

It was starting to drizzle. I wiped a gathered tear of rain from his cheek and said, "As soon as I can." A moment later I broke into a run and headed into a dark alley.

I felt a drop of water run down my face and I wasn't sure if it was me or the rain. It didn't matter. I roamed the streets dotted with city lanterns and sickly trees. The cold moon followed as if mocking my pain with a twisted snarl on her face. The rain halos around the street lamps tainted with memories of Brooklyn, things I tried to hold back but couldn't -- waving goodbye to my mom from the car as she stood on the stoop, never thinking it would be the last time I saw her. This image I couldn't shake, no matter how long or far I walked.

I hadn't noticed time slipping by or the pounding of my footsteps or the chill of the rain soaking through me until I hit the Potomac and I stared at the obstacle it posed on my quest to lose myself. I had walked at least five miles, and I knew I had to get back before Ira started a vain attempt to find me. It felt like the edge of the earth and the edge of time. I was crashing and splintering like a fine piece of porcelain hitting concrete.

And then I saw them. A woman about my age, in her early thirties, holding a small, limp girl in her arms and struggling to walk the rain-slicked stairs.

Logic told me not to -- they could have been afflicted with some new plague, or a crime may have been taking place, but I ran toward them. Something compelled me. And for the first time I can remember, I discarded logic and apathy.

By the time I got to them the mother was struggling to put her dying child into the car. She was about to lay the girl on the sidewalk to open the door when I took her from the woman's hands. She looked at me as if I had always been there, like some sort of guardian angel. We said nothing. She opened the door and I slid the girl into the back seat. Seconds later the woman was backing out of the driveway, barely getting the driver's side door fully closed as she sped down the street.

On the way home I wondered about them, whether the mother had gotten the girl to a hospital in time, if the girl would survive. Helping them had, for a moment, made me feel a little less helpless. And I treasured that feeling through my personal darkness.

Ira was fully dressed and ready to start his search when I let myself in. It looked like he had been crying. The flatscreen behind him was a cacophony of devastation.

"If I wasn't so happy to see you I'd strangle you right now," he said, grabbing me.

"I'm not a child."

"And what? You didn't think I'd be worried? Why are you punishing me like this?"

"This isn't about you, Ira."

"Yes, it is. It's about you not letting me in. I want to help you, but you make it impossible."

I nodded. He put his arms around me and held me until I couldn't be held any longer without breaking down again. "I'm sorry," I said.

The news cut to a clip from a press conference with none other than Paul Lamont. I sat down to watch.

Lamont looked too put together. He wore a suit that would cost an average person a year's wages. He was unnaturally relaxed for the circumstances. "There has been a rush to judgment by the scientific community about the Atlantic's rise in temperature and climate change. For years I've pored over countless studies, reviewed thousands of reports and culled through all the supposed proof. I've never found a correlation. The evidence is overwhelming for a natural shift in the Earth's climate. This has occurred many times before human history. It's unfortunate that we happen to be living during one of these intense global changes."

I yelled at the screen. "Motherfucker! That one, just one study, was done by oil companies."

Lamont then took a question from Surnow. "What about the ozone hole?"

Lamont responded, "Another natural phenomena caused by radiation imitated during solar storms. We've seen evidence of holes before in layers of igneous rock. And it's been repairing itself over the past forty years."

"Bullshit," I said.

Ira cautioned me. "Just hold on a minute."

Surnow asked his followup. "Are you suggesting all the horrible tragedies that have occurred over the past 40 years are simply a result of natural earth changes?"

"Absolutely," Lamont said. He waived away any further questions and left the podium.

Ira sat down beside me. "I saw it this afternoon, but I don't get why they're still trying to cover up the climate change thing when it's been proven countless times."

I hit the rewind button and replayed Lamont's comments, freezing a medium shot of him and examining it carefully. "There's something strange about this. I was taken in to see him this morning at work."

A curious Ira walked back in. "You were?"

"Strauch was there, too."

"The president was at Digibio?"

I continued to stare at the screen, trying to determine what exactly was different about Paul Lamont. Was his hair a little longer? I went through the catalogue of images fresh in my mind from the boardroom meeting. Yes. But without a physical picture, I couldn't be sure. His clothes were obviously different. The suit most patently was not something he would wear to work. Of course he must have changed. Then I noted something that confirmed my suspicion.

"This was prerecorded," I said.

"What makes you think that?"

"When I saw him this morning he had a cut on chin." I paused the image and zoomed closer, pointing to his chin. "There's nothing there."

Ira squinted. "They knew this would happen."

"And they didn't give us any warning."

"But why?" he asked.

I shook my head. "I can't think about it right now."

THREE

Gale-force winds and thunder, garbage cans crashing over, objects slamming into walls and fences, and Ira slept through all of it like a kitten cuddling at his mother's breast. But not me. My mind and heart were on fire.

Chi followed me, meowing for treats. It was cold downstairs. The angry wind forced its way through door and window cracks. I grabbed Ira's ratty old sweater, the first present I had given him. It was the only thing left from that period of his life, perhaps a small reminder of how far he'd come since the penitentiary. I barely knew him then. We had dated about a year. He told me he worked for an internet research corporation, a consumer watchdog group that kept an eye on the defense department. It had some crazy name I forcibly forgot.

There was never any question. I was instantly in love and hopelessly naive about human nature. Turned out he was part of a watchdog group of hackers who stole classified information and sold it to reporters for a premium. To him it was noble: the people had a right to know, and he had a right to make a living. Really, it was closest to intellectual prostitution, although he saw himself as a 21st-century Robin Hood. He could have been building something great instead of hunting down and exploiting government weakness. But who was I to judge? I knew his heart was good and his intentions were pure. And I loved him. He loved me. So I waited.

We avoided talking about it. And if we had to refer to that period there was a code, words that lessened the pain or importance for both of us. Anything to make it less real than it was. Usually, if I referred to it, I said, "When you lived in the country."

He usually said, "During that time."

When I was hired at Digibio, they ran a background check. Nothing came up in the preliminary. A month later they revoked access to anything but the chlorophyll research lab and the cafeteria. But it didn't really bother me.

The kettle was singing. Only one bag of chamomile left; I hoped it would help put me in a coma. And I could wake tomorrow discovering it had all been a horrible nightmare.

The lights browned. The drawer had only three emergency candles left from the previous storm, which had just ended two weeks prior. It lasted thirty-five days straight and the power had consistently gone out during peak hours. According to the weatherman, another hurricane was due to hit North Carolina. But other than the historic value, there was nothing there. Both Carolinas were dead -- the states didn't have money for scrims, and except for folklore about people surviving off the land in the forest, there wasn't a soul within a hundred miles of New York or D.C. And now all that was left was D.C. There were reports of a smattering of survivors in Seattle, but the numbers were low.

I walked to the sofa and stared out the window, sipping my tea. Chi sat on my lap. The rain was fierce and reminded me of New York, in my mother's old brownstone. There had been a very bad storm when I was ten. We had both awakened for different reasons. The thunder and lightning had cast shadows of monsters on the wall, scaring me out of the room.

Meanwhile, Mom contended with a real beast. She was setting buckets all over the living room to catch the water oozing out of the fissures and cracks in the ceiling. Later, I found out she had been afraid the whole damn roof was going to cave in on us. But at the time she pretended it was a game – a fun thing to do together. She had me searching for bowls, buckets and hats, until each little fissure was represented on the hardwood floor. And when a bucket would fill, she would grab one of the mongrel cups or bowls from my loot while pouring the bucket's contents into the kitchen sink and then dutifully replacing them.

But even though she presented a calm, rational exterior, I knew something was very wrong. And I remember admiring her. She was fearless, capable and godlike. Nothing could harm me with her protection. She was able to keep the world away with her mind. Her brilliance was so powerful it worked on everyone who neared her circle of influence.

But that night I saw panic when she didn't know I was watching. It was complicated, seeing it and not wanting to see it. So I chose to believe the buckets were a game, knowing it was a protective lie - a lie - affirming her love for me.

The streetlights flickered in the rain. Some of the UV scrims down the block looked as if they'd been sliced by a colossal box-cutter. They flapped in the wind like serpent-shaped kites.

D.C. was tolerable. It was cleaner than New York and had a much more reliable and quick-acting body pickup service. New York just had Corner Hut Drop-Off Centers, which were always teeming with mutant flies and reeked of decaying flesh no matter how often the workers cleaned them out. It was an ineffectual system and a health hazard. But you hardly ever saw the dead on the streets here in D.C.

Maybe it was a bit healthier here, but I preferred New York. It felt more like an old city, with people doing all different sorts of things besides just working for the government or on some government-related project. More than anything it was my connection to a personal history I missed. Even if New York barely resembled the one of my youth, even if it never snowed anymore and the winters felt like warm fall days from childhood. I knew it. Somewhere under its fading, wilting petals, the stem was the same.

And despite the elaborate scrim maze providing the best UV protection in the world (or so we were told by our government), I had preferred shabby New York. If only I could have gotten my mother to move. But that was like asking lead to turn into gold. And even though it got tiresome - always wearing a protection suit or carrying a UV umbrella or coating my skin with titanium dioxide, which made me and my mom break out like hormonal teenagers if we so much as looked at the stuff - she would hear nothing of the virtues of my new city. She desperately loved all that was left of New York.

On the steps of the apartment building across the street a black shape moved. It was big enough to be a person but could have been a box or a piece of furniture left out for trash pickup that was instead caught in the gale-force wind. Most likely it was one of the infected. A crack of lightning lit the street clearly and I saw the woman. Blood oozed from everywhere. She was in the last throes of the Skeleton Plague - a tragic sight to witness. She had probably escaped quarantine to try and see her family one last time, but either they couldn't open the door or they thought they'd risk exposing everyone in their building. No final goodbye, just people crying behind glass as they watched their loved one go from a pale skeleton to one blue-black bruise with blood oozing from her pores.

To me this was the most heinous lie our government had perpetrated until today. I could never understand why they did this. I suppose it was a way to separate out the sick and do research on them. But it hardly mattered anymore. If New York were gone, it wouldn't be long before something came for D.C.

I called the health department and a few minutes later I saw a hazmat team take the body away. No fanfare, no ceremony. Life reduced to inconvenient garbage. It hadn't always been like that. I could almost remember a different time. Mom told me crazy stories about her childhood and what seemed like an Edenic period at the turn of the century. I never really believed her until I was in college and studied history. They thought they had it bad then.

When I first started dating Ira, I brought him to Columbia to meet my mom for lunch. We decided to stay afterward to see a documentary she was showing for her sociology class. Ira and I both burst into laughter after just a few minutes of the film. It looked so ridiculously naïve: their biggest worry was crime. What was it? A thousand people died each year from gun violence? Something remarkable like that. I couldn't believe it was real, and Mom nearly kicked us out because some of the supposedly "shocking" statistics being thrown out about the death rate and natural-disaster escalation seemed like a statistic seen on one good day. A year? It was shocking. Shockingly cushy and they were shockingly lucky and shockingly irresponsible and shockingly ignorant. It was hilarious. But Mom didn't think so, and it took a while for Ira to live down the incident and make up for his "insensitive behavior." I had been the one making all the noise but, being her daughter, it was OK for me.

His saving grace was his Jewishness. No way mother would have forgiven him if he were a gentile. Not that she was religious. Try the exact opposite. She passionately hated any and all organized religions and pooh-poohed all forms of spirituality. So the emphasis on being Jewish always struck me as bizarre. She explained her obsession as a desire to keep the genetic lineage alive. Why that was important in my case was silly since I couldn't bear children - nor could more than half of all New Yorkers, due to our parents' and our own radiation or UV exposure - but she kept her hopes up.

When I was a teenager, my rebellious phase included going to temple with my orthodox friend, Rachael. You'd think I was found plotting to kill the Pope. Even then my mom probably wouldn't have been so angry because she hated the Pope as much as all religious leaders. To her they were devils poisoning minds and using fear to enslave the masses. The first time I got a six-hour lecture about the evils of organized religion and a history lesson about the estimated quarter of the women's population of Europe who were brutally murdered by the Catholic church during the Dark Ages.

The next day was a four-hour lecture on the raping, killing and pillaging of the matriarchal temples of the original Jewish people (the temples were dedicated to Astarte and later, in an obvious political move, she was turned into the demon Ashtoreth in the Bible) by the followers of Jehovah who later became modern Jews. Then came the lecture about the slaughter of Christians and Jews by Muslims and the rise of terrorism in the Middle East at the turn of the century - tens of thousands were murdered in God's name as revolutions spread like a virus. She was sure to point out the irony that they were all fighting over the same god, Jehovah.

The next week was devoted to the Hindus and other so-called Pagan religions who didn't fight over the politics or names of gods, because to them, "all gods are one." So she told me that if I were going to study any religion, the only kind - in her opinion - worth its salt were the shamanistic traditions of either old Europe or the Americas. But as far as she knew, all those teachings had been wiped out by genocide and political warfare. So being a shaman was a dangerous business, and she didn't condone that, either. Best to stay with science, the functional universe and the now. Religion was too messy, spirituality too dodgy and philosophically too abstract to be useful. These feelings, Miriam claimed, came from studying sociology. But I don't think the cause of religion was helped when her rabbi father walked out on her orthodox mother, who later denounced Jehovah as a god who only cared for selfish men.

So in my family, God was a dirty word used to divide families and punish mothers. I couldn't help picking up a distaste for Him after watching my favorite biology professor's research project shut down by the university because of pressure from Jessie and Sandy Applegates' Wrath of God Inc. Biological waste was used in some of the experiments, and this meant there was some fetal tissue. Hordes of fundamentalist Christian zealots picketed and screamed for months on campus. The university had been pretty good about ignoring them until one strapped a bomb to his back and blew up the lab.

        The Wrath of God Inc. denounced the suicide bomber once the university slapped a lawsuit on them; and, of course, they weaseled out of that because they practically owned the U.S. They were the biggest religion in the world - what was left of the world, anyway. My mother called them "a twisted hip-hop carnival of Christ." They made me sick, and if Mom wasn't enough to turn me against religion, their very existence shut, locked and buried any religious curiosity in me.

FOUR

The next morning, Ira cooked grits for breakfast. I didn't particularly like them, but had gotten used to the taste during the last food shortage. "Why do you think President Strauch was at the board meeting?"

Ira shook his head. "Don't know, but I could ask around."

"Who would you ask? One of the guys you lived in the country with?"

Ira pushed a strand of his shoulder-length hair away and nodded. "And?"

"And you know what I think about that."

He poured his gruesome concoction into two bowls and threw spoons into the corn swamps. "My friends are just a sorry bunch of geeky hackers who got caught being hackers. I don't see why you freak out every time I…"

"Forget it."

"Psyche, we need to know. This is big. I can feel it." He handed me breakfast and walked past with his, through the living room and toward the basement.

"Where are you going?"

"To get to the bottom of it."

"No." I chased him down the stairs. "Stop!"

He ignored me and went straight to his terminal and linked up. "Don't worry. Malone showed me where I went wrong."

"Really? When did he instruct you, before or after he disappeared?"

He strapped on the goggles. "Bite me."

"I won't be able to if you're one of the hundreds of hackers who evaporate into thin air every year."

"He's not dead." He waited for this to sink in. "Trust me." And then put his nose plugs in and glared at me. "If either one of us are going to continue living, we have to know how to play this."

I frowned. He was right. There was every indication Digibio was connected to a black operation or it was a cover for one.

Certainly the company was taking every precaution against leaks, even with their own scientists. Now the importance of my research had put me on their radar, and leaving the company would be dangerous. I grimaced and went back upstairs to track down information about my mother.

In the living room I clicked on the screen. The hurricane had settled into a tropical thunderstorm. Several hundred people were stuck on top of a high-rise in downtown Manhattan. The water was rising around them. A rescue helicopter was pulling up a woman and her baby; when the winds changed, the basket cracked against a satellite dish, twisting around the base. The helicopter sputtered and whined, crashing into the water. A crack of lighting singed the sky and the picture blew into digital noise.

My hands went numb. I was in the throes of an anxiety attack. Breathe. Just breathe. Chi brushed my leg and followed me to the sofa, where I sat for a moment, trying to shake things off. He jumped on me as if he knew I needed him. "Thank you," I whispered.

I dialed my mother. An error message from a computer-generated voice said, "All systems down."

A number flashed on the bottom of the TV. It had been set up by the Red Cross for relatives of the missing, the injured and the dead. After a few tries I got through to a computer and punched in my mother's name. The recorded voice said, "Miriam Johanna Hershenbaum is reported injured and being treated at St. Mary's Hospital. The number there is 3-569-987-4500."

After dozens of attempts to get through to the hospital, I finally tracked down my mother's ward. The nurse asked, "Are you family?"

"Her daughter," I said.

"Hold a moment, I'll look up her chart." Bad electronica, wallpaper posturing itself as music, rubbed my nerves raw for fifteen agonizing minutes that felt more like fifteen days. The nurse came back on. "I'm sorry but she passed away this morning. The cause was internal hemorrhaging."

"But the com..."

The nurse interrupted, "I'll forward your call to the morgue."

My feet and hands turned to ice and snow clouded my vision like an old, broken TV. The last time I talked to Mom she was more animated than she had been in years. Her last paper had been nominated for a prize.

The man at the morgue was gruff – hostile, really. He answered with a curt, "Yeah?" In the background I heard voices and metallic screeches, things bumping and thudding.

I sputtered out, "My, my, mother her..."

"Name?" he said.

"Her name i..."

"Yeah, her name. I'm busy here."

"Have some compassion."

"No time for that, I can't tag bodies fast enough."

"I'm sorry."

"Whatever." The phone muffled while he screamed orders. When he came back I managed mom's name. "You got an out-of-town funeral home set up?"

"Excuse me?" I said.

He sighed. "A place to ship her."

"I'll have to arrange that."

"Goddamn it. The nurse just put you through, then, huh?"

"Yes."

"You'll have to call back." A click, then silence.

Life and death had become an inconvenience - a mark on a piece of paper, a check on a form. A wooden box stuffed with the anonymous shipped to the anonymous. No time to look back, no energy to acknowledge our common humanity. People were as sick as the planet. Both cause and effect of the cancer created by technology. And this made me grieve for more than just my mom. I grieved for all the now-mythical creatures that once roamed the earth, for a time when people could bask in the sun without being burned alive by it.

For the first time, I felt the pain of the Earth itself, and the tears of all who had loved this planet like their own mother. I wept for all we had lost. Maybe it was easier to weep for the world because mom was all I ever had and I couldn't let myself face being orphaned in this hostile world. One made even more hostile and violent, evil and sick by my latest discovery. We hadn't been unwilling victims. We created this. Our government had vigorously participated and ignored the ecological disaster to come out of greed. They had, in effect, murdered all life and the planet herself.

So this was humanity's legacy? Whatever future alien intelligence discovers this barren planet would know only the worst parts of us, the crazy, out-of-control monkeys whose brains were eminently clever and whose hearts were shriveled from lack of wisdom and maturity.

The born-again Christians had been right - this had been the end of days, but they had brought the rapture and no second coming. No Christ, no Jesus had ever appeared. Perhaps He had thought better of wasting the kingdom of heaven by crowding it with His sick followers. Perhaps He was as disgusted as I was and He decided to let them rot in the cesspool they had created.

Perhaps if there were gods, this was heaven's insurrection and the Bible had not just been used on earth for political gain to subjugate humanity, but served the same purpose in the heavens by a trickster god. Maybe Jehovah had better access to us because of our small monkey minds, which could only comprehend viciousness, not the true Creator's unconditional love.

All these years I had looked through microscopes and marveled at the beautiful complexity starting with cells, then atoms and electrons and quarks. My heart would sing with praise for the intelligence behind it all. A peek at the night sky between the scrims was enough to confirm there was so much more to the universe than I could ever pretend to understand. I was less than a speck in the vastness of all that was, with its tapestry of layers in every direction, from the smallest to the largest, with its simultaneity of time to the unquantifiable infinity of dimensions. There was no way any religion on earth, interpreted through our smallnesss, could grasp even a wisp of the truth. This was the one thing I was ever sure of. Atheism had been the bone my mother chewed on, but this was mine.

Anyone who claimed to have the answers was either a liar or completely deluded. We could only hope to find a tiny key for personal development. All great spiritual leaders had focused on things we could control, such as our emotions, our minds. The lessons of holy men like Jesus, Buddha, Mohammed and countless others were forgiveness, love, respect, kindness, compassion. And their teachings were always misused, misrepresented and misunderstood by those who sought power in the selling of redemption.

The Applegates were such people. The type to pervert the message of a spiritual genius into a set of proscribed rules, laws and doctrines that had nothing to do with the true meaning of the message but, rather, were a way to control others through fear and intimidation while pretending to offer salvation. The Applegates hadn't been the first to do this, just the most recent and most extreme. They miniaturized all others with a bloated circus of uneducated, infantile literalism and corporate greed, crushing all other major religions through sheer aggressive proselytizing, arrogance and war.

Maybe Jehovah had appeared to the terror-stricken Jews wandering the ancient desert and demanded absolute and total loyalty to Him before the true God had a chance to sweep down and emancipate our sad little monkey brains from our shame and humanness. Maybe Jehovah was a trickster god who really meant to plant the seeds of destruction and had been working the whole time for it so we might be forever be enslaved to Him. In the short period of time he showed up, the world had quickly gone to shit. And of all the historical forms of God, He was the only one who claimed singularity and obedience to just Him. It was He who inspired people to kill over His name alone. It was He who ruled with the iron fist of fear.

Perhaps the Garden of Eden symbolized the Edenic period before He showed up, when the world had been matriarchal and the people had worshiped all of creation, both feminine and masculine. Perhaps He was the collective gestalt of the wandering men kicked out of their tribe for crimes against humanity, made real by their worship and forced on their people through rape, destruction and pillaging of the ancient temples and their women. Perhaps He was more akin to an angry god of warring gangster men hell-bent on taking over the turf of the Middle East, and not the true God after all.

Maybe the true God was far too complex to reveal Itself to us in Its truth. The Cabala, which predates Jehovah and is one of the oldest theological systems of mankind, has two pillars on its tree of life, one feminine and one masculine. Beyond the highest point of our understanding lies Kether, beyond an unfathomable gulf where the true majesty of the Creator lives. The gulf represents our inability to understand the Creator, too powerful for our minds and perhaps even not advisable to access with our limited capacities; like plugging a computer into the sun, all our circuits would fry. This is why I gave up trying to understand these things so long ago, not just for my mother's sake, but because I knew I wasn't capable. I could only look into a microscope and, using what powers of mind and concentration

I had, help humanity take one more baby step in its database of knowledge.

But now I had to do something, not just curl into a little ball as I had so many times before.

Ira came leaping upstairs, panting and carrying a stack of papers. His dark eyes looked like smoldering charcoals. "Check it out," he said, throwing the papers on the coffee table.

There was a strange stillness inside and a chill as I read the first line: Classified - Black Midnight - Operation Environ - Top Secret. I scowled at him. "If they find out..."

"I didn't leave a crumb behind."

A thud in the kitchen startled me. "What was that?"

Ira poked his head around the corner. "Nothing. Just the cat." He sat beside me and grabbed my hand. "You're really scared, huh?"

I nodded.

"I know what I'm doing," he whispered. "I would never do anything to put you in jeopardy."

"I'm worried about you, not me," I said. "Your involvement with me already makes you a target, and now this. They still need me, but they could use you."

Ira rubbed the tense muscles at the back of my neck. I tried to allow myself to relax, but it wasn't working and he gave up. "Malone is the one who modified the old firewall system for the Department of Defense and set up their encryption codes. It's the paradigm for all private-sector and government computer systems."

I pulled away and stared hard at him. "And how do you know that?"

"You don't want that answer." He picked up the first sheet, the one I had abandoned, and said, "Just read it."

There were a bunch of codes, scrambled numbers and then the text unfolded before my eyes: "Global warming refuge - Planimal structure, self-sustaining, nano technology, computer system merged in cellular structure - read: self repairing structure, internal and external monitoring systems, controlled sustained climate, feeding - chlorophyll based, capable of conversion – omnivorous - unsolved reaction to excessive ultraviolet – update - securing usable specimens."

I gasped. "Oh my God. They're using my research to perfect an escape hatch."

"When did you start believing in God?" Ira quipped.

I pointed to a line. "What's this?" It read:

"Geneco – transported - 300 strong."

Ira shook his head. "Some kind of company code. I haven't had a chance to decipher all of it."

I continued to read: "Mars - unattainable, colonization costs prohibitive, risk factors too high, conversion of climate unalterable. CODE 5 ALERT - life unsustainable. CDC reports malaria outbreak is uncontainable on East Coast - vaccination prohibitive - estimation 5 million deaths - Department of Agriculture - crop mutation, pestilence and flooding of Project Northern Planes - estimation 10-15 million deaths due to lack of resources - NWS predicts: volatile hurricane conditions off the Eastern Seaboard – Ninety-eight percent probability of total or near total devastation to NYC. Escalation of F5 tornadoes across the middle wasteland expected to wipe out remaining pockets of life."

I couldn't believe what I was reading. The horror blazed through me. "Extinction."

He frowned. "There are entries dating back to the turn of the century."

"Impossible. You must have read the stats wrong," I said.

"No. If you finish reading you'll find references to the inception of the Final Plan, as it's referred to in the documents, going back to the spring of 2002. The Final Plan entries became very active just before the war." Ira searched through the documents. "It reads: Project Pipeline - security threatened. Deposing King I. going ahead without little brother roundtable or slick economy is belly up."

"Read it again," I said.

He passed me the paper. "It's a lot to absorb."

"Is this old Pentagon?" I asked.

"No. I pulled this from the Strauch Dynasty's hard drive. It was in an encrypted reference log which I traced through their web host."

"So this is private information?" I asked. He nodded. "Did you check files at the CDC or the NWS? Or any government sites?"

"Yeah, there's a suspicious lack of information on any of them," Ira said.

"Fuck. They're lunatics."

Ira stopped for a moment to smile at my feisty new attitude and then continued, "I found references to Lamont dating back twenty years or more. And some turn-of-the-century data has reference to the Mole Man. I think its code for the guy who was vice president during Strauch 2's reign. He was integral to the Final Plan's development and instituted the groundwork, from what I could tell."

"So you're implying that this group of rich, powerful plutocrats formed a cabal to protect their own personal wealth. And they consciously knew their plan would destroy life on earth?"

"I'm not implying it. I'm stating a fact. It cost too much to reverse the trend, so why not squeeze every last remaining bit of gold out and live like kings until the end?" he said.

"What about their kids? Their grandkids?"

"That's what Digibio is for. I don't know exactly how the Environ functions, but I do know it's a self-sustaining biosphere. And it's their way out. The foxhole or bomb shelter, so to speak, for the ecological disaster they knew they were creating. They kept it away from government agencies for obvious reasons - a military coup, or a citizen uprising if it ever went public. I also found a partial encoded list of those they deigned worthy enough to live," he said.

I covered my face and rubbed my temples. "How big is the Environ?"

"Don't know."

"Where is it? How many people are going inside?" I asked.

Ira shook his head. "I couldn't find those details. Digibio isn't connected to the net."

"But we have an internet research room."

"Tried it. Those are separate search vehicles only. Not hooked up to the mainframe," he said.

Ira walked into the kitchen and poured himself a cold cup of coffee. "From as early as the 1980s there were rumors about the Buildaburgers and a secret project known as MJ12. I don't know much about it - the information was always sketchy and contradicted itself - but one thread ran through it." He walked back into the living room with his mug. "There was a group of powerful plutocrats, extremely wealthy people who secretly controlled the world governments. Historically the theory was always blown off as a..."

"Conspiracy theory, I know." I stopped to push at the crook of my neck to work out a knot steadily growing there. "The Environ, the Final Plane, none of it makes sense. Why would a group of people who thrive on having power over others knowingly destroy their own kingdom, so to speak?"

Ira chortled from behind me. "You really don't get it?"

I shifted positions to make sure he got a good look at the indignation on my face. "No, I don't. How could I? It's not logical."

"Psyche, it's perfectly logical. Those kind of guys only care about money and power, right here and now. None of them gave a shit about some far distant future because they weren't going to be personally living in it. It was an abstract problem for someone else to solve." I arched my eyebrow and stared critically at him, letting him know I still couldn't believe him or it. "Don't look at me like that," he said.

"Like what?"

"That's the problem Psyche, you think everyone is like you. You've lived in a safe world of ideas where empirical data and logical conclusions have been elevated to the status of demigods."

"It's not that I don't believe you or the facts, because they're sitting right here in front of me. It's just that I can't believe anyone would do something so stupid."

"Yeah, well, people do stupid things all the time. Especially politicians," he replied. "Denial has definitely worked to their advantage."

"No. It goes way beyond that. A person in their right mind could never conceive of this. Greed so perversely blind that it's mutated into ecological disaster and genocide. The scale of this atrocity is mind-boggling."

I paged through more of Ira's research. There was another reference to the Environ, one that said they expected to secure a solution to their problem and would soon inhabit. "How long, do you think, the Environ could sustain life?"

"Who knows? They're probably hoping it's just long enough for the problem to go away, and then..."

I cut him off. "Then what? They'll have everything - which will be nothing - all to themselves?" I was furious. I just wanted to stand on the stairs of the Capitol and scream. I imagined the joy and relief of pummeling Strauch's face with a baseball bat until his features were a bloody pulp and his skull blasted open like a squashed pomegranate. And then I felt a sickening nausea and intense guilt.

"Don't look at me," I yelled at Ira, as though he could see the shame of violence playing out inside me. "You're making me sick."

"Just take it easy, Psyche. Relax." He sounded frightened.

"Fuck you. Don't tell me what to do. Don't tell me to take it easy. The whole fucking world is being lit on fire like a sack of garbage and the fuckers who did it have a fireproof vault to crawl into."

Ira went pale and sweaty and sat down on the sofa. For a moment I worried he was having a heart attack. "Are you OK?"

He nodded.

"I'm sorry. I'm really sorry. It's not you..."

He held up a hand to stop me as he interrupted, "I know. She was all you had."

I went limp. He knew me so well and loved me anyway. I was horrible. I had been so cruel and yet he saw through it and diffused it in one swift poke. "I'm so sorry," I said.

I wished I were one of those women who could just cry and get it all out and let people see who I was and what I was really feeling. But I couldn't. I had never been like that. I was a mystery even to myself. I never really knew why or how I was feeling or what triggered my emotions. Sometimes I didn't even realize I was feeling at all until I was in the middle of a sentence and it was coming back at me as if someone else were speaking. It was miraculous Ira could read me. In the eight years we had been together I had learned more about myself from his interpretations than in the twenty-two years before him. And slowly, with his help, I had started unraveling myself. "It was always easier to be objective about other people," Ira said whenever I marveled at his uncanny ability.

But I wasn't a good people reader. I had no talent for it. My mom had said I had been diagnosed with highly functioning Asperger's, once considered rare in girls until they figured out girls exhibited differently. She didn't believe it and warned me never to put faith in any label. She told me that it meant nothing. I read up about it in college and some of it fit; then again, so did a lot of things. But Ira taught me how to be better and through him my empathy for all beings deepened.

Ira shrugged. "What are we going to do about it?"

"I don't know yet. I still have to figure out what to do with the remains of my mother. This is too much for me to handle right now." I stopped dead and felt myself go blank. I rolled my head and my neck cracked. "I can't remember what she told me about her wishes. I guess I didn't want to hear it."

"Cremation. She wanted her ashes scattered from the Brooklyn Bridge," he said.

FIVE

Weeks after I had requested my mother's ashes, they arrived. There was no Brooklyn Bridge to herald her departure beyond the veil of death, so instead Ira and I put on our UV suits and went to Memorial Bridge over the Potomac River, where Miriam's ashes drifted peacefully in the wind, scattering like a gray mist over the water.

There was no prayer, only silent grieving. The way Miriam would have wanted it. I leaned over the railing with the support of Ira and watched the river's current gobble up the last of my mother's dust.

As we walked back to the Lincoln Memorial I wondered how mom had stayed an Atheist after all the places she had been and all the people she had seen and studied. In my scant years of researching nature the conclusion I'd come to was that a greater logic existed to the universe and everything in it. My mother's voice argued inside me, "Religion devours logic and excretes dogma." But there had to be something true, at least in the desire for a greater being. The yearning for a transcendental experience of the divine, this was inherent in all people. And I felt so hungry for belief, but in memoriam to Mom, I swiftly hunted the clawing beast inside and killed it.

Other kids had celebrated the passing seasons with Christmas and Easter or Passover and Hanukkah. Being an only child lent itself to comparisons with my friends' lifestyles. Embarrassing as it was to admit, even now, the presents and attention other kids received during holidays had made me jealous. But Mom never acquiesced. She never pandered to me, or social pressure. This may have made childhood lonelier, but it also made me stronger.

The parking lot was empty, just one car in a vast geometric pattern of white lines and meters. The sun crested the Washington skyline, above it cloudless blue like polished turquoise. It was a rare, tranquil afternoon and I wanted to hold it forever.

There was a long silence in the car before I asked, "When you were growing up, your parents celebrated the holidays, held Seders, that sort of thing. Didn't they?"

"Sure."

"Did you like it?" I asked, watching the White House fence pass by.

"I don't know. I didn't think about it, just something we did."

"But you sat shiva for your mom when I first met you."

Ira nodded. "And my father before that. Last I heard, Charles still practiced."

I nodded. I wondered if it was because Charles was the youngest or maybe because he had children and wanted to pass on the tradition. I didn't know him very well - Ira wasn't close to him. Last we heard he was in upstate New York and that was just before Ira's trial. Once I had left a message for him when Ira was still in prison, but he never called back.

"Do you ever wonder what happened to him?"

"I think about him and the kids all the time, but there's nothing I can do. He hates me."

"He doesn't hate you."

Ira took his eyes off the road momentarily to berate me with his bleak, give-me-a-break expression. "He disowned me, moved, went unlisted and warned me never to contact him again or he'd press harassment charges."

I knew they had had problems, but this was the first I'd heard of threats. "Why didn't you tell me?"

"I don't know. It was early in our relationship and you were already freaked enough. I guess I thought it would scare you. Was I wrong?"

I shook my head. "I don't know, it might have."

"I'm glad I trusted my intuition."

Ira pulled the car into the garage. I stayed inside for a moment and watched. He was a good man, a decent man who had a pathological dislike of authority. Not because he didn't believe in rules. He did. He just didn't believe in our government.

Ira walked over to my side of the car and opened the door. "Are you OK?" he asked in a gentle voice.

I nodded. "Just thinking."

He held a hand out to me. I took it.

Inside I collapsed on the sofa. Chi seized the opportunity to nest on my stomach while Ira made supper. I was perpetually exhausted these past few weeks since mom had died. Work had been hard to concentrate on and my signature fastidiousness had temporarily gone lax. Since discovering the secret Environ, a keen resentment was building in me toward Digibio. Fantasies of sabotaging my chlorophyll research haunted me while I peered under microscopes and set up slides. Today, at the end of my shift I had to talk myself out of dumping a canister - holding the last two months' research - into a vat of sulfuric acid in lieu of putting it back in the freezer.

It was only a matter of time before I had to quit - find something better to devote myself to. The world was dying. I had undeniable proof, no more lying to myself. If I could get hard evidence the Strauch dynasty was in cahoots with Digibio Technologies and their plan was to abandon ship, only giving life rafts to the richest and most powerful, then I'd have something to take to the scientific community. Finding more information about the Environ project was key.

I went into the kitchen to watch Ira cook, but from the looks of it he was finished. I sat down at the table and waited. "Has Malone ever done iris modulators for scans?" I asked.

Ira put his famous noodle kugel casserole down and started cutting. "Doesn't do optics, but he's got a dealer." He handed me a piece and then poured himself a glass of fermented grape juice, which he liked to refer to as wine. When he started to pour mine, I motioned for him to stop.

"I'm not interested in drinking 'the science project that went awry.' "

"It'll still get you drunk," he said. I hesitated. "Just a little. It will relax you."

I waited for him to fill half the glass and then said, "Great, that's enough." It was hot and bitter. There was an acrid metallic aftertaste, which made me gag. I made a sour face.

"It's not that bad," he said.

"Could Malone get a contact lens of Lamont's iris made?"

Ira stared hard at me. "It's too dangerous. I don't want you doing it."

"It's the only way were going to be able to break into the system at Digibio," I said.

There was silence as he weighed my words. I knew it wasn't just the danger of getting caught that scared him - I had changed. This was not something I would have entertained a month ago. There had been numerous arguments between us over the years about his disrespect for rules. Now he had won the debate. I was, in effect, admitting and sanctioning his past actions. He knew something had shifted inside me. My personal paradigm had twisted back onto itself. There was a long silence. We were about to step off a cliff together and we both knew there was nothing left to lose. It was as sad and daunting as it was exciting. For the first time, I felt really alive.

Ira let out a sigh and said, "I should be the one to do it."

"Impossible," I said. "And you know it."

He hesitated. I knew he was really worried and was searching to find some way out for me. But there wasn't one. He studied me for a while. I had never felt such resolve. I stared at him with a keen stubbornness of purpose. There was nothing he could do except go along. "I'll see what I can do," he finally said.

It took nearly a month to get a copy of Lamont's iris made and Ira had to drive to a remote part of Virginia, where he parked by the side of the road near an abandoned farm. He waited nearly two hours for one of Malone's men to do the exchange. The price was steep, wiping out most of our savings, but it was our only hope.

He got home late that evening, expecting me to be asleep, but I had waited up and was sitting on the sofa re-reading the documents he had taken off the Strauch website.

"I was getting worried," I said.

"Here," he said, handing me the brown paper sack.

Inside was a jewelry box. I opened it. A gold ring with a large amber jewel stared back at me.

He took the ring and popped the stone off the setting. Inside the gold mount was a secret compartment where the contact lens was stored.

I scooped it out. "Ingenious."

There was a mirror set up on the coffee table and I went to try the lens on when Ira pulled out a small bottle of solution and said, "You'll need to clean it off first."

He sprayed the lens and I popped it in. It stung and my eyes watered so much it kept popping out, but diligence paid off. In order to trick the scanner, it had to be an exact duplicate of Lamont's open iris and required opacity. In effect, it left me blind in that eye.

I stumbled around trying to get used to it and ended up stubbing my toe on the sofa. The pain brought tears and I rubbed my eyes, making the burning worse. I limped into the bathroom and popped the lens into my hand. Ira followed me.

"You'll have to practice for a while," he said. "Give your eye a break for a few days."

"I'll be fine," I snapped.

"This is serious shit, Psyche. You can't draw any attention to yourself," Ira said.

I raised a brow. "I'm very aware of that."

"I don't know..."

"We need evidence."

"What are we going to do? We haven't come up with a plan yet."

"I have," I said. I took him downstairs to my workstation and pulled a list of names out of my desk drawer. Next to each was a line or two about their area of specialty and a number.

He studied it for a moment but couldn't make out my reasoning. "What is this?"

"I'm going to contact these scientists and start a collective. With all our combined efforts, I believe we can come up with an alternative strategy of survival. The goal being to save and preserve as much life on this planet as possible and ultimately find a way to reverse the damage."

He smiled. "Genius. But what if some of these people are screwed up or are in cahoots with Digibio..."

"That's what the numbers next to their names are for. It's a grading system. Some of them I've found enough information on the internet to know they are not just great scientists, but ethical people. But, of course, we'll also have to conduct extensive interviews," I said.

He looked over the list one more time - less than a third of them had numbers. "There's no way."

I took the paper from him and scanned the list. "See here?" He nodded. "I've already talked to La Donna Washington."

He was horrified. "But..."

"I didn't tell her anything yet, just that I was looking for a good shrink. I wanted to get a handle on her personality. She seemed perfect for this, very fiery, but fair. I liked her. I'm going to approach her first. With her background she'll be instrumental in helping us weed through our prospects."

"This is a monumental task," Ira said.

"There's no other way."

A week later I decided to try out the iris scan. It was rare for a new researcher to be left alone in the lab, but my chlorophyll experiments were the pinnacle obstacle for Digibio, and time was of the essence. When I purposely lost the key sample cell for a few hours, my time was bought. I had taken it to lunch that afternoon and left it in my paper sack until enough time elapsed for Geraldine to be sufficiently worried. Then, during a break, I arranged for it to look like it had fallen out of its category in the bio-fridge. A fellow researcher found it an hour later on top of a vat of cockroaches, and by then the chain of events was so convoluted it didn't arise any suspicion.

Geraldine's office was a glass cube near the entrance of the lab. At five o'clock I went in to see her. "After that mix up today I'd like to stay and get back on top of my research," I said.

Geraldine grimaced. "Yes, that was very unfortunate. With the long weekend coming up it would be advantageous to get the bulk of the work done." She paused to mull it over. "Very well, I can authorize you for another, say, three hours?"

I nodded. "I'd really like to get this finished before next week. I'm close but..."

"How about four, then?" Geraldine looked me up and down for a moment. "I was sorry to hear about your mother. Are you going to be OK to do this?"

I straightened up and nodded.

"Work can sometimes take your mind off things like that," Geraldine added when she saw my resolve.

"It's the only thing I can do," I said.

"I'll let the guard at the front gate know. But don't stay any later than nine." Geraldine turned to leaf through some paperwork on her file cabinet.

I worked diligently to finish my research. I had plenty of time because I had held back results for weeks in preparation for this day. Herb was the last one to say goodbye and asked if I needed any help, more out of politeness than actual work ethic.

"No, you have a family to go home to. Don't worry, I'll be fine," I said.

"Right then, good luck," he said, turning off the overheads with the switch near the door, leaving only my sector bathed in light. Everyone was gone. I finished writing my observations down and grabbed the specimen and went to the storeroom. I slipped the specimens into the bio-fridge and opened the ring. The light was dim but I managed to pop the lens in. I went back through the lab and flipped off my section's lights and waved a hand over the heat sensor.

The hallway lighting was at ten-percent capacity. It was dark and my peripheral vision was severely impaired. It took a while to feel my way to the break room, where I tested the iris lens first. If the lens were defective it wouldn't set off the alarm because authorized visitors were allowed. But the scan would be stored in a digital database if the computer didn't register Paul Lamont's name. This would make getting into the secure sector a bust and within a few days I ran a serious risk of being caught by security when the visitor scan logs were checked against sign-in sheets and the iris database.

I took a deep breath. "Please let this work." I stepped up to the camera's eye and put my chin on the rest. The shutter clicked and my heart skipped. The flashing red letters moved in slow motion: READING... HELLO PAUL, WELCOME TO THE BIO LAB COMMISSARY. The wall opened and I walked through, took a deep breath and walked out again into the corridor.

Through the twisting concrete I headed toward the mainframe. An echo of my clicking shoes trailed like a ghost chasing after me. At every intersection of hallways I listened for unfamiliar footsteps. Noises traveled like whispers through pipes in the sub-city and half a mile later, just blocks away from the mainframe I heard movement around a corner. But there was nowhere to hide. My heart leapt sideways and a whoosh of blood screamed in my ears. Maybe it was a night watchman or another scientist working late? Whoever it was, I waited until their clip grew faint before moving.

There was no sign heralding the mainframe room, just a galvanized metal door and an iris scanner. An antique plaque, unchallenged since the inception of the company, hung next to the chin rest. It warned: Maximum Security Area Criminal Prosecution to All Unauthorized Personnel.

If ever there was a time to believe in God, now was it. *To anyone up there who might be listening, I'll believe in you if this works.*

This iris scanner was a little different and when I put my chin on the rest - a clamp came down holding my cranium in place. *Is it measuring my head?* And the purple laser light was intense enough for me to see a fog of it behind the opaque contact lens. It moved slowly from one side to the next, catching every detail and analyzing it. After it made its first pass the clamp didn't release; instead, the laser passed from left to right again. I knew I was caught and started squirming as another pass of the laser measured the fake iris up and down.

An alarm sounded, and a bolt of terror paralyzed me. The clamp released. The digital readout welcomed Paul Lamont and I nearly missed the opportunity to enter because my heart was pounding so hard I saw stars.

The only light inside was cast from a wall of digital screens and illuminated buttons. I caught my breath and took inventory before settling at the main terminal's board.

Ira had compiled a list of codes. Some were guesses, others traced from the Strauch website and some suggested by Malone. I had weeded through the best of them at home. Malone had warned Ira - too many tries triggered the security system. Two wrong codes in a row got the computer to record any input. Next a silent alarm sounded. This could happen as early as the third or fourth try.

Now that I was staring at the keyboard, all the data looked like shrapnel. I went over each possibility and weighed it again. The crunch of time was on. More than an hour had passed since leaving the lab.

I decided on Mildred, Lamont's mother's middle name. It looked promising with a statistical probability of ninety percent, according to Ira's calculations. My hands quivered on the keys. A sharp buzz came from the speaker and red letters popped across the top of the screen: NOT IN USE. That had been my best bet. Perspiration rained from my hairline and I wiped it away from my eyes.

Most likely Lamont changed codes daily, meaning he'd have a hint page. There was no way of remembering hundreds of different codes without one. I scrolled through a directory and found it hidden in the maintained file. The question read: Your favorite P. system?

Did the P. stand for personal? Practical? I racked my brain and browsed through my purse for my tablet. I scanned through pages of codes... permanent system? No that didn't make sense. Political system? I found one reference that wasn't part of the code list. It was a note to myself, a word, "plutocracy," floating in the margins. Another try might not set off the silent alarm but it would trigger the system's default and if anyone looked over the records they would question Lamont and figure out someone had broken in. The room was cooled to sixty degrees but felt like ninety.

I looked at my watch. It was almost seven. Only two hours left to download, to get to my car and say goodnight to the gate guard. The more I stared at the question on the screen the more sure I was that the word fit. Of course a plutocracy would be Lamont's favorite political system. It was the one he had spent his life building.

I held my breath and keyed in, P then L then O. Each letter more confident then the next, until the file opened like a blooming lotus and page after page of text came up.

I connected my tablet with a wireless, low-grade digital receiver that was not traceable and downloaded all the pertinent biological specs on the Environ and its history. Next I had to locate the digi side, but since I was hacking through the bio's mainframe there would be top-loaded files that had to be wadded through.

It was a tangle of information and every time I thought I was close to finding the digi files I'd open something useless, maintenance schedules or security reports. After meandering for more than half an hour I started to worry that my only recourse was to physically try to get to the other side of the sub-city where the digi mainframe was. But I didn't know my way around that area and finding it would probably take longer than I had. Just when I was losing faith, I happened upon a small file folder of corporate officers. I didn't think it would lead anywhere but opened it anyway. It demanded another code. I was onto something. I tried Mildred again. It worked. All corporate offices were listed with the Environ's funding and shareholders. I copied the files and searched further. My tablet was running out of memory. There was too much information to store. I had the bulk of what I needed. I didn't have the digital structural underpinnings of the Environ's makeup but I read enough to get the general gist and made some notes on a piece of paper. It would have to do. I looked at my watch - it was twenty to nine and if I didn't hustle the guard would report me.

I backed out of the system, hit the restore, gathered my belongings and got up, making sure to leave everything as I had found it. I quickly moved to the doorway and triggered the sensor. The wall opened.

I bolted down the long twisting corridors until I got to the elevator. It was just five 'til and an eternity passed waiting for the elevator to clink down into the shaft. I punched the button and the doors closed. I leaned against the cool metal, out of breath and thankful to be on my way home.

Inside the car I popped out the lens and hid it in the ring. I revved the engine and speeded down the ramp. At the final twist, right before the guard gate, I slowed and eyeballed myself in the rearview mirror. Perspiration had gathered at the base of my hairline. I wiped it away.

The guard gave a suspicious nod. "Working late?" he asked.

"Yeah."

"Name," he said.

"Psyche Hershenbaum. Geraldine Shumaker approved my overtime."

He scanned the put out orders on his computer screen. A few minutes later he came out with a receipt and said, "You'll want to keep this in case they forget to pay you."

I smiled. "Thanks."

The gate arm lifted; on the other side was relief. I zoomed down the street and onto the expressway. Near my exit it became a parking lot. The Friday before the Fourth of July and D.C. was gearing up for its celebration on Monday. The timing was perfectly ironic for contacting my list of scientists with hard evidence Democracy had been poisoned and, in its weakened state, subverted. Our government had had a long-suffering, quiet, unnoticed revolution. Here was proof that America the beautiful had been drugged, raped and broken by oligarchs and push-molded into a corporate plutocracy.

Throughout downtown, people were camped along the streets to watch the next day's National Pride Parade, as if there were still a nation to be proud of. The people were ravaged, emaciated and dispirited, but still chose to believe in a mythical America. A country where a single voice was heard through a vote and the average person was represented on the Hill.

A few days earlier I had found a copy of a history journal my mother had sent. I had stashed it away to read at a convenient time. Its theme had been the turn of the century. I read it voraciously, as if it were a letter from beyond, and it made me wonder if she had always known about humanity's demise but, like the rest of us, had to deny it.

According to one article, the seeds of our destruction were sown at the turn of the century when corporations had a stranglehold on Washington and a quiet gentleman's coup had taken place via the judicial branch, subverting the will of the people and their right to representation through the ballot box. People who questioned the coup were marginalized and shut down with patriotism.

There always seemed to be people screaming along the sidelines of history about the breaking of America but, like Cassandra, their predictions and protests were ignored. Perhaps it was the only way to live through the overwhelming unraveling of the world, to face the end without facing it.

The Second Amendment - the right to bear arms, a provision against potential political corruption bestowing the people with the ultimate right to revolt against a broken system or an autocrat, theocrat, oligarch, king, anything that took away their God-given right to freedom and democracy - the self-destruct button was built in by the forefathers because they knew from experience that power corrupts and, given enough time and conniving, another revolution would be inevitable. Of course, they didn't foresee nuclear weapons or the military industrial complex.

America was a singular superpower bending in on itself. My mother had told me a story about a Native American shaman who had written a book of prophecies back in the early 1980s. The shaman had had a dream: a hideous dog walked a city street walled with stalled traffic. Out of the dog's anus were two sticks used as stilts. The lower half of the body was missing and it was eating its own intestines. The shaman wrote that the dog was a symbol of America and its people. The traffic-infested city, a metaphor for the world and its reliance on fossil fuels; the missing half of the body, a symbol of the disintegration of ideals and the Constitution. The sphincter controlling its ability to walk on stilts was a crude metaphor for the precarious road America was headed down, where money (excrement was synonymous with money in dream language) controlled America's movement. And eating itself was a clear way of saying that it was cannibalizing its own people, resources and life, eventually destroying itself in its shortsightedness.

My mother had often recounted this story, which she had found as fascinating as Native American culture itself, but I hadn't understood it until now as I drove through D.C, passing monuments that seemed as pertinent as the bittersweet relics of the Roman Empire. There was no here here. Democracy was a phantom, stalking shadows in an abandoned house. All that we had pledged allegiance to was as gone as the ozone layer, as dead as the billions eaten away by plague, as real as the morals of the oligarchs, as concrete as the second coming that never came, as strong as the desire for the rich to protect the poor, as fair as the lies we wanted to believe - the lies that were sure to kill us all.

SIX

"What took so long?" he asked. "I was getting ready to hack into Digibio's system to see if you were spotted, but I stopped myself."

"I left a little after nine as planned but... traffic," I said.

He shook his head. "I forgot."

I smiled, took his hand and led him upstairs to the living room. "I got most of the Bio side, but couldn't fit all the Digi stuff on the tablet. I read through what I could and wrote some key points down."

Ira sat down. "That's not important. We just need evidence."

I sat beside him and pulled my tablet out, then combed through my purse and found my tablet and handed it to him. "We're going to need supplies and money to start this thing."

He nodded. "I've got some of that figured."

I stopped fiddling with my tablet. "How?" I asked.

"The rest of the funding for the Amazon project was confirmed. The team of techs I've assembled will relocate to the temperate rain forest in northern Oregon. They'll build shelters and set up camp. We have the ultraviolet scrims arriving in a few weeks."

"But if they find out..."

"I've enlisted the help of a few friends at Williamson Pharmaceuticals; we're working on changing the scope of the drug. I'm going to write up a new finding calling for cultivation in the Northwest. The project will be less expensive to fund, and with some documentation I can make the case," he said.

"Do you really think they'll go for it?"

"There are a few scientists working for Williamson who would make great candidates for the Collective. Once we get the information translated, distilled and make a presentation to them, it shouldn't be a problem," he replied.

"Who?" I asked.

"Xin-Yi Chan and Zoe Campbell. Zoe comes from an anthropology background. I've used her in unfamiliar cultures. She's very thorough and helpful and has unshakable ethics, besides being a tree hugger. Xin-Yi is relatively new, but extremely intelligent, hard-working and known for her philanthropic work," he said.

"What about Aine Flanagan? Didn't she work at Williamson?" Psyche asked. "She was a big environmentalist. Did she move back to Dublin?"

"No, she's working on shoring up the windmills and solar panels in the Southwest and what's left of California up into Washington."

"If we get this together maybe she could help get power to our site."

He nodded.

In front of me was enough information to fill a thousand Bibles. "We still have to talk to La Donna and go through all those names."

"Feeling overwhelmed?" Ira asked.

"Yeah," I said. "I can't stay at Digibio much longer."

"When are you going to resign?"

"After I turn in my findings. I hope you have leads other than the Amazon project. If they don't buy it, we're screwed."

A crooked grin eclipsed Ira's face. He nodded. "You know that if there's money to be found, I've got my fingers on it."

SEVEN

La Donna's office was in one of the worn-out parts of Georgetown with only patchy inhabitance. Whole blocks were abandoned and scorching in the sun. Holes in the scrims had gotten too large and expensive to fix. I was taken aback by the damage. Full city blocks looked like they had been put in an oven and left to bake for ten years. Bricks and cement were charred. Tar had bubbled up, turned soupy and melted, running like slow, molten water into antique gutters. Apartment buildings crumbled from exposure like decrepit gingerbread houses. Broken shells of grocery stores and banks were blown apart by the elements, their ancient signs and lettering a jumble of unintelligible letters. Nature had waged her war to survive us.

The satellite map hadn't been updated in years and didn't take into account streets that were now too decayed to drive down. I resorted to an online atlas to find alternative routes. And we got lost for a while, taking one street which led to another impasse. I was nervous we wouldn't make it in time. After a bunch of missteps and bad information that turned into bad directions, Ira decided to quit listening to me.

"That atlas is worthless," he said.

I had argued vehemently for its use but by now Ira had proven his point. It was supposed to be updated every month and logically it should have panned out, but any disaster could have visited the webmaster or the pages' sponsors in a month.

Ira's driving scared me. He took random turns and sped through yellow lights and changed his mind at the last second. I tried to zone out and focus on the scenery outside. We had tried things my way. And now we were stuck feeling our way with only half an hour left.

"Are you sure this is a good idea, Ira?"

"Shh, I'm trying to tune in," he said. Anxiety, which felt like a coiled dragon nesting in the pit of my stomach, lashed up. I quickly suppressed it before saying something I'd regret. My jaw clenched tight and the vinyl armrest submerged my fingernails. Relax, I told myself, but even I couldn't listen to me. I never trusted intuition, no matter whose it was.

Seven minutes later we were looking for the closest parking place and I had to ask myself if perhaps Ira had something that was beyond my understanding. But those musings disappeared when I went over what I would say to La Donna on our walk to what looked like an abandoned medical building.

There was a running elevator but it squeaked as it descended and made a loud thud when it reached the lobby. When the doors opened only halfway, I suggested, "It's only three flights."

Ira nodded. "I need the exercise."

There was a buzzer outside her office door. Ira hit it. A few seconds later we heard, "Yes?" from the intercom.

"It's Ira and Psyche," he replied into the box.

La Donna opened the door and I was taken back. She was as beautiful as she was physically imposing, with dark chocolate skin and eyes. She wore a colorful African-pattern scarf and dress. She shook our hands. "Nice to meet you," she said, in a husky, beguiling voice.

Ira opened his tablet and I took a stack of paperwork from my briefcase and handed it to La Donna. "This is strictly confidential material," I said. "I need your word that you won't discuss this with anyone until the appointed time."

La Donna nodded. "You have it." She looked over the paperwork. Almost instantly she appeared shocked as she read and the longer she read the more shocked she seemed. Periodically she shook her head with disgust and/or disbelief.

"As you can see, the lists of suitable candidates for admission into the Environ are based on economic investment or contracts with workers assigned to keep the Environ running," Ira said, watching her.

She held up a paper with only graphs and numbers on it and asked, "What's this in reference to?"

"Those are statistics showing the rate of decline for habitability on earth," I replied.

"Doesn't look good, does it?" she said, studying it more carefully. "They don't expect anyone to survive except possibly very small pockets?"

I nodded. "We're talking about an extinction-level event happening here, now," I said.

La Donna stared at the paperwork, reading the information over and over, trying to absorb it. "Are you sure these calculations are accurate?" she asked. I nodded again. She looked at me in disbelief and horror and said, "Climate change did this?"

"Yes," I said. "But steps can be taken to reverse the trend. I'm not going to lie, we may not see it turn around in our lifetime, but we can at least try to save our planet so eventually life will be sustainable again."

"Even if we get a group of scientists together to form a community in the Northwest, what are the chances we could survive there?" La Donna asked.

Ira stood up and turned his tablet screen toward La Donna. On it was a detailed map of the coastal rain forest, stretching from Northern California into Canada. He pointed to a section near the center of Oregon. "We've selected this area as a starting place, but this whole region has excellent possibilities. The rain forest, although it's changing and becoming more tropical, still has an abundance of thriving plants due to a canopy of ancient dead pine trees and vines which help provide a natural filter, cutting down the UV exposure. There's also a concentration of oxygen-rich air and a regular rain cycle, which provides drinking water and helps regulate the climate so that it remains relatively temperate."

"We have plans for shelters and want to put into action a breeding program to sustain and encourage animal diversity. This is very doable - we just need the right people," I said.

La Donna reached for a glass container filled with mints. She offered them to Ira and me. I shook my head but Ira paused to inspect them. "Go ahead," she said, and smiled.

"So you want to build an ark?"

Ira grabbed a candy and said, "I suppose, if you want to be Biblical about it."

I continued. "My main concern is not just the ability of candidates to perform their functions within the Collective, but how those individuals will interact with one another. This is the most important aspect to setting up the project. We're all going to have to live together, get along. We can't have people that..."

"Turn out to have psychological or social problems," La Donna said.

"Right," Ira replied. "We want you to be in charge of interviewing."

"We are in the process of going through potential candidates," I said.

"People who won't rat us out," Ira said, smirking. "We have no idea what the Strauch administration would do to us if they knew. We can't risk anyone telling, or nobody survives this thing - even them, in the long run."

La Donna nodded. "It's a lot to process right now. I'm finding it difficult to wrap my head around it. My whole life has been here in Washington and it's not an easy thing, you two popping in here and telling me we're in an ecological Armageddon. I have a family and uprooting them..."

"It's far worse to let them die. There's only one choice if you want your kids to have a chance to have children, and someday, when the earth regains her strength, it will be your great-great grandchildren inheriting a livable earth. I know how you feel. I didn't want to see this either. But something has to be done not just to save ourselves, but for the good of life on this planet, for the survival of our world," I said.

"Bottom line is, your family won't make it unless you join us," Ira said. "Unless, of course, you're secretly a trillionaire and gave billions to the Strauch dynasty that we don't know about."

The room went silent. La Donna sat down in her chair and stared hard out the window for a long while, as if she were taking in the tattered scrims and broken pavement, abandoned buildings and unrelenting Washington sky for the last time. She knew we were right. But I felt for her. We were asking her to take her head out of the sand and not just see the obvious but throw herself into an unknown world with strangers and come to terms with her and her family's mortality all at once.

There is nothing more devastating than the true, honest revelation that the one thing which has always supported you, been there before you were a twinkle in your great-great-great-great grandmother's eye, is as vulnerable and delicate as you are. There's an unexpressed feeling we all share - counting on the permanence of our mother earth and all that we've built upon her. Our skyscrapers, houses, roads and bridges promote the lie of mastery over her. But we are not separate from her suffering.

Science has told us the sun will burn out eventually and all its children will become frozen rocks without its heat, but we don't really believe this. How could we? It goes against everything our biology and life-experience tells us. This reality is as invisible to the naked eye as a quark, as much a belief system as a religion. Faced with this illusion, it feels like losing a psychic compass we never knew we had. It is mind-shattering.

As scientists we are asked to hold the abstract idea of the death of earth in our minds and this is possible, but what is impossible is feeling it. And so, like a child, we refuse. We're incapable of perceiving her mortality just as a gadfly is ignorant of the horse it feeds from. We desperately need to believe the earth was here before us and it will be here after us, as if immortal.

We were asking La Donna to clear all old models and dreams, and her way of life, and embrace a dark, horrifying abstraction. No matter how clear the signs and signals or the physical evidence, we had all learned to shut down and function in denial generations ago. We lived in a culture of easy dismissals and mandatory detachment, a code we all followed as much my method or Ira's or La Donna's or those of the billions who died by the shadowy hand of corporate greed's spoils. We were asking what should never be asked of a person, to face the mortality of everything at once. And the pain and fear were chiseled in the lines of her face.

"I was trained to see my contribution to the survival of mankind in a personal way - having a family, children, grandchildren, providing for them, giving them a good life. I've done all that. Now you're telling me it isn't enough? That my kids won't be able to survive on this planet fifty years from now if something isn't done?"

The tension in my neck was giving me a headache. "I'm afraid it's worse than that," I said.

She gave me a confused look. "It's more immediate," Ira said.

"I need some time to absorb all of this," La Donna said. "To think about it."

"We understand," Ira said.

La Donna replied, "It's all just very hard to accept."

I nodded. "I know."

"Let me talk to my husband. I'm going to need to convince him as much as myself. Can I make copies of the statistics?" La Donna asked.

Ira turned to me, and although I was worried, we both knew we had to trust her. I nodded and Ira added, "Just don't show them to anyone else."

"OK," she replied. We started for the door. "There's just one more thing before you go."

We turned around and waited. "Yes," Ira finally said.

"If I do say yes, I'd want to bring on a woman named Tuwa Redhawk. I trust her instincts more than my own."

"Who is she?" I asked.

"She's a brilliant psychologist. More specifically, a Mapper."

"A Mapper?" I asked.

"It's a newer science pioneered by an anthropologist who had gone to live with the last remaining Hopi Indians and Aborigines of Australia about thirty years ago," she said.

"They're closer to shamans than they are psychologists, aren't they?" Ira asked.

"Well, they're both. Once you meet her you'll understand," La Donna said.

"She's trustworthy?" I asked.

"Beyond trustworthy. She's a holy woman," La Donna said.

Ira and I looked at each other for a moment. "Whatever you need," I said.

EIGHT

On the drive back from the meeting with La Donna, I told Ira, "We're going to need a plan B."

"I don't think so. She'll do it," he replied, turning into an alley to avoid the parade.

"But if she doesn't..."

Ira reached over and patted my knee. "She will. She's a smart woman, she cares."

I stared out the window. Another one of his hunches. I loathed the arrogance accompanying his hunches. But I didn't say anything. At this point there was no way to win him over with logic. In a few days an answer would come and in the meantime I needed to proceed with organizing supplies and researching potential Collective members.

When we reached home I was exhausted. I still had to write a resignation letter, but my mind was caught up in future plans. If only there was a time machine. But even if I could go back, where would I go? An assassination of the first in the long line of the Strauch dynasty? No. The problem was there long before Gerald Strauch had cemented humanity's suicidal fate. It dated back 100 years earlier, during the birth of the industrial revolution. But there was no simple answer, no easy solution - only a fantasy of closure that I desperately longed for.

As I lay on the couch with Chi purring on my stomach, Ira called to me from the basement. "Psyche, take a look at this."

I hoisted myself up, carrying Chi over my shoulder and down the stairs to Ira's workstation. From behind him I read the screen: Psyche Hershenbaum Code 3. I felt my mouth fall open. "What does that mean?"

"You've been officially designated a suspicious employee," Ira replied.

"And?" I retorted.

"Digibio suspects you of company espionage. It seems they think you've been hiding your UV-resistant plant-cell research," he said.

"Shit, I must have let too much out at one time. I just didn't think I would make such quick advances."

"Be careful how you word the resignation letter. Don't tip your hand. If they find out about the Collective they'll know we broke into their system and..."

"I know," I said cutting him off, not wanting to think about how much danger we were in.

He tried to hide his anger, but I could see it. I was absent-minded. Early in our relationship he thought it was cute - the adorable genius who can't dress herself - but in this context it was a fatal flaw. Going to the market with two different shoes on is one thing, but blowing our cover because I was distracted by putting together the Collective were two entirely different end results of the same flaw.

He stared hard at me and annunciated with the deliberation with which one would speak to a child. "We have to be careful."

As if I didn't understand the gravity of the situation. "I'm not an idiot," I retorted.

"No one can know about this project until after the interview and selection process."

"Well, you didn't seem to have a problem trusting La Donna, so don't lecture me."

I was in a determined mood. There was no changing my mind and he knew it. Besides, I could argue circles around him. He turned back to the computer and started working.

There was a thick streak of white growing out of the crown of Ira's head. I fingered it, realizing it hadn't been there a month ago. Suddenly I felt a stab of guilt. I had done it to him, all the sneaking around, the weight of building a new world and a new society in the shadowed milieu of conspiracy, the stress of my mom and the world dying around us. There was no use making life any worse. I kissed the top of his head, wondering how we would survive such a formidable undertaking - putting together, populating and sustaining the Collective. I had been lucky so far by deciding to think it out one tiny step at a time, keeping it small enough to digest, but Ira's personality didn't afford him that luxury.

I went to my computer station to search databases and biographies of some of the candidates. It was rare for both of us to be working downstairs at the same time. He was usually relaxing on the sofa in front of the flatscreen when I got home and I would sneak downstairs to finish a paper or do some extra research. I couldn't stand sitting around, and added to my already workaholic personality was Ira's obsession with flipping through TV stations. In his contorted, estrogen-deprived mind, he believed he could sum up the entirety of plot, substance and importance in milliseconds, even during commercial breaks. And he was always filled with awe when I found something interesting. Yet he never learned the secret of my keen ability - it was as simple as reading the description at the bottom of the screen and watching for a few minutes to see if the program lived up to its hype. But despite this unbelievably annoying habit, I loved him more than I had ever loved another human being except for my mother. Which, of course, was an entirely different thing altogether.

Now as I stared at all the biographical information about different scientists and their families, I wished Ira and I had gotten married while my mother was alive. It had always felt like a bureaucratic institution. But my mom, despite her left-wing anti-religious rhetoric, had a soft spot for marriage and she never quite understood my stance, no matter how I explained it. The funny thing was, now I couldn't remember what the argument against marriage had been.

In retrospect it seemed more like a rebellion against convention that turned into a point of pride. Ira was the best friend I ever had. We were true equals and partners in every way. Maybe it was the idea of making a public spectacle of ourselves that threatened our hermetic way of life. But it would have made mom so happy to see us settled and the silly piece of paper I had so disdained may have helped me feel that way, too. I remember an old college friend telling me, "Your husband is the only family you get to pick." She was right, but I was too young to fully understand it then. And now the time had passed, the subject long-since put to rest.

I signed off the internet and stared at the blank screen. A resignation letter was in order and I tried to think of an explanation that wouldn't raise a red flag, but my mind did flips. Images of the past bled through and I saw the familiar line of brownstones on our Brooklyn street, the slate steps to my childhood home and my mother reading a bedtime story shortly after father had left us. She had struggled for years without him, working two or three jobs until she got her degree. It seemed there was never enough time for the two of us.

If only I had gotten Mom out before the hurricane. If only I had focused my training on stopping global warming, maybe this future could have been the one unchosen. The data was there but I hadn't looked at it. The truth was bitter - I had allowed myself to be blinded by personal ambition and denial. But I hadn't been the only one.

Ira snuck up behind me and rubbed my shoulders. "How's it going?"

"Not very well. I haven't written anything but Dear Ms. Geraldine Shumaker." I shrugged. "I can't think straight."

He pulled at my chair and offered, "Let me start it for you. Go upstairs and take a nice, warm bath. You need to relax."

I pecked his cheek. "You're too good to me."

"I know," he said.

I smiled at him, collected Chi, who was sitting on my desk, and went upstairs.

After I put in my resignation, every workday was formidable. There was a constant, nagging fear of being found out. An excruciating week went by before word came from La Donna - during which time tension built between Ira and me over finding a psychiatrist who would be an appropriate replacement. I was anxious to start and I made a list of names, confronting him with it at dinner every night. But he deflected with my own weapon of reason. There was no one better for the job, and my impatience didn't serve the bigger picture. I really couldn't argue with him.

It was a Saturday afternoon and Ira and I had just had a blowup. I had gotten Ira to admit his intuition may have been off when it came to La Donna and he agreed to give my list a real look.

The phone rang. I answered abruptly, "Hello?"

"Psyche?" La Donna said.

"Yes." I waved Ira over, mouthing to him, "It's her."

Ira nodded and picked up the wireless extension. "Hey, have you made a decision?" he asked.

"Yes. I'm glad both of you are on phone."

I braced myself for the bad news. "Well?" I asked.

"I'm in." La Donna's voice was deep and sensual. It massaged the ear with a reedy resonance. "I've gone over it a million times. As much as I'd like to bury my head in the sand... I can't."

Ira cheered so loudly into the phone the sound waves stabbed my brain. But I was so happy I almost didn't care. "That's great news," I said.

"You can email the list and I'll look it over. How does this Monday at five sound for another meeting?" La Donna asked.

"Perfect," Ira responded.

"See you then," I said, hanging up the phone. There was a strange sensation flowing through me - a mix of excitement, as if I had just graduated from college, and an arresting shot of fear. I wasn't sure if I should pop open a bottle of champagne or curl into a ball and cry myself to sleep. So I did what I always did, froze my feelings, stuffed them into a jar inside myself and proceeded with my business. There was too much left to be done.

NINE

In the Oval Office, Paul Lamont sat opposite President Reginald Strauch, waiting for Strauch to finish a phone call. The American flag hung just over Strauch's shoulder. It seemed like an ironic twist to Lamont. He was well aware of the implications of the Environ, even at its inception. Although he was not a man of ideals, he felt uncomfortable every time he set foot in the White House for all it represented to the dying hordes of Americans naive enough to buy the plutocrats' cover stories.

Lamont tried to ease his conscience with a strict dose of reality. On his wristcom he dialed up Psyche Hershenbaum's data.

"Good to see ya, Paul," Strauch said, smiling. "What can I do you for?"

"We had a bit of a security problem at Digibio. It seems that a young scientist, Psyche Hershenbaum..."

"Who now?" Strauch asked.

"She's the one who did the breakthrough research on the Planimal's chlorophyll..."

"Right, right," Strauch said nodding. "The Jew. What about her?"

"She broke into the database about six weeks ago; since then, she's resigned," Lamont said.

Strauch leaned back in his chair. "That doesn't sound good."

"No, sir, it isn't."

"Well, is she the talkative type? The kind who might be a problem?" Strauch asked. "She seemed kind of mousy to me. But why take chances? I'll put my boys on her."

"We've been tracking her. It seems she's been collecting scientists. But those we've contacted don't know much about the project except that it requires a stint in Oregon."

"Well, that's good. At least she's not talkin' yet," Strauch said, scooting forward.

"If you're willing, I think in this case it might be best to wait before taking action. We'll keep a watch on her, but as far as I can tell, she's smart enough not to expose the Environ project and we're close to operation date."

Strauch shook his head and put a thick, stubby finger to his chin. "We don't want panic. And we don't want every slimebag, low-life taxpayer thinkin' it's their goddamned right to get into the whatchamacallit. We don't have room for every stinkin' moron left in the U.S."

"Granted," Lamont said, taking a deep breath. "But I have a suspicion her project has to do with saving the temperate rain forest, and since the Environ biosphere is going to be located 300 miles southeast of that forest, it might not be such a bad idea to let her preserve it in case it's needed as a resource later."

"What are you talkin' about?" Strauch said.

How many times had he tried to explain the Planimal structure to Strauch? The man was bordering on mentally challenged, but Lamont smiled coolly at Strauch and dug in again. "The Environ is a Planimal, comprised of plant and animal genetic information. As you know, it is a living creature. That means it eats, moves - albeit slowly - and breathes by converting sunlight into chlorophyll..."

"Stop with all the science horseshit. Just get down to why we need to let the kike live," Strauch said, fidgeting.

"In approximately 100 years the Environ will eat its way through Northern California's gold country, up to the border of Oregon, and..."

"A hundred years? That's a long fuckin' time. What do I care what happens in 100 years?" Strauch said getting up from his desk to walk over to a mirror. He stood facing himself, combing his hand through his dark hair.

"Most likely your son will still be alive," Lamont said.

"Well now you're talkin.' I can understand that," Strauch said, fixing his tie. "Fine, do what you think is right." He turned briefly to face Lamont. "But if one word about the Environ comes out, I'll hold you accountable."

Lamont nodded. "I'll see to it that it doesn't."

"Good boy. I have a press conference startin' in about ten minutes, so if you'll excuse me…" Strauch said, grimacing at himself in the mirror.

TEN

We were drinking coffee and had our lists spread across the kitchen table when La Donna arrived that morning. She seemed more unsure of herself than she had in her office and a little nervous, even a bit morose. Ira took her coat and showed her in.

"Is everything okay?" he asked.

La Donna nodded, but clearly everything was not all right.

"You sure?" I said.

She nodded again. "This is just really depressing."

There was a palpable and instant congeniality among us. We were three of the only people on earth who knew the truth, and we were trying to stop it. "You have to keep your mind trained toward the future and the changes we can affect for the better," I said. "That's the only thing keeping me going."

La Donna nodded. Ira pulled out a chair for her and she sat beside me, looking over the long list of names. "Remember I told you about Tuwa Redhawk?"

"Yes," I said.

"I asked her to join us today," La Donna said. Ira and I glanced at each other unsure what to do or say. "That was the condition of my joining."

"You really trust this woman?" Ira asked.

La Donna nodded. "She'll be here in about half an hour."

"You certainly mean what you say," I said.

She chuckled and then screeched, "You know it."

"We've already decided on some of the scientists, unless you see some problem with them." Ira handed La Donna a file. "This is all the data we've collected on Aine Flanagan, Hyunae Gaffney and Zoe Campbell. Psyche and I know Hyunae. She's a good friend. Aine and Zoe I know through Williamson Pharmaceuticals. They were both instrumental in getting the funding shifted to the Northwest."

La Donna put on her reading glasses and leafed through the paperwork. "They look fine, but the only way I'll know for sure is if I interview them. Statistics, health records and career accomplishments don't really tell me much about how they relate or if there are any personality disorders."

Ira nodded. "We'll arrange that."

The doorbell rang. I answered it.

Tuwa had strong, bold features and piercing eyes. I felt like she was staring through me and I momentarily forgot where I was. There was definitely something uncanny about her, as if she were lit from inside. She seemed to glow.

"Tuwa," she said shaking my hand. "You're Psyche."

"Yes. Follow me," I said motioning her into the other room.

Ira didn't look up from the paperwork. "Scott Baxter is out. La Donna thinks it's between John Samuelson and Naomi Goldberg. What do you think?" he said, finally acknowledging us. "I'm sorry. Tuwa, right?" He stood up and shook her hand. She nodded.

"I thought Samuelson had worked for Weber Oil," I said.

"Ten years ago," La Donna said. "Other than that he has an impeccable reputation."

"I don't know. Naomi doesn't have one blot on her record. She's perfect," I said.

"But we haven't met her yet," Ira retorted.

La Donna handed the paperwork to Tuwa, who sat down and looked it over for a moment and then closed her eyes and ran her fingers over Naomi's name and then John's.

I was about to ask La Donna what the hell Tuwa was doing when La Donna shook her head at me and motioned for me to be quiet. Ira seemed fascinated by the whole thing, but I wasn't amused. This was nothing short of voodoo, and it wasn't the way I had envisioned picking candidates. Tuwa might as well have thrown a pair of dice or flipped a coin.

"You're not going to like this, Psyche." Tuwa was suddenly staring hard at me. "It's not going to seem logical, but Naomi will cause trouble. If you pick John, things will go smoothly. He's the right choice."

I didn't say anything.

Ira pushed the hair back from his face, a sure sign he was engaged and curious. "Was that a Mapping technique?" he asked.

"Yes. It originated in shamanistic practices."

"What did you just do?" I asked, trying to mask my indignation.

"I scanned their energy," Tuwa responded, looking me straight in the eye with proud, calm defiance.

"Um, I suppose I'm not used to this mapping thing, but this is not, as far as I know, any sort of scientific method," I said.

"What matters is results," La Donna said. "And I can show you her accuracy rating. It defies science, too, but you can't argue with success."

"What is it?" Ira asked.

"Statistically impossible, so much so you probably wouldn't believe it if I told you. I'll give you a copy of the study," La Donna said.

"I'd like that," replied Ira.

"Who did the study?" I asked.

"A team of researchers at Georgetown University," La Donna said.

"Your mother lived in Brooklyn?" Tuwa asked. I nodded. "I'm sorry for your loss."

"Thank you," I replied.

Long after Tuwa and La Donna left, Ira was poring over the Georgetown papers and suddenly asked me, "Did you tell La Donna about your mother?"

"No, I assumed you had."

Ira handed me the last page of the report, with all the hard statistics about Tuwa's abilities. I set down the list of names to look at it. According to the research her accuracy was between eighty-seven and ninety-nine percent, depending on the test taker and how they interpreted her information. When it came to hard studies without interpretation, such as the Zener card ESP test, her accuracy rating was just shy of 100 percent, which the parapsychological researchers claimed had never been seen in any test subject in the history of the science.

ELEVEN

I reviewed the Georgetown papers a hundred times, and each read confounded me more than the last. If the lead researcher's reputation hadn't been impeccable I would have dismissed Tuwa's study as a fake. The science of Mapping appeared to meet between quantum physics and psychology, a long marginalized area of science. But in recent years, as answers and reasons eluded humankind and the march backward into religious fanaticism took hold of the world, the study of such phenomena had taken center stage.

Sometimes I thought this trend was a desperate attempt by scientists to strike a balance between the cruelty of the world and their need to believe in something bigger while still satiating their desire to have intellectual mastery - the one driving ambition of all people of science. This trait usually led to a dictatorial and rigid streak and often created roadblocks for scientific truth-seekers. On rare occasions this intellectual acquisitiveness was carved so deep it bore the rare scientist whose breakthroughs turned history on its ear. But even those men and women's minds locked on a paradigm and repeated the mistake of their lesser colleagues. No mind, however strong and keen, could operate in a vacuum for long without the burglary of madness.

According to my research, Mappers were trained in what was once called "remote viewing," and besides studying psychology, mythology and shamanism, they used a sophisticated computer program inspired by twentieth-century biofeedback machines, though with unparalleled nuance and subtlety. The program, called Neuropathtronics, was able to tag and track thoughts in the participant's brain and helped strengthen the ability to "connect with the collective unconscious," using it as a way to read minds, time travel or see anything, anyone or any place hidden.

While all of it was fascinating, Mapping was still in its infancy, and from what I could tell, there wasn't a lot of empirical data - making Tuwa the exception, not the rule. One individual with extraordinary powers does not provide truly empirical data. I finally had to conclude, after studying the Georgetown papers, that Tuwa did have some remarkable ability, but whether she was a skilled trickster or an anomalous fluke was completely unknowable.

For the sake of the project, I tried to keep my cynicism in check. Ira seemed convinced after several meetings with her. Research and time were waning, and I felt the pressure to put aside questions until later and follow, for once, Ira's lead to trust. La Donna was key in making the Collective work, and if her judgment was off we may as well have given up. And we couldn't afford to face that possibility.

Weeks went by interviewing, checking references, scanning the internet, and reading psychological profiles. Although I had grown accustomed to La Donna's quick decisions, often based on Tuwa's intuition, the process was difficult to embrace. La Donna was charming, warm and friendly, but occasionally her candor was brash, sometimes off-putting. No rational argument dissuaded her once she had formed an opinion.

I was the odd man out, arguing against Ira and La Donna's "gut feelings" and Tuwa's visions. This, more than the grueling work, wore me out. I didn't like fighting and always tried to avoid conflict. Ira and La Donna's minds tracked the same way. It was beyond frustrating - it was exhausting. Both relied on some indefinable feeling from data and interviews and, of course, when Tuwa was consulted, it was as if they were consulting a sibyl in the hub of a majestic oracle.

I alone took into account all data and strategized a person's likely behavior. Their evaluations were personally biased and potentially jeopardized the safety of the Collective. La Donna's phrase, "You have to learn to think outside of the box, use your right brain, be more creative in your choices," was a vexing mantra. We needed balance and I had a plan to acquire it.

Over dinner Ira and I looked over the paperwork and I said, "I'm bringing Hyunae in. We're desperate for another voice. This process is too important for gut feelings alone."

Ira looked up from one of the biographies he was reading and said, "We don't have time. It might deadlock us. The timing is too crucial to screw around."

This was an argument of inconvenience and I countered, "This is my project. She's in," I said.

Ira raised his eyebrows. It was uncharacteristically brazen and he gruffly mumbled, "Fine," and went back to reading.

Several weeks of indoctrinating Hyunae into the methodology of picking suitable candidates went by before she had any say in the decision-making process. But once she started voicing her opinions she was a valuable ally, in favor of hard, cold research, the assessment of facts and consultation of background to determine a candidate's facility. Often this process frustrated La Donna and Ira. Tuwa appeared unfazed. Ira felt it was too lengthy. La Donna thought it unnecessary. But on several occasions our checks shed light on candidates who might otherwise have slipped through.

Our biggest clash was over Naomi Goldberg, whom La Donna, Ira and Tuwa had a "bad feeling" about, first from reviewing her file. Later, resistance to her got stronger after meeting with her. They refused to budge. But Naomi had an impeccable reputation as an environmental activist. They all wanted John Samuelson, but he had strong ties to Bill Weber, a fossil-fuel proponent who had sued several Japanese carmakers for patent violations on hydrogen cars – the suits turned out to be completely unfounded and just a way to continue staving off the proliferation of alternative-fuel sources so the fossil-fuel industry could suck one last drink of blood from the dying planet.

I wouldn't stand for anyone who was in bed with Bill Weber, no matter how reformed they pretended to be. Logic finally won out after Hyunae and I dug in our heels.

After selections had been made, Ira had second thoughts about the division leaders - they were all women, and after a heated discussion among all of us, he conceded that the core group was the most qualified and represented a diverse set of experiences and cultures despite their lack of maleness. He would just have to represent those issues if any came up. But this was only after Hyunae asked, "If these candidates were all male except perhaps one woman, would anyone think twice about it?" His silence was our answer. Besides, as far as I was concerned, these were not only the most morally upstanding, capable people for the jobs, it would be easier to hold panel meetings if there were no sexual tension between members.

The first group sent into the temperate rain forest of Oregon comprised engineers and workers; the second tier was a party of assistants who came after the building and walkways had been constructed. The laboratories, computers, software systems and access lines, cameras, monitors, etc., were all set up before the core group of scientists relocated.

The department leaders (or the core, as we became known) drafted a mission statement, which wasn't easy because it had to encompass a new world view and the foundations of a new society and a new civilization which would hopefully last for many generations.

After several months of deliberation we managed to come up with one: *It is our mission to protect, save and nurture life on our planet, with honor and respect for all cultures, all species and the earth itself. We dedicate ourselves to this cause and to finding a reversal of man's abuses against the environment while sustaining whatever life is left, so that it may thrive now and in the future.*

> *Psyche Hershenbaum*
> *Ira Cohen*
> *La Donna Washington*
> *Hyunae Gaffney*
> *Tuwa Redhawk*
> *Xin-Yi Chin*
> *Zoe Jones*
> *Safia Brahma*
> *Kimi Toyota*
> *Fayza Alavi*
> *Eva Rodriguez*
> *Aine Flanagan*
> *Naomi Goldberg*
> *Marina Balas*

Before the core made passage to Oregon, it was decided that I, despite my desire to shirk titles, was named chief. I had final say in breaking all ties and had the ability to veto the panel's decisions. So I officially became the Collective's leader. In case something happened to me or I was incapacitated, Ira would become acting chief until the panel nominated, and subsequently elected, a new leader.

TWELVE

It was achingly verdant and wet - full of possibilities and hope. We trekked through the brush. I had Chi sedated in his cat carrier. Ira was behind me, followed by the rest of the core. The majesty of this new world was overwhelming, leaving me to wonder how mankind could have ever thought to cut down a single tree to make paper.

But it wasn't all pulchritude, unfortunately. Signs of acid rain, ultraviolet damage and various ramifications of climate change flourished. Despite the fact that the substantial canopy of wounded trees generally provided a thick filter, the damage was surprisingly extensive, all the way down to the forest floor. An assay of local biological materials was the first order, along with a catalogue chronicling rainfall cycles and their effects on the detritus.

About half a mile from the metal parking sheds where our jeeps were housed was a maze of pathways to a series of structures perched on top of an absurdly steep hill. The site had been selected in case of a tsunami or overpowering rains. But the cost of building roads up the hill had been too much for our budget.

We needed transport mainly for future scavenging trips to Portland or Seattle. Both cities were ghosts now.

Portland had shrunk from six million people to 200, and that was before an onslaught of sleeping sickness - the most hopeful estimates two years ago only considered the possibility of a few survivors.

Seattle, which had a long history in computer technology, had suffered a widespread autoimmunity-based plague. It had killed so quickly there wasn't enough time to study it. The city was thought to be devoid of life. There was some speculation that the unidentified disease was related to a large hole in the ozone, one that had shifted downward from the Arctic. All America's cities were thought to be specters now. We hoped unknown pockets of life existed, but it was only a hope.

Indeed, the Collective's first order of business had been to develop a UV shield. The series of bridges, walkways and gardening areas were covered in an opalescent mesh scrim that reduced the UV radiation by 85 percent, but members were still required to wear heavy sunscreen because burning would occur after thirty minutes, even under the shields. And if anyone were to venture past the scrims, UV suits were required. This was the new world's first rule, and nobody argued with it.

The thirteen core scientists and I made our way up the series of redwood ramps to the central building, which housed the meeting hall, cafeteria and dorms. La Donna had already nicknamed it the Nest, and the name caught on quickly.

The building was simple, large and square. The exterior's lack of character made it difficult to imagine what the inside would look like, even though I had seen and approved the blueprints. I was the first one at the door. After punching in the code, there was a click and it opened.

"Oh, my, this is ugly," Hyunae said, following me in.

"No, just plain. It will be beautiful once our families are here and those amongst us who are artistic have decorated it," Tuwa said from behind Hyunae. Hyunae turned and raised a speculative eyebrow at her. Tuwa added, "It just needs some life."

Safia heard the discussion and said, "I have some beautiful tapestries from India. I'll take on the project of decorating the public quarters if no one is opposed." She was diminutive in stature, but not in style. Her long, thick black hair was elaborately braided and she wore modern adaptations of traditional saris, which were joyfully colorful and intricately beautiful.

A petite, red-headed woman came forward from the small crowd gathering in the entryway and stuck her hand out toward Safia. "We never formally met. I'm Aine," she said.

"Pleased to make your acquaintance," Safia said, taking her hand and giving it a firm shake while flashing a toothy smile and friendly, glowing amber eyes.

"I'd be happy to help move things, arrange, whatever you want. I love decorating, but I admit I'm not very good at it. I'm not the creative type. I would love to learn, though," Aine said.

The smile on Safia's face never wavered; she beamed and nodded. Xin-Yi shook her head with a grim expression, which was too serious for the situation. She whined, "I don't think that's fair."

This was not a good beginning for our new communal home. Xin-Yi was unexpectedly immature and I flashed back to her profile. She had been born in China but was raised in America as an only child of wealthy, indulgent parents. This had raised a flag early on to La Donna, and we had argued about whether her background and emotional inexperience would be a problem. There had never been a serious relationship in Xin-Yi's life. She had lived alone and was in her early 30s. Work was her life, her only life. The argument was settled by Xin-Yi's remarkable record of accomplishments as a genetic engineer and her dedication to idealistic university projects which focused on benefiting mankind. Many corporations had tried to lure her away with huge salaries, but Xin-Yi had stayed true to her vision of making a difference.

I said in a calm steady voice, "Why don't we retire to the meeting table in the next room? And we can all discuss this."

The room was large enough to hold the entire community – all the lead scientists, researchers, technicians and family members. A large table was set up panel-style at the back wall, where the lead scientists were to hold meetings both open and closed. A stack of folding chairs lined the walls, waiting to be used.

I sat in the center, Ira on my left, La Donna on my right. Everyone else grabbed seats in random fashion, except Tuwa. Tuwa watched Naomi struggle to find her place and then sat down next to her. All the scientists - La Donna, Hyunae, Aine, Safia, Xin-Yi, Ira, Tuwa, Eva, Marina, Zoe, Fayza, Kimi, Naomi - waited patiently for me to lead our first discussion.

Naomi flung thick, curly salt-and-pepper hair off her shoulder and said, "Safia aren't you a software designer?"

Safia nodded.

Hyunae stared at Xin-Yi with determination and said, "I nominate Safia. She's the most creative, besides being the best dressed."

Marina said in her usual stiff manner, "I certainly wouldn't want to do it. There are plenty of more important things. I don't see why we're even wasting time discussing it. If Safia is offering, we should be happy she's taking on an added responsibility." Everything about Marina seemed older then her 54 years. Her eyes were set in dark circles and her dark hair was more salt than pepper.

Ira shifted in his seat and said, "Since we're going to be living together, eating together, working together, I think every issue is an important one."

Zoe pursed her thin lips and raised her hand like a dutiful child. It was a ridiculous gesture among peers. Before I called on her,

I was instantly struck by her painfully frail physique, pasty complexion, washed-out blue eyes and dishwater-colored, lackluster hair - perhaps it was mild malnutrition. I nodded at her and she spoke in a slow, wispy voice with a faraway quality, "I second Hyunae's nomination for Safia."

Fayza glared critically at Xin-Yi and said, "Are you satisfied?"

I hoped Xin-Yi wouldn't catch the bitterness in Fayza's voice. There was a harshness that came with Fayza's honesty. She was incapable of hiding emotion; feelings danced across her face at every thought. I wondered if this had anything to do with her time as a young woman, when she had been in a radical feminist group in Afghanistan before fleeing to the U.S. Maybe being so young and in such an extreme environment had trained her to be reactively forthright and outspoken, or perhaps the inhumanity she had witnessed left angry wounds. But her frankness would be a virtue in the Collective. We needed honesty above almost all else.

Xin-Yi did not prickle at Fayza's words. Instead she sat straighter in her chair and said, "What if I don't like it? I want a say."

With a sharp creak, Tuwa pushed back from the table, got up and circled Xin-Yi. She said, "We are all anxious, afraid of our new life. We left our world and everything we have ever known to start anew. This group – this room – needs to be smudged. We all have grief, even if some don't know it yet. This is a petty thing, Xin-Yi, masking a larger anger. I sense it growing inside you. Let me help clear it. And if you still want to help because of your joy in participating, rather than your fear of being excluded, we will all support you."

No one spoke for a while. Tuwa's words hung in the room, like shadows lurking, ready to be born inside us. What she said was true and brought tears to my eyes, although I held them back. Finally, La Donna said, "You're right. Does anyone disagree?"

Around the table everyone's heads shook except Kimi's. She shuddered. When she spoke, her words sounded thin and veiled. "I don't know what smudging is. Will it hurt?"

Tuwa laughed. "No, it's an ancient Native American practice. I use it as part of my practice. Rituals help us to connect, make talk therapy more real. In this case we have already gone through a group therapy of sorts. There will be many issues brought to the meeting table and smudging will help clear the air, help us move on and let go of anger."

"So is it like meditation or prayer?" Kimi asked. Her shoulder-length black hair appeared glued to the edges of her face as her eyes followed Tuwa's movement around the room.

"Yes, it is a mutual prayer, more like a visualization grounded through waving the smoking sweetgrass and sage," Tuwa said, stopping when she got to Kimi.

Kimi nodded, looking down at her folded hands. She was a quiet person, soft-spoken. Her pale ocher complexion was now splashed with embarrassed pink. Tuwa knelt beside her and whispered, "Of course, if you're not comfortable with it you don't have to participate."

Kimi studied Tuwa. Tuwa was mesmerizing, with powerful features and ageless eyes that defied the etched lines of her face and the gray, skunk-like streak in her hair. "I trust your wisdom," was all Kimi said.

La Donna's voice boomed, "I nominate Tuwa for the position of arbitrator. She not only has a strong background in Jungian psychology, but is by far the most spiritually adept among us. Her ability to see the long-range good of the whole has been well documented in her work among the Hopi and the Pueblo communities."

"Would you be willing to act in that capacity?" I asked her.

Tuwa stood up, walked back to her seat and said, "I would be honored."

"Fine then," Ira said. "Let's get to work setting up the research committees."

After a long night of discussion it was decided Eva would head up the marine biology division, Aine would lead zoology and they would work in tandem with Naomi, who would head botany. All would collaborate with the genetic-engineering team chaired by Kimi in botanicals and Xin-Yi in animal and human development. Marina, whose many years as a physicist had crossed over into environmental gasses, would collaborate with Fayza's work in geology and Hyunae's research in astronomy and astrophysics. La Donna and Tuwa, both having psychology backgrounds, would collaborate with Zoe and Ira. Ira was trained as a sociologist/ethnobotanist and Zoe an anthropologist/archaeologist. Safia would design and maintain all computer systems. I'd oversee all projects keeping the bigger mission on track – sustaining, nourishing and restoring life with the ultimate goal of reversing the effects of global warming.

We had a lot of work to do, setting up our labs over the next month in preparation for our forthcoming staff. Safia would have the added adventure of trying to decorate the Nest so that it seemed homey and comfortable for all the families and pets that would be arriving a few weeks after the staff.

It was a tremendous job and I wondered if we would be up to it. My main concern was the ability for everyone stuck in this tiny new world to navigate around one another without animosity.

THIRTEEN

Reginald Strauch and his wife, Camille Pamela, walked from the aircraft toward an immense, gelatinous sphere. Surveying his new empire, he said to her, "Look at what money can buy." He put his hand to the fleshy gray exterior but quickly pulled it back and wiped the slimy residue onto his pants. "Remarkable."

Although Camille Pamela was dressed in spiked heels, her hair and makeup done as if she had just walked off the set of a silent movie, she wobbled closer to the Environ and mimicked her husband's gesture with one of her fuchsia-lacquered claws. "Ick," she said, pulling it back to examine the goo under her fingernail. "I thought I felt it breathe."

"You might have," Strauch said, shrugging. "I'm told it's alive, but don't ask me how the hell it works -— that's what we paid the scientists for."

Paul Lamont, who had been conversing with the pilot near the aircraft, finished and walked toward the couple with a small briefcase in hand. He opened it and handed Strauch a small gold card with a chain attached. Engraved on it were all the override codes for the Environ.

Strauch looked at it and said, "Couldn't this have waited until we got inside?"

Lamont shook his head. "I wanted to show you how it worked in case of an emergency."

"Emergency? What kind of emergency?" Camille Pamela asked, fingering a stray golden lock that had blown free from her thick layers of hairspray.

Lamont didn't dignify her question; he merely shot her a cool look and proceeded with his explanation to her husband. "The top code will disengage the mainframe's command. The second will open any door you punch into the local nerve center."

Strauch examined it carefully, then inched closer to the keypad. There was no definable door, but rather a discoloration in the Environ's flesh, indicating an opening could be formed. He shot a furtive and nervous look to Lamont and said, "Is it OK to try this out right now?"

"That's the plan. Go ahead," Lamont replied, looking at his watch. But Strauch hesitated, so Lamont added, "They know the time of our arrival – the lab is expecting the interruption." Strauch nodded, then, slowly looking at the inscription, punched one number and then the next, until a red beam flashed, lighting up the inside of the gray flesh. "Now the second code," Lamont instructed.

Strauch was a little more confident this time and his fingers moved nimbly across the keypad. Lamont then stuck his gold card into the slot. The orifice of flesh opened and Strauch smiled in surprise at his sudden power. "This is great," he said with a dim Texas accent. "My card does that, too?"

Lamont nodded.

Once inside, Lamont stepped close to the keypad near the orifice. "For the sake of time, just watch me," he said, pointing to the third set of numbers on his gold card. He punched them in, making the Environ seal itself. "This code reengages the mainframe and seals the orifices. The extra set next to it is not to be used unless you want to lock all exits." He stuck the card into the slot again, quickly pulling it out, and then slipped the chain around his neck and hid the gold card under his shirt. "I suggest you wear this at all times," he said to Strauch.

"When do I get one of those?" Camille Pamela asked.

"You don't. Your husband and I are the only people authorized. I'm sure you understand... knowledge is power," Lamont, said, snickering to himself. "It was hard for me to get one."

Strauch tried to assuage his wife's future vengeance. "That's true, darlin.' If he wasn't lead scientist in charge of all this... whatever the hell it is, he wouldn't have gotten one. But I guess he needs it if somethin' happens... you know, some scientific crisis."

Lamont pulled Strauch aside to change the subject. "I need you to look over the Geneco files. We've had the group stationed at the caves near the mine. They seem to be doing OK there."

"Right. How's the breeding program goin'?" Strauch asked.

"Fine. The egg cave – as the wranglers call it – has produced another 50."

"How many of those ugly lizard-bastard clones are there now?"

"Nearing 400 and still hatching," Lamont replied.

They walked down the corridor. It was dank. The sun filtered through the Environ's skin, and it cast a strange, gray light. As they moved toward the heart of the giant beast, only the ceiling provided illumination. Walls of flesh had been constructed to set up a variety of different rooms. Camille Pamela said, "It's so morbid."

"Maybe you can think of some way to cheer the place up, Mrs. Strauch," said a young woman who came out of a room and started toward them.

"Kaitlin, is that you?" Camille Pamela asked.

The woman shook her head. "Yes, ma'am."

"Well, for God's sake step away from that wall, it's casting a shadow. I can't see you. Where's my boy?" Camille said.

"Jacob is in the nursery with the corporate nanny. I came to meet you," Kaitlin replied.

"You're a little late for that, huh, honey?" Camille said.

"Yes, ma'am," Kaitlin said stepping into a gray shaft of light. Her long, shiny chestnut hair glistened even in the unflattering light. She was a slight woman in every way. Her perfectly formed features and porcelain-like skin were as perfect as a David painting. She seemed to be the direct opposite of Camille Pamela. She was natural without a stitch of makeup, whereas Camille could have started her own cosmetics corporation with what was presently on her face. "Would you like me to show you around?" Kaitlin asked.

Lamont was impatiently checking his watch. He gave Strauch a tired look. Strauch said, "That sounds like a fine idea, Kaitlin." He then turned to his wife and said, "We're going to go to headquarters. I'll see you in our suite later." Before Camille Pamela had a chance to reply, Strauch and Lamont disappeared down the long corridor.

"Well, this is certainly going to be an adjustment," Camille said, taking Kaitlin's arm to steady herself on their walk. "Is everything here this depressing?"

Kaitlin nudged Camille down the next series of corridors. "No, the garden is absolutely beautiful. Would you like to see it or Jacob first, Mrs. Strauch?"

"I need some cheering up. Jacob will be fine," Camille said.

After a series of hallways, which reminded Camille of being inside a giant, diseased intestine, she asked, "Where are all the rooms?"

"They're everywhere, ma'am," Kaitlin said.

"Then why don't I see any? When we first came in there were all these openings with large rooms inside, filled with furniture," Camille said.

"Those were the common areas you passed. This is the private wing. Each discoloration you see on the corridor wall is a door. Iris scanners allow the inhabitants inside to look out, kind of like a keyhole. And of course, it acts like a key, automatically opening the door for the occupant," Kaitlin said.

"Good Lord, I'm never going to get used to this. Everything looks the same to me," Camille said.

Kaitlin walked up to what appeared to be the end of the hallway just before it ran into a perpendicular corridor. She waved her hand in front of a blinking red light and the orifice opened.

"How did you do that?" Camille said, staring at her.

Kaitlin nudged Camille inside and said, "Everyone has access to this area for farming. We're all supposed to put in at least twenty hours a month as part of our payment to Digibio for letting us live."

"I suppose we all have to eat," Camille replied, still keeping her eyes on Kaitlin. Once she realized how much brighter the room was she turned her attention toward the ceiling, which was different than anything she had seen so far in the Environ. It had an ambient, fire-like glow. "How come it's so much brighter in here?"

"I asked the same question when Jacob and I were shown around by one of the scientists," Kaitlin said. "He told us it was because this room, while connected to the rest of the Environ, was uniquely developed to compensate for the oxygen created by the plants – and, of course, they needed more light, too. The biological material that the ceiling is made of extends all the way around and loops to the main body."

"Well, why didn't they make the whole thing like this? It's so much nicer. Did he tell you that? Those men are such fools sometimes. People need light too, not just a bunch of damn plants."

"He said it had something to do with the UV rays. I guess it's not safe enough for people to live in all the time. It might cause birth defects. They aren't really sure, so they played it safe. He described this room as sort of an eyelid and the rest of the Environ as the body. The membrane here is much thinner and the plants have been genetically engineered to resist the extra UV. We're supposed to wear sunscreen if we're going to stay in here for more than half an hour. And because the membrane is so thin they couldn't run the digital rods... I think that's what he said. Anyway, it could be dangerous in an emergency because there's no way out except back through the main body of the Environ."

They walked around for a few minutes and Camille spotted a handsome, thickly muscled man walking hand-in-hand with a tall, thin, willowy woman with colorless blond hair and eyes which were placed so far on opposite sides of her broad face she resembled a bottom feeder. "How could a man that gorgeous fall for a woman so grotesquely ugly?" Camille said, more to herself than to Kaitlin.

"There are park benches past the corn – near the herb garden at the start of the pines," Kaitlin said, pointing at a dense array of foliage.

"Let's head over to the nursery," Camille Pamela said. She threaded her arm through Kaitlin's, shuddering. "Ooh, I can't look at them. Just get me out of here." Kaitlin and Camille snaked around a path toward a charcoal gray wall. Camille's eye caught the pulsing red beam and she ran her hand across it this time. The wall opened like a biological shutter. Camille grimaced. "I'll never get used to that."

"You did great, Mrs. Strauch."

Jacob was in the middle of a tantrum when Camille Pamela and Kaitlin arrived at the nursery. The corporate nanny was holding a small boy in her arms to shield him from the barrage of wooden blocks Jacob was throwing. The boy had a red spot on his temple and was curled against the nanny, with a pacifier in his mouth, rubbing his head. He had obviously been crying but was worn out. The corporate nanny was in the middle of saying, "Jacob, calm down."

"You know Mommy doesn't put up with this sort of behavior," Camille said. "You are to be a good boy, no more throwing blocks."

Jacob smirked. He wasn't quite three years old, and his expression appeared too devious for a child of his age. He picked up blocks in each hand and threw them with all his might toward Camille Pamela. One whizzed past her ear, the next whacked her shin. The smack of it on her bone sent a wave of shock through her body. Her vision went red and she jerked him off the floor, screaming, "You little bastard!" Before Kaitlin could stop her she was punching his little shoulder with one hand and shaking him so hard it looked like his arm would break.

The expression on his face had instantly changed from self-satisfaction to utter terror and his eyes reached out to Kaitlin, who was frozen. Finally, Kaitlin said, "Let me take him, Mrs. Strauch. Why don't I have Josephine take you to your room?"

The corporate nanny came forward, putting a gentle hand on Camille Pamela's forearm. She jerked her hand back, still seething with anger. She pointed her finger at Jacob and said, "Little mister, you'd better pray I don't get a bruise."

Jacob shuddered; he reached for Kaitlin's hand. Camille made a swift motion toward him and hissed. He recoiled and started crying. "I'll teach you yet," she said.

Kaitlin tried not to look horrified. She had learned early on that suggesting a calmer tone or implying a kinder method of discipline incensed Camille and thus made it far worse for Jacob. Instead, Kaitlin would do what she always did when Camille was through with her tirade – hold Jacob close, rock him on her knees and sing him a lullaby.

As the corporate nanny, Josephine, was escorting Camille through the corridor, she said, "We don't spank children in daycare, and we usually don't have a problem."

"Save me your liberal bullshit. Spare the rod, spoil the child, that's what the Bible says. The Applegates beat the hell out of their kids, and they were the best-behaved children I had ever seen."

"Had?" Josephine asked.

"The most famous televangelists in the world, and you never heard their kids died of the plague?" Camille Pamela was indignant, her face screwed into a sneer. "What? Aren't you a Christian?"

"Yes, of course. I just didn't understand the reference. I knew that," Josephine quickened her pace so Camille couldn't see her directly. Some people had blamed the Applegates for not taking the kids to a clinic fast enough, and Josephine was one of them.

In the Environ, everyone was a Christian, and no one was allowed in, with the exception of scientists. And then they were made to join the Wrath of God Inc. The Applegates were the Environ bishops, or so they called themselves at the mandatory Sunday service.

"You'll have to forgive me, but I don't have access, of course, to your quarters. So I'll leave you to retire," Josephine said.

Camille looked at her suspiciously before leaning into the iris scanner. While waiting for the orifice to open, she dismissively waved her hand, letting her pink lacquered claws flop like two flags dropped by the wind. "Well, go on," she said.

Her room was better than she had expected, considering the hideousness of the environment. Strauch, thank God, had had the good sense to mask the horrible gray with sheetrock. It looked, by all accounts, like a normal home if you didn't examine anything too long. Most of the White Houses furniture had been brought in – what could fit, anyway – and the suite was big. It had three bedrooms, two bathrooms, a study, living quarters, a playroom and a den. Funny how White House furniture could brighten a room.

The orifice opened into the living room and Camille spied the bar and made a beeline to it. She poured some bourbon into a thick, ancient-crystal tumbler and kicked off her shoes. She wondered what Sandy Applegate was up to right about now. Maybe she'd like to come over for a drink and to do some scheming.

She sipped her drink, fell back onto the leather armchair and called into what looked like a vocaphone, "Give me Sandy Applegate, please."

A soft male voice replied, "That is cell 33, hold... ringing."

"What the fuck?" Camille said aloud to the computer. The mention of being in a cell jolted her. She had almost forgotten she wasn't back home.

"Hello, Sandy speaking."

"I'm having a nice drink, my feet are up on the ottoman. I thought you would like to come over and join me... you know, do some planning," Camille said.

I'm so happy you made it, Camille. I prayed for your safe journey," Sandy said.

"Oh, cut the bullshit. Your secret's safe with me. Come on over and lets have a grand ole' time."

Sandy snickered. "What cell you in?"

"How the fuck should I know? I just got here and don't use that word... cell ...it's so distasteful. Computer... whatever the hell you are exactly... disengage the call."

"Disengaged," the computer mimicked.

Camille was pouring herself another drink when she heard Sandy's voice outside the orifice. The computer voice announced, "You have a visitor."

"I fucking know that. I can hear her," Camille screamed into the air. "Hold on, Sandy," she yelled as she set the bottle of booze down on the marble surface of the bar top and walked to the orifice. She waved her hand over the red blinking laser and it opened. Sandy stepped in, hair teased and piled high like lavender cotton candy, her pink dress dotted with rhinestones accentuating a pastel print of doves with olive branches, and a thick cake of makeup that had more in common with masks and clowns than other women. She looked like a demented Cabbage Patch doll with caterpillars for lashes and plump pink pincushions for lips.

Camille Pamela stretched out her arms and the two women embraced in a stiff hug. "What happened to your pink hair?" Camille said, returning to the bar to pour their drinks.

"I had it for so many years in Vegas I guess I just got tired of it and decided last week, when we got to the Environ, that it would look better purple under this grayish light. Besides, purple is associated with spirituality," Sandy said, sitting on the couch opposite the armchair.

Camille walked around the coffee table and sat down next to her, handing her a drink. "Since this is my husband's company, I think we should set a no-abortion policy," she said, taking a sip of her drink as she rotated herself toward Sandy. "Don't you agree?"

"Absolutely, no pre-marital sex, either," Sandy said. "Technically, the Bible says it is better to lie with a whore than to cast your seed to waste."

"So, no condoms," Camille said, leaning back into the cushions of the sofa.

"No birth control of any kind, right..." Sandy stopped for a moment and said in hushed tones, "But we don't have the resources to support many more people than we already have."

"Well, those who can't live by the rules can fend for themselves outside, or if they're too afraid of a long, drawn-out death, we can aid them out of this world, so to speak. Of course, you can really help with that," Camille lifted her glass and met Sandy's eyes with a snarling smile.

A slow, dark grin spread across Sandy's face. It was starting to hit her. She held her glass up to Camille's and clanked. "Of course, there's to be absolutely no adultery either."

"Oh, yes, yes, I agree. But I do think the women should be held more accountable than the men. We all know how men are. They just can't help themselves," Camille Pamela smirked.

"Those desperate, desperate men - bless their hearts. How awful it would be if they couldn't get laid. And what would we do if all those handsome scientists were punished? I sure couldn't fix this

Environ," Sandy said, her southern drawl deepening with the bourbon. "I'll have another one," she said, holding up her snifter and giggling.

"I'm so glad we're on the same page," Camille said, getting off the sofa and walking over to the bar. As she grabbed the bottle, she said, "In this little kingdom we have, I want you to back me up with the moral side." She sat back down next to Sandy. "You know, we don't want any backlash with the people. It would cause utter chaos. And we certainly can't have all those worker bees running wild." Camille poured more drinks.

"I hear you darlin'. You know Jesse and I have always backed you guys on policy from the beginning of Reginald's career in politics. Nothin's gonna change now," Sandy said.

"Just checking, because it might not always be easy," Camille said.

"Oh, hell, don't worry about it. We'll get this place under control," Sandy said.

"You have a visitor," the computer said.

"Who is it?" Camille shouted.

"Jacob and Kaitlin," it called back within moments.

"Shit, let them in," Camille said.

The orifice opened and Kaitlin walked through, holding Jacob. "I'm sorry, ma'am, we didn't mean to bother you, but it's time for Jacob's nap. I'll put him to bed and I'll head to my cell. If you need me, I'll be here in a flash," Kaitlin said.

"Go ahead." Camille feigned a generous smile and said, "Please, no more talk of cells. It's your room, OK?"

Kaitlin smiled and nodded back. She and Jacob exited the living room and entered Jacob's bedroom.

Sandy shook her head and looked deep into her bourbon. She lifted the glass lovingly to her lips and reveled in the fiery warmth as it went down her throat. "My, my, you're going to have to watch that one. She's a real temptress," Sandy said.

Camille Pamela stared for a moment at her, then slowly bent over the coffee table and refilled her own glass. Sandy continued, "We had a real pious girl, never wore a stitch of makeup, clean as the day is long - you know the type - well, she turned out to be a real troublemaker with the menfolk. Seems they all wanted a piece of her - she was a 'challenge'."

Camille looked hard at her. "Gilly? The assistant?"

"That's right. She fucked Jessie's brains out while I was ministering in Florida." Sandy met Camille Pamela's eyes and took a sip.

"That little bitch. I would have killed her," Camille said.

Sandy laughed with a slight snort. "I would have, too, if I could've gotten away with it."

"Well then, I guess we know which rules have to be set in place first," Camille Pamela said.

"We sure do," Sandy said, raising a toast.

FOURTEEN

All the family members and crew scientists arrived without incident. At first, the dozens of family cats and dogs were isolated to their owners' quarters, but over a period of months they were socialized until, in their own time, they were given free reign of the Nest. There was a special sheltered outdoor area they had access to through a few electronic doors. Chi loved going outside - he had never been before. In D.C. the scrims were unreliable, torn in places. People knew where they were, but anyone who loved their animals didn't allow them outside unaccompanied.

There had been several town meetings in the Nest. At one, a family member brought in an old flatscreen TV and we watched as the lone station in D.C. reported people flooding into emergency rooms with severe burns. A Category 5 hurricane with winds of 220 mph had hit the North Carolina coast and broke into a fierce tropical storm, spinning off dozens of tornados. Washington was ravaged, buildings torn apart by winds, and of course the city's scrims were completely destroyed. The reporter looked like he had suffered second- and third-degree UV radiation burns. People were literally frying to death, and there was no one to help. The doctors were in as bad a state as their patients.

Europe had long-since seen its demise from the mini ice age of the '30s, and Africa had been rendered uninhabitable, ravaged by drought, disease and famine starting at the turn of the century. The next time we watched the flatscreen there was only a test pattern; a few weeks later, only static. We tried an old radio, but it was no different. Whatever was left of the world's population had vanished within weeks.

At the next series of town meetings we established rules and regulations. The basic principles were simple - have respect for every member of the community and live by the Golden Rule. This, of course, was more easily said than done. La Donna and Tuwa developed resolution techniques and a form of group therapy, as well as individual counseling sessions. Everyone was encouraged to take advantage of both. Because of Tuwa's background, she took the role of spiritual advisor, organizing rituals for those who wanted to be involved.

My first concern was preservation, and I concentrated most of my energy into Aine's breeding program for rescued animals - some had been shipped in before the core scientists arrived and were cared for by a skeleton crew of techs who were setting up the labs, but most animals were indigenous, collected from the area shortly after we arrived. The farming animals - chickens, cows, sheep, etc. - were first on the agenda for obvious reasons. They had genetic mutations caused from ancestral UV exposure; most of the problems manifested as infertility. This was Xin-Yi's area of expertise. In her 20s she had solved the crisis of rapid aging associated with earlier clones, and ten years later she found a way to double the normal life span of a sheep. This sheep was still alive, safe in the Collective's UV-sheltered stockade.

But there was a trickier problem to solve - repairing damaged DNA and reversing infertility so animals could repopulate without human intervention. Soon we would lose this opportunity with less and less genetic variance, which would make repairing the problem virtually impossible. Kimi, back in D.C., had already started this monumental task, but her government funding had run out and the study was never completed.

There was growing concern about Naomi and her botanical project. She refused to incorporate strains of lab-created UV-resistant DNA to the Collective's edible plant garden. After nearly a dozen leadership and community meetings, she conceded to a specialized oversight committee, allowing them to decide. The committee was comprised of fourteen scientists, seven of the best on her botanical team and seven from Kimi's genetic-engineering staff.

The committee concluded the UV-resistant strains were perfectly safe for consumption (which had been Naomi's argument against their incorporation). They presented their conclusion to Naomi and she refused to accept their findings. I had to call a community meeting where the oversight committee presented their evidence and the whole Collective voted 437 to 1 to implement their recommendations; six people abstained from voting feeling they didn't understand the subject well enough to vote.

A backlash against Naomi was swift on the heels of her controversial stance, and the botany staff presented a petition for her resignation as lead scientist of their department. Out of fairness to everyone, she was put on a three-month probationary period, with her performance to be reviewed at the end. This placated her staff, but Naomi wasn't happy about it.

Naomi called a closed leaders-only session. After listening to fifteen minutes of her argument, La Donna interrupted. "So, basically what you're saying is that you don't think you've been treated fairly?"

Naomi nodded and added, "No one on my staff has anywhere near the level of expertise that I have on the subject. I've put in 25 years of research on edible plants."

"And that's why you're still lead botanical scientist," I said.

"Probation is humiliating," Naomi hissed.

"There has to be a repercussion for betraying the agreement you made," I said.

"I was forced to agree to that?"

"This is ridiculous," Fayza shouted. "You're acting like an insolent child. You have no idea what unfairness is, what punishment really means." She got up from the table. "I can't listen to any more of this nonsense."

Fayza was almost to the door when I said, "Wait a moment."

"I'm in complete agreement with Fayza," Kimi said. She stared hard at Naomi and said, "Ever since we got here you've acted like a total prima donna."

"How dare you," Naomi retorted.

Maria chimed in, "I don't agree to name-calling, but in this case Kimi's right."

And then all hell broke loose. There was yelling about Naomi's stubbornness and arrogance, and other people telling people to calm down, and things just kept escalating. No matter what I did, I couldn't get everyone to relax. If it were a group of men it would have erupted into a mass fistfight.

The door slammed shut and the room went momentarily silent. Everyone turned to Tuwa, who had just walked back in with a smudging wand and a hand drum. She lit the smudging wand and started singing in what I suspected was her native language, Cree, and handed La Donna the hand drum. La Donna looked befuddled at first, but as Tuwa's singing grew more intense, she joined in. Tuwa moved the smoking wand around the room and then over each individual.

A few minutes later everyone sat down again, five more minutes and a peace crept over the room, half an hour later everyone was calm again.

FIFTEEN

Eva's project was also going to be difficult. It required marine specimens and access to the ocean - meaning trips to the seashore in our trucks, which would deplete our energy storage and require scavenging trips to Portland or Seattle to replace what was lost. But antidotes needed to be developed to a host of problems plaguing marine animals. It was an ambitious, long-term project, but necessary to the grander mission of restoring balance to the earth. And without ocean health, the future would remain bleak.

The sun was rising as I set off on my rounds, checking the research at the various facilities and collating it to be used for my staff. The information was to be tracked, making sure no department went too far off the goal of the Collective's mission statement. This required combing through findings, identifying links in research and putting bridge teams together, when necessary, to share expertise. It was a difficult task and I was feeling the stress of it.

I finished scanning the previous day's report into my wristcom and took a break to let Kimi show me the cattle pen where the animals grazed.

"Aren't they cute?" Kimi said. "My favorite is that Holstein near the fence with the black band near her eyes. She's feisty," she said, pointing.

"Feisty?" I said.

"For a cow," Kimi replied. "They all have different personalities, they're just subtle. You have to pay close attention to notice."

I smiled at the idea and then turned to walk back into the lab, but Ira rushed out toward me, stopping a few feet away to gasp for air. "What's going on?" I asked, rushing to him.

"You've got to see. Even I had no idea they were capable of something like this," he said, grabbing my arm.

I was completely confused and his frantic behavior scared me. "Who are they?"

"Digibio, I didn't understand the reference to it in the downloads. But I've re-examined it, looking for clues," he said, walking me over to the Nest.

I shook my head. "I still don't know what you're talking about," I said as we entered the foyer.

"Brace yourself, try not to show any emotion," he said escorting me into the meeting room.

On a sofa near the window was a little knobby-looking humanoid with lizardlike skin, eyes and coloring. If I didn't know better, I would have sworn it was of extraterrestrial origin, except for Ira's caveats and ramblings about Digibio.

"Hello, ma'am," it said, getting up to bow its head at me.

I looked at Ira, who was staring in fascination at the green man. I stepped forward and extended my hand to him. "Hello," I said.

The lizard man was horrified by the gesture, shook his head, and took a step backward and bowed. "I'm Psyche," I said. But he didn't respond.

Finally Ira said, "This is Geney 199. He's been trained to answer only direct questions."

I directed another question to the lizard man. "Where did you come from?" I asked.

"Cave near Environ, ma'am," Geney 199 said, looking up at me.

"I mean..." I started.

"He was manufactured in a lab somewhere in Florida by an arm of Digibio called Geneco Wave. They spliced together an amalgam of human, reptile and fish strands to make a mining slave-race for the Environ. He's clone number 199. Officially they are called Geneco, a registered trademark to Digibio and Geneco Wave, but among their own they call themselves Geneys."

"What are you mining for?" I asked Geney 199.

"Gold and metals. We serve creators," he said, bowing his head again.

"How did you get here?" I asked.

"Mine wall collapse working. Friend Geney 178 and 200 die, I scare, hurt arm and I walk for long time then no can I walk no more," he said.

"If you'll excuse us, we'll be right back," I said, tugging at Ira's arm.

We stepped into the foyer and closed the door. "It's unbelievable," I said.

"I know. They're sick bastards," Ira replied.

"He seems intelligent. I doubt he's had any kind of education. He must have picked up English from the scientists," I said.

"He looks mostly human. I bet they wanted the Geneco to look scary so no one would question their use as slaves. But it's doubtful he has very much non-human DNA."

I nodded. "He does look odd. Some members might be scared by him, especially the kids."

"Yeah, well there's nothing we can do about that except explain," he said.

"Let's get some blood from him and do a workup. And get someone from medical to do a physical, make sure he's OK from the accident."

Ira nodded, adding, "I'll get Kimi to do the workup on his genetics to see what's up."

"And he needs to be quarantined for the time being, until we're sure he's not carrying anything."

Ira moved closer and stared at me. "You realize he can't go back."

I nodded. "I know."

SIXTEEN

"Oh, Lord have mercy!" Jessie Applegate screamed into the wireless headset mic while prancing around the stage of the chapel in his electric-blue polyurethane jumpsuit flagged with rhinestones. The room was packed to capacity. And although Digibio law required all inhabitants attend each Sunday, the Applegates seemed orgasmicly inspired by their audience.

"Lord have MERCY on your SOUL!" Sandy screeched, throwing her arm into the air in a mock square dance with Jesus. Her outfit mirrored her husband's except for the layers of stiff plastic lace puffing out in every direction, causing her to resemble a blowfish. Her finest feature – seductively handsome legs - were exposed, luring most parishioners and even her husband to give her bottom half their attention. "Heal us of our SINS!"

The karaoke music started to play and Sandy and Jessie clasped hands and sang, "Jesus, oh Jesus, you are our one and only. Jesus, oh lord Jesus, dying for our sins! Jesus, oh good Jesus, God gave us his only son!"

Sandy broke free of Jessie, clapping her hands at the crowd to pump them up. "Come on, all together now!" she screamed. "Jesus, oh Jesus..." They continued singing with the gathering steam of their parishioners.

Lamont was at the back of the church, leaning against a curtain that butted against the wall. He rolled his eyes thinking, *what a tacky burlesque show. Couldn't the Strauchs have picked someone more dignified, like the Pope? They have money. But I suppose Americans bought this crap up. The least they could do would be exempt the scientists from this fiasco.*

When the song was finally over, Sandy went behind the pulpit and read a passage from the Bible and then said, "The Lord, he gave us life. That life is sacred, precious. It should be valued above all other gifts. When a man spills his seed, that is a sin. When a woman kills the baby growing inside of her, that is a sin - the worst kind of sin. It is murder. When we lay down with another for any other reason than to give that precious gift of life to a fellow human baby, that is a sin."

Jessie chimed in, "As soon as that sperm leaves your body, that's the hope of life - that's a baby - a human being. That's why the Lord said it is better to lay with a whore than to spill your seed."

Sandy gave him a strange glare then said, "That's why, to stop that baby from coming into this world with condoms or pills or anything, even the rhythm method is a sin. Because that's the hope of life - a baby wanting to be born."

Lamont rolled his eyes again, hoping no one could see disgust cross his face. *Don't these people realize there's only so much room in here? After we mine enough metal it will still be at least 10 years before we can get the Environ to reproduce, and even then it will take another 10 to mature. Even with natural biogrowth we'll run out of space in here in just a few years if these people start procreating like rabbits. There just isn't enough physical room for this policy.*

"God creates beautiful little baby spirits in Heaven and they need a home here on Earth. We can't murder those precious little baby spirits just because we want to get off, now can we? If you don't want to tempt the Lord with a home for His baby spirits, then you have to say no! No to sex of any kind," Jessie said.

"Amen to that!" Sandy said.

"Amen!" the believers cried.

"When a wanton woman comes to you with desire in her eyes, looking for a place to sleep, you just say no!" Sandy said.

"Amen!" Jessie shouted.

"Amen!" the crowd repeated.

"When you're full of pride because a pretty lady pays you a compliment, remember the Lord!" Jessie said.

Sandy shook her big purple beehive. "Amen."

"Amen," the crowd said.

"When you feel that itch of lust, pray to Jesus!" Sandy said.

"Amen," Jessie said nodding to his wife.

"Amen," the audience retorted.

Lamont looked at his watch. *How long were these idiots going to rage on about the Lord?* He had work to do. Scanning the crowd, he spotted the Strauchs sitting at the front of the stage in special gold-plated chairs. This is a sideshow, he thought looking for a way out. He scooted toward one of his techs sleeping in fits on a folding chair near the orifice. He whispered into the Asian man's ear, "Is there a secret chamber out?"

The tech woke in a start. "Why don't you use the restroom near the back? You can use your ID to get out the other side into the hallway." He smiled. "Most of the scientists already escaped that way."

SEVENTEEN

The room was crowded, and in order to accommodate the town hall-style meeting, the table was moved out and chairs were placed close together in rows. Even still, many techs who hadn't been officially brought in lined the walls out to its perimeter. Kimi stood at a makeshift podium and read Dr. Harold Candell's report to the crowd. "Geney 199 shows no signs of disease and is indeed physically robust. Genetically, his makeup is infinitesimally different than our own, with only the most minor adjustments having been made in the DNA strand controlling the skin organs, reproductive systems and digestive systems. Nearly all his genetic material is human, and I would classify him as such. However, because of these alterations he is also quite alien, sharing some characteristics with reptiles, of which Eva, Xin-Yi and Kimi's combined report will detail."

Kimi took a seat behind the podium and made way for Eva to speak. She scowled at her papers, muttering to herself before she began. "I don't entirely agree with Harold's report. Yes, humanoid but not quite human," Eva said quietly before she started reading from the report. "Geney 199's body temperature fluctuates with the environment, allowing for adaptation to extreme heat. He has also been genetically altered to be physically stronger than an ordinary human being and requires feeding just once a month, like a snake."

Eva looked up at the crowd for a moment to make eye contact before she began again. "Normal human reproduction has been exchanged for one closely resembling lizards, from conception to gestation in an external egg. According to Geney 199, there are some mammalian traits shared, such as nursing. Genetically, however, there seems to be no difference in the construction of his brain, and scans confirmed it appears perfectly normal in every human sense of the word." Eva sat back down.

I came to the podium. "La Donna Washington gave Geney 199 a standardized IQ test and found him to be slightly above average, but she felt his potential, with education, would have changed factors to raise it at least another 10 points. The potential she thought might be higher, she couldn't be sure. Overall, his cognitive skills were good. The problem we face now is in the definition of human life. And while our charter doesn't speak of the liberation of a genetically altered slave race, we have to consider not only what we will do with Geney 199, but others who might wander into our encampment. I'll open the floor to discussion now. Yes," I said, pointing to Tuwa, who was sitting in front of the podium.

"All life is sacred and must be protected. I see no difference or exception here," Tuwa said with authority.

Naomi stood up, asking, "May I speak?"

I nodded.

"Our mission statement was drafted to save nature. This creature is, in my opinion, a genetic amalgamation created by a corporation, not a life form that would or should have existed in the natural ecosystem. Who knows what kind of havoc it - he and his kind - could wreak if protected by us."

Aine shook her head. "Life is life, he's here now. I've worked with all kinds of people across the globe, and I'll be frank Naomi: You sound like an early white settler in Australia, someone who would hunt Aborigines."

"That's kind of extreme," Kimi said. "I don't think Naomi's comment implied violence toward the Geneco."

Naomi arched a thick brow and said, "This situation is quite different."

"You don't think working in mines as slaves is serious?" Aine spat back.

Kimi replied, "No, I do… it's just not the same as hunting people for sport."

"It's just as horrible," Aine retorted.

Naomi started, "How can..."

I spoke over her, "All of you, please. The reality is, Geney 199 is here and he's staying here."

Naomi said, "Who decided that? I thought that's what this was all about."

"He can't go back. He would be murdered," Ira said.

"You don't know that," Naomi replied.

"Please," I said. "Let him finish."

Ira walked over to the podium. "We do know, based on what he told us. If a Geney so much as faints from exhaustion, he's killed. If he misidentifies a location or speaks when not spoken to, he's beaten to within an inch of his life, then made to go back to work, often dying soon after," he said.

I scanned the crowd. Many of the scientist shook their heads in disbelief. "Do you doubt the moral corruption of Digibio?" I asked.

Hyunae said, "No. But what do you propose we do about it?"

"We keep him. Assimilate him into the Collective for now - retrain him," I said.

But Naomi shook her head. "There's no way to do that. He's too different, the children are afraid. My boy saw him and had nightmares."

Tuwa said, "Are you proposing segregation?"

"What's wrong with that? The animals are kept separate from us. Why not him?" Naomi responded.

La Donna got up from her seat and strolled to the head of the crowd, in front of the podium. "There was a time not so very long ago when my people were enslaved. And even after we won our freedom we were segregated, undereducated and ghettoized because of the color of our skin." She shook her head. "It was wrong then and it's wrong now. What's wrong is wrong."

"But..." Naomi started.

"What about the history of your own people? You're a Jew. Don't you remember your Bible stories? Or the Holocaust?"

"La Donna is right. We cannot allow ourselves to make the same mistakes our ancestors did. The children will get used to Geney 199 and others of his kind who join us. We will incorporate them into our community. Young people are resilient and adapt quickly. I will train him in the arts of healing. He is a gentle soul and there is no need to be frightened of him," Tuwa said. Her calm demeanor and spiritual wisdom descended on the meeting like a cool spring shower. She was quickly usurping my power not because she was trying to, but because she was the wisest among us. All those who had sought her counsel or came to her rituals found genuine peace in her presence. She was a stabilizing force and her ancient practices had quickly been adapted into the life of the Collective over the eight months we had been settling.

Even the most rigid scientists were converting to her brand of spirituality because of the miraculous things they had witnessed her do. One of the strangest stories, something I didn't witness, was of Tuwa healing the broken leg of an 8-year-old girl. Supposedly the girl had fallen off a chair while during a play in the recreation room. Everyone heard the chilling sound of the break and subsequent scream of pain. The girl's shin was bent in two as though it had grown a second knee. Tuwa reset her leg and after chanting (some said 10 minutes, others said an hour - people said it was as if time had skipped backwards) the girl was perfect again. This one event instantly converted everyone in the room.

But I didn't see it and I resisted Tuwa's circle. Besides, if there was a God, he had to be a real bastard. Allowing all of the Earth creatures to suffer and die in the horrible twisted ways I had seen the 30-odd years I had been alive. Not to mention what he did to my mom.

Religion caused wars, fed on fear and kept people from being rational enough to save themselves and the planet. No matter what, it was a bad game. I'd made it through far worse without the shelter of an omnipotent being. Why start now?

Mom had been right.

EIGHTEEN

Reginald Strauch clipped through the orifice, past the waste reassignment and to the brain, as the scientists called it. It was his first time in the eight months of running the Environ that he had to come to Lamont. Once he got there he asked a lab tech, "Where's Lamont?"

The tech pointed him toward the central nerve center. Strauch walked up to it and felt around for the sensor, but there wasn't one. The tech called to him, "You'll have to use your code, sir."

Strauch let out a sigh of exasperation and pulled the gold card from under his shirt. It resembled a dog tag just a little too much for his taste. He squinted at the sequence, slowly punching the numbers into the keypad and sticking it into its slot. "Why didn't you people put iris scanners in here?"

"Budget. I guess Mr. Lamont didn't think it was worth it, since he's usually the only one in there," the tech replied.

Strauch grimaced at him, then turned to walk through the orifice. Lamont was sitting at a luminescent wall of gray flesh. It was called the nerve center because all the Environ's systems ran through the board in this room, like the base of a brain stem. Strauch took a seat and Lamont finished what he was doing before saying, "I take it this is urgent."

"Damn right," Strauch replied. Lamont betrayed no emotion. He simply stared at Strauch's cold, blue eyes, waiting for the tirade. This drove Strauch to the brink of madness. Lamont showed no fear, a quality he didn't like in men. "Camille tells me your people have been duckin' out of services and she said you haven't even bothered showing the last few Sundays, not even for roll call." Strauch could barely control himself. His voice cracked and whined with anger.

"Yes, that's all true," said Lamont.

"Well, you mind tellin' me why?" Strauch hissed.

"I've been kept very busy these last few weeks. It seems Geney 199 has turned up missing," Paul replied.

"So?" Strauch demanded.

"Missing as in no dead body. It seems he escaped. I put a tracker team on it. We used one of the wrangling jeeps and they turned up evidence he went into the rain forest near the Oregon border."

Strauch stared indignantly at him, "And your point is?"

"The Collective is located there. If he runs into them it will constitute a breach in Geneco security. Chances are, with that band of bleeding hearts, they'll hatch a rescue operation, seeing them as a slave race – which, of course, they are. Who knows what else? With all the liberal jibber-jabber, they might want to destroy the Environ because it eats, drinks and sucks the life out of everything it contacts, leaving a trail of toxic waste in its wake. They might not like that too much. After all, they are trying to save the Earth."

Lamont was sarcastic in his tone, and Strauch didn't appreciate it. If he could have disposed of Lamont he would have by now, seeing as how the man had absolutely no respect for him. But he was the only scientist who held all the pieces of the Environ puzzle. And as Lamont had aptly said himself, "Knowledge is power."

Strauch sat back in his seat, staring at the multicolored lights blinking in front of him. He had absolutely no idea what any of them meant. Finally, he said, "You're a scientist. I respect that, but I'm a politician and a CEO. I'm a decider and when it comes to governin', you have to show me the same respect. The church is the founding principle in our system of government. It provides the moral underpinnin'ens for our people. We can't have a bunch of nobodies runnin' around doing whatever they please, screwin' off. We need organization in order to survive not just here, but period. If you or your people keep buckin' the rules then everybody else will feel it's OK for them to do the same. You understand?"

"Yes, but there may be certain crises my people will have to deal with. I don't think we should be penalized for taking care of these difficulties. After all, without our ability to sustain the Environ you'll have no world to govern," Lamont said.

Strauch nodded. It was an intricate game of chess. He waited for a moment for his anger to subside, then said, "Granted, but in those cases why don't we agree to a tech representative givin' a brief statement at the beginnin' of service..."

"Why not just exempt the scientists? They are of greater use doing their jobs," Lamont said.

"Damn it, Paul! It was mandatory for admission. You and your scientists agreed to play by the rules," Strauch said. The veins in his neck bulged and his face burst scarlet. He took a deep breath and continued, "Now, if we have a code system that could be announced at the beginnin' of service, the people would know and those members of that particular branch, or team or whatever the hell you call it, could do their job, but still be held accountable."

"Very well then, a code. I'll come up with something simple," Lamont said.

"But I want to make sure your people are at least represented. No more of this sneakin' out through the lavatory."

"Fine then, very good," Lamont said.

"Don't give me that horseshit! I mean it! The next time one of your techie nerds sneaks off, he'll get a public beatin'. "

Lamont nodded indifferently.

"And if that same son-of-a-bitch does it again, I'll cut off his testicle or tit and shove it down his or her goddamned throat. Got me?"

"Well, that certainly won't be necessary," Lamont replied.

"It'd better not be," Strauch said, getting up in a rush to exit.

Strauch was too pissed to go straight into his meeting with Jessie - he stopped back at his cell to have a Scotch. While he was pouring himself a double on the rocks, Kaitlin walked in and said, "Jacob's down for his nap. May I be excused for a moment to go to my cell? I forgot to bring him the digi-fingerpaint scans that I printed out this morning. He's so proud of them."

"That dress is very becomin' on you, Kaitlin," Strauch said turning toward her with a strange glimmer in his eye.

Kaitlin backed up. "Thank you sir."

Strauch sauntered close to her, peering down at her breasts. They seemed riper than he had remembered. "You've put on a little weight?"

She smiled. "Yes, thank you."

He ran his finger up from her navel until it came to rest on her sternum. Flattening his hand he reached inside her dress and fondled her. She stiffened. Her fear excited him and he pushed her down onto an end table near the orifice. "You don't have a boyfriend, do you, Kaitlin?" He whispered into her ear as his hand reached under her skirt.

"No, sir," she said shaking.

"I suppose you're too young and pure for that sort of thing," he said smiling.

She scooted back and tried to lift herself off of the table. "I..."

"Shh," he said, putting his sticky finger to her lips. "We don't want to wake Jacob, do we?"

Tears streamed down her face as he yanked down her panties and stabbed inside of her with such force it felt like she was going to break in two. She bit down on her lips to suppress her anguished screams. She tried to slide away but he threw his weight on top of her. Her head cracked against the corner and she bit through her lip; blood flooded down her chin. She whimpered in pain, half conscious.

Jacob heard the commotion and walked into the room. He stood by the entrance watching. Kaitlin reached out a hand and muttered, "Go back to bed."

But he didn't move. Instead he stood crying, screaming. "Daddy, leave Kaitlin alone! You're hurting her!"

Strauch screamed, "Get the fuck out of here!" Jacob scurried away and with one wrenching twist of his sword-like penis, Strauch cut so deep into Kaitlin she felt his rumbling in her stomach. When he pulled out there was blood on the back of her dress. "Better take care of that. Don't want you getting' sick, you have to get up bright and early," he said, belting his pants on.

Sloppily she slid off the table and put a hand to her head. Her hair was matted together with coagulated blood. "Don't worry," he said to her. "You'll get used to it."

She backed toward the orifice and turned to open it, leaving to go to her cell.

When she was gone Strauch poured himself another drink and went to the bathroom. He cleaned the blood off his penis and changed boxers. Kicking off his shoes in the living quarters, he put his feet up and called, "Computer, turn on the flatscreen, dial up the spy movie that came out a few years back with that actor Bill Surnow."

" 'Code 5,' sir?" the computer asked.

"Yeah, that's the one.

"And make me a drink while you're at it."

"Sir?" the computer said.

"Ah, fuck," he said, getting up and sauntering over to the bottle of Scotch he had left open on the bar. He grabbed it and brought it back to the couch with him.

The orifice opened. He looked over expecting to see Kaitlin, but it was Camille. He turned his attention back to the screen. "What are you doing home?" she asked.

"Had a rough day. I talked to Lamont about the BS goin' on with his scientists and the church," he said, taking a gulp.

"You don't even notice anymore," she said, pushing his legs off the coffee table to walk past. She sat down next to him. He glanced at her. "I've been at my geneticist's and plastic surgeon's all day."

He looked more closely at her. "Nice eye color, almost a violet, but your voice, it's not much huskier."

Smiling, she took the bottle out of his hand and placed it on the coffee table, then put his hand onto her breast. "I had them push me up two cup sizes."

He looked perturbed. "I thought we agreed to six? And I want your voice to sound like it's massaging my cock when you talk."

"It takes time once they make the changes. My voice will get lower and they'll be growing for the next few weeks. They'll be there by the end of the month," she said.

"You should just go the old route, you change so much. Plastic surgery is faster," he said, staring back at the TV. "And your hair's still blond."

She took a deep breath. "That takes time to grow out, too. I can color it to match, but I have to wait a week to see how it's going to turn out first. Red is tricky. Damn it, Reginald, what's gotten into you?" She looked around the room for a second and saw Jacob curled near the entrance to the dining area. "Where's Kaitlin?"

"I just saw her a minute ago. She went back to her cell," he said.

"Her place," she corrected.

"Yeah, to get somethin' for Jacob. She'll be back," he said.

Camille went to the bar and poured herself a glass of bourbon. She watched him staring vacantly at the flatscreen. He seemed different, smelled funny. Her eyes wandered the circumference of the room and she noticed the end table was out of place. A coaster was dropped next to it on the floor. Something happened, but she wasn't sure what. She brought her glass with her back to the couch and they watched the film, engrossed in the action.

Halfway through, just as Surnow was about to have his big death scene, Jacob tugged at her arm and said, "Mommy, I'm hungry."

"Tell Kaitlin. Mommy and Daddy are doing something important right now," she said, not taking her eyes off the screen. "Oh my lord, it's so realistic. I love 3-D. And Bill is so good, we'll have to tell him over lunch next week."

"He's a damn good actor," said Strauch, taking another sip of his Scotch.

"Mommy..."

"What?! Leave us alone!" Camille screeched, giving Jacob a 'don't make me hurt you' look.

Jacob recoiled and said, "But she's not here."

"Who's not here?" Camille quipped.

"Nanny Kaitlin."

"Well, that's a great way to treat the people who saved your goddamned pathetic little life!" she said, throwing her hand up. "Jacob, fetch the handheld for Mommy."

When he brought it back to her she gave the computer Kaitlin's cell number, but no one answered. "What the hell has gotten into that little tart? When I see her I'm going to chew her a new asshole."

"She had an ouchie," Jacob said, pointing to his head.

"You mean a headache?"

No, he mimed. He pointed to a cut on his arm. "An ouchie."

"What, did she fall down or something?" Camille said. Jacob took a step back with his fingers in his mouth. "Maybe I should check on her." Jacob nodded.

Across the corridor was Kaitlin's cell. She waved her hand over the orifice and let herself in. "Kaitlin?" she called. The room was small, drab and very gray - standard issue, no frills. The absence of noise drew Camille's attention to the squishing sound of her heels on the Environ's flesh. She wrinkled her nose at the reminder of its vulgar life. She walked toward the bathroom, which had only a washbasin and toilet. Kaitlin was passed out on the floor near the john. The first thing Camille noticed was the blood soaking her dress between her legs. Then she saw a trickle down her lip, across her chin and chest, and the dried, matted blood in her hair. She shook her, but

Kaitlin didn't come to. "Computer, get Dr. Harris over here immediately. Tell him it's an emergency."

Camille stared for a moment at Kaitlin's body. She was breathing. Walking into the other room, Camille sat down on a chair and waited. Somebody raped her, she mused. Who would have the fucking nerve to do that here in the Environ? Before she could mumble the words aloud, she knew the answer.

Dr. Harris let himself in and Camille pointed to the bathroom. While he was administering the nano pill, she said to him, "I was warned about her past promiscuous behavior before I hired her, but she swore to me it would stop. I had no idea she was into that M&S stuff, though."

"You mean S&M?" Dr. Harris asked.

"That's right," Camille replied.

"Don't worry, her secret's safe with me," Dr. Harris said.

"Good, keep it that way. We can't have people thinking we hire degenerates."

"Right," he said nodding as Kaitlin started to come to. "She's going to be just fine."

"Thank you for coming so quickly and for your professional ethics," Camille said, walking briskly toward the orifice.

NINETEEN

A full, bright moon illuminated the sky. Tuwa was bringing larger and larger groups of people out to the edge of the encampment and into the rain forest for rituals on mild nights - a chance to be in nature without the worry of UV. It was as close to the old ways as the people of the Collective could get. A "normal," in the pre-ecological disaster sense of the word - many went simply for that reason. People brought their children for a chance to see what the world had been like. The children whose imaginations were ripe were taken on magical journeys through other realms during Tuwa's ceremonies, which drew heavily on ancient symbolism - stories of Buffalo Women and trickster coyotes, the Rainbow Snake and the Dream Time burrowed from her stint with the Aborigines. For the kids, storytelling around the fire was the best part of life in the new world.

Over the course of the year the ceremonies had became more elaborate as members wanted to participate and other traditions entered into the mix. But tonight was Geney 199's welcoming ceremony. He was becoming a member of the Circle of the Great Spirit. After the bonfire had been lit and those who wanted to tell the stories of their ancestors had spoken, Geney 199 was brought to the center of the crowd. Tuwa took out her smudging wand and waved her hand at La Donna, who beat on a drum. Anyone with noisemakers was encouraged to follow.

The ensemble moved around to the music, dancing and laughing. Tuwa waved her smoking wand over Geney 199 and sang in a sweet, deep voice, "Tonight you are born into your own being-ness. From the darkness of aloneness you are born into a tribe. We sing for your becoming. And celebrate your new life. A life given by your own doing and at one with divine holy will."

When she finished, La Donna put down her drum and came forward to stand next to Geney 199. She grabbed his hand and triumphantly lifted it skyward, then said, "Welcome, friend!"

"Welcome, friend!" the members repeated.

La Donna let his arm down and grabbed his other hand. She looked into his small, amber eyes and said, "Those of us who wanted to shed ourselves of the past have given ourselves new names." She nodded at a young woman standing across from her and said, "Redhawk in her old life was known as Mary. Flying Eagle was known as Max. Do you wish to take a new name?"

He smiled, saying, "I do."

Tuwa said, "And what is that name?"

"Freeman Fred."

"Welcome to your new world, Freeman Fred," Tuwa said.

"Yes, welcome," La Donna said shaking his hand and stepping back to allow each person to have their chance to greet him.

I had refused to go. Instead I leaned on the rails of the front porch near the front door of the Nest, waiting for Ira to come back from the ceremony so I could hear all the details. I looked out over the sprawl of simple white buildings dotting the landscape. The same structures that held an assortment of labs, offices and development rooms somehow they looked different tonight. I was the only person left at the encampment and the extreme quiet was something I had almost forgotten. Chi came up and marked my leg, and I bent down to pick him up, petting him until he purred.

I knew the ritual was important for Geney 199 to feel accepted. I had talked about it with him many times over the course of the past month, but I explained I wasn't religious and had never taken part in ceremonies. I wished I could have gone for his sake, but I didn't feel it would be respectful when my feelings were so mixed about issues of spirituality.

I heard an amalgam of laughter and voices in the distance toward the southern perimeter. I took one last stroll across the porch with Chi and sat on the stairs, looking up at the moon just beyond the scrims, peeking through the canopy of trees. It was a pleasant night, cool but not cold, and I waited until the voices came closer before heading back inside the Nest to the cubicle where Ira and I slept. Chi followed me in.

It was tiny, just big enough for a full-sized bed on one end and a wall of cupboards on the other for clothing. I sat, pulled off my boots and lay down, staring up at the ceiling.

The door opened. The Nest was quiet. I sat up, surprised to find Ira standing at the doorway. He came in and sat next to me and said, "You really should have been there. It was so moving. I don't know why you're so stubborn. You don't have to believe in anything to go. It's just a way for everyone to share stories and bond."

"You know that's not true," I responded.

"It is for a lot of people, and there's nothing wrong with it. Tuwa has a way of making everyone feel connected to something greater than themselves. What's wrong with that?" he said.

"Unfortunately, I don't believe in anything else. Besides, don't all religions do that?" I said.

"No, believe me. This is different. You have to see for yourself. We're having a welcoming feast in the meeting room. Why don't you just pop in, if for no other reason than Freeman Fred and I want you to go?" he urged.

"Freeman Fred? Is that Geney 199's new name?" I asked.

Ira nodded, smiling to himself. "Isn't it sweet? Everyone else takes such grand names, like White Wolf Running, and he picks that. He just wants to have the chance to be like us. It's kind of sad, really," he said, then nudged my leg. "It would mean so much to him. Just come. Nobody's going to bite."

I shook my head.

"Don't be so ridiculous. If I have to, I'll stay here and stare at you until you agree." He waited for a moment and then added, "Think of it as research."

I propped my head onto my hand. "Fine, but give me a second. Let's wait until everyone is settled in. I don't want La Donna seeing me sneak in."

Ira snorted quietly. "What is it with you two?"

"She's been on me for so long about getting involved. I don't want her to think her methods are working," I said.

"Fine, we'll wait," he said, lying back. He grabbed my hand and massaged it, kissing my palm tenderly. "I regret not marrying you."

I frowned and looked down at the comforter. "I regret it, too."

The long meeting table was pushed against the far wall and lined with food. There were banners woven together out of broken branches with handmade signs reading, "Welcome, Friend." The walls were filled with the children's drawings, detailing different stories Freeman Fred had told their classroom about his life in the mines. I was struck by one that depicted dozens of eggs cracking open, with a frogish woman holding one of her new babies. The scene was so alien, yet the child had somehow rendered it like one of those pictures I would have drawn of mother, myself and our brownstone back in New York. It almost made me cry, but I stuffed the pain down where it burned until I saw Freeman Fred. He was so elated I had come. He broke out of his usually cautious demeanor and hugged me. I laughed and said, "Congratulations!"

"Thank you, Miss Psyche," he said, beaming.

Ira patted him on the back and said, "We're all very proud of you, Freeman Fred, for being so brave."

Tuwa waved a rattle near the banquet table. The room quieted and she said, "We welcome him into our family and feast in celebration of his heroic journey. Freeman Fred has seen the dark side of human nature and has found inner strength when others would have cowered. He has risen to the challenge of hard lessons won and has walked hundreds of miles to liberation. But his journey is not over. It is only a new chapter in the book of his life. One we will fill with pages of laughter, joy, and happiness in this - his new home, among his new tribe of loving friends."

La Donna beat her drum then said, "Now eat drink and be merry!" She let loose a belly laugh, jiggled her hips and said, "Let's paaaaarty!" She started around the room and I hid behind Ira.

For a brief moment I felt a pang of grief for not allowing myself to belong. I wondered why I had been so stubborn. But hadn't history proven religion a source of intolerance, war, suffering and pain? It had always been antithetical to the humanitarian views which were woven into the very cells of my being. I looked around at all the stodgy scientists and their families dancing with noisemakers in their hands. Their children painted and laughing. The freedom they had in union with each other and the acceptance, warmth and love lighting everyone's faces.

Maybe, just maybe, this really was different. I wondered if there could be a religion based on love, celebration and togetherness - one that allowed for diversity and acceptance, and fostered individual growth? I found myself wanting to believe there could be.

TWENTY

Camille Pamela was careful to hide her transformation to the Environ public. She spent most of the month feigning illness so she wouldn't have to go to the Sunday ceremonies, and instead Sandy came to "preach" to her later in the afternoon. She stayed sauced up on bourbon, hanging out in her "flat." During Kaitlin's recovery, Jacob spent nights with "Aunt" Sandy when he wasn't in corporate daycare. Strauch had given Kaitlin a nasty, near-fatal kidney infection, among other things.

Camille's hair was now flame red, her eyes a bright lavender and her back fat was pushed down into her buttocks, creating two perfect basketball-shaped cheeks. She was closing in on her husband's six-cup size-up request. The growing pains made a great excuse for Dr. Harris to siphon the precious and limited supply of oxycodone earmarked for the critically ill; but, of course, Camille was special.

The gene-o-plastic surgery was remarkable. The structure of Camille's face had broadened, her features spread apart and in the case of her eyes there was so much room between them she was almost wall-eyed. Her nose had shrunk and changed shape, rounding into a ball at the tip. Her lips were now as thick and bulbous as a pair of copulating earthworms, and her waist had shrunk to a third the size of her hips. Her reflection in the mirror made her horny. There was no reason all her pain and beauty should be reserved for just one ungrateful man. And after the Kaitlin incident, regular old B&D just wasn't enough for him. She didn't care for his new style of lovemaking – or, more accurately, his lack of lovemaking. He was no longer interested in a willing partner. Unless she let him beat, cut or strangle her, he couldn't get it up.

It was address day and Strauch would be busy taping his message to the Environ until late evening. She put on a red, skin-tight dress, tousled her hair, gave her neck a spritz of perfume and headed to the garden. It was community-service week for the Geney wranglers. They were the hottest men in the Environ, six-pack abs and fine, hard man-breasts. She had one man in particular on her mind, the one she had seen on her first day, when Kaitlin was showing her around. Through Sandy, Camille had found out his name - Nick. He was dating the horrible-looking wretch. She was sure she could snag him. Before the Environ he had a reputation for being a lady-killer. And Sandy had checked his confession lists - he had many adulterous thoughts.

When she made it into the garden the light nearly knocked her back. It had been a while since she had seen anything outside her flat, and her new eyes were still adjusting. But before long she spotted him transporting a 60-lb potted plant to his work area. He started digging. She sauntered into his line of sight and as soon as he caught a glimpse of her he stopped his work and stared in foggy awe. She inched closer and he repositioned himself to appear cool, leaning on his shovel and trying to break eye contact, which was impossible. Camille was a beguiling siren in the gray dimness of the Environ milieu. She was every man's wet dream, designed to erect any penis at her slightest glance, made by science to be more perfect and dangerous than nature could have allowed.

She said in her new deep, husky voice, "Hi, I'm Rose. You look so... hot." She fanned herself, looking away briefly as she undid a button near the ledge of her breasts and rubbed her hand over her cleavage. "How about we get a nice cool drink together?" she said, smiling at him.

"I can't say no to that," he replied, staking his shovel into the soil.

She walked ahead of him, making sure to wiggle her hips. They stepped through the orifice toward the worker cell area. It was the first time she had seen it. "How about your place?" she said. "I'm married. Wouldn't want any problems."

Nick smiled, putting his arm around her waist. "This way," he said, angling her down another gray corridor and through the orifice to his tiny cell. It was smaller than Kaitlin's, with a toilet and sink opposite the bed. She sat down on his bed and crossed her leg so the slit would expose the length of her seductively curvy legs. He stared at her. "You're too good to be true," he said handing her a glass. "All I have is whisky."

"That's fine," she said, undoing another button on her dress. He gulped his drink down and let the bottle and glass fall onto the squishy flesh of the floor.

"I've never seen you around here before," he said, sitting close and gently rubbing the small of her back. When she didn't resist, he lifted her hair and between planting kisses on her neck said, "I'm sure I would have noticed."

"Well, I've noticed you," she said, smiling.

He smiled back as he undid another button. "You have?"

She nodded and did a slow striptease, undoing one button at a time, licking her fingers and smiling seductively. With her shirt undone she slipped one perky, watermelon-sized breast out at a time, turned around unzipped her skirt and wiggled her bare ass before turning to give him a full view of her amazingly ripe body. He shook his head. "You've got to be the most beautiful woman I've ever seen."

"And for today, I'm all yours," she replied.

He couldn't take his clothes off fast enough. He was ready to burst before he even had a chance to touch her. The last time he had felt that way he had been a lovesick teenager. For a moment he wondered if he were still alive or if he were hallucinating. Maybe he had died and gone to heaven? No, heaven was full of angels, not hot porn queens.

She put her thick, warm lips to the tip of his penis and suddenly he was in a world of warm, wet flesh. He had to push her away. He wanted time to savor her. He touched her for a while, tasted the nectar of her flower, until he gathered enough strength to look at her amazing body again. When he did she spread herself open like a blooming flower; he stuffed himself inside and buried his face in her mountains. She moaned like a wild woman and he had to take himself out, count to 10 and wait before he started again and again and again.

She was every fuck fantasy he had ever had, every wet dream rolled into one, every gooey lap dance, every pornographic image he had ever seen, all exploding inside at the same moment in time-space.

A month later Nick was in the viewing room waiting for the taped address from the CEO's wife. Everyone in the Environ was dying to see what kind of transformation Camille had made this time. Nick had made a wager with a fellow worker she had gone for an exotic look, having been a blonde for a while. Bill Surnow, who now co-headed the entertainment department for the Environ, came on saying, "Without further adieu I now present the fabulous Camille Pamela Strauch!"

The view shifted to a black curtain and out popped Camille. His heart sank - Rose? He had been screwing her nearly every afternoon for the last month. How could he not have known? He was in deep shit. He was suddenly queasy. He ran to the public bathroom and puked out every last morsel of his cheese fries and beer.

TWENTY-ONE

In a small boardroom in the genetics division, I listened to a presentation Marina, Fayza, Naomi, Xin-Yi, Aine and Hyunae had put together regarding speeding up the reduction of greenhouse gasses. They had pooled their various expertises in physics, botany, genetic engineering, geology, astrophysics and anthropology to work on a plan. Because Xin-Yi was the main presenter, they had picked her department room for the meeting.

"We can build tiny spore-like plants which are resistant to UV. They'll have an increased carbon-dioxide input and heightened oxygen output. They will not only act as a natural air purifier but will also provide a layer of protection encouraging the growth of natural unaltered plant life, much like the canopy we live under now," Xin-Yi said.

Hyunae took out a large digi-print and tacked it to the wall. "Look," she said, pointing to a breakdown in the layer between the atmosphere and stratosphere. "They can be so microscopic and lightweight their natural resting place will hang just above the atmosphere, and because they are UV-engaged they will migrate toward the ozone holes. If those holes heal, then they will seek out radiation disbanding out of the stratosphere. Eventually, they will drift closer and closer to the sun," she said.

Marina unlatched her briefcase and unrolled a large, crude, handwritten graph. "Forgive the mess," she said, trying to get it to stay straightened against the wall. She opted for holding the bottom down as Fayza taped the top. "The increased production of oxygen will help stabilize the ozone depletion. This is world-forming technology and could lead to a breakthrough in making uninhabitable areas inhabitable. From my calculations it will take almost 100 years for the spores to proliferate and blanket the Earth's atmosphere, but there will be enough to filter approximately 30 percent of unwanted solar radiation in about 20 years. The problem, of course, will be erratic weather patterns, which we cannot predict at this moment, and increased rain schedules, which will grow exponentially for the duration of their life, cycling the planet until they disband."

I raised a brow. "That could be a disaster," I said.

"It will encourage more rain forest and that will also encourage more wildlife," Naomi said. "The only real worry is those possible pockets of human life that maybe struggling in areas we don't know about."

"That's a big if," Aine said. "But the fact of the matter is that any human colonies would be made up of survivors, which means clever people, capable and adaptable. We'll just have to hope that Darwin was right and the strong will survive the changes. If we don't put forth this plan, chances are all life will die out, including human. We have a better shot at saving them if we give them a chance to grow food, hunt and avoid genetic mutations and the various cancers caused by excessive UV. The fact is, supplies will run out no matter how prepared anyone is unless we ultimately reverse the damage."

"What other options did you look at?" I asked.

Naomi responded, "As you know, this started out as a joint venture between Xin-Yi and my department for the obvious reasons of creating UV-resistant plants. But the more we examined the models, the more we realized this new species could ultimately spread so quickly it might cannibalize its natural parents. Or worse, destroy the delicate ecosystems which are now desperately trying to survive."

"You'd get a more-severe version of the Australian cane toad epidemic from the last century," Aine said.

I nodded and said, "Well, I think you're ready to make your presentation to the community." I smiled at Marina and continued, "I would suggest, however, that you make a print of that graph. It's unreadable."

Marina shrugged. "I was so busy."

"Well, it's important for everyone to understand what we're going to be working on next. Especially if we plan on dedicating 90 percent of the workforce to this project."

The two looked to each other and smiled. It was more than they had even dared to hope for.

The meeting adjourned. As I strolled down the hallway of the genetics building, Aine jogged up next to me and tapped my shoulder. "I've been meaning to talk to you about Freeman Fred."

"What about him?" I asked, stopping near the exit.

"There are reports he's been having trouble adjusting," she replied.

My eyes narrowed as I scrutinized Aine. "I can't believe it. I've been meeting with him regularly. He's been here almost a year and this is the first I've heard of it."

"Well, it's a recent development. He stopped attending ceremony last month, and when Tuwa asked why, he said it was because his people had no history except being born slaves. When she tried to explain many people throughout history had been subjected to slavery, he retorted with something like, 'Yes, but we were created solely for that purpose. We have no culture but to breed and work until we die for our masters. I have nothing to offer in the Circle of the Great Spirit. It did not make me, man did.' "

"Huh," I said.

"And when she tried to convince him all living creatures had souls the Great Spirit created, he said, 'Not everyone believes that.' "

"That's true. Is it really so important for him to go to circle?" I asked adding, "I don't."

Aine nodded. "That's one of the reasons I wanted to talk to you."

I stared at her. "What's the other?"

"He's been having night frights. His screaming is so loud he's awoken several of his bunkmates. He's also been withdrawn lately and he refuses to see La Donna. It seems he's depressed and feeling guilty for his freedom."

"I'll talk to him," I said, opening the door.

Aine put a hand on my shoulder. "Tuwa believes that Freedom Fred feels a special connection to you. He sees you as a bit of an outsider because your beliefs and position keep you separated from the group. She thinks that if you come to circle, so will he."

I went on with my duties, checking lab reports at the various departments, but my mind never wavered from thoughts of Freeman Fred. There weren't many people who had made an effort to know me personally because I had ardently defended my autonomy. But with Freeman Fred I felt different, maybe because he was so much like me in some ways. We had often taken walks at night around the encampment, talking about the Environ, his old life and the egg cave, as he called it. The egg cave was literally that, a place with hundreds of eggs in a warm, moist cave guarded by a female Geney whose job it was to nurse recently hatched Geneys, then send them off to be weaned and inspected for work.

The nightmares he had been having were mostly about "the rock," a six-foot tall circle made of metal with straps. The wranglers used it to keep a Geney restrained as he or she was lashed, burned or beaten. I wondered if the cosmic circle cross Tuwa used in circle was tugging at this memory. His life before the Collective had been so unimaginably bleak that his will to survive awed and inspired me.

When I was finished for the day I tracked him down. The sun was setting. He was sitting alone on a rock just outside the vegetable garden. I sat down next to him. "It's hard being the only one of your kind. I know, I've been thinking a lot about the two of us. We have a lot in common," I said. "Sometimes I think you understand me better than my mate, Ira."

He turned to me. A bitter yet soft smile warmed his scaled face. "But you have past fill with memory of mother, love educate, politic history, person history, even if not a spirit one."

"Yes, but I also have a past filled with regrets, loss and sorrow, not unlike your own. And visions of a tomorrow that could never be realized," I replied.

Freeman Fred hit his chest twice and looked at me. "I speak from heart and tell you only truth. You my deep friend." He turned away in thought and I waited for him to continue. "If my soul as Tuwa say is created by Great Spirit than aren't souls of my kind also made by It?" he said casting his eyes down at a row of young hybrid cornstalks.

I didn't say anything. I waited, musing about the gesture he had made. It seemed significant, as if it were second nature and genuine. Although I had never seen him make it before, I knew it was deeply symbolic in some way, like a handshake, but done with the reverence of a person genuflecting.

"But maybe you right and there is no Great Spirit. No thing above man..."

"And his atrocities and creations," I whispered, reciting my words to him on our walk six months before.

"If that is so I wonder why bother live? I never thought these things before. I only try serve with no beating, no pain best I could. I no chance to think about these things and now I know, these confuse me. The suffering of Geney is very great. How could Great Spirit allow this if It is what Tuwa say, all knowing love?"

"I can't answer these questions for you. They're the same ones I've struggled all my life to figure out. Perhaps you should ask Tuwa," I said.

"I have," he said, looking at me. "She say Great Spirit create us, but no intervene in way of Its creation, like a painter who finish work. Done it take on own life – pass from wall to wall, slow decay until disintegrate and turn into something else. But I no understand this." He shook his head and peered down at his thick, knobby hands.

"I think she's saying, once we are given life each being has his own journey," I said.

"Yes, but how Great Spirit give evil men knowledge of creation? So they make people for only work and suffer, and die with no love, no freedom?"

I put my hand on his shoulder. "Perhaps that's why you made it here – so others could follow you out of the darkness of the mines. Maybe the Great Spirit sent you to us so we could help."

He looked into my eyes. "Think so?"

"I do," I said.

TWENTY-TWO

Strauch had just gotten back to the flat when Camille assaulted him with, "She's pregnant, you asshole!"

"Is it a boy or a girl?" he asked, walking to the bar and pouring a Scotch.

"Bring me one while you're there," she said. "Twins."

He nodded while walking to the sofa and handing her the glass. "A single mother, we can't have that," he said.

"No shit!" Camille said, slamming down the Scotch.

"Can't have the minions breedin' like bunnies."

"I'm aware of that. She'll start showing by next month. I've got Sandy working on the moral-high-ground tart thing," she said.

"What have you got?" He smiled. He could count on her – always did.

"The groundwork was laid the first time you fucked her. I told the doc she was into perverse S&M shit. Then I leaked it to a few nurses and my beautician. Of course it spread like wildfire and over the last eight months people have added to it with gems such as "She fucks everything in sight - doesn't care if it's man, woman or child." This morning it hit the net and I publicly fired her."

"Good, that's good," he said.

"That's just the start," she said.

"Excellent, I can't wait to see your handiwork," Strauch said. "Computer turn on the flatscreen. I want to watch the news."

On the following Sunday, Camille was the first one to chapel. She was excited. The ceremony started with a show of brilliant spotlights zooming around the room. They stopped on the purple velvet curtain behind the pulpit. The karaoke music played and Sandy popped out with a wireless headset mic, singing, "You died for our sins, Jesus Lord on high."

As if he were being birthed out of the vacuum of a black hole, Jesse appeared from the curtain to rap the next line, "We are low, small little nothings, bound in a prison of the devil's flesh!"

Together they clapped and encouraged the audience to chime in on the next line, "Without the great scissors of Jesus to cut us from our unholy original sin, we would be nothing, but food for the worms!"

Sandy pulled Camille from her golden viewing throne and handed her a mic, rapping, "Every seed is a gift from the Lord waiting to praise the Son of God, and those who don't know or worship Him are damned to the eternal suffering of a burning, fiery hell."

Camille sat back down while the congregation sang a reprise of "God is a jealous God, full of vengeance and spite, but Jesus will intervene for us, 'cause he loves us with all his might."

"That's right," Sandy said when the song was over. "Jesus does love us. He will take us to Heaven if we let him. But those who smite the commandments of God will not be tolerated among us."

Jesse leaned forward, casting his hand above the crowd. "It has come to our attention some of you have not been obeying your commandments! There are those who've been sneaking out of service, only to lie and say they didn't!"

Sandy said in a squeak, "And those who've done the unthinkable; laying with another outside the sanctity of marriage!"

"This is a horrible crime against our Lord and Savior! And a sin punishable by the laws of the Environ, for those who don't repent and make peace with the Lord through his advocates here on Earth, you will feel the wrath of the Lord Almighty!" Jesse said.

"He did not select us to live in order for us to be sinners. Those who don't live up to the highest moral code will feel his vengeance here in the Environ!" Sandy exclaimed.

"Make your peace with the Creator! Repent! For those of you who admit your mistakes, and ask for forgiveness, the Lord will have mercy on your soul," Jesse said raising his arms to the gray, gelatinous ceiling.

Sandy said, "Some of you have come forward and talked to Jesse or myself. You've told us of lust in your hearts, of problems in your marriage. We are all sinners. Jesse and I are here to help you make your peace with God. But we can't help you unless you come forward with any and all your sins against the Lord. Too many of you have not used your confessional software, and even more have not come to us with your problems."

Jesse said in a deep baritone, "I respect those who have had the courage to face the devil, look him in the eye and let loose the lion of God. We are that lion."

"Hallelujah!" Sandy said.

"Hallelujah," the congregation echoed.

"No sin is too small or too big for the ears of this lion. Tell us your troubles. Take a load off your soul. Let Jesus hear your cries of atonement."

Sandy went to the podium and read from a printout, "We're cutting sermon short today because of a special announcement from our CEO, Reginald Strauch, and his wife, Camille Pamela. We want to honor them now with a small prayer."

Jesse took her place at the podium, looking out somberly over the parishioners. "Jesus, Reginald Strauch is a great man, a worthy man. He reminds me of another man from the Bible named Noah, who built a ship, with two of every kind to repopulate the world when the great flood subsided. In much the same way our CEO has saved us. Even if that flood outside never relents, humanity will survive, thanks to him. We want to take this time to thank you, O Lord, for working through Reginald Strauch and for giving us him (and his lovely wife Camille Pamela) in our darkest hour. Without him, our lives and those of our children would be rotting in the wasteland that lies outside. Amen."

"Amen," the parish repeated.

"Go ahead, Reginald, Camille, stand up and take a bow," Sandy said, urging them out of their gilded seats. Strauch waved and smiled to the crowd behind, as did Camille. They then made their way through the aisle and left to go to the broadcast studio.

Bill Surnow was waiting with Ellis Rush in the booth. Their heady conversation about the best digital background to use came to a screeching halt upon the first rumblings behind the orifice. When Strauch and Camille appeared, Gibson quickly hustled them to the stage. One of his daughters gave Strauch a fast powder, and Gibson pushed aside a harried DP to look briefly at the shot on the monitor, with the superimposed backdrop of the Environ flag to the couple's left and the American flag to the right. He yelled to the cameraman, "Pull back, the shot is too tight." And then watched the monitor until he gave a satisfied grunt.

An assistant strolled next to Strauch, out of the shot, and asked him, "Are you ready?"

Strauch nodded.

"OK, let's do this," the assistant said giving the thumbs-up to Gibson.

"Roll film," Gibson said. "One, two, three ... and action!"

Strauch began, "I hope all of you enjoyed the wonderful sermon by Cardinal Jesse Applegate and Bishop Sandy. I know I did, and I want to thank them for their kind prayers on my behalf. But that's not what this address is about.

"Over the past year in our new world, many issues have arisen, things we did not plan for. While no system or people are perfect, I have laid down certain ground rules for participation in our society. When all of you were selected for service it was not just for your expertise but also for your good Christian values. Unfortunately, it has come to my attention that some of you have not been fulfillin' the social contract we made with you upon entrance into the Environ."

Strauch waved a hard copy of the contract at the camera. "I've highlighted certain excerpts from which I will read." He skimmed the first page and then read aloud, "I promise to uphold the ten commandments. If I should falter from this commitment, I will willin'ly leave the Environ or take the punishment to be decided by the CEO and his council.

"Jesus Christ is my Lord and Savior. I herby promise to attend services every Sunday except under extreme illness or cases of emergency. If, for some reason, I do not attend, I shall seek private council of the clergy or attend special services durin' the week."

He looked up from his paper and said, "I'm disappointed that attendance records contradict this. Tonight will be a lesson to those who think they can buck the system. Let this remind you of your civil contract and commitment to God."

Gibson slashed the air. The first cameraman pointed at the camera opposite the sound stage. The audience saw a seamless transition to the second point of view. Two large ex-Marines donning their old uniforms walked forward holding a small, frail Asian man, clearly a scientist. The two men secured his arms and legs to a circular metal rack with a cross inside. The device had been brought in and cleaned up by the Geney wranglers before the broadcast.

The camera swung around. One of the Marines took a utility knife to the scientist's shirt, cutting it in half. The same man took out a small box and set it on the ground. He played with the dial at the device's base. The other Marine applied a clear gel to the scientist's back.

The first Marine pushed a button. The Asian man writhed in agony. Gibson instructed the first cameraman to get a close-up of his face as it contorted in agony. The next shot was of the steaming welt left on his back. The second Marine lifted the tentacle-like wire and placed it lower on the scientist's spine. Again, volts sent him into convulsions. He screamed, "I repent! Have mercy on my soul sweet Jesus!"

Strauch nodded to the Marines. The second turned the machine off. The first let the scientist out of the harnesses and walked him off the soundstage. The camera tightened on Strauch. "Praise the Lord, this sinner has been purged of his arrogance."

Jesse and Sandy Applegate came through the orifice from the makeup cell and stood in front of a green screen, which superimposed a digital portrait of Jesus looking heavenward with his sacred heart exposed to the viewing audience. Jesse said, "Let us pray. Holy Father and Son, we humbly exact your will on Earth. Guide those sinners among us to the sanctity of your life. In Jesus's name keep us from the devil's fiery Hell of damnation."

"Amen," Sandy replied.

"And cut," Gibson said.

"This concludes Digibio's public service override; regular programming is now available," the computer said.

A tech from the booth waved his arms at Gibson and shouted, "You've got to see this!"

Gibson strode over to him, "What?"

"The ratings readout... It's phenomenal. At the start of the broadcast only half the monitors where engaged, but when the prisoner was tortured, every monitor in the Environ went on."

Strauch walked over to the huddle. Gibson turned to him and said, "They loved it - lapped it up like sweet cream."

"Good," Strauch said.

Camille's ears pricked up and she walked over. "If they liked that, wait 'til they see what else we've got. This is just the beginning."

TWENTY-THREE

"I want you to help me," I said, moving Chi so I could flop over in bed and face Ira. "It will be hard convincing people."

Ira nodded. "It would go a long way if you went to circle."

"I know," I said. "Do you think Tuwa would support my plan?"

"Yes," he responded.

"I'm going to circle tomorrow," I said.

Ira lit up. "Really?" He paused for a moment. "It's not just because..."

"No. I need to get over my... resistance... my prejudice. The Circle of The Great Spirit is the soul of the Collective."

"Have you talked to Tuwa?" he asked.

"I don't want it to be a big deal. I need to get comfortable. I don't want a welcoming ceremony," I said.

He nodded. "I know it's not easy for you, but I'm proud. It's a huge leap forward, not just intellectually or physically, but..."

"Spiritually," I said completing his sentence.

"Yeah." He wrapped his arms around me. "You don't know how happy this makes me."

I whispered, "I always thought we were so much alike, until we came here. Did you change, or did I?"

"I stopped feeling alone, like I had to be at war with the rest of the world just to survive. And going to circle allowed me to feel oneness with everything – something I had always been looking for, but didn't know it," he said, stroking my cheek.

I wanted to cry, but couldn't allow it. "I didn't know that."

"How could you? I didn't understand it myself," he said.

I nodded. He took my face in his hands and kissed my forehead. I felt my eyes watering, my throat throbbing. I tried to distance myself, but a tear trickled down my cheek. He wiped it away, saying, "You're the strongest person I've ever known."

I flashed on my mother, Miriam, walking up the steps of our Brooklyn brownstone, her dark hair sticking out from a striped knit cap, carrying a stack of papers to grade from her class at Columbia. Another image of Miriam pointing to the first diagram of a molecule I had ever seen. I was seven.

Once, mom had brought home a dying fern. She taught me how to nurture it back to life. Every day I watered it, made sure it didn't get too much sun from the living-room window. She had stroked my head and told me how proud she was of me - what a remarkable green thumb I had. I wept.

I hadn't allowed myself to grieve. The last time I had cried this hard was when my father left us, never to return. I was three. I lay down. Ira cradled me. I tried to remember my father's face but couldn't, and as the shadows of my life in New York faded, I fell asleep.

The next day was long and difficult. One of the Petri dishes with spores ready for testing had been dropped in the lab. Kimi was furious and nearly got into a fistfight with the tech who had tripped and broken the dish. I had to spend the day arbitrating – half the Collective was as angry as Kimi, the other half felt there were plenty of other samples and all was basically OK. In my estimation it was an accident, but an inexcusable one after a year of our effort, spending every available resource to develop the spores. With one careless tech's mistake we were set back months.

But I couldn't take sides. I had to be neutral. I wanted to strangle the idiot. In the old world, people got fired over much smaller infractions, and I so wished we were back there. All I could do was demote him to a less-responsible position. Maybe I could retrain him for gardening with the agricultural sector. At least then his carelessness wouldn't matter as much. The tech was inconsolably apologetic to everyone. But his reprisals upset people more and arguments flared all over the encampment. I was run ragged smoothing things over. It wasn't until the tech tried to apologize to Aine that it got really hairy. Tuwa, La Donna and I all had to arbitrate. Tuwa had to physically restrain Aine from hitting the man.

Aine kept screaming at him, "How could you be so fucking stupid? Just tell me how! After all we've worked for? Just tell me how! You stupid fucking bastard!"

The tech slinked away as Tuwa grabbed Aine and said calmly, "Be still, you're making it worse, causing more dissension."

Aine stopped her ranting to stare at Tuwa. Tuwa went on to say, "You have a right to be angry, it's an emotion we all share, but let it pass. It's a disease and must be released before it sickens all of us. We must stay focused on our goal if we are to achieve it." Aine relaxed and Tuwa continued, "Let it go, yes, visualize a calm wave washing over you, sweeping away the anger." When Tuwa was satisfied, she released Aine.

"Thank you," Aine said.

Tuwa nodded. As Aine, La Donna and Tuwa started off back to their sectors I caught up with Tuwa. "I want to thank you for stepping in."

Tuwa nodded.

"I'm going to circle tonight, but I don't want..."

"Anyone to notice," Tuwa said finishing my sentence.

"Right."

Tuwa smiled. "We'll make you invisible then."

I laughed. "I thought I already was."

"Will you be bringing Freeman Fred with you?"

I nodded and Tuwa continued, "Ask him to start compiling his list of stories for me, will you? He doesn't think there are any, but any group of people become a community after a short time, and stories happen. Remind him it's the repeated ones I'm most interested in."

"Why?"

"Because those become oral tradition, and oral tradition is the precursor to religion and the beginnings of culture."

"You think patterns already started to emerge?"

Tuwa nodded. "Of course, it happens on every level - individually, among families, lovers, co-workers, friends. Freeman Fred is in his mid-20s, right?"

"That's our best guess."

"And if there are 198 ahead of him, their zygote civilization is at least 25 to 30, right?"

"Right. I see your point."

"There's a seed in there. I just have to find it."

Circle was just getting started when Freeman Fred and I snuck in behind everybody at the edge of the encampment. The area had become a regular meeting spot and some Collective members had dug a fire pit and made a circle of stones around the perimeter. It had the aura of a sacred place, like an ancient temple. It felt open and inviting. I could tell Tuwa noticed us, but she didn't let on to the group.

Tuwa walked around with the smoking sweetgrass and sage, smudging everyone. There was a deeper note of piety in the attention of the circle members than I saw when Freeman Fred was welcomed 18 months before. It struck me as odd that this group of people, mostly scientists and their families, had found such solace in these ancient practices. It seemed so antithetical to their training. But I felt it, too. There was something magical about Tuwa; even her voice had some strange effect on people, as if she were reaching inside with it and stroking the soul of whomever she was talking to.

I felt something shift inside as I watched Tuwa walk the circle. She projected a feeling of love, a compassion that reached across the void of our separateness. It felt like a communion, as if she were creating a psychic loop making us all one.

Tuwa was triggering something deep inside, a belief that perhaps had always been there but I'd never allowed to flourish. Like the preverbal connection to your mother, or looking at a dissected flower for the first time and marveling at its complexity, its design, and wondering how chaos and chance could create such amazing organization – an overwhelming feeling of awe, appreciation, warmth and sublime beauty defying all words to describe it.

Tuwa chanted and something was awakening in us. Its energy lifted us. I felt it. It gave me a feeling of freedom I had never known. It released me from the chains of rationality into the deep abyss of knowingness and feeling. The very thing I had fought so hard against. This was when I realized why I had never come to circle before. I was afraid – afraid to feel anything, even if it was exaltation.

Tuwa encouraged the others to chant along with her, and as they did, the experience deepened for me. People around me began to sway, dance, move, drum, and I felt my own body responding, relenting to the overwhelming power of unity. I had never felt so present and so connected.

Tuwa led us around the fire pit, where we settled down. She said, "Fayza has a story of the past to share tonight. A story we must keep fresh in our hearts and in our children's, because it is one of many stories mankind has repeated throughout generations. We must keep alive all our trials in hopes that we don't repeat them."

Fayza sat in the talking chair near the fire. It was a simple bench constructed out of a makeshift log, reserved for the evening's storyteller. "Back in my country, my homeland, I was raised to read and think. My mother was a doctor and her mother before that. There was never a question about my calling in life. I was born a scientist. I had a passion for it ever since I was a little girl.

"But one day, while I was in class at the university, a group of armed men, guerillas, came. They rounded up all the women and threw us into the basement boiler room. It wasn't big – there was no room to sit, and barely any room to stand. We didn't know what was happening. One of the women began to cry. She said her father had warned her about a rebel group of zealots who had threatened to overtake and destroy the government, so they could force us all to return to the old ways, where women were not allowed to walk freely or be educated and a man could kill a woman without repercussion.

"When the other women began to ask questions, one of the guerillas came in. He ripped her out of the crowd by her hair. She screamed. Blood ran down her face where a piece of her scalp had been torn. He dragged her upstairs and opened the door. A blinding shaft of light shone in. We watched as he beat her lifeless and then rapped her with a knife. We huddled together crying in silence, scared to death. He yelled down to us, 'The next one of you who talks will have a fate worse than hers!'

"That was the beginning of the enslavement. The zealots took over and the schools became closed to us. We were made to cover every inch of our bodies in cloth, with only small holes through the mesh so we could see enough to walk without falling. We were not allowed to leave our homes without the accompaniment of a male relative. Women were raped and their own family members were ordered to kill them. If they did not, the whole family would be exiled, starved to death. Men ran wild with power – even the gentlest among them seemed to be sickened by it. They killed us without reason and suffered no consequences. They held the thread of our lives in their hands and it drove them crazy for blood. Many women committed suicide rather than live through the horrors they saw around them. Women getting stoned in the street and raped, only to be murdered by their brothers later."

"They told us we had no souls, that we were worthless animals. When the white women came in secret to smuggle us away in their trucks, I wrote a note and pinned it to my door: it said, 'If I am a worthless animal, then what are you who came into this world through my loins?'

"When we piled into their trucks that night, a dear old friend of mine could not fit. I cried and begged her to wait until the women came back for her, but she said, 'I will be dead by then.' I told her, 'If you take your own life, take as many of them with you as you can.' She nodded. She was a chemist before the revolution. I heard she strapped a bomb under her garments and went to the market alone. When a group of the evil men started to stone her, she took them out with her. I was happy for her revenge, even if it meant her death. That is how defiled I was, how filthy with anger.

"Those that stayed behind had their spirits killed, and to think of it I still feel the rage of their injustice burning me. This is the world where I came from. I am free from it now, but the wounds are still tender, even though it has been many years."

Tuwa put her arms around Fayza, who was shaking. "Thank you for telling us. We will remember this always so it does not happen again."

The circle disbanded, its members lost in reflection. We walked silently back to the encampment. I wondered about the cruelty in the hearts of human beings. It was unimaginable, yet we were facing a similar situation. The Geney were slaves, beaten and treated worse than animals. Could I be one of those brave women who had come to save Fayza? I turned it over all night, knowing that if we did save them, we might destroy ourselves in the process.

TWENTY-FOUR

"It's time. I've got more than half the Environ ready to stone her," Camille said, pouring a hefty glass of bourbon. She took a seat on the recliner across from Strauch, who was sprawled across the couch.

"Is it really necessary to use Kaitlin as the first example?" he said, lazily swirling his Scotch before taking a drink. "There must be others more deserving?"

"The babies..."

Strauch cut her off, "Babies, yeah, right."

"Twins, and they are more than viable now. What better way to show we mean business than to publicly execute someone so close to us? It will most certainly put the fear of God into 'em," she said.

"The polls look good," Strauch said, rubbing the back of his neck. "What about the Applegates? Are they on board?"

"Don't be ridiculous. When haven't they been? Of course they are. I made up the list with Sandy." Camille knocked back her drink.

"Great. What have you got?"

"Well, let's see..." she said, picking up a tablet in front of her. "Hanging." She looked up at him for a second – he shook his head. "Your instincts are right; it came in last on the survey we circulated after service."

"Too old-timey. Boring," he said, sitting up.

"Then we have poisoning, also a bad choice, I think, no drama in it. Stoning, but that's too Muslim. I kinda liked the tasering. Electricity is pretty gruesome, but it wasn't preferred," she said.

"What about a firin' squad. I always thought that was romantic," he said.

"Don't be an idiot, Reginald, it would cause too much damage to the Environ. Besides, what would we use? Your grandpa's old rifle?"

"Well, you don't have to get pissy about it. I just love those old westerns." He poured himself another shot of Scotch and said, "And, by the way, we do have a militia."

"A ragtag group of ex-military men with guns and tasers doesn't really count as a militia." Camille looked back at the report and said, "Number one on the list was stabbing. People felt any other way would jeopardize the babies," Camille said.

"Good point. Well, it seems like you have it all figured out. Why don't you arrange it and I'll give the announcement?" he said, getting up to sit on the arm of the recliner. He ran his fingers through her hair. "I like the black better. It goes with your tits."

She smiled. "I think so, too."

He put his hands on her watermelon-sized breasts and searched for her nipples, pinching them until they stood at attention. He was growing fond of her new body. The older he got the harder it was to adjust to her changes. When he was younger it was exciting, like being with a new woman, but as time went on he felt more pressure to perform than excitement, and he often wished she would settle on something. Constancy was a comfort to him. No matter what Camille did to her outside, she was still the same woman and the sex always fell back into old patterns.

What he wanted more than anything was what he had with Kaitlin – power. Fear was the greatest aphrodisiac. He regretted being indiscreet. He wouldn't make that mistake again. Once Camille had found out, she made it difficult, and after Kaitlin got pregnant, Camille vanquished her. Jacob and one of the corporate nannies had been given a suite on the other side of the Environ, and when Strauch was home they were ordered to stay away. The nanny was allowed to bring Jacob home only when Camille was there and he was out. No more easy access.

Camille sensed he was preoccupied as he nuzzled her neck. "What's wrong?" she asked.

"Nothing."

She pulled away and stared at him. "Just spit it out."

"What are we going to do with the kids?" he asked.

"Raise them, of course. Isn't that the Christian thing to do?" she said.

He smiled deviously at her. "You are a genius. Have I ever told you that before?"

"Almost every day." She chuckled. "Why don't we go into the bedroom? I'll let you use the chains. I know how much you like playing servant and master."

He ripped open her dress and clawed at her bra. "Put on the leathers. I'll be right in."

TWENTY-FIVE

Kaitlin had been in the holding cell for two days. Once in custody her long, dark hair had been shaven. No new clothes had been provided since her nanny days months earlier, and her ill-fitting gray uniform was soiled and full of holes. Her ripe, naked belly spilled out in the gap between the waistband of her skirt and the tails of her shirt.

The holding cell was tiny and had been meant for a prisoner to wait momentarily, not for days. There was no bathroom and no place to sleep except on the sticky, squishy, wet, gray Environ floor. There was one plastic chair she had chosen to fold herself into in order to sleep, rather than on the ground where she was forced to relieve herself. The Environ would absorb the waste eventually but it released a foul, acrid smell in the process.

This was hell. The waiting. Waiting in the claustrophobic cell, encased in its sweaty, gray flesh. Sometimes she would stare so hard at the walls, she swore she could see the monstrous Environ breathing. She imagined herself as Jonah waiting to be absorbed by the belly of this beast.

Her unborn babies were the only reason she wanted to live now. The thought of Camille raising them was a fate worse than their death. Their lives would carry unspeakable pain. If Camille could treat Jacob with such malice, she wondered what torture her babies would endure. She contemplated suicide. It was a mortal sin and killing her babies… She never believed in abortion, but now she wasn't sure – a life of unspeakable abuse and torture versus the innocence of her unborn babies' souls? Jesus would surely welcome them and maybe forgive her. But she couldn't be sure.

By the third day, Kaitlin had refused all food and liquid. But the guard had orders to force-feed her. He tied her to the chair, stuffed bread into her mouth and forced her to chew and swallow. She finally complied, eating enough to satisfy him so he would go away and leave her to figure out her next move. Starving wasn't going to work; there really wasn't enough time for it, anyway. The chair was the only thing in the room. She turned it over and looked for sharp edges, metal bolts – nothing. Maybe if she tore her skirt and used it to hang herself, but there was no way to secure a rope of any kind to the ceiling. Perhaps if she lay naked and still on the Environ floor it would absorb her.

After an hour of keeping her breath shallow and pressing herself into the Environ, she felt the beast discharge a jelly substance – it burned so badly she twitched in agony and the substance receded, leaving a film of goo on her backside. She wiped it off with her dirty underwear and put her clothes back on. It was no use. She resigned herself to death at the Strauchs' hands. Maybe there was a way to save her babies during the execution.

The days in isolation were hell. Her mind flipped between escape, resignation, fear, anger and profound motherly love. Everyone in the Environ had turned against her. She was branded a sinner and a whore. Even the corporate nannies had refused to speak to her, and they knew she had been set up. Only Josephine, the woman who took her job, acknowledged her presence. She told herself that someday they would see. She would be greeted at the pearly gates by a fleet of angels and the Lord himself, as one of his most holy martyrs.

Kaitlin had loved the Strauchs' son, Jacob, as if he were her own. Those long days and nights alone, she wondered, how could the Strauchs do this? They had been surrogate parents to her after her own had died of plague. They had taken her in at 16 to be their nanny. She had spent much of her childhood hearing wonderful things about them from her parents, who had been friends and supporters of the Strauch campaign for years.

She reflected on the papers they had her sign. At the time she didn't understand she was turning over all her parents' assets to the Strauchs for the privilege of being their nanny. She hadn't really minded because she felt like part of the family, but in realty she had been an indentured servant buying her life with her parents' money – nothing more.

Kaitlin had always been a true Christian, willing to turn the other cheek, have compassion for the downtrodden and lend a hand to anyone who needed it with love, not resentment. The Strauchs and the Applegates had turned her religion inside out, perverting it with abject hatred, using whatever Bible quote they could find to support their case – usually from the Old Testament. But as a Christian it was the New Testament Kaitlin had been taught to live by. The Applegates and the Strauchs didn't seem to suffer under the same high standards. To them, religion was a cover for lack of personal responsibility, a way to absolve sin after sin without thought or repercussion.

Before Kaitlin's mother had died from plague she had warned Kaitlin about the Strauchs – at the time, her fever was 105 and Kaitlin thought her mother was hallucinating. But now her mother's words came back to haunt her: "Don't trust the Strauchs. They hide behind the cross, but they worship only power and ego. They are morally bankrupt. Worse than that, they haven't a clue what morality means." Camille and Reginald had been two of her parents' closest friends, and the truth was, she wanted to live. She had chosen to ignore the truth. She was ashamed of herself.

She knelt on the slimy flesh of the Environ and prayed: Dear Lord, please give me strength to endure the pain of death and come swiftly for me. In the name of the Father, Son and Holy Ghost, amen.

When the soggy footsteps of the executioner were heard outside the orifice to her cell, she recited the Lord's Prayer. *Our Father who art in heaven, hallowed be thy name.* ... The orifice opened. *Thy kingdom come.* The executioner came in dressed in a black hooded jumpsuit.

He was a volunteer from the security department – a Neo-Evangelical zealot and ex-military man. He put the shackles around Kaitlin's wrists and clamped them tight. *Thy will be done* ... The Applegates assured him of his special place within the church because of his sacrifice and he was excused from community gardening for six months as payment.

On earth, as it is in heaven. The executioner tugged at Kaitlin's chains and she followed him, stumbling out of the orifice. *Give us this day our daily bread.* He led her down the dim gray hall. *And forgive us our trespasses as we forgive those who trespass against us.*

The executioner waved his hand in front of the wall and the orifice opened to bright white light. *And lead us not into temptation, but deliver us from evil.* The executioner pushed her toward another man waiting in the green room. *For thine is the kingdom, and the power...* A young woman came in and powdered Kaitlin's face and glossed her lips with cherry-flavored color... *And the glory for ever and ever. Amen.*

She waited there with the executioner, repeating the prayer until it was time for her entrance.

It wasn't a huge studio. Only 30 guests were allowed in besides the Strauchs and Applegates. The scientists who had been invited refused the invitation. That's when Camille and Sandy came up with the idea of a lottery for the workers, who then filled the audience seats.

The spotlight belonged to Strauch. He gave a brief speech. "Let this be a lesson to all the evildoers among us. We have no tolerance for your kind. This is a good, Christian community and we'll do anything to keep it that way."

The executioner tugged at Kaitlin's chains. They entered through a velvet curtain, she in her soiled, bedraggled nanny uniform – a sharp contrast to Strauch's dapper suit and Camille's couture dress, covered in diamonds.

Center-stage on a platform was an enormous aluminum circle mounted to a lead base, with leather straps on each side. The Geneco wranglers had adapted old exercise equipment to create it. It kept the Geneco stationary while being beaten, whipped or tasered, and looked like an updated medieval-torture device.

The executioner pushed Kaitlin onto the platform. Two hooded men came forward and positioned Kaitlin inside the device. Her ankles were tied together and fastened to the bottom. Her arms strapped into the wrist cuffs, spread into a cross inside the giant steel circle. The executioner checked the security of the buckles and gave thumbs-up to the stagehand.

The Applegates came forward, standing to the right of Kaitlin's shot. Sandy said, "Your death will be swift and your twins saved."

"Do you repent?" Jesse asked.

"I was raped," Kaitlin said, secure in the knowledge that nothing could save her now, even if they accepted her "confession of sins." She would be cut open like a sow, her babies stolen, and then cast out of the Environ into the blazing desert sun, where her flesh would sizzle into third-degree burns as she was left to die a slow, painful death.

"Still won't admit your sin," Sandy said.

"I was raped," Kaitlin said with a disarmingly steady, cool and confident tone.

Jesse worked himself into false righteous anger, "Lying won't work now, missy!"

"I asked if you repented, made your peace with the Lord," Sandy said calmly.

"The Lord loves me. I am and have always been true to him," Kaitlin said. "You should ask yourself these questions."

Jesse shook his head. "Ain't that somethin', the whore calling the righteous into question."

"Only the Lord can judge who is righteous," Kaitlin replied.

The studio was dead silent. Both Applegates knew Kaitlin was making people think; she was winning. "Poor, lost soul," Sandy said, dabbing Kaitlin's head with holy water.

Jesse said, "If only you were strong enough to repent, you and your babies would be safe."

"Liar," Kaitlin retorted.

The crowd let out a collective sigh of disbelief and the Applegates knew they had turned the tables. Jesse wrapped it up with, "May the Lord have mercy on your soul," and the Applegates returned to their seats.

Kaitlin started to repeat the Lord's Prayer in a hoarse whisper, "Our father who art in heaven..."

The executioner looked at Strauch.

"Hallowed be thy name..."

Strauch nodded back.

"Thy kingdom come..."

With one swift movement, the executioner's blade was thrust into Kaitlin's side. Kaitlin screamed, and then silence. Blood poured like wine from a pitcher, taking the color from her. The executioner used the blade to filet the area from her rib cage down in a circle to her pelvic mound and around back to her chest. In a roping motion her intestines spilled to the floor and then her stomach, uterus and organs fell in a pile of gore. She was dead – her body still upright, strapped to the device. A giant hole was all that was left of her middle, cut pieces of flesh clinging to her spine.

In the booth, Surnow fainted and Gibson doubled over, projectile vomiting. It caught on like a yawn; one after another in the booth let loose. The smell permeated into the audience and the vomiting spread.

The Strauchs and the Applegates, on the other hand, seemed strangely unaffected, even as a noxious odor bubbled from the

Environ floor as it worked hard to absorb the influx of stomach acids, blood and partially digested food.

The executioner stayed focused on his job of combing through Kaitlin's gore to find the babies. He pulled out the first baby, cutting its cord, and then the next, and held each by their tiny feet, like prize pigs. A few people in the audience managed a cheer before the hooded assistants took the babies to a makeshift medical unit behind the curtains.

Strauch gave a brief closing speech and a crew of bio-waste workers unstrapped what was left of Kaitlin's body.

"Remember, crime doesn't pay," Camille said.

Strauch smiled warmly at the cameras and said, "This concludes our missionary act of mercy."

A spotlight hit Jessie and the camera zoomed in on him. "Keep poor, lost Kaitlin in your prayers. Ask Jesus to pull her from the gates of Hell and take mercy on her soul."

"And cut," the assistant director said. Gibson had found a toilet and was still incapacitated.

The audience filed out of the studio. Camille took Strauch by the arm. Smiling at him, she said, "Well, I think it was a complete success. We'll look at the numbers tomorrow. But what will we name the twins?"

They made their way down the squishy hall toward their cell and Strauch replied, "I don't know, something Biblical," he said. The Applegates followed after them for a victory celebration of booze back at the Strauchs' place.

"What about Elijah and Jezebel?" Camille said.

"Oh, those are perfect names," Sandy said from behind. "Jezebel, lest we forget the whore who begot her."

Camille nodded. "A prophet and a wicked woman. I could use kids like that."

TWENTY-SIX

After the setback, everyone in the Collective had been forced to work such heavy schedules that tempers flared daily - people were cranky. There had been less time to meditate, cleanse, do spiritual work and bond through circle.

When it came time to do the second experiment, Kimi and Naomi did not agree about how to release the spores. Kimi wanted to build a balloon and set the sample in a time-released box, but Naomi simply wanted to release them outside the encampment and measure how fast they floated upwards. They argued around the table at the board meeting in the genetics building while all the division leaders were present.

"But we did that! We already have that data. It's just a waste of precious time!" Kimi snapped at her.

"Empirical data takes more than one trial. I don't think I need to tell you that," Naomi quipped back.

"It's true," Aine interrupted. "But in this case time is of the essence. The longer we wait, the more the spores will have to compensate for damage. It will take more resources, strategy..."

"We don't really know..." Naomi started.

"Kimi's team has already built the time-release, the launcher and the balloon. Are you suggesting we let all that work go to waste?" Marina said, scooting her chair closer to the table.

I shook my head. "Let's not get too excited. Everyone keep an open mind and consider the good and bad in each plan."

"I, for one, say sooner is better than later," La Donna said in a low rumble. "No time like the present."

"We have enough data. We've been working on this for over a year. The first experiment was a success. I've always believed in moving quickly," Ira said. "We all know from past experience how opportunities can turn into liabilities if not acted on fast enough."

"Or just the opposite," Naomi retorted.

"The weather could change. A storm could come and interfere with the test if we keep this up," Hyunae said. "The conditions are perfect right now. From what I saw this morning, they will be for the next few days, but it's very unpredictable."

"With all our expertise and research, I think we can go forward to the next level of the experiment. If it saves one more animal, human or tree, it's worth the risk," Fayza added.

Tuwa, who had been leaning against the wall, came forward. "She's right. Everyone seems to be in agreement except Naomi. And my spirit speaks: 'It is time to follow the heart.' "

"Amen to that," La Donna said, slapping the table. "Let's put an end to all of this ridiculous fighting. We're all on the same side."

Safia offered, "I've programmed the time-release capsule with an override. I've tested it many times and it has never failed."

"Fine, then we go with Kimi's plan," I said.

Kimi smiled.

We set up the launcher and balloon. Everyone in the encampment stopped what they were doing to watch or participate. I took Ira inside and applied UV block to every inch of his skin, making sure to check and recheck for holes. He put on a thick cotton unitard, stepped into a treated jumpsuit and picked up his UV helmet. We rejoined the group waiting near the assembled launcher.

It was small but awkwardly shaped and cumbersome. Ira picked up the launcher and walked several yards outside the encampment to the site where a part of the canopy had been cleared the night before. He engaged the meters, monitor and tiny computer, then hit the launch button.

He ran back to the encampment and half a minute later the capsule sprung into the air. We watched as it catapulted above the trees. Safia hit a button on her wristcom, engaging the balloon. It took a few seconds for the communications to come in. There was nervous silence as we watched. She smiled, giving the thumbs-up. Cheers and laughter erupted in the crowd.

We had done it – created an ozone bandage. It wasn't going to reverse 200-plus years of raping the earth, but it was a start. For the first time - there was hope.

TWENTY-SEVEN

Lamont put on his UV suit and followed the Geneco wranglers outside to the mines. It was the first time he was to visit their camp. He had been too busy setting up the Environ to pay attention to his pet project. But the Geneco had been under-producing since the mining accident. Geneco 199 had gone AWOL from it. If the low production numbers continued, the Environ would have a metallurgic crisis. Paul preferred to leave the dirty business of slavery to those more familiar with suffering and sadism.

At first, Geneco 199's disappearance had been only a mild concern, but in the past week Lamont had put a special-ops team on the case. They found evidence of 199 crossing into Oregon. A few days later, his men tracked 199 to the Collective, where they saw evidence of 199's assimilation.

Lamont had recently reexamined the case files of Collective members. He suspected they would eventually raise objections about the Geneco enslavement – if memory served, which it always did in Lamont's case, they were a bunch of overzealous, tree-hugging idealists. He worried 199 would eventually come back with Collective members to free the Geneco.

The head wrangler, a man named Johnson, helped Lamont into the hovercraft. "Where do you want to go first?" Johnson asked.

"The reproduction cave," he responded.

Johnson leaned forward, instructing the driver to head across a dried-up riverbed toward a cave about two miles north of the Environ. They entered a makeshift docking bay. Lamont and Johnson got out. "You'll have to excuse me if I'm not very good at being a tour guide. I've never done this before," Johnson said, leading the way through the twisting cavern with his electric lantern.

It was relatively cool and dark, so dark it was difficult to see. His helmet obscured what little light Johnson's lantern gave off. They hugged the side of the cave, trying to keep track of their footing.

At the next bend, a wave of heat hit Lamont. It was so intense and sudden the UV suit didn't protect him from it; even the air visibly changed. The heat lamps glowed an eerie red in the chamber's blackness. The cavern floor was lined with pale eggs that reflected the glow of the lamps, making them look like embers. But under the scrutiny of the electric lantern, they were a pale yellow.

A female Geneco was sleeping on a platform with two newly hatched lammys suckling at each of her breasts. The baby Geneco had been nicknamed lammy by a scientist back in Florida, early on in the project and the name stuck. Lamont thought it was funny, but it had the adverse effect of creating compassion in him for the babies.

The female reminded him briefly - despite her abhorrent lizardlike features - of his first wife nursing his child. The color of the room added to the mirage, changing her normally green complexion to a warmer, more-human tone. Lamont couldn't help but see the humanity in the nursing mother and felt a twinge of guilt before he reminded himself of the trillions of dollars, other people's dollars, they had cost to create.

They were company property – nothing more. They weren't even real animals. They were soulless creatures bred and made to work. They were an abomination. Anger surged through him. If only they could have taken away all mammalian traits, it would have been so much easier.

Lamont asked, "Is she the only Geneco you have for all these eggs?"

Johnson laughed. "No, they take shifts. They change every 12 hours."

"Where's the training camp?" Lamont said.

"It's next to the brothel," Johnson replied.

Lamont raised an eyebrow. "Brothel?"

"A little joke among the wranglers. We call the female Geneco milkers and egg layers, whores. And the one-stop sleeping quarters and nursery is the brothel," Johnson said.

"It's repulsively hot in here. Take me there."

They wound east through the cavern. In this area there were small electric lights posted along the wall. Most had gone out, but it was a little easier to see with the aid of Johnson's electric lantern. There was a simple white sheet at the entrance of the brothel. Johnson tore it down, grumbling, "This is not permitted."

Some of the female Geneco were sitting in a circle, talking, while several others were teaching the lizard children mining techniques. Johnson became furious upon seeing some talking and not training and he screamed, "At attention!"

The females jumped, visibly shaken by his command. One of the Geneco came forward and said, "Sir. Sorry, sir, for Geney relax time. Those fems be dutiful, short break, sir, after meal just end."

"Break over," Johnson said.

"Yes, sir," the female replied, saluting.

Lamont surveyed the quarters. It was filthy, dank and smelled like rotten food and baby diapers mixed with wet earth. He wondered how long it would be before these females developed a more complex language of their own, maybe even a written alphabet.

All the earmarks of an emergent culture were there. Women being made to function in a group - not unlike early humankind's development, where women developed language to communicate about plants and child-rearing. There was hard evidence the outgrowth of this begat women's development of the written word. This was thought to be the reason why modern women tested better than men in language skills and generally used more words with greater intricacy on a daily basis.

Lamont hadn't given those theories much thought, but seeing the Geneco fems made him nervous. He was watching a uniquely human primal force break through the carefully orchestrated world of the Geneco – a need to connect, communicate. Next would come a weaving of tales to rationalize the irrational, to create safety and control when there was none, to order a universe of random chaos. And then, with or without the Collective and Geneco 199, the Environ would be in trouble. There would be more Geneco than people, and eventually they would find a way to revolt – after all, they were mostly human.

He considered separating them, but it would most likely exacerbate things. He flashed to the original intent of his brothel visit – the immediate threat posed by 199 and the Collective. How would he stop a mass exodus? For the future of the Environ, it might be better not to. The Geneco wouldn't be able to take the eggs, and the lammys could be bottle-fed. A new crop could come up, the Environ would have to conserve, but it was doable. And while the lammys were being reared, a new system could be developed to keep them isolated from one another. Strauch would never understand it, but he never understood anything. There was more to think about than just

Strauch's whims and ego now. Lamont's son's survival was far more important.

As Johnson led him to the hovercraft, Lamont considered the microchip idea. It had been cheaper to brand them and keep their information on computer. Developing the chip had been bagged many years prior to implementation because all resources had gone into the development of the Environ. Maybe he should revive the plan? But it would be a hard sell to Strauch, who had thought the Geneco too barbaric to be of any real concern. Without education and knowing no other life, they had been an easy group to control. But now, things were changing. It seemed dangerous that they lived on the outside and had time to themselves. After all, they were designed to be intelligent, at least as smart as an average person, and that was now a liability, not an asset. Besides, tracking the Geneco to the Collective would start a war, and the Collective's work to restore balance was the only hope for his future grandkids. The Environ wouldn't last forever. It was, after all, a living creature, and all living creatures eventually have to die.

Lamont and Johnson got back into the waiting hovercraft. The sleeping quarters were about half a mile away in an eastern cave, closer to the mines. After docking they headed into the mouth, which opened to a large space. The floor was lined with simple, dirty white bedrolls. Under some was dried grass. Johnson shook his head and picked up a handful of it in his hand. "They're forbidden to do this," he said.

Near the back of the cavern's room a small group of miners were sleeping - those who had been beaten too badly to be of use for the day. Johnson started for the area, but Lamont pulled him back and said, "Let it go for now. There are more important things to worry about."

"Being one of their creators, perhaps you're just a little too soft on them. I don't like insolence," Johnson said as they headed back to the hovercraft.

"Neither do I," Lamont warned.

The mines were not far, only a few minutes away via hovercraft. Although Lamont had approved the systems, he was struck by the bizarre scene in front of him. It could have been 3,000 years earlier, except for the mix of wranglers in space-age UV suits. The Geneco, although lizardlike, looked so human from far away. They could have been the Jews and the wranglers a modern version of the Egyptians, with silver-colored helmets standing in for gold cornets.

Of course, the Geneco's humanness disappeared with every footstep closer. He reminded himself, they were beasts – manmade beasts. Each filthy, green, with knobby skin and elongated, pointy faces, small reptilian eyes and thick, semicircular slits for breathing, holes on the sides of their heads for ears. Their hairlessness gave them a particularly gruesome look. They were monsters.

The wranglers had taser guns, cattle prods and whips - each preferring his own weapon of fear. The Geneco worked half-naked and without any protective gear. To the right of the mine, only a few hundred feet away from the entrance, were dozens of devices like the one used to execute Kaitlin, each modified a little differently – metallic circles, some with dilapidated wooden boards crossed in the center, others with straps or central metal crosses – all used by the wranglers for beating, tasering, strangling, shooting or whipping the Geneco. They would wither there or be left to die - or not, depending on the wrangler's will.

Surrounding the circle crosses were the remains of dozens of Geneco in various states of decomposition. It was a reminder to work and stay within the confines of the rules. All Lamont could think about was the waste. Was there no other way to control them, or were the wranglers just sadists who enjoyed torture?

"How many Geneco have your men killed?" Lamont asked Johnson.

"Somewhere around 80," he replied.

"You don't know? You don't have accounting for each death?"

"Yes, we do. I just can't remember offhand," Johnson said.

"I'm not happy about this. It's wasteful. Trillions of dollars went into their development. You need to control your renegade group of cowboys or someone else will," Lamont said.

"We have a job to do here, and when a Geneco isn't doing it, we have no other recourse," Johnson said.

"Perhaps more discretion - tasering should be uniformly used. It causes less cellular damage and is extremely painful. And it won't kill them," Lamont replied. "Your cowboys are too comfortable with destruction."

"You design a system, we'll implement it. Boss."

"Get the driver. I need to get back to the Environ," Lamont said.

TWENTY-EIGHT

While Hyunae made her rounds to the various temperature gauges and observation posts, she began to become concerned with the dramatic climatic changes reflected in the data. The spores had been released six weeks earlier, but no one had accurately predicted their effect. Naomi had thought it would take a year for the spores to settle and start reproducing. Xin-Yi had been more optimistic, along the lines of six months, but six weeks was way too fast.

Hyunae made her way to the genetics lab.

Xin-Yi was in her office, hunched over her desk reading lab reports, when Hyunae walked in. "What, you don't bother knocking first?" Xin-Yi said.

Hyunae tried to hold back a roll of the eyes. "I have something to show you. It's very important." She took off her wristcom and put it on Xin-Yi's desk. "Read the output."

Xin-Yi smiled. "Faster than I thought."

Hyunae let out a sigh and shook her head. "The spores are creating instability."

"In the short term, yes. But, I don't see a problem," Xin-Yi replied re-gluing her eyes to the computer screen.

"Well, I do. It's creating an unstable jet stream and is greedily collecting moisture. Which means only one thing – storms and more storms… flooding to be specific. We aren't prepared for it," Hyunae said.

"Well, bring your findings to Psyche, she's in charge of everything. Why did you come to me?" Xin-Yi said.

"Before I go to Psyche I want to make sure there isn't some sort of defect going on with the spores. Is it possible they mutated?" Hyunae asked.

"Anything's possible… But not probable. We were too rushed. We just miscalculated our projections."

"Just? This isn't a theoretical paper, it's the balance of the Earth at stake," Hyunae retorted.

"Don't be so dramatic," Xin-Yi replied. "It will right itself."

"I hate to admit it, but Naomi was right," Hyunae said.

Xin-Yi laughed. "No, Naomi is never right. She's one electron short of a molecule."

This time Hyunae's eyeballs got away from her and rolled with the exasperation of a teenaged girl listening to her mother. "Just figure it out," Hyunae said.

"Yes, ma'am," Xin-Yi said, mocking a salute.

"What is with you?" Hyunae asked.

"Nothing, I'm happy our spores are a success," Xin-Yi said.

"I know astrophysics and meteorology aren't your strong suits, but I don't think you understand how potentially deadly this could be."

"We knew it would cause flooding. What you're telling me is it will happen sooner rather than later," Xin-Yi said, smiling.

"And it could be potentially a lot worse than we originally thought, so I need that data. OK?" Hyunae said.

"Fine, I'll get on it," Xin-Yi said.

Hyunae found me in the garden with Naomi, examining a new genetically engineered corn hybrid – a hardy variety more resistant to harmful UVB and UVA rays than any we had previously. But despite the minor breakthrough, a few generations down the pike would lead to the breed's sterility if we didn't fortify it with the UV-resistant DNA sequence I had discovered back at Digibio. I had been trying to reproduce it in our labs, but due to the secrecy at Digibio, much of what had led up to the acme of my research was withheld and I was now guessing at combinations that weren't cutting it. I kicked myself for not having the foresight to steal their technology while I had a chance.

Naomi and I were in the middle of discussing alternatives when Hyunae physically grabbed me away and walked me into her lab without a nod to Naomi. Hyunae was rambling on about a devastating rain unlike anything seen before by humankind. Naomi looked put off until I nodded in her direction. I didn't dare interrupt Hyunae's verbal spew – I'd never seen her so agitated.

Once we hit her lab she laid it out for me. The charts and graphs she had prepared on the fly were hard to follow. "There will be so much rain… So much. I'm not sure we're at a high-enough elevation to avoid flooding," she said.

I examined them carefully and did some calculations. We were at the highest point of the temperate rain forest at just over 4,000 feet. "The water should run down the mountain, but erosion could be a serious problem."

Hyunae nodded. "And what if we run out of supplies? We won't be able to get into the dead cities to scavenge."

"A couple of weeks should be OK," I replied.

"For all I can tell it might be a couple of years before this storm ends. I can't see any end to the clouds. It's massive, like something we would see on Jupiter, not on Earth as we used to know it," she replied.

"I'll call a meeting," I said somberly.

Hyunae wasn't prone to exaggeration or alarmism and her warning grew inexorable roots. Within hours a multiplicity of moral-imperative weeds needed attending, weeds that might destroy the uniformity of our ideological flowerbed. The Environ was crawling around in the desert below us. Could it survive this deluge? Maybe. Surely the Environ scientists would have taken into account flooding. But certainly the Geney caves couldn't sustain a flood – the Geney would likely drown.

We had to save them.

I stewed over every possible scenario for hours. Where we would put the Geneco; what their long-term impact on the Collective would be; how to accommodate the basic necessities, housing, food, clothing; and how they would contribute to the Collective. These were all going to come up in a town-hall meeting which we were going to have to have so the community would take them in. The majority would have to agree – preferably, everyone would agree - or we'd save them physically only to become a tiered hierarchical society like the Environ. And if we became them, the Earth might as well stay dead.

But we couldn't turn our backs, either, or we'd be guilty of genocide, and again we'd be as bad as the leaders of the Environ. I had to convince the Collective to follow our charter, to take a leap and rise to another challenge, to use vicissitude in the face of a life-threatening crisis. My facts had to be in order, just as they had been at the start of the Collective. I didn't want to see our shadow ugliness in the meeting – that in itself would ultimately undermine us.

Tuwa popped into my head. It was late at night and thundering when I found her alone in the recreation room. It was lined with bookshelves – everyone had brought their library, along with every other type of entertainment: a trunk full of board, virtual and simple computer games; a huge flatscreen hung on one wall with almost every film ever made, downloaded onto pods for Collective members' viewing pleasure; and of course, everyone's favorite and not-so-favorite music was catalogued in an elaborate database. Several scientists had made it their mission to gather as much of the old culture as possible to bring with us into the new world. Usually the room was full of noise and people talking, but Tuwa was silent and alone, sitting in a glider, deep in thought, knitting.

Her wolf-like amber eyes refocused and reached inside me. I shifted my weight and looked away to defuse it, if only for myself. It didn't seem to matter, though. She was incapable of staying inside her own skin.

"A darkness has settled inside your heart." She patted the chair next to her. "Come, sit, tell me what's going on."

Sometimes Tuwa made me nervous. This was one of those times. There was a strange, indigenous formality to her speech and way of being that came from living among tribal people. In their world everyone had a place; there were elders and shamans and fools, but all were treated with respect, the sort of respect never accorded someone in an urban world full of anonymous people who prefer to stay strangers. I supposed the formality was a necessity for survival – a way to keep adult egos satiated and children hungry for assimilation.

I sat down. "The Geney…"

"The storm won't be as bad as Hyunae thinks, but it will drown them if we don't do something. I've been having dreams," Tuwa said. "I had hoped they were metaphors."

"We have to save them. It is a moral imperative."

"Agreed," she said.

I replied, "Convincing everyone isn't going to be easy."

"Leave that to me," she said. "Focus on where to put them and how to take care of them until we can set up a sister community."

"You don't think they should live with us?" I asked.

"For the short term. But they need their own culture, time to develop, and their own identity. Assistance from us will be fine only in the short term, but ultimately they won't want to live among us. They won't trust us. And why should they?"

"I hadn't thought of it that way," I said.

"Their species and culture are in their infancies now, but once they are free, their sense of self will develop quickly. While we should stay deeply connected to them, we would reinforce their sense of inferiority and dependence if we simply took care of them," she said.

"You're probably right," I said.

"A people stripped of an identity are a lost people. They become misfits to the world they are trying to inhabit – this is why alcoholism and suicide were so high among Westernized indigenous people like the Native Americans and the Aborigines of Australia."

"We don't want that," I said.

"No. We don't. We'll work with them, but not rule them. They should develop their own government; make their own mission statement. And both our nations will have to form and ratify a treaty."

"You've been thinking about this for a while," I said.

Tuwa nodded. "Since Freeman Fred joined us." She smiled at me like the Mona Lisa and said, "We both knew one day we would have to take action and free his people."

I nodded. Freeman Fred had become my closest friend. I felt his survivor's guilt. The pain of personal freedom was unbearable when its price tag meant those you loved were left behind to suffer. My agony was the same. I had pleaded with Ira in private to help me devise a plan for Geney emancipation, but he felt there wasn't enough support for it and didn't want to divide the Collective over the issue. But it was different now that their lives were threatened and Tuwa was with me. She could convince the devil to buy fire.

TWENTY-NINE

With the new babies, Elijah and Jezebel, there had been no choice but to take Josephine on. Camille certainly wasn't going to raise the children - she hadn't even raised her own. Although Camille didn't much care for the head corporate nanny, she was the most qualified for the job and was by far the most unattractive of all candidates. Camille didn't want a repeat of the Kaitlin episode. It was hard enough covering Reginald's tracks the first time, and a repeat would be nearly impossible.

Unfortunately for Camille, her husband had accidentally discovered her daytime entertainment. Strauch had come home unexpectedly to discover Camille gone. It only took a couple days for Strauch's henchmen to track her to Nick's bed. A few days later a high-level computer key code was found, scrawled on a piece of paper, in a pocket of Nick's jacket in his work cubby at his waste-management post. Everyone in the Environ knew early on this was considered a capital crime for a multitude of reasons. The first was obvious – stealing – and with this code Nick could give himself as many credits as he wanted. In the Environ this was more effective than old-fashioned bank robbery. Second, the crime of hacking carried a sentence of anywhere from five years' isolation and hard labor to, in extreme cases, death.

In the Environ anything offending the upper echelon of the hierarchy was considered a capital offense. The first caveat when entering the Environ, written in bold letters on every brochure, "All laws are subject to change and are set by the CEO." Further into the snarl of information, the pamphlet admonished, "All inhabitants of the Environ serve at the CEO's pleasure."

The Environ, of course, had no judges or lawyers, eliminating the messy cost of expensive trials and the inconvenience of fairness. It was a true corporate theocracy. And, to be fair, the literature was forthcoming with the social contract – either submit to the rules or die. Most who were offered sanctuary in the Environ chose the former. Heaven might be a great place to hang out someday, but why rush it?

Camille's vindictiveness spawned a mission to ensure Strauch's sexual anguish: As long as she lived, access to other women would be impossible. Josephine would have to wear a leash so tight it would leave a permanent mark. She was to become a ghost presence in the Strauchs' life.

Josephine brought Jacob with her to report for duty, interrupting Camille's hot-wax treatment. The wax was being slathered on Camille's new mustache (a side effect of the exotic look she was cultivating) by a nubile, upstart esthetician who had been the toast of the fashion world pre-Environ. Camille pushed the fashionista away as though she were a bum looking for a handout and snapped, "I need privacy," as if mind reading were taught in beauty school. The esthetician scampered into the hallway to wait.

Camille put a grave face on and warned Josephine, "You are not to talk to Reginald for any reason, and if he should come home while you're with the kids, leave with them for the daycare center. Do you understand?"

"Yes, ma'am," Josephine responded. She was a frail, unhealthily thin woman with a churchgoing demeanor. Josephine's gut told her there was something very wrong with the request. "I'm to report at 8 a.m.?"

"Unless Reginald is still home. Call first," Camille said.

Camille must have read the slight raising of Josephine's brow as condemnation because she raised her voice in indignation. "Do you have a problem with that?"

"No, ma'am," Josephine responded.

"Send in what's-her-face," Camille said. Josephine called the fashionista back in.

The esthetician touched the hardened wax and said, "It's time to pull it. Are you ready?"

Camille held up a finger. "Hold on. You'd think for all the fucking money I spent funding that genetic cosmetic line those fucking doctors could eliminate this crap," she said.

"Shall I take Jacob to his playroom?" Josephine asked.

Camille nodded.

"When will the twins be out of the hospital nursery?" Josephine asked.

"How the fuck should I know? I'm not a newspaper or a doctor. The only thing you need to worry about is staying away from Mr. Strauch. You understand? If you hear the slightest peep you are to leave immediately through the opposite orifice and bring Jacob with you."

The esthetician ripped the wax off and Camille screamed. "Goddamn it! That fucking hurts! I'm going to rip those doctors a new asshole."

Josephine nodded and bent down to grab Jacob's hand.

"No contact, understand? Anything suggesting you disobeyed me will result in your immediate termination," Camille said.

"I understand." Josephine exited with Jacob.

"Or worse!" Camille yelled after her, getting up to walk toward the bar. She poured herself a bourbon and said to the esthetician, "OK, now what can you do with this China-girl hair? I want some body in it."

The playroom was filled with every toy imaginable. It was a mess. As Josephine straightened up, Jacob sat in the corner, playing with a set of dolls.

The memory of Kaitlin's hideous execution washed over Josephine. It was brutal, barbaric. She was beginning to have doubts about the nature of the Environ. The eye-for-an-eye mentality and the strange bloodlust whipped up at Sunday services – it was positively un-Christian.

Josephine had been raised Catholic and was taught that the New Testament trumped the Old, that Christ's teachings were meant to mollify the Jews' perception of God – going from vindictive, jealous and angry to a kind and loving God. She'd converted when she married, and although her husband had died of Skeleton Plague just two years later, she stayed in the church to honor his memory. Since entering the Environ, the Applegates had really turned up the fire and brimstone. Josephine's years in CCD taught her Jesus preached the golden rule, love, forgiveness and turning the other cheek. She wondered if the Applegates were ignorant or something more sinister. Now she worried she'd made a grave mistake.

After Josephine finished picking up, she sat down next to Jacob and noticed something that at first she couldn't allow herself to believe. He was using an action figure to hump a half-naked female doll and relentlessly repeating, "Fuck me, bitch!"

After the shock wore off, Josephine pulled the dolls away and asked, "Where did you learn that?"

"Daddy," he said.

She was speechless. It took a moment to think of an appropriate response. "You're not allowed to use that kind of language," she said.

"But if Daddy said it, why can't I?" Jacob asked.

"Daddy is an adult. You're a child."

"I hate you!" Jacob boxed the air and bawled. "I want Kaitlin back!"

Josephine wondered if Jacob knew about the execution – or saw the broadcast. Maybe this was why he was so disturbed.

He shrieked in one long, deafening tone that morphed into, "Where's nanny Kaitlin? I want my nanny Kaitlin!"

She tried to draw him into a hug, but he fought her. She managed to grab his hands and get him to look at her. In a calm, even tone she said, "Kaitlin's in heaven now. She's with God."

"No!" Jacob screamed, tearing his arms away from her and throwing his little body to the squishy floor. "Daddy promised! He said her ouchie would go away."

"Shhh, be quiet, Jacob. Your daddy will get angry." Jacob became sullen, sucking his thumb and rocking himself as if to keep his tears silent.

"It's OK. You're OK," Josephine said, sitting next to him and holding him to her breast. "You poor thing. It will be OK." She pushed the hair out of his eyes.

"Daddy said not to tell. Don't tell or bad things will happen," he replied.

"You don't have to worry about Nana Josephine – whenever you need to tell a secret, you can trust me. I will never tell," she said, rocking him.

He nodded, almost imperceptibly.

"Nana Josephine will always love you no matter what."

Jacob looked up at her in disbelief, as if he'd never heard such a thing before. Her heart sank – such a small boy without even the familial pretense of unconditional love. He was a helpless tortoise without a shell, so frail and alone in a family of sadists. It was no wonder he was a bully with other children.

Josephine took his tiny hand in hers and rubbed it. "My sweet little boy. No more worries. I'm here to protect you."

THIRTY

The sky had darkened at the western edge of the forest and storm clouds loomed there, stationary for days. The radar showed them gathering strength, getting bigger and growing fiercer as two pressure systems violently collided, crashing against each other with unprecedented force. A crude radar system was all Hyunae had to decipher the storm. She speculated dozens of waterspouts were forming under the densest clouds north of Seattle and approximately 500 meters off shore.

I asked, "When will it hit us?"

Hyunae shook her head and replied, "We have a week, max."

I nodded and said, "I want you to be in charge of battening down the hatches. Make sure all roofs are leak-proof and that there are no places for moisture to collect around any of the structures, including the garage."

"Maybe we should consider towing some boats back when we get supplies from the dead cities," Hyunae said.

I nodded. "You think the flooding will be that bad?"

"There's no way to know."

I called an emergency town-hall meeting. Hyunae presented the bad news. Once the room had thoroughly processed the gravity of the situation, I took my place at the podium.

Generally I ran cold. Ira had always said it was because I was so slender – it was his nice way of saying ghastly skinny and awkward. Tonight I felt my scalp sweating, a brand-new sensation of which I wasn't fond. I disliked giving speeches, but this was worse than usual – I looked out at the sea of familiar faces and drew a momentary blank. It wasn't until my eyes rested on Tuwa that I remembered my speech.

"We've managed to live through what would have been extinction if we hadn't taken action. We've saved thousands of plant varieties in our gardens and hundreds of animal species in our zoology department. We've invented technologies to reverse CO2 levels while shoring up the spotty ozone layer.

"This Collective has some of the finest minds humanity has ever known. We have created a miracle in the face of humanity's biggest disaster. We are remarkable. And all indications are that we will achieve our ultimate goal of restoring the Earth to a habitable state.

"We did not abandon the Earth by climbing into a controlled environment and hoping for the best. We took responsibility. We made a commitment and upon entrance into our new world, we all agreed on our mission statement."

I pulled out our founding document and read it: "It is our mission to protect, save and nurture life on our planet, with honor and respect for all cultures, all species and the earth itself. We dedicate ourselves to this cause and to finding a reversal of man's abuses against the environment while sustaining whatever life is left to sustain, so it may thrive now and in the future." I held up the document and pointed at the long scrawl of names that followed the initial 14 department leaders' signatures.

"There's no way we could have known our technology would have its own ecological blowback and that the very thing that would ultimately heal our planet would endanger the lives of a people we didn't know existed… I'm talking, of course, about the Geney."

I looked around. The faces staring back were a mix of surprise, annoyance, fear and sympathy – all tempered with shock and pride. I wasn't sure what to make of it or how the discussion would take shape. I took a deep breath and continued.

"We are faced now with the first test of our mission statement. Approximately 300 miles southeast of us, in the valley of the desert, live the Geney. Their progenitors live in a comfortable controlled environment, the Environ, but the Geney spend their days mining and their nights sleeping in caves. With the torrential rain we expect, the mines will flood and, of course, their caves, too, leaving them homeless and defenseless against this monster storm."

The marginal coughing fits and shifting in chairs ceased. All eyes were glued to me, hanging on each word. "If we are to live up to the ethics we have set forth, then we have no choice - it is our imperative duty to save them."

As I gathered my notes, a smattering of applause arose to a roar. Marina, Fayza, Ira and Freeman Fred stood up and soon the whole room was on its feet in a standing ovation. I was shocked and suddenly very aware of myself. I scurried back to my seat while Tuwa floated effortlessly to take my place.

She waited for the applause to die down and then said, "I had planned a speech but...." She closed her eyes for a moment, as if scanning the crowd. "You have something to say, Naomi?" she said opening her eyes.

Naomi looked shocked. "I..."

"Don't be afraid, there are others who feel as you do," Tuwa said. "Come here."

Naomi hesitated for a moment, as if looking for reassurance. Her eyes met those of Xin-Yi, who motioned her to the podium. Naomi took her place next to Tuwa.

"Certainly we can't let the Geneco die, but contacting the Environ would be very dangerous," Naomi said.

I stood up and said, "I'm not proposing we talk to the Environ."

Tuwa said, "The Geney need to be free."

I walked back to the podium and said, "I propose a five-step plan. First, we vacate them from their caves during the night..."

Naomi interrupted, "That's stealing. We can't just go in there and take them. They're property of..."

"No living thing is property," Tuwa said resolutely.

"But they wouldn't exist if it wasn't for Paul Lamont or Digibio," Naomi said. "They are his brainchild."

This caught me off-guard. "How do you know that?" I asked. It wasn't in any of the information we had, and Freeman Fred had never mentioned Lamont.

She glanced at me nervously and continued, "Even if we did steal them, where would we put them?"

Tuwa's nostrils flared in anger. "They are sentient beings with feelings, thoughts and exceptional intelligence. They are our biological children. The Great Spirit created them as He did all of us."

"They were manufactured in labs," Naomi squealed.

"The way they came into being has nothing to do with their creation," Tuwa retorted. "They are divine beings with souls and spirits and minds, no man can create that!"

Naomi was silent.

Xin-Yi came to the podium and said, "If we do this, we risk war with the Environ."

I nodded.

A wave of mumbling washed over the crowd. Ira stood up and said, "Then we'll assemble an army."

Naomi jumped in, "If we save the Geneco, the Environ scientists will develop another creature, and then what will we do? Rescue that new life form, too?"

Aine stood up and yelled at Naomi, "That's a ridiculous argument – the slippery slope."

Fayza yelled, "If we don't save them, we are no better than those cowards!" A wave of affirmation burned through the crowd. "Let me be the first to offer myself as a soldier."

A young man of 20 stood up and saluted. "I was stationed at Quantico when we were abandoned by our commander in chief. We heard about Strauch's cowardice while on our mission to save the people of New York. The driver of our supply truck told us there was no more aid coming. A new plague had wiped out Congress and most of the executive branch. General White sent a team to recover the President and discovered he was gone."

Another young man stood and said, "I was there. Meeks and I are the only survives of our battalion. Some went back to their hometowns to be with their families. We buried the others during the recovery effort. We were just lucky to be orphans, I guess, and to hear about the Collective. I, for one, would lay down my life without question for this place, and for what we stand for. We're what America was supposed to be – a democracy."

The two young men sat back down to a round of applause. "They're right," I said. "The only thing that separates us from Strauch and his people is our willingness to honestly live by our principles – making excuses about what we choose to do or not do, for the sake of our convenience, is the primary reason mankind extinguished life on Earth."

Both Naomi and Xin-Yi crept back to their seats without another word. And with that I knew we had won. My eyes met Tuwa's. We smiled victoriously.

THIRTY-ONE

Before the rain came, a mist settled around the mountain. Aine started calling the Nest Avalon; it was so shrouded in fog you literally had to bump into the building to find the door. Luckily, the garage was further downhill and we were able to take one of the military surplus hoverbuses out for a trip to the nearest ghost city, Portland.

Ira had assembled a group of half a dozen high-ranking former military men: Robert, Max, Todd, Jack, Dave and Kevin. Robert, Fayza's husband, was a retired five-star Air Force general and took the reign of command at the men's request. Max had been a brigadier general 4th class upon retirement to the Collective at 28. Todd, also a WWIII veteran, had started as an enlisted man, private first class, and had spent his life working his way up the chain of command. Jack's background was also in the Army, retiring to join the Collective at 38. He had served as a command sergeant major class 9. Dave had gotten to a Navy captain 3rd class before his forced retirement at age 32 due to the dissolution of the service, and fellow seafarer Kevin served as vice admiral 9th class in the Coast Guard until its end.

Since Ira had no military experience, he became a liaison between the Council of Department Heads and the newly formed military strategy coalition, officially named the CAT (Collective Army Training) division, by its founding members. They picked the acronym, first for the cat's mystical powers as well as because cats had the highest kill ratio.

Ira, Aine, Fayza and I went along with the six officers on a weapons-recon assignment. Among council members, the five of us decided it would be important to get weapons training to better understand the military and assist in a time of war.

The whole thing struck me as absurd – we might have to kill other survivors in order to live. It was nature's cruel law turned against us at a brutal time, when all of humanity should have been working together, but would not, might never. I pushed the pessimism away momentarily to study the oddity flanking the broken old 5 Freeway.

On the western side was a wall of encroaching gray mist as far as the eye could see, and underneath that a renewal of verdant forest. To the east the sun bore down on scorched ochre earth and patches of dried vegetation. The old 5 cut like a knife between opposite worlds. The way the sky and land were split reminded me that either side had an equal chance of winning. A shiver ran through me. A war was being waged and I felt like a white blood cell watching the battle for my host's life begin.

After all we had sacrificed and all we had worked for it might come down to humanity's greed, once again. I must have looked upset because Ira put his arm around me and said, "We're going to win. The good guys always do."

"Hitler," was all I managed to say.

"And we won that war," Ira replied.

"Not until 26 million people were murdered in the Holocaust," I replied. "I'd call that a pretty major loss."

Ira stared blankly - no witty comeback, not even a hint of what to say sparkling in his eyes. He turned away to look at the scenery whizzing past at nearly 200 mph.

Soon we crested the mountain and were headed downhill, barreling through the outskirts of the ghost city. The gray sky receded further west, away from the blazing sun. What was once suburban sprawl was now a deadly quiet specter — rows of lookalike houses melting in the afternoon sun like colored marshmallows.

We drove into the heart of the city. We followed the bend of the old 5 all the way to the Oregon-Washington River and got off, much to Ira's chagrin, on a distressed, antiquated frontage road running between the river and the Smith, Bybee and Ramsey lakes. The further we drove down it the more cracked and cratered it became, with at least two holes bigger than our hoverbus. This was where it seemed everything came to die; corpses and animal carcasses in varying states of decay flanked both sides of the broken highway.

Ira leaned into the front seat and said, "Thought we were going to stay close to the 5."

"We are," Robert said.

Movement near a wrecked energy station caught my eye. A wild dog, or maybe a coyote, was running for cover under the station's broken roof with a decayed human arm in his maw. As the hoverbus wound closer to the first in the set of lakes, I caught a glimpse of his scraggly pack tearing apart a half-dead woman. Nausea hit me like a lightening bolt and before I or anyone else could open a bag, I had heaved too much for my cupped hands to hold.

Ira ran to the back of the bus and grabbed an oily old towel and helped me clean up. I had seen a lot of horrible things in my life but never realized how desensitized I was until that moment. It had been nearly three years since we left the old world inundated with the dying.

The long nights surrounding my mother's death came back to me as sharp and clear as seeing the coyotes – hurricane Xavier was pouring out its load. At the time I had watched a broken woman waiting to die on the street as if it were a biology experiment. I felt suddenly nauseous again. Ira was prepared this time and held a small trashcan to my face. I shook it off.

Fayza came at me with a pair of fatigues and a tank top big enough to fit five of me. I stared blankly at her. "The sickness will attract the dogs. Change before you suit up."

I nodded. "Where did you get those?"

"From an old supply box under the back seat, next to the first-aid kit," she replied. And before she could sit down Aine had brought the kit and was searching for antiseptic wipes to take away the smell. But each one she opened was dried out.

The hoverbus came to a stop at an old Coast Guard base. Ira covered me with his UV suit while I changed out of my soiled clothes. I really wasn't keen on nudity, ever, and despite everyone being more than polite and averting their eyes, I was embarrassed.

Despite my best effort I still smelled of the sickness and Robert said, "Think it's best for me and some of the boys to go ahead and grab the weapons first. Maybe you could stay behind, inside with Fayza and the other gals. Keep in contact via wristcom."

I wasn't much for sitting on the sidelines, but endangering the group was just selfish. "I came here to learn about weapons."

"Oh, you will," Robert said. "Once we've got guns and can scare off the coyotes or dogs or whatever those things are."

I nodded.

"We'll find a place to practice. Guarantee you those little monsters won't want anywhere near the sound of a gun."

Aine, Fayza and I sat on the hot bus and watched the seven men rush the headquarters combat-style. Within moments the men were back outside still without any arms except an axe. They seized upon a broken-down shed. One of the youngest ex-militia, Todd, struck the first few blows against the door until he was too tired and another ex-soldier, Max, took over. A few more hard blows and the wood splintered enough for him to reach inside and unlock the door. An enormous cache of weapons, a variety of guns too sophisticated for me to discern, glowed like gold at the end of a rainbow.

But to our horror, the noise had awoken an angry pack. The men were instantly surrounded. These were definitely coyotes, but much bigger and scruffier than any I had seen — they had to be some sort of mutation. The alpha went face-to-face with Max and blocked entry to the shed. My smell alone would be enough to distract them. I made a run for the bus's door, but Fayza grabbed my arm. "No, it's too dangerous. The men will be fine, they have size and an axe."

I pulled away, "Just hit the button when I run for the door."

"But…" Fayza started.

I let myself out into the searing heat and sun. The noise and smell momentarily distracted all, even the alpha coyote, but instead of baiting the pack away from the men, my presence raised their hackles. Two coyotes inched toward me, growling, and the alpha barked at the men as if protecting a kill. That's when I noticed a female, her teats enlarged, creeping out of the shadows inside the shed. She didn't look happy. Her presence drove the alpha to lunge toward Max. The men stepped back but the alpha managed to grab hold of Max's arm and he dropped the axe.

I ran screaming to the shed, with the sound of my voice amplified and echoing back inside the UV helmet. The mamma coyote rushed to her pups at the other end of the shed. They were hidden inside a hole in the wall, which I assumed was how she got in. I grabbed a box of bullets marked .22, another marked .45, and took several nearby rifles and handguns, hoping they would match.

Ira had grabbed the axe and was using the blunt end to hit the alpha's nose. I threw ammo and weapons to Robert, Todd, Jack, Kevin and Dave's waiting hands. Ira managed a strong blow to the coyote's nose and he cried in pain and released Max. Max was trying to keep pressure on the bite, but blood was oozing from his ripped UV suit.

I went through a cache of bullet clips looking for a match to the handgun I'd grabbed. I fumbled with a box that looked right and tried to snap it into place. The mamma heard the yelp of her mate and came growling toward me. The clip didn't fit. It was too small. I grabbed a fallen magnum from a different box that had spilled open onto the ground. It clicked in, melting into the steel like it was built into the gun.

I looked outside at the men, hoping one of them would have secured his weapon, but they were still struggling with the same predicament I had had. The alpha male leered at me, ready to clear me from the path to his mate.

I raised my hand up and clicked the trigger, but nothing happened. The alpha inched closer and I managed to remove the safety and aim again at the ceiling. The gun went off. The bullet tore through the metal roof in a deafening screech. Both coyotes scattered – her through the hole in the wall and the alpha zipped past the men, with the pack following him.

Aine and Fayza were out of the hoverbus by the time I exited the shed. Aine took Max Back to the bus and wrapped his arm and prepared an inoculation gun to prevent any infection.

Fayza and I helped the men commandeer the cache. Max waited on the bus while the rest of us picked out weapons to practice with and stuffed the surplus into the bay of the bus. There was more than enough for each member of the Collective to have a gun and ammo, if need be.

I had no idea what any of the weapons were, but I overheard Todd telling Jack, "Most are practically antiques. Looks like all the handguns are old 911 Glocks released more than 20 years ago." Jack nodded in agreement.

Robert set up some simple paper targets on the long side of the shed and from about 100 yards we stood and emptied out round after round. I was the only person who managed to unload ten rounds without hitting my paper. I managed to hit Ira's, which were two targets away. I was great at decimating the aluminum siding but couldn't get anywhere near the target.

When I hit Jack's target (he was next to Ira) he studied me for a second and realized I was in serious need of instruction. He tapped my shoulder and motioned for me to hand over the weapon, which I did without hesitation.

"You don't have any control," Jack said.

"I noticed," I replied.

"Here, try this," he said pulling a small gun from his belt. "Hold it straight." He motioned to the top-center part of the gun and said, "Now line up your shot."

I did as requested and managed to actually hit the bottom corner of the paper.

"Keep your hand steady this time," he said.

I tried again and actually hit the outer part of the circle. We didn't stay long due to Max's injury, but by the end of Jack's lesson I had enough command of the gun that I was no longer dangerous with it.

Ira corralled us. We made a check and headed back to the bus. This time Ira insisted on driving. I warned, "Don't go too fast."

Ira grunted from behind the wheel, "We'll be fine."

"It's OK," Robert said. "I'd prefer to get to work on strategy. We don't have much time before the rain hits."

I nodded.

The men huddled around Max at the back of the bus. Aine had done a great job. The bleeding had all but stopped. He'd need stitches and a few more inoculations, just to be safe, but he'd be fine.

I stayed up front to make sure Ira didn't push the vehicle too hard. He was anxious to get back. I started to drift off, but bloody images of the silver circle cross devices the Environ used woke me in a start. My eyes wandered to the vehicle's instrument panel. We were doing over 400 mph. "Ira," I said.

"I'm being safe." He wasn't about to slow down.

THIRTY-TWO

Inside the Environ's nexus - the brains of the beast and the only proper lab area - notorious genius hacker Malone labored over a series of numbers, trying to crack their code. Malone had always been a free agent, working both sides of the fence for the government and the people. Ira had known him as a fellow ex-con and rebel. Lamont knew him as the greatest computer whiz alive.

Malone was cocky enough to think he'd gotten into the Environ with donated money and his false Christian conversion, but it had been Lamont who had saved Malone's ass without him ever knowing.

For years Lamont had watched Malone from a distance, wanting to invite him to participate in Digibio, but he couldn't risk exposure. Malone had an idealistic streak and would have blown their cover far too early in the project. Lamont knew it was Malone who had helped Psyche and Ira. In fact, it was one of Lamont's men, Herb (Psyche's co-worker at Digibio), who had made the false iris scan at Lamont's command and handed it over to a man Malone had done time with.

No one in the Environ knew, would ever know, that deep down, hidden under the veneer of coldness and greed, Lamont wanted the Collective to succeed. He believed someday they would find a way to save the planet.

Lamont was in a resource meeting when Malone entered their huddle. Herb was in the middle of explaining, "There isn't enough vegetation to sustain the Environ in the valley for more than 10 years. We'll have to aim toward the Oregon border."

"I'd rather we didn't," Lamont replied.

"The UV-resistant hybrids take too long to mature," Herb said. "We've got to reset the coordinates."

Lamont nodded. "OK, if we have to."

The meeting disbanded. Malone caught Lamont's attention with, "Are you sure we have the right numbers from the satellite?"

"They were checked and rechecked. That's why I brought them to you," Lamont responded.

"There's no way the information could be right," Malone replied, shaking his head. "It would mean there's a storm system headed our way that stretches all the way to Australia. It's impossible."

Lamont looked gravely at him. "A hundred years ago, if you said hurricanes would reach speeds of 400 mph you would have been laughed out of the room. Anything's possible. History isn't applicable anymore."

"What do you want to do with these findings?" Malone asked.

"I'm not sure yet, just keep it to yourself for now. I'll talk to the engineers, make sure they planned for a flood," Lamont replied.

After hours of discussion with the lead Environ engineer, Lamont was assured the beast was a truly amphibious creature. A world made entirely of water had been one of the parameters the engineering team had considered. The only foreseeable problem was the energy issue - because the Environ was a living creature, it needed to eat. Northern California had been picked because it had once been wet and lush; subsequently, it had turned into a relatively thriving desert, with enough migrated Joshua trees, sage brush, chaparral and various succulent plants. They, along with a large variety of roaches and rodents – all extremely adaptable - would sustain the Environ's immediate appetite

The air hole on the Environ's top could still breathe, but if the arroyo remained flooded the beast's method of feeding would be disrupted. It would no longer be able to slither over its prey for a snack. The only feeding method for extended periods of time in water was from the inside. This had already been tested; those who died naturally were taken to a feeding orifice located in the garden, was hidden by a dilating mucous wall flap.

Disposal attendants laid dead bodies just outside the flap. After a few hours the flap fully dilated and a tentacle would slither out, wrapping tightly around the body and dragging it inside, to be masticated by two opposing walls of bone. The broken body then slid down a series of tubes into a digestion pit, where highly concentrated acids broke what was left of the body into liquid form in an enormous turbo-powered stomach.

The policy for the executed was exposure and humiliation after death. They were left on Geneco decomposing piles to bake in the sun, their bones a reminder of their misdeeds. If flooding occurred this would have to change. But, of course, Strauch would whine about it. He enjoyed watching the bodies of his enemies torn apart further by the elements. Camille would get it. Lamont decided to convert her first.

Lamont worried Camille would suggest other methods if the flooding lasted more than a month – the kill ratio wouldn't be great enough to meet energy demands. He imagined the Geneco rounded into a pen and cannibalized, or worse. If Strauch didn't want to shelter the Geneco somewhere else, due to his characteristic lack of foresight, they'd be left to drown in the caves. Either way, many more citizens would be executed in the near future under spurious claims – their blood used to keep the hungry beast alive - the least valuable members first, most likely the wranglers who'd be useless without their slaves. Next would come the labor force, equipment operators, metal processors, cooks, housekeeping staff, nannies. Most scientists were pretty-well protected - they were needed to keep the beast running - but technicians would be threatened if it continued, and then, who knew. It could become a free-for-all.

It was Friday and Lamont's ex-wife, Tricia, was supposed to drop off their son, Bryan, in less than an hour. Lamont made his final rounds, checking each station to see if any problems had arisen. All was fine. But before he left work, he asked Malone and Herb to come with him to his cell, where there was a modicum of privacy. They agreed.

Lamont's cell was not typical, more like the Strauchs' than any other scientists'. There was a living area, kitchen, bathroom and bedroom, and he had commissioned a designer to decorate and put up actual sheetrock walls. It was simple, clean and very beige, other than the hint of gray flesh poking between throw rugs.

Malone said, "I should have worked for Digibio."

"It wouldn't have made any difference," Herb said. "My cell sucks, too."

"Can I offer you fellows anything to drink?" Lamont said, heading into the kitchen.

"Whiskey on the rocks," Malone replied, taking a seat on the sofa across from Herb.

"I'm fine," Herb said.

Lamont came back with two glasses and a bottle of Jack Daniels. He poured Malone's over ice and handed it to him and dispensed one straight-up for himself, managing to knock it back before Malone had a chance to taste his.

Lamont pushed a button on the side of his coffee table and a holographic chessboard appeared, complete with holographic pieces fashioned after historical periods – the black pieces after Henry VIII and his first wife, Anne Boleyn, and the white after Queen Victoria and Prince Albert.

"Technically, Albert wasn't a king, but in chess the Queen has all the mobility and real power," Lamont said.

"Why'd you pick Victoria?" Malone asked.

"I've always been fascinated by that era. They were poised on the brink of the Industrial Revolution and the enormous advances that ultimately put us in the spot we're in now," Lamont replied.

"And why Henry VIII and Anne Boleyn?" Herb asked.

"They have a lot in common with the Strauchs."

"Did you call us here to play chess?" Malone asked, taking a sip of his whiskey. Lamonat relaxed into the sofa and tried to wipe the creeping indignation from his face. Malone squirmed. "I was just kidding."

"Such a rapier wit," Lamont said.

Malone grabbed the whiskey bottle. "Maybe you should have another drink, loosen up."

"I'm loose enough," Lamont replied. He took a deep breath and started over. "Either of you play chess?"

"Not much," Malone replied.

Herb shrugged. "A little with my dad when I was a kid."

"Then you know it's a game of strategy. I'll keep it simple so both of you can follow along," Lamont said pointedly. He looked over his shoulder unconsciously, as if someone might be listening, and continued, "The king can only move one step at a time – he's a useless liability, hidden away and protected – a figurehead without a mind. The queen is the most valuable asset on the board; without her it's nearly impossible to beat your opponent."

"Rudimentary," Malone said. "What are you getting at?"

"Imagine this as a metaphor. Imagine we're not the only players on the board," Lamont said, staring hard at Malone and hoping his body language could convey what his voice couldn't for fear of being monitored.

The two stared for a long moment; finally, a light of recognition flashed in Malone's eyes. "If we're not alone, who would our opponent be?"

"That's the wrong way to think about who we're playing. They're less like an opponent than a teammate. They have a strong, decisive, rational queen with a weakness for idealism and Cupid."

"Psyche?" Malone asked. Paul shushed him. "They survived?"

Paul nodded subtly. Herb jumped in, "It worked?"

"Be careful," Paul said nodding to Herb.

Malone studied them, realizing he'd been played and all this time in the Environ he'd felt guilty for making a few bucks off an old friend with the knowledge that he was a goner. "You could have told me. It would have saved me a year of migraines," Malone finally said.

"It could have cost my life," Lamont replied. "Besides, if you knew, you might have gone with them."

"Damn straight," Malone said with a note of melancholy.

"I picked both of you for your personal connection and understanding of the importance of this… extraordinary teammate. In order for chess to be played, we need our board intact. Their team excels in repairs," Lamont said.

He had their attention now, both men focused on his every twitch. "So far we've been lucky enough not to play a match against them, but I have reason to believe we will soon. I need both of you to be my loyal teammates. Can I count on you?"

Both men nodded.

"Good," Lamont said, getting up and activating the orifice. "That's all for now. We'll resume our chess lesson later." Herb and Malone were buried deep in thought and left without another word.

Lamont poured himself another drink and looked at his watch. Bryan would be delivered in moments. Lamont knew Psyche had studied the scientists she picked to join her in their new world and he was certain they knew about the upcoming rain and had already hatched a plan to save the Geneco. It was their nature. They were more than mere scientists, unlike his crew - they were humanitarians.

In the old world it was an uneasy mix, science and compassion – one that came with consequences, usually to the detriment of the scientist's career. It was hard to pay the bills solving world hunger, cleaning the air or saving the planet. It was much easier to make one's way attached to corporations, and their motivations were always the same – bottom line, profits and greed.

"Your son Bryan is here with his mother," said the cold female voice Lamont had assigned to his monitor. He had gotten tired of hearing Tricia's name and liked keeping her where she belonged in his life, as the vessel of his progeny and nothing more.

"Open up," Lamont called to the air.

The orifice dilated and his ex-wife and son walked in. Tricia let go of Bryan's hand and encouraged him to walk over to his father. She still had her long, beautiful brown hair and those sad, almond eyes that had sucked him in 15 years earlier. He was always shocked at how beautiful she really was, as opposed to the wicked hag she became in his mind when she was absent. One look at the ivory skin of her neck or the soft crescent of her lips made him angry at all she had denied him.

"He's all yours for the weekend. It'll be nice for him to stretch out and play. There's no room in our place to do anything except stare at the flatscreen. We don't even have enough…"

Lamont completed her sentence, "… room for a virtual-game station. So you've said 100 times."

"You could help us if you wanted," Tricia said.

"If he's too much of a problem for you I'd be happy to take him off your hands," Lamont replied.

"That's not what I mean and you know it," she spat back.

"Why can't Dick get you a better cell? He's Jessie's right-hand man," Lamont cooed.

"Let it go, it's been three years," Tricia said.

"Technically, it was two years and nine months," Lamont said.

Tricia bent down to Bryan and exchanged hugs, giving him a peck on the cheek. "Have fun with your dad, little man."

"I wish you'd stop calling him that, it's so repulsive," Lamont said. "He's a child, let him be one while he can."

Tricia glared at her ex. She threw a kiss to Bryan and said, "I love you, sweetie," and without another word to Lamont, she let herself out.

Lamont stewed. Dick was a perfect name for his old rival. The irony of ironies was Tricia and Lamont's conversion to the Wrath of God Inc. The supposed bastion of family values had been the very thing that had torn the family apart. Looking back on it, Paul was sure Dick had finagled himself into being his family's spiritual overseer. All new candidates were given one minister to work with, and Dick had always seemed interested in much more than just Tricia's soul.

The moment the family had stepped onto the headquarters' unassuming cement path, Lamont's stomach did a flip. At the time he thought it was just his lunch not agreeing with him, but once they entered the flat, square stucco building and Dick greeted them, he knew. He saw the way the "minister" stared at Tricia, laughing at her inane jokes and avoiding eye contact with him. It was as if he had suddenly disappeared and his wife hadn't noticed he was gone.

After a few months of torture Lamont tried to reason with Strauch about the church. But Strauch informed him his family would not be able to enter the Environ without becoming members of the Wrath of God Inc.

Her husband's ambivalence toward the church confused Tricia. He had been the one to insist on the family's involvement and once she was genuinely converted, he debased her beliefs at every chance. Even as he saw what was most important to him slipping away, Lamont kept the secret. He had to, for the sake of his wife and child's survival. He even kept his mouth shut after he found her in bed with Dick.

Some men might have been blinded by revenge, but even in his darkest moments, Lamont placed the safety of his family above all else. If he let Tricia know the truth, she and Dick would have been killed by one of Strauch's men - and even though his heart was torn to pieces, he still loved her.

Sometimes Lamont consoled himself with the lie that Tricia was just that kind of woman – it would have happened eventually. But it was a fleeting wish and couldn't be sustained. If he could have been honest with her from the beginning, if she had known he was saving her life, maybe her love for him wouldn't have been drained dry and their marriage would have worked. He hated them and the Strauchs and even himself for this.

"Dad, can I play world builder?" Bryan said.

Paul grabbed Bryan's hand and walked him away from the flatscreen and the control gloves. "I was thinking we could do something else together," Lamont said.

The chess game was still on when he brought Bryan to sit opposite him at the holographic table. "What is this?" Bryan asked, reaching for one of the pieces but finding his hand go through it like a ghosts. "Am I dead?"

Lamont laughed. The boy had never seen a hologram before; his mother was too poor to provide such games, his stepfather too stupid to figure out how to make one. "All you need to do is say, 'E2 to E4.'" Miraculously, the red coat marched ahead two spaces.

Bryan laughed and clapped his hands together. "Do it again," he squealed.

"I can't, it's your turn," Lamont, said motioning for the boy to lean closer so he could whisper, "Tell the computer 'C7 to C5.'"

"C7 to C5." Bryan squealed again, this time delighting in his power to make his medieval soldier advance.

"Now you have to learn to think ahead. Every decision you make will ultimately affect whether your soldier lives or dies," Lamont said.

Bryan winced and retreated. He had seen too much death in his young life, and Lamont instantly felt sad for the loss of his child's innocence and angry with himself for causing any inadvertent pain. His poor boy knew too well the anguish of a dying world and the loss of everything dear to him by the tender age of eight. And a broken family, with both parents desperately trying to shelter him with their love but incapable of doing so. No child should have to grapple with a world full of such heavy contradictions. It was too much for a developing mind to conquer. Watching Bryan brought back the intense heartache Lamont felt when Tricia left. His chest tightened.

"Daddy, what's wrong?" Bryan asked.

"Nothing. I'm fine. Maybe we should play this some other time," Lamont said. "When you're a little older."

Sometimes, just before Lamont fell asleep, he was unable to suppress his most shameful thoughts – a wish Bryan had never been born. Not because he didn't love Bryan – he did, with an intensity he'd never felt for anyone else - but the pain of that responsibility made Lamont do things that put himself at risk.

"Don't feel bad. I know you and Mom tried. All things have to die," Bryan said. "Even the Earth."

Lamont was shocked. He had said this a thousand times to himself but couldn't remember ever saying it to another soul. Had he let it slip when Bryan had asked him an impossible question, or about the reason Jesus was so important to so many? He may have, but he had no memory of it. "How do you know that?"

Bryan shrugged. "It's true. Sometimes it makes me sad but only for the animals. We killed everything. We're bad. We're sinners."

Lamont knew where Bryan got this last bit of disinformation – Dick - and it made him ill. He berated himself, wishing he'd been brave enough to do what Psyche had. If the Collective would accept him he would gladly steal Bryan and make a run for their encampment. But he knew they could not, and even if they did, Strauch would do everything in his power to destroy them, even if it meant sacrificing the Environ and everyone in it – except, of course, himself.

Lamont finished explaining as much of the game as Bryan's attention span would allow and then put the boy's PJs on, read him a story and tucked him into bed.

There was still so much to think about with the upcoming rains – what would he do if the Collective came for the Geneco? Lamont walked into his kitchen and made a cup of tea. It would be a long, lonely night of strategizing. He wanted the Geneco and the Collective to succeed. He hadn't worked for 30 years, splicing genes together to create a race that could withstand the increasing global temperatures, CO_2 levels and UV-A and UV-B rays, only to see them destroyed.

He couldn't help but love and hate the Geneco in the strange way a painter loved and hated his paintings or a musician his songs. The creatures themselves offended his aesthetic sensibilities and he wished he could have made them more beautiful, not so monstrous. But when not confronted with the vileness of their appearance, he loved them like they were his children – after all, they were the culmination of his life's work.

If only he could find a way to let the Collective save them. But, of course, this would cause war unless, unless...

THIRTY-THREE

The herbs had been harvested and some of the staff and community members had decided to try something different for dinner. The lead cook had asked Safia if she had any good meatless-curry dishes she might pass along, since there was now a plethora of fresh spices. The meal was an unusually good one. Everyone sat quietly around the dinner table until their plates were clean. It felt like any other night, with the exception of Tuwa's absence. She was praying and fasting in preparation for the mission. It was more comforting to see the lack of conversation as symptomatic of the scrumptiousness of the meal and not because of the underlying apprehension.

Naomi began clearing the table and clearing the air. She said to me, "I don't believe the emancipation mission is a good idea."

"Neither do I," Kevin echoed.

All eyes focused on Kevin. He was, after all, a member of Operation Bare Bones and had been a high-ranking officer in the Coast Guard before its demise. He looked around the room squarely and said, "Diplomacy should always be the first step. I suggest we send an envoy to warn them about the upcoming storm so they can protect the Geney. Otherwise they will perceive our rescue as a hostile act and let loose a war. We can't afford to lose any of our members. This will endanger our greater mission to save the planet."

"But our mission is to save all life," I said.

"If we can't fight for our principles now, then when will we?" Ira added.

"Kevin's right. We don't want to start a war," Kimi said. "I want to help the Geney, but we have to think about our own survival."

The table erupted in heated side conversations. The noise level became so loud I banged my fist on the table and said, "Please, everyone, settle down." For a moment there was a hush. "Nobody wants a war, but does anyone honestly think diplomacy has a chance of working with the people of the Environ?"

"If they see the Geney as their property, won't they want to protect them?" Safia asked.

I was thankful Freeman Fred needed to feed only once a month and that tonight he had turned in early to prepare maps to the Geney encampment in the morning. He would have been heartbroken to hear these people, his friends and now his family, talk about him indirectly in this way.

La Donna shook her head and groaned. "Girl, I'd like some of what you're on. You think these people are logical? If they had an ounce of reason we wouldn't be here, let alone discussing the Geneco."

"But even if we do save them, what are we going to do with them?" Xin-Yi asked. "We barely have enough room in the Nest to sleep and eat. There are almost a dozen pregnant women right now, and hopefully more to come. We can't accommodate a hundred-something Geney."

"We build," Fayza announced with resonant authority. "There's plenty of land around us. We're high enough in the hills to ensure against flooding."

Hyunae had been quiet. She hadn't said a word to anyone in days. She had a tendency to go deep into analysis, almost to the point of catatonia, answering only in monosyllabic grunts indicating yes or no when she was thinking through a problem. Her voice was weak and frail, cracking from non-operation. "It will take anywhere from a month to a year for the rains to stop. We have no idea. Construction can't begin until it is over. Where will they live in the meantime?"

Fayza's husband, Robert, cleared his throat as if to say something, but she shot him a look and he kept quiet. Instead, she spoke. "Robert took me target shooting. About 600 meters to the southwest there's a burn area. The trees have been cleared."

"Yes, and we found a half-dozen cave entrances on the northern face of the mountain nearby," Robert added. Fayza looked at him neutrally, as if he'd apologized for an argument she hadn't quite forgiven him for. "If we had an overflow problem we could house some in there until we finished construction."

Ira had spent every waking moment on that question and had come up with a plan. "The observatory will be down due to the weather, so the astronomy wing can be converted for the time being. And then, when the rains clear and we start construction, we can park the vehicles outside and use the garage, maybe set up some tents nearby for overflow."

"That sounds like a very doable plan," Aine said.

"Because it's not your fucking lab that's going to shut down," Hyunae said. Her unusually emotional outburst sent everyone left at the table into shock.

Fayza responded in an even, calm tone, "We're not shutting your lab down because we want to, Hyunae. It's just not going to be operational due to the circumstances."

"There are plenty of other things we can do. We can gather information on the storm and do calculations…"

"But none of that's going to matter," Aine said.

"We have hundreds of mathematical problems to solve. We have just as much work as everyone else," Hyunae said. "How can we guarantee our equipment will be OK with over 100 Geney living in our space? You tell me that."

"It will be fine," Fayza said. "We can do our calculations in the Council Office."

"There won't be enough room!" Hyunae said, pitching her voice in an uncharacteristically shrill way.

All order broke down and Fayza lost her temper. She and Hyunae went at it while everyone else split into side arguments. I tried to pound my fist again on the table, but to no avail.

I caught Robert's eye across the room and went to him for backup. "We've got to do something to calm everyone down," I yelled to him over the escalating noise.

"This is what happens when you don't have a military in place. We need protection and strong rules," he said.

"With only a few thousand human beings left, war games and nation building weren't foremost on my mind when I envisioned the Collective. The primary concern was survival."

"That's why women never ran the world," he retorted. "They can't think long term."

"Really? Because, as I recall, you boys raped, pillaged, warred and destroyed everything. I hardly think you can make a case for men's ability to think long-term on that record."

Robert grunted and walked away. I was furious. This was his repayment for the little bit of power he'd been given. We'd entrusted the formation of a military to this man? If I had more time I would have worried about his arrogance and a possible coup d'état. But I didn't have time. The situation was escalating. The possibility of violence felt tangible. I never thought I would see the day when a group of rational, logical, cool-headed scientists and techs became as out-of-control as an English mob after a soccer match.

I escaped the dining hall without anyone noticing and ran swiftly down the corridor to the front doors of the Nest and around the pathways, past the labs and barns to a free-standing, windowless shack, originally built to house gardening tools but cleared out and given to Tuwa for meditation and spiritual work.

No one was to enter this sacred space without being invited unless it was an absolute emergency. I hated having to disturb her, but at this point, Tuwa was the only member of the Collective everyone listened to. I knocked but there was no answer, so I let myself in.

The room, which wasn't more than 10-by-10 feet, was thick with burning sage and sweetgrass. I could hardly breathe. A circle divided inside by a centralized cross had been painted on the floor, each quadrant filled with a different color – southeast was red; southwest, blue; northwest, yellow; and northeast, white.

Tuwa had told me six months earlier that the medicine wheel varied in color and meaning for each tribe. The Cherokee divided it north, south, east, west, below and underworld, with different colors assigned to each direction. But Tuwa had made her medicine wheel in the Hopi tradition, the tradition she had been taught since childhood, even though she grew up on a Creek reservation in Oklahoma. Tuwa came from a mix of different tribes, nearly equal measures of Cherokee, Choctaw and Creek.

Tuwa was deep in meditation, sitting at the center of the wheel, chanting and swaying in a resonant language that washed over me like ocean waves lapping at the shore. I'd never heard anything like it and assumed it was probably Hopi.

I desperately wanted to speak to her, but something stopped me. Instead I watched and listened, waiting for the feeling to change so I could interrupt her. Instead the sounds penetrated my body and I felt something shifting inside, as if I were being cleansed by what felt like a pulsating electrical field. It was strange. My insides buzzed and the air seemed filled with a blue-and-white haze.

I had never been to a temple or a church or a mosque or any religious ceremony, except my one visit to circle. And that did not have the same strange sense of privacy and intense communion.

There were no words for what I felt. All I knew was that the feeling was foreign and it was making me strangely lightheaded and separated, as if I had stepped into someone else's dream.

I felt I had to leave before whatever was happening to me got too far out of my control to reign in. But a split second before I turned, Tuwa made a motion to me and said, "Stay. Close your eyes and pray with me." I was about to protest, say I didn't know how to pray, say I didn't know what to do, when Tuwa spoke again. "Just follow me."

So had Tuwa known I was there all along? What else could I do? I closed my eyes and went along with it. After all, I had come into this space uninvited and there was an obligation to play by her rules, even if I didn't know how. Once I followed her song, there was a sense of peace. At times the unintelligible words and sounds stuck in my throat, but they held an unattainable mystery in the melody I could feel coursing through the air.

"I'm singing for guidance, for strength, for support of our mission. Hold the Geney's emancipation in your mind's eye and sing with your heart - whatever comes," Tuwa said.

"That's what I came here for," I said.

Something in my voice snapped Tuwa out of her trance and she looked at me with hawk-like clarity. "They're fighting?"

I nodded.

Tuwa grabbed a yellow medicine bag and ran out the door. I had a hard time following her. She zipped through the garden, a shortcut I never took, and into the Nest, then through the corridor to the dining hall. I arrived a few moments after her, panting and out of breath. She was fine.

Everyone was still fighting. I'd half expected them to have calmed into the mature adults I had always known them to be, but they hadn't. It had gotten worse. Dave and an ex-Navy captain were inches away from ex-Coast Guard vice admiral Kevin's face, both taking turns yelling so hard they were spraying each other with saliva.

Naomi had corned Aine and was angrily gesticulating. La Donna was in a sarcastic showdown with Xin-Yi. Hyunae was giving the evil eye to Fayza. Ira was pointing his finger in admonition at Safia.

Tuwa and I watched. She was drinking in every scene, studying where to crack it. I was shaking with nerves. Strange, dusty memories glided across my inner eye – my mother and father yelling.

My dad, a tall, thin, dark-haired man, grabbing handfuls of his clothing and throwing them into boxes, carrying the small bedroom flatscreen downstairs and into the back of his hatchback. My mother holding back tears, showing only rage and then absolute silence as we watched him putter away.

While I was lost in the past, Tuwa had lighted some sage and was making her way around the room, singing in her native tongue. At first no one noticed - they continued battling - but as she went up to each couple and waved the smoking sage and sweetgrass wands around them, their expressions changed, as if they'd been slapped across the face in a fit of hysteria. There was almost a shock effect and a sudden grounding that seemed to take place so quickly they became literally dumb.

Within a quarter hour the room had gone from an angry, hostile den of fierce lions to a calm, brooding pen of lambs. Next came a long, tiresome group meditation and then grievances were aired and rebutted by her. By the end of the long night only a very small minority remained unconvinced (chief among them Naomi), but their voices were now meek, modest, unsteady and unsure. Their minds were cracked open to what now seemed imperative, even if dangerous, hostile to the Environ or inconvenient. All who left there had a deep belief that despite whatever that was about to unfold, it would ultimately be OK. They had been like children afraid of the monster in the closet, then calmed by their mother into sleep. A part of them still believed in the monster, but the authority of their mother and her resoluteness had been enough to tame them.

THIRTY-FOUR

We were getting the first roll of clouds, which were more gloomy than wet. The storm was moving leadenly across the sky, more like a snail carrying a wet wool blanket than the quick violence of a time-lapse film. In the short term this was good, providing us time to organize our mission and prepare. In the long run, it was disheartening. A storm of this magnitude, moving inches a day, meant it would stick around for months unless some miraculous change in air or ocean current shifted conditions enough to speed it along.

The rest of the Collective cleared out the observatories and the three labs which had been dedicated to reading radio telescopes and deciphering old satellite feeds; makeshift beds and lounging areas were set up. Tuwa kept me at her side. She insisted on personally training me in several meditation techniques. I was intrigued but resistant and asked her, "Why now?"

"The Great Spirit insists. The mission cannot be accomplished if you aren't ready," she responded.

If everyone else was making sacrifices, then how could I not? Yes, I had wanted to honor my mother's beliefs and carry her spirit into this new world, but the philosophies she ascribed to had made less and less sense the longer I lived in the Collective. This world was nothing like the one my mother came from, and her rules didn't apply. There was no more capitalism and thus its foil, communism, seemed just as ridiculous. Marx and Freud and Hegel, and Kierkegaard, Plato and Sophocles - all had interesting points and observations, and while all had something to give under any circumstance, it was as applicable as a Christian parable was to a Sumerian tribesman. Of course, there were kernels of truth in all philosophy and all religion, but what I had been taught was no longer practical or sustainable.

Saturday, a week and a day before the mission, Tuwa asked me to fast after sundown. She had a lesson planned for me in the morning. I was to meet her in the meditation shack just before sunrise.

I didn't normally eat much after dinner, anyway, but somehow, knowing I couldn't eat anything made me hungry and slightly obsessed. I found myself standing in the middle of the pantry, looking through shelves of corn, peas, beets, carrots and beans all canned by Collective members. Another shelf housed at least 50 jars of homemade jams and pickled tomatoes, cucumbers and things I couldn't readily identify. The pantry was huge and in the two-and-a-half years we had been cultivating and harvesting, we had shown ourselves to be extraordinarily adept at providing sustenance for our group. A strange mix of emotions welled in me - melancholy, pride and fear. Tears burned my eyes, wanting to escape, but I knocked them back.

I got the stepstool from the kitchen and went deeper into the pantry, taking inventory of the "nuclear food," a nickname for all the preserved food still edible despite its age – processed cakes, gum and stale candy, stuff people eat ritually for birthdays and holidays like Christmas and Easter. It was a way to bring some familiarity, some bit of tradition, into our new world. Rarely if ever did I enter the pantry, and the packaging of these treats drew me in. They were like edible relics, more beautiful than an Etruscan necklace or a Minoan vase.

I grabbed a box of candy bracelets, probably rescued from a ruined Portland store on one of the scavenging trips. The box was colorful and decorated with cartoons of big-eyed girls wearing bright bows and happy dresses.

Inside was a sea of six- or seven-dozen multicolored pastel bracelets in cellophane. I grabbed one and tore it open, rolling it onto my wrist – the band stretching tight, leaving spaces like a used line on an abacus.

A memory swam back from the deepest recesses of my mind – skipping down De Kalb Avenue to the corner store at Fulton Street (before the area was swallowed by the East River) with my best friend, Janette. We had instantly bonded during recess in fourth grade, when the girls divided themselves up into teams to play kickball without us.

Janette was my opposite - chubby, blond, short - and her mother, Cloris was a devout Anglican. I met Janette after her father died and she and her mother had moved into her grandmother's studio apartment. Janette loved to eat. She'd eat anything, but she especially loved sweets, and that day her grandmother had given her $20 to buy some staple items from the corner store - milk, bread, bottled water and whatever lunchmeat she could afford - but instead of lunchmeat and bread, Janette bought four chocolate bars, two packs of bubble gum and both of us candy bracelets.

It was the first time a friend, or anyone aside from my mother, had cared enough to buy me anything. I thought the bracelet was the most beautiful thing in the world and wore it until the candies were gray from dirt and pollution and sweat, baths and rain had worn it to nibs on my wrist. Even after my mother noticed it was giving me a rash, I refused to take it off. One morning I woke up and it was gone, reduced to a single grayish pink disc on the sheet where my wrist had been.

I combed the bed for evidence, like a detective looking for a murder weapon, but couldn't find the elastic string, leading me to the conclusion that my mother had cut it off while I was sleeping and thrown it away. But when accused of the crime, my mother denied any involvement. When I wouldn't fall for her disintegration theory, she told me it had probably been chewed off by a rat and taken back to its den. This stopped me from any further line of questioning. The idea of a rat walking across my bed and drooling on my wrist as it sawed the string with its little teeth gave me the shivers.

Years later, when I was on summer break from college, she admitted cutting it off of me and I got so angry I didn't speak to her for three days. It wasn't just that she had taken a prized possession against my will, but that she had made up such an creepy lie. She tried to explain how irrational I had been and how tired she was of arguing over something so trivial, which only upset me more. The candy-bracelet incident stood as the biggest argument between Miriam and me.

The Nest was dead silent except for the tightly held sound of my weeping on the pantry floor. I hadn't seen or smelled or felt any of the hallmarks of my childhood in years and all that had been physically left of it was emptied into the Atlantic Ocean. This silly candy bracelet was the closest thing to a touchstone I would ever have. It was like finding a precious heirloom and my favorite teddy bear and a baby blanket after living in a desert full of aliens. My heart broke.

I woke before sunset and made my way to Tuwa's meditation shack. The air was charged with the looming storm. The sky was dampened by the heaviness of the wooly clouds, fresh and sad all at once. I had forgotten how silent the world was when everyone was asleep.

When I arrived, the familiar scent of sage and sweetgrass wafted from the cracked door in a long, inviting ribbon. She must have heard my soft footsteps through the dirt because she said, "Come in."

The shack was glowing amber. At the far end, a horseshoe of candles bordered a small, central altar decorated with crystals, a wide variety of feathers, a small smoking cauldron, a statuette of a cougar and a thick set of cards placed face-down.

Tuwa grabbed a glass bottle of oil, motioned to a pair of pillows on the floor and said, "Sit."

Before sitting next to me, she dabbed her finger with oil, massaged it into my forehead and sang a sacred Hopi song. This was the language she used in circle, her medicine language. Her mother had learned the ancient ways as a girl from her adopted Hopi mother and passed the tradition to Tuwa, initiating her into shamanism almost as soon as she could speak. Perhaps this was why she was so remarkable; she not only had the Gift (as La Donna called it), but had been trained to use this unusual talent so early in life her brain had to have formed differently from other people's.

"Close your eyes," she said, waving sage and sweetgrass in circles around me. "Clear your mind. Let the sweetgrass, sage and song float you into deep peace inside yourself."

Images, numbers, letters, snippets of skylines and pieces of buildings I had lived in all flashed strobe-like inside my mind's eye. There was no peace, and the more I searched for it, the more images flashed, changing like lightning, leaving nothing to hold onto except anxiety.

Tuwa must have sensed it. She broke away from her song to say, "Clear your mind. Imagine your consciousness as a pearl floating in a pool of dark water. Let it sink lower and lower. Concentrate on your breathing."

For some reason, this worked, and the images dissolved into blackness. My mind settled, the voices dimmed – my breath, heartbeat and the sound of Tuwa opening a bottle, followed by the hiss of herbs hitting the charcoal inside the cauldron, was all I heard. I was fully present.

Meditation wasn't entirely new to me. Ira had gone through a Buddhist phase right after he had gotten out of prison – not wanting to discourage him from getting his life back together, I went with him to the Shambhala Center in Manhattan every morning for almost four months. My ability to concentrate greatly improved, but the speed and agility of my mind changed – facts and information that used to swim close to the surface of my mind had to be dug up and plucked with what felt like a dull blade of logic. I didn't like it, felt like it was changing me too much, interfering with my analytical ability, and I quit. Two months later, Ira quit, too.

Tuwa was close: I could feel her. She whispered, "See white light pouring down from the sun, from the moon, let it fill you, cleanse you, wash away the dark places." She touched my forehead in the place Indian women wore bindis; this time, the oil on her finger tingled and burned my skin. I felt a strange jolt of electricity pulsating through her finger before she pulled her hand away. "See from here," she said before lightly pressing a finger to my throat. "Speak the truth." She put her hand over my heart and said, "Sing with the light inside."

Each time Tuwa did this, I felt myself open a little and fall deeper into an altered state of consciousness. The light felt more real, the sweetgrass and sage seemed more potent, and the troubles and pressures dissolved into a mist and lifted away.

Tuwa sang in a gentle and warm voice. The song had only vowel sounds, which rolled from one to the next effortlessly, but without logic to them. When she was finished she waved the smudging wand around me and said, "Open your eyes."

How was it that I felt OK, even optimistic, about the mission? But a strange flash of dread gripped me, and a man's voice whispered, "A sacrifice is required." Of course, there was no man. I stared at Tuwa, trying to regain the peace I had felt just moments before.

"We will all have to make sacrifices," Tuwa said.

It was as if Tuwa plucked the words out of my mind. How did she know, and who's voice had that been?

"I don't recognize the voice. Perhaps he is a spirit guide, an ancestor, or maybe a time fragment," she said.

I stared dumbfounded at her. "How did you know what I was thinking?" She was reading my mind, there was no other possibility.

"Oh, I'm sorry. I thought I heard you speak."

"I didn't say a word," I replied.

"Sometimes, after meditating with others, I hear their thoughts," she said.

There was an uncomfortable feeling of violation, like being walked in on while in the restroom.

"I know, I'm sorry. I wouldn't like it either," she said.

"You're still doing it," I said, aghast.

Tuwa shook herself. "I need to separate," she said, stepping outside and shutting the door of the shack behind her.

After ten or fifteen minutes I began to wonder if perhaps I should leave, or if I were supposed to be doing something. But Tuwa had made me promise to spend the day with her, so I waited and entertained myself by reading the homemade labels of dried herbs and incenses that lined a wall of shelves.

It looked like some of the jars and their contents were as old as Tuwa was, others looked freshly ground. If the names on some of the powders weren't kava kava or cayenne, one would have assumed they were painting pigments.

I marveled at the primitive-looking ingredients that I knew had cured several Collective members from certain death when standard medicine didn't work. Tuwa had cured a tech that had developed a mysterious disease that no diagnosis fit. She had brought him into the shack and prayed over him for weeks, feeding and giving him special teas until he emerged renewed.

Another incident involved a young girl thought to have contracted a mutated form of Ebola after going with her parents on a trip to the ghost city of Portland to scavenge clothing after she'd had a major growth spurt. The girl was quarantined and after a few weeks of trying everything the doctors could think of, they gave up and were pumping her full of painkillers, waiting for her to die, when Tuwa asked the family if she could try to save her. Curing the girl seemed to take much out of Tuwa. Due to the contagiousness of the disease Tuwa worked alone in the quarantine area. She was made to wear a suit to avoid spreading the disease, which she complained made everything more difficult, but after a couple of months the child's symptoms subsided and a few months later she was completely healthy again and released to her parents. These were just a few of the miracles attributed to Tuwa.

The jars were meticulously organized via an impenetrable code. I was staring hard, trying to puzzle out the logic, when Tuwa re-entered the shack.

"Good, you're still here," she said. In her hand was a small white pouch. Embroidered in red was a circle with an equilateral cross inside. She handed it to me.

Inside a variety of stones - quartz, lapis lazuli, coral and a small piece of turquoise - sat in a mixture of sage, sweetgrass, a root of some kind and other herbs I couldn't identify. "Keep it with you always. It is for protection," she said.

"I'll be fine," I replied, trying to hand it back.

She shook her head and closed the medicine bag in my hand. "If you should find yourself in trouble, hold it tight, close your eyes and listen." She pushed my fist back.

There was something of a warning in the way she spoke that sent a chill down my spine, as if she knew my fate and was trying to ease or protect me from it. I put the medicine bag in my pocket and promised to keep it with me at all times.

The rest of the day was spent teaching me songs and prayers. She insisted on my ability to recite them perfectly, although she never said what their meaning was. Native American customs were intricate and complex, and I assumed my day with her was a sort of initiation - she was preparing me for leading the group into "enemy territory," to free the Geney slaves. And because I was not only the leader of the Collective and the mission, but also the only member not initiated, it seemed reasonable she and the rest of the Collective make a tribeswoman or chief of me before I led them all into imminent danger.

That night I had intense, colorful dreams. My mother, Miriam, came to me looking healthy, vibrant, younger than I had ever seen her. She was beautiful, wearing a navy suit and white shirt. Her black hair was cropped, short and curly. I had never seen her look so good. But she never said a word. She only smiled when I talked to her and went about her business of cleaning up the Nest, which was empty except for the two of us and Naomi. Everything looked and felt so real, except for a staircase. In reality, there was no second story to the Nest. And there was a bright light coming from the top of the staircase, casting a long, dark shadow at the bottom, in front of the steps Naomi sat on.

I woke the next morning comforted but very confused about the meaning of the dream. I didn't normally remember them.

THIRTY-FIVE

La Donna, Aine, Tuwa, Freeman Fred, Fayza, Ira, I and Robert's militia group, CAT, prepared the hoverbuses with water, food, blankets, some basic medicine and rafts, in case there were any mechanical problems and one of the buses broke down in a floodplain. We had seven buses and each could carry up to 50 passengers. But with all the extra equipment, only 40 could comfortably fit – but that would be plenty. We figured there were less than 200 Geney alive.

The lead scientists were bus drivers and were paired with at least one member of CAT. Freedman Fred couldn't drive but he was our liaison. A young CAT recruit named Sam offered to drive and Robert went with them.

Anyone who volunteered had to be trained in using a firearm. Freeman Fred, La Donna and Tuwa submitted to training a few days before the mission. La Donna and Tuwa protested, but I insisted on everyone being armed, just in case. I wanted every chance available for my people's safety and the safety of the Geney.

Freeman Fred had spent the last two weeks working on maps of the area from memory. He didn't know or remember how he had gotten from the mine to our encampment, so we relied on old AAA maps found in Seattle on a scavenge to get us to the general area. Once we got there, Freeman Fred's drawings and schedules were to be used. They were very detailed, from when the Geney worked and slept to where the wranglers congregated, when they started work, when they had lunch and shift changes. The one thing he wasn't sure of us was the presence of border guards, since the Geney were locked up in a cave at night.

Robert felt they might have one or two night guards. But most likely there wouldn't be any, probably just an electronic fence or alarm in case one of the Geney exited the caves. I agreed with him. It seemed doubtful the Environ would waste resources on a guard when electronics were more reliable and could be monitored, along with everything else, inside the Environ.

We ate dinner with everyone that night. The Collective was nervous but excited for us. It seemed everyone had finally come around to the mission. I credited this to a series of rituals Tuwa had led, where members were asked to fly to the Geney encampment and see through the eyes of their brethren. The attitude shifted dramatically: People had come to me over the course of the week telling me what a hero I was for insisting on helping the Geney and relating their experiences.

One woman said she had seen a line of Geney entering the cave and her consciousness went to a young, confused Geney girl who accidentally hit her thumb with a mallet while she was trying to carve out a bit of silver. The woman said she felt an excruciating pain in her thumb, the bone crushed, and then felt herself being yanked out of the cave by a large man in an orange UV suit, who took her outside and whipped her until she could no longer feel her back. The woman began crying as she retold the story.

I had asked Freeman Fred if the things people were seeing in the rituals were true. "Yes," he said with such a profound sadness in his eyes that I had to turn away.

The dinner was especially good. One of the turkeys had been slaughtered in a sacrificial ritual that morning. "It was its time, soon, anyway, and at least it served a purpose," Tuwa had said when I asked her if it was really necessary. "All creatures are sacred and in honoring the animal's spirit we honor our own."

I couldn't really argue. We did have to eat, but something about animals being sacrificed felt barbaric to me. I suppose everyday animals were sacrificed in the old world, we just did it without honor and while no one was looking.

The Thanksgiving-style meal was topped off with a chocolate cake Naomi made for us. I was surprised. It was delicious and afterward I thanked her for it. She gave me a hug and said, "Good luck. Be careful."

Shortly after dinner we gathered the last of our supplies and headed to the buses, followed by most of the Collective. I gave Ira a hug and kiss before we went to our respective buses. He took Max; I took Todd; La Donna was paired with Kevin; Aine with Jack; Dave and Tuwa with ex-Green Beret and new CAT recruit Gavin.

As I waited for my turn to exit the garage I watched the crowd. On the whole they looked anxious, scared and excited. I noticed Naomi standing with her son in front of everyone. She looked dazed, more afraid and somber than anyone else. She gripped her son's hand tightly, so tightly he seemed to be wincing and trying to pull away, but she didn't notice. She was in a far-away world. It struck me as odd, but I had no idea why.

One by one we exited the garage, following Robert, Sam and Freeman Fred. I felt like a soldier going off to war. When my bus passed by Naomi, I waved to her. She looked right at me but it was as if I were a ghost, invisible. She didn't respond.

It was a three-hour ride to the mouth of the valley where the Environ was situated. The buses could only safely travel 100 mph without overheating, so we kept our speed down and followed the broken remnants of the old 5 Freeway that had taken motorists all along the West Coast, from Mexico to Canada.

A few minutes after a sign welcomed us into California, the rain went from a fine drizzle to steady rain. The deeper we plunged into California, the harder the rain fell and the more difficult it was to see the line of buses ahead of me – or, more importantly, the road. My wristcom had run out of juice and was charging. I tried to use the bus communicator to let the others know I wanted to slow down, but the storm was causing interference so I flashed my lights and honked the air horn to get the attention of Gavin, Tuwa's driver and team member.

I worried momentarily that they would think something was terribly wrong and try to pull over, but luckily it was Tuwa in front of me. I calmed myself and concentrated on her. Once I felt a connection was made, I visualized the bus speedometer slowing from 100 to 60 mph. It seemed to work, because in a few minutes we had slowed to a careful pace, close to what I had envisioned.

A swarm of lightning revealed Mount Shasta looming close by. I had seen it once before, on a trip down the West Coast to visit Yosemite with my mother when I was a kid. It was seductively beautiful, but there was something eerie about it. My mother had told me some people believed extraterrestrials lived underneath it, and I remembered thinking I could see why. It had an unnatural feel, cold and predatory, almost as if it were staring at you passing by. Later I chalked up my fear to an innate sense of danger because it was a volcano. But now that we were passing it again, I felt like there was something more to it. Tuwa had told me shamans and psychics had called it a power center, like an earth chakra. Another strobe of lightning convinced me Tuwa was right.

We were getting close. Ira had spent more than a month going through all the old data on the Environ and found a coded reference to its longitude and latitude, which he then located on a map. When the topography was explained to Freeman Fred he agreed with Ira's assessment. I hoped Ira was right, because there was no way to find it otherwise. The area was far too large, and from what we knew about the Environ, it was a dark-colored biological entity that would most likely blend into the environment.

I followed the line of buses onto a small, two-lane highway, catching a decayed sign a few miles down the road that read "Highway 89." The rain became thicker and the lightning more continuous. We had been descending into a valley and as we continued, the roads were washed out, making it hard to tell if we were still actually on the highway.

There was static coming through on the bus communicator. Todd changed the frequency several times and fiddled with it until we could hear an exchange: Ira was asking, "Are you sure? Because the map we agreed on says it's another 10 miles before we head off the 89 south."

Freeman Fred crackled through the radio, "Just beyond hill. I positive. Sure 100 percent."

"OK," Ira said.

And we all turned south off the highway into the darkness. Already there were patches that looked like little lakes and streams. But we kept descending, and I worried that once we got into the basin it would be a river and the caves would already be flooded. If the Geney were in a panic it would make it more difficult to rescue them. More than anything I hoped we'd find them all alive.

THIRTY-SIX

The Environ was across the valley, several miles from the Geney caves. We could see it during the lightning strikes. Its gray, gelatinous skin shone like a slime-covered slug. From what Freeman Fred had told me, it was marbled with dark-gray veins and appeared almost translucent in daylight.

The Geney caves were within its sights to the north. The rain had advantages. We were hard to spot and the thunder and lightning covered our noise.

We parked the buses on the side of the mountain, out of the Environ sightline, by way of a short walk to the caves. Todd loaded. I put on a raincoat and galoshes and met everyone outside.

We huddled together under a protruding rock for shelter. "Do you have the sample key?" I asked. Ira nodded and pulled out a square black module made to fit into any computer port. The sample key was programmed with hundreds of override codes he and Safia had programmed.

Ira asked Freeman Fred, "Where's the entrance?"

Freeman Fred took the lead. We followed him around an outcropping of boulders at the bottom of the hill and sloshed through a knee-high puddle rapidly forming into a pond.

"Beast behind next corner," Freeman Fred said. Ira signaled for everyone to turn off our head lanterns.

The lightning had slowed to a momentary stop. A tear in the clouds revealed a full moon, giving us much-needed light. We rounded the corner of the mountain. Across the plain I saw the dark, shiny beast, parts of it glowing from inside. It had a terrifying, predatory charisma. And the eerie moonlight gave it the illusion of a face, even though I knew it wasn't possible. It looked like the strange beast was watching us.

Freeman Fred had seen the wranglers fumble with something on the eastern side of the mountain, before and after the Geney were let in and out of the caves, but he didn't know exactly where the keypad was. La Donna, Tuwa and I walked to the general area and felt our way along the mountain's face. We divided the area into thirds to investigate. Everyone else crowded into a dry crevice, protected from the wind and rain.

The wall was slick and jagged; one wrong slip toward the rock formations could cause a fatal head injury. It was pouring so hard I couldn't see a foot in front of me, and the rain had such high acid content it was burning any small patch of uncovered skin. Despite the rain goggles my eyes were watering and burning, making it impossible to see clearly. The insensate blinking caused me to keep losing track of any unique features in the rock, which normally would have guided me. It was very disheartening. I was sure we'd never find the keypad.

I grasped for what I thought was a rock formation until I felt Tuwa's plastic rain slicker. She laughed. "Hey, watch it. You're gonna poke my eye out."

"What are you doing over here?" I asked.

"We're not far from the keypad, just follow me," she replied.

I almost asked her how she knew, but decided not to waste my breath – it was like asking a spider how it wove a web. For Tuwa, it was so natural she couldn't explain her abilities. She stopped about 10 feet from where I had been feeling around.

The rain started beating harder and the lightning started up again. I watched it crack against the sky in the distance, followed by the low rumble of thunder moments later.

"It's here," Tuwa said.

"Stay there, I'll grab Ira," I said, breaking into a jog. The wind was fierce. I hardly made any headway against it on my way back to the refuge in the mountainside. I ran to where I thought it was and looked around, but couldn't distinguish anything human in the darkness.

"Ira," I called.

A muffled, "Over here," came back. I followed its trail, calling Ira's name until his voice came back clearly and I reached the refuge.

They were huddled close together with barely enough room to breathe, let alone move. "We found it," I said. It took a moment for Ira to squeeze out of the shelter.

Ira secured his goggles and cinched his raincoat's hood strings tight. He followed me through the sheeting rain in search of

Tuwa. Once we got close to where I remembered leaving her, I called out. Her voice guided us through the rain.

Ira shielded the sample key from the rain as he gently fit it into the keyboard's port. An eternity shuffled by without any response from the gate.

The rain died down and several hulking black shapes emerged in the distance. "Hey, what's taking so long?" Robert said, making his way to us. Behind him were Todd, Max, Kevin and Dave.

"It's searching for the right codes," Ira replied.

"Let's just shoot the keypad, rush in, get the Geney to the buses and get on with it," Max said.

"You serious? That would trigger an alarm for sure," La Donna said. "And we'd all get out butts killed. Uh-uh — no way!"

"We don't even know if there is an alarm," Kevin said. "We're wasting time."

"Just be patient," I said.

Dave opened his mouth to speak and Tuwa put a finger to her lips. "Shhh," she said. "If there weren't an alarm, this wouldn't be taking so long."

Another fifteen minutes went by without any sign we were close to unlocking. The CAT division members were antsy. Clearly, they were used to the instant gratification of explosives, nukes and gunpowder. As the rain gathered momentum, Todd's frustration mounted. The lightning and thunder drew closer together. Todd finally stepped between Ira and me.

"We can't wait out here all night. The codes aren't working," Todd said.

Robert heard Todd's plea and said, "It's time for Plan B."

"I told you, this could easily take an hour," Ira shouted back over the rumble of thunder. "Just relax. Go back to the shelter if you don't want to deal with it."

Both Todd and Robert made sour faces, as if Ira had attacked their manhood. Maybe he had, but he was right. I looked at my wristcom and said, "It's only been 40 minutes."

Robert and Todd fell back into a huddle with the other CAT members, Max, Kevin and Dave. It struck me as funny how bent out of shape they were while Tuwa, La Donna and I waited patiently. I'd always heard women had a greater tolerance for pain. It had to be true: The thrashing from the rain and burning irritation of my eyes and skin had all but disappeared into the numbness of the moment. I hardly noticed it at all, but Ira still winced and remained bent over like an old man with osteoporosis. My attention turned to Tuwa and La Donna. They were turned away from the onslaught of water, unbothered. Only the volume of their speech was louder, as if carrying on a conversation in the middle of a crowded nightclub.

Another 10 minutes or so went by and the men became antsy again. This time they took out their weapons and, instead of asking Ira how long it would take, loaded their clips. I got very upset and rushed to Robert's side.

"Tell them to stop," I said.

"We have to be prepared," Robert replied. His eyes flashed cold and predatory in the lightning.

"For what? What are you planning to do?" I demanded.

"Whatever we have to," he said.

I yelled, "You think you can just shoot the keypad off and jerry-rig the thing so it will open, and then what? Shoot whoever responds from the Environ and leave with the Geney intact?" He pulled out a second gun and loaded it, ignoring me. "This is not some old Western, Robert. Hundreds of real lives are at stake."

He looked up at me with the glaze of combat in his eyes, a strange, unnerving stare. As a kid I had seen it on an old soldier who had been in Iraq. "You don't think I know that? You don't think I've dealt with life and death a thousand times before? You may have brought us to the Collective, sweetheart, but America wouldn't have survived at all if it hadn't been for guys like me."

This was the first time I'd ever really been afraid since living in D.C. We'd had disagreements in the Collective, but we'd always reasoned them out. This was the ugly side of human nature, the unchecked I – the runaway ego married to its dark half-brother, the Id. I was rendered speechless by its rearing.

Tuwa must have seen me staring dumbstruck at Robert loading his weapon because she materialized. "Just because we can't see it doesn't mean we aren't making progress," she said to Robert, trying to mollify the tension.

"Just because you say so doesn't make it true," he responded.

"Hey, everyone, get over here," Ira yelled. "It's disarmed and it looks like the gates are starting to open."

Robert stared me down and sauntered over. We had come close to something very dark. Tuwa and I stared at one another for a moment as if to make sense of it and give comfort. Ira called out again. We made our way to him.

THIRTY-SEVEN

We stormed into the caves, against my better judgment. But stopping CAT members from their agenda was as doable as teleportation. Calling it impossible wasn't quite fair, but thinking it achievable was foolish. Robert and his men had their weapons loaded and at the ready. Even though Freeman Fred had told them there were no guards inside the caves, they felt it best to be prepared. Arguing was pointless - they had no respect for non-military-style strategy. Disagreeing with a soldier about a potential combat situation was seen as foolish. The thing was, it really wasn't a combat situation, but there was no way to tell if it would become one. Thus, my authority in the situation was undermined and Robert took over.

The caves were surprisingly dark, not a hint of ambient light anywhere. Robert and his men stepped back toward the mouth of the cave where they could see. They were about to engage their head lanterns when I said, "Freeman Fred can see. Maybe we should let him guide us. The head lanterns will panic the Geney - they'll think we're wranglers."

Robert's mouth twitched as if to disagree when Todd said, "Great idea." He pulled out an old-fashioned flashlight and said to the men, "If we need more light, we can use this until they get used to us."

The men uniformly grumbled in agreement and stayed close behind Freeman Fred. The rest of us held onto the tails of each other's jackets for safety. The tunnel felt long. The end opened to a mouth where three openings in the rock faced one another. A soft, red glow softly sprayed light on us. An intense heat came from inside. It was the Egg Cave, and it felt worse than the hottest day in the Devil's Punchbowl.

The door next to the Egg Cave was the nursery, where the Geney mothers lived while nursing babies and caring for toddlers. It was here Tuwa and La Donna felt we needed to go first. If we could get the mothers to understand and go along with us, then everyone else would follow without incident. After all, in the Geney culture they were the only individuals with any kind of authority – aside from the wranglers.

Freeman Fred, Tuwa, La Donna and I had planned to go in and talk to them alone, but Robert kicked up. "It's not safe to assume they're all alone in there. You need to take us."

"No," I said. "You'll scare them."

"They no have men," Freeman Fred said.

"But it could be a trap," Robert continued.

"This isn't Iraq," La Donna said. "The Environ has no idea we're here."

"But…" Robert started.

"No," Tuwa said. "You will wait here with the men. If something happens we will call for you. There's nothing to fear."

"I can't be responsible if something happens," Robert said.

"I take full responsibility," Tuwa said.

"As do I," I said.

"Same here," La Donna echoed.

"Fine," he said with macho exasperation. "I'm just trying to do my job."

"And we deeply appreciate it," Tuwa said. This seemed to placate him and he relaxed.

There was some light inside, enough to see the women asleep on torn rags, some with babies swaddled close by, others cradling toddlers in the crests of their arms. The gentleness and love of these women was remarkable, knowing the torture they had endured and the hopelessness they must have felt while raising their children. Their children literally had no future. They were slaves – less than slaves, really, because slaves at least had worth to their masters. These people were treated like machines, yet I had never seen such humanity and love nestled in one place.

The Geney culture was young. La Donna had pieced together a tapestry of stories from her sessions with Freeman Fred. Together with Tuwa they found the nursery wasn't just nurturing the next generation of Geneco, but also the start of a spiritual/religious system, or what post-Westerners called mythology. The plan was to use their emerging mythos to convince them to leave.

The mothers had developed the ideal of a mythic Freeland shortly after the Geneco were taken to the caves. Over the years it had developed into a richly symbolic story of redemption and Edenic freedom. The culture was still very young and the stories wavered between it being a real place somewhere beyond the horizon line to a place the soul traveled upon emancipation from the body. We had to convince them of the reality of such a place, even though we looked like the enemy.

There was a woman sleeping alone. Freeman Fred nudged her. She startled awake. "What you here?" she said, alarmed, waking some of the other women around her with the pitch of her voice.

"No harm. I bring the special ones. We go Freeland," he said.

She rubbed her amber slitted eyes with the backs of her scaly green knuckles. "Sleeping," she mumbled to herself, lying back on her nest of rags.

"No," Freeman Fred said. "Real. Freeland Real. I 199."

"199 dead," the Geney woman lying nearby said. "No play trick. Go bed."

Freeman Fred asked me to turn my head lantern on. I did and he stood at the center of its beam. "See, 199. I bring Special Ones, take us Freeland."

The women gasped and nudged their sleeping neighbors awake. And the cave erupted in a chorus of whispers. The voice of the first woman stood out among them: "They smooth skin. Special Ones no be smooth skins."

"Special Ones save me. Telling no say Special Ones no smooth skin. These Special Ones," Freeman Fred said.

"Freeland no have smooth skins," another woman said, the gash where a human mouth would be constricting in a funny expression I couldn't read but Freeman Fred did.

"Telling say only Freeland where Geney free. I free now. Go from Geney 199 to Freeman Fred. Special Ones good, no afraid of Special Ones, good smooth skin. Take all to Freeland."

I came forward and explained the Collective as best and simply as I could, telling them they would have their own place if they wanted and we would help build it. I wasn't sure if the women could understand everything, but the more I talked the more everyone relaxed.

Tuwa broke in to ask them about their stories of Freeland. It was a paradise they were taken to after one of the Geney came back to life to take them there with the Special Ones. It was strangely prophetic; perhaps the Geney woman who had originated the story was a natural psychic or shaman, like Tuwa.

La Donna's thoughts were along the same line as mine. She tried to trace where and when the first stories of Freeland were from, but none of the women could remember. They just said the story was always there, like a truth or absolute.

By the time we finished talking with them, they were leaning toward the idea we were the Special Ones and had come to take them to Freeland. Even the more skeptical of the bunch admitted anything was better than living strictly within the confines of the cave and giving over their babies to slavery. But there were two women who were very afraid of change and didn't want to leave what they had known their whole lives – these same women were attached to the eggs and didn't want to abandon them, which of course we couldn't take with us for many reasons, not the least of which was that the eggs would not have survived transport. The mothers agreed to help us establish trust with the others and let the individual Geney make up their minds about going with us. It was all we could have hoped for.

The mothers went into the sleeping quarters first, without us. We heard them retell the story of Freeland and of the Special Ones and make claims that the Special Ones were now here to take everyone away to Freeland. They prepared the Geney for the inevitable shock of seeing 199 alive again, and the bigger shock of the Special Ones being smooth-skinned like their nemesis, the wranglers.

Everything went well at first. We got them to gather up whatever they wanted and line up to get onto the hoverbuses. A few White Shirts were resistant to leaving because they had been given a modicum of power by playing snitch and "foreman" to the other workers. The wranglers relied on the White Shirts to be their eyes and ears inside the mines and to keep the Geney in order. It was extremely rare for a White Shirt to face disciplinary action. They had no other special privileges or compensation except the assurance they wouldn't be beaten to within an inch of their lives, which was a strong motivator.

One of the White Shirts, Geney 132, appeared extremely apprehensive and shaky. He dropped the small satchel of his belongings half a dozen times on the way to the buses. I asked him if everything was OK, but he didn't say much, just nodded. Tuwa tried to get him to talk, but he resisted her as well.

The buses were parked in a row alongside a wall of jagged boulders at the foot of the mountain, around 300 meters from the cave entrances and out of the Environ's site. The Geney walked in the straightest line I'd ever seen, tighter and more organized than an army unit. The lightning and thunder had rolled further west, along with the heavy surge of rain, but the mist was starting to turn into drizzle.

We broke the line into four, one for each bus. Freeman Fred spoke to each group, telling them not to be afraid of the machines and what to expect on the ride – how it would feel and how long they would be traveling. They asked questions about where they were going, which he answered.

I walked back to the other side of the bus to grab some supplies for the ride when I heard a faint moaning coming from the black vacuum of the desert. I grabbed Ira, who was waiting patiently near his bus, and pulled him to the area where I had heard the sound. But there was nothing, and then…

"Hurting, hurting…" the female voice whimpered.

I engaged my head lantern and ran toward the moaning. Ira followed, stumbling over a pile of jagged rocks shortly after he started off. He fell but wasn't hurt, and then gathered himself up, turning on his light and being more careful. He found me bent over a Geney. All he could see of the Geney were her bloody and scabbed green feet poking out from behind my silhouette.

"Go get Freeman Fred and some of the Geney men, we need to move her," I said, ripping what was left of the soiled tunic on her back. The lash marks were deep and beginning to fill with puss. Ira started running back. I yelled at him, "And bring the first-aid kit; make sure the antibiotics are inside."

Ira came back with a crowd of Geney. He had tried to tell them it was best for only a few to come with him, but they were insistent and he had relented for the sake of expediency. Tuwa found the antibiotics and the first-aid kit and brought La Donna with her. The men of CAT decided it was best to guard the area and keep a lookout for a possible Environ security patrol. It was the first decision they made that everyone agreed with and were happy to accommodate.

I was surrounded by a crowd 10-people deep in each direction. It took a bit of jostling for Tuwa to reach me through all the deeply concerned geney. It struck me how much emotional they were despite their faces' inability to show it. I could see the worry through their body language, which I had learned through my intense friendship with Freeman Fred.

Profound sympathy was expressed through the dilation of their irises and bowing of their thin lips into a subtle O shape. They slumped when very emotional, and their tongues hung out of their mouths while their eyes watered like dripping faucets. Their collective fear and grief was palpable. They didn't hide it one bit. Some of the women moaned along with 218, as if in an eerie empathic chorus. Some of the men grunted as if socked in the gut. Perhaps it was because their culture was so young and unabashed that they showed such compassion, or maybe it was something genetic.

I administered a shot of antibiotics to the young woman and Tuwa cleaned up the wounds as best she could. But the woman was far too ill to travel three hours on the hoverbus back to the Collective encampment. She was on the brink of death and we needed to stabilize her first. She needed an antibiotic IV, which we'd have to manufacture, and the four hours we had until sunrise, when the wranglers would come around, was quickly approaching.

I motioned for Freeman Fred to come close and whispered to him, "In order to save her we're going to have to wait until tomorrow night to take the Geney. Will they be able to keep the secret?"

Freeman Fred nodded, "Geney keep many secret."

"But this is a big one. If anyone tips the wranglers off, we could end up embattled. People could die," I said.

Freeman Fred pondered this. He knew the responsibility I was foisting on him, the decision to save this young Geney woman's life at the risk of everyone else's. And he was the only one of us who truly knew the Geney well enough to know whether waiting was a viable option. He sat next to me, gravely pondering the potential outcomes, while I continued to inspect the woman for any other signs of trauma.

Finally, he spoke, "We wait. I talk to Geney. If I see no understanding we go tonight."

"OK," I said. "But first we have to move her to a secure location."

"Ira and La Donna look for cave. They be back soon," he said.

Tuwa and I continued working on the woman. I placed a thermometer in her ear – her temperature was 102, five degrees

warmer than normal for a Geney (they ran cool, usually around 97).
It was far too high and I found a pack of liquid analgesic and
prepared a shot while Tuwa went through her medicine bag for an
herbal balm she could apply to the skin until she could make a proper
poultice.

Freeman Fred gathered the Geney in a group and explained
the situation. Ira and La Donna came back with Kevin and Dave.

Once Kevin and Dave had heard of the sick young Geney,
they made a makeshift stretcher out of one of the hoverbuses'
bathroom doors, some emergency blankets and rope. They had
expected to bring her on board, but understood the need to stabilize
her before moving on and brought her to the nearby cave without
incident.

Freeman Fred talked to the Geney for over an hour. They
promised him over and over no one would say a word to the
wranglers, but instinct kept telling him otherwise. He knew saving the
young Geney woman would inspire confidence in his people and
allow them to trust his new friends, making the transition into the
Collective easier for everyone. He was torn. And decided to explain it
again, hoping the feeling would go away this time. The Geney assured
and reassured him of their loyalty and eventually he came to believe
them. Even if they didn't trust his new friends, at least they all
wanted the well-loved young Geney woman they identified as 218 to
live.

"We go night tomorrow," he said. "Go sleep now and
remember keep silence."

The Geney disbanded, walking back to their cave slowly.
None had ever been outside at night and they marveled at the
brilliant, swirling tapestry of lights now visible due to the storm's
momentary lapse. Freeman Fred heard them wondering how and
what the pinholes of light were, and heard one of the mothers say,
"Lights of Special Ones. Put up in dark to find way home."

The desert floor was bumpy with small dust dunes blown into
rows by the wind. There was no living indigenous plant life except
the occasional dried-out stump or the gnarled bones of dead, ancient
scrub oaks.

Boulders around the valley formed a protective horseshoe
where the Environ was located. I caught a glimpse of it on the way to
the cave. It was far enough away to look more like a slug than a
biosphere. Its dark gray skin glistening unevenly in the moonlight, a

black trail of what looked like crude oil left behind marked its gradual movement.

Aine and La Donna scouted the area and found a canyon 20 miles north to in which to store the buses. They worked together to hide them and redistribute supplies into one bus, which they stored behind an outcropping of boulders on the western face of the mountains. It was close enough to the cave we were bunking in to utilize.

Tuwa and I followed the men carrying Geney woman 218. It was about a mile to our encampment and the men were sweating and fatigued by the time we got there. The mouth of the cave was low and the men had to improvise a sleigh to push her through.

Inside, somewhere far in the distance, water rushed and trickled. It may have been under us, or around a lacy wall. It was so dark that the head lanterns and flashlights felt useless against the dense blackness. I felt a tap on my head and nearly jumped out of my skin. A few drops of water had collected enough momentum to fall just as I was walking under them. I didn't like it. Not at all. I had never been much of a fan of small, dark places, and although I would never have admitted it to anyone, the cave scared me.

Medicine and a bed had been prepared for 218, but La Donna and Aine hadn't a chance to do much else. Tuwa pulled a bag she was wearing from under her shirt. Inside were strange roots and herbs.

"What is that?" I asked.

"Medicine. I'm going to make a poultice and this root…" She held up a dark, earthy brown, pepper-shaped twig, "A natural anti-inflammatory, antibiotic, and it stimulates cell regeneration."

"But she's not fully human. It might be dangerous."

Aine overheard our conversation and interrupted. "It was found in the last patch of Brazilian rainforest in 2024. If found earlier and the FDA allowed testing, it would have saved millions from the Nidor Improbus strain of Ebola. Initial European studies showed it sped recovery time anywhere from 95 to 600 percent.
Early on it was tested on a wide variety of animals - lizards were the earliest group. At the time there was an epidemic of Paramyxovirus and it was tried as a last resort. It reversed the disease in 86 of 100 cases."

Tuwa opened a can of Sterno and filled a pot with distilled water. "I'm too simple to understand all that."

"How did you know about it?" Aine asked.

"A friend gave it to me as a medicine gift."

I followed, asking questions. "Why did you bring it?"

She smiled enigmatically. "I was told to."

"By?"

"Every day I meditate and talk to the Great One. Before the trip there was much to pray about."

Aine was as intrigued as I was about Tuwa's strange process. "So how did you know it was an antibiotic and stimulated cell growth?

"Like I said, it tells me its gifts. I learned the art as a small girl from my Hopi grandmother. She could listen with her hands better than anyone, better than me."

"So you hold it? Like psychometry?" Aine asked.

Tuwa nodded. The water was coming to a boil and she stirred in the root, along with dried, cut green leaves that looked like basil.

La Donna had been tending to 218 in the meantime. She had administered pain relief to her once she had been laid inside the cave.

Ira and Todd turned 218 over and cut the shredded, sack-like tunic, peeling it back from the matted blood. It was a hideous sight, her pale green skin lashed with such ferocity the wounds were like bloody ravines; in some, we could see bone peeking through the coagulated red. One of the wounds across her shoulder blade was filled with puss and turning an off-yellow. It was all I could do to keep from running outside and vomiting – more due to the implicit cruelty than the wounds themselves.

Robert waved Todd over. The CAT members inspected their weapons and huddled together, strategizing how to keep the encampment safe. Todd and Dave were ordered to prepare our nearby bus for an emergency escape and firefight. Robert ordered them to sleep and guard in shifts. After Max, Jack and Gavin were finished checking maps, guns and rations, they followed Robert out to survey the area.

Tuwa had finished stirring and preparing the poultice. It needed to cool down. She hung it from a stalactite to drip dry, careful to keep it from the path of the natural, erratic drip of water.

Ira glanced up from cleaning out the wound and saw my wan face. "Get some fresh air. You're not going to be much help otherwise."

I nodded and quickly left, bending under the jagged archway

of the cave's mouth. Tuwa followed me. A gentle breeze caressed my face. The storm had cleared and the sky above was cloudless for the time being. The stars and full moon were captivatingly bright against the inky-black sky.

"It used to be so peaceful – so beautiful here," Tuwa said. "This desert teemed with secret life when I was a kid."

"I thought you grew up in Santa Fe."

"I did. But my father's mom lived a few hours from here, near the Klamath River. I spent a few summers with her, learning her ways. She was a funny mix of Achomawi-Shasta and Navajo blood. She invented her own medicine and mixed many legends. She told me stories of this valley. It was a paradise before the turn of the century, from here to San Francisco and east to the border of Nevada."

I leaned against a cold, hard boulder. An icy gust of wind hit my face. I shivered.

"It won't be cold tomorrow. Close to 130 degrees, and in the UV suits it will feel like 150," Tuwa said, reading my mind. It no longer shocked me, and the intimacy felt comforting in this strange place.

On our walk back, the moon started to set and the stars glowed ever brighter. I marveled at the tapestry of time they represented. A time that no longer existed. Some of them were long dead, having blown into supernovas, collapsing into white dwarfs or even black holes by now. But I got to see them in their glory. It was an enormous historical painting only a handful of other creatures were privy to now. This little blue egg had a particular vantage point, a unique cross-section of time, place and space. If we ever were alone in the universe, then we had been the only creatures to enjoy the vast spectacle of creation. There was too much majesty to waste on dust and open space; the universe needed an audience as much as we needed to live to enjoy it.

"The Great Spirit deserves it," I said. This time I was the one talking about the Great Spirit and uttering a half-spoken phrase, but Tuwa understood. She nodded.

"Now you understand. We are the eyes, ears, nose and touch of the Creator. The Creator experiences Its life through Its creations. We are one and the same," she replied.

Until this night I had never thought about the universe this way, and that tenacious piece of my skepticism finally faded into the desert wind. God had never been real. He had resided on some distant cloud in the nether-regions of imagination. But if God were intelligence itself - the intelligence in all the universe, the math behind understanding a black hole, the law governing the way a flower blossomed, the crash of the ocean against a sandy shore or the unpredictable way in which a quark reacted to glass - then I had seen God all my life. God was everything and everything was God.

Tuwa said, "This is what the myths are for, to break down reason and allow us to access the god/goddess within - the part of us that feels the oneness with the All. It is the feeling some get from nature, or others get from seeing a baby born or from a beautiful work of art. It is All the One - the expression of ourselves. We are all mirrors of one another and all reflections of the Great Spirit."

I contemplated this on our walk back to the cave. I felt something moving around inside, transforming me. A change so profound it felt like a physical burning in my heart and a sort of strange, ecstatic rapture. A peace and happiness overwhelmed and engulfed me, as if I were suddenly in the embrace of my mother. Tears ran down my face before I could stop them. Tuwa put her hand on my back as we walked.

"You are feeling your destiny. The Great Spirit is stirring within. It is Her love you feel."

It took me a few moments to get a hold of myself, and when I finally did, I took Tuwa to task. "Did you mean it was my mother I felt?"

"Yes, but not your biological mother. It was the spirit of the world, the Animus Mondi. She was thanking you, as you more than any of her children have fought for Her and for life."

I didn't quite understand, even though I was really trying to, and Tuwa sensed this. After giving me a little while to process it, she said, "Maybe it is because your mind has been more pure than most, that you were able to clearly see what the rest of us could not let our hearts believe."

"What's that?" I said.

"That she was dying. We were all in a state of denial - we emotional creatures. In the nearly 30 years of being in the healing and mental-health professions I encountered only one man who was truly honest with himself and didn't fall into denial. He was dying of cancer and continued to fight for more time even as he prepared his loved ones to let go. This is true bravery. Not climbing Mount

Everest or hunting a tiger or jumping out of a plane - that is recklessness masquerading as bravery. No, he faced the absolute truth naked, without even the blanket of faith to hold him. For him, death was just an ending, and he accepted it with grace and dignity.

"Accepting limitations can be as great an act of bravery as pushing past them. Knowing when to concede is often the hardest part of a lesson because it requires raw, naked honesty. The gruesome facts were available for all of us, but only you would look at them. This is why you are the chosen one. You have the eyes to see."

"If you want to say circumstances chose me, then I suppose I'd agree."

Tuwa shook her head. "You did what no one was willing to do. You accepted responsibility not just for yourself, but also for mankind. You looked at the facts unemotionally and figured out how to solve the problem. No one was willing to do that, not even our president. Change is very frightening, and the only reason you didn't balk at it is because you have control of your emotions - your mind is disciplined. I admire you greatly. I could never have done what you did."

"What are you talking about? You're the real leader, the center of the Collective, not me," I said.

"I calm the mind and give people meaning in their new life. But you gave them life."

We were silent for the remainder of the walk, except for the occasional pointing out of environmental features. I was deep in thought as we approached the cave and was quickly taken out of it when I heard Ira's voice. "Tuwa, the poultice is cool enough to use. La Donna gave her another antibiotic shot along with some acetaminophen, but her fever hasn't come down much."

Tuwa nodded and quickly made her way toward the cave. We bent down and I followed her through the jagged layers of concentric circles that got smaller and smaller before opening into the encampment.

Tuwa took down the poultice and patted the gummy residue left in the pan onto the cloth. "I can take care of her from here," she said, relieving La Donna for the night.

She put the wet poultice on 218's head and began singing an ancient Cree healing song. I had heard moms sing it to their sick kids around the Collective. It was a haunting minor-key ballad that stirred visions of open planes and Native Americans dancing with smoking sweetgrass around fevered children.

Tuwa broke away from the song and, nodding at me, said, "I would like some privacy, please." I nodded back and ushered everyone out through the cave's mouth.

We huddled outside and La Donna said, "I'm not sure we're going to get all the Geney out tomorrow. We had the element of surprise in our favor tonight. People don't like change."

Incredulous, Ira asked, "You think they'd rather stay enslaved?"

"It's all they've ever known. We're asking them to take a big leap. And some of them, those White Shirts…" La Donna shook her head. "We'll have trouble with them. They have an elevated position here. They won't want to give that up."

"What should we do? We can't just leave them here to die…" I said.

Robert snuck up behind and broke into the conversation. "Damn straight we're not leavin' 'em here."

"We can't force them to go," I said.

"Sure as shit we can't."

Every muscle in my body tightened. "Are you suggesting we use violence?"

Robert shrugged. "We have weapons."

It was everything I could do to restrain myself from screaming at him. I clamped down my jaw and said through my teeth, "For those who won't come with us, we'll make an exit plan to higher ground and leave a map and communicator, so if they change their minds, we can come back for them."

Robert shook his head and sniggered. "That's just stupid." He leaned in close to my face. "If we leave them behind they'll be able to identify us, which would cause a war," he said, drawing out the word "war" for impact.

La Donna, Ira and Aine closed rank around me. Their puzzled looks at Robert had become antagonistic glares. But Robert didn't seem the least bit phased by the enmity – he glowed as if he enjoyed it.

Kevin and Gavin had finished scouting their portion of the perimeter and joined our huddle near the outcropping of boulders a half-dozen meters from the cave's mouth. Kevin asked, "What's going on?"

"Put a woman in charge and this is what you get – they change strategies like they do outfits."

Ira got in Robert's face. "If you have a problem with our leader, go ahead and ask Reginald Strauch if the Environ will take you in. I'm sick of your shit. Keep this up and we'll have to resort to Lakota tribal justice."

"And what the hell is that?" Robert snapped.

"You will become invisible to everyone," Aine answered.

Kevin wore a familiar disappointed expression – one he often seemed to have when interacting with Robert. He apologized to us with his eyes and said to Robert, "We'll need your help mapping an escape route."

Robert glared at him, but Kevin's face was blank, leaving Robert to grumble off into the cold desert night with his men.

Ira grabbed my hand. "Let's go for a walk."

I nodded.

We went southeast through the canyon toward the Environ. The earth was loose and dry like sand beneath our feet; ahead was a grove of dead scrub oak, their gnarled branches stark against the glow of the setting moon and swirling stars.

"Thanks for backing me up."

Ira stopped dead and stared in disbelief at me. "Psyche."

"I'm sorry, it's just a lot to deal with. And it means so much that you believe in me, because sometimes I don't."

"How can you say that? You're a great leader, one of the best the world has ever known. You're brilliant, fair, kind, honest, diplomatic."

"I don't know. I guess I don't feel like a leader. I feel more like an outsider." Walking in the sandy soil made my calves ache. "I'm so tired."

There was a small boulder, rounded down by the wind and rain, just a few meters away. Ira walked me over to it. We sat down, holding hands and looking up at the stars.

"I can count on my two hands all the times I've stared at the naked sky. The scrims were already up in most of New York when I was born."

"Same," Ira said. "They're so beautiful, it makes me sad our generation missed out on what we should have been able to take for granted."

We sat in silence for a while. The wind picked up and he drew me closer, wrapping his arm around my shoulder. He pushed the hair off my face in a tender gesture and said, "There's only one thing I regret."

"What's that?"

"Not getting married. I don't know why, but I feel like it would have completed something."

"It doesn't matter. It wouldn't change how we feel about one another," I replied

"Maybe it would have made me feel like you would always be mine."

I pulled away to look him in the eyes. "What? You don't feel that now?"

"I don't know. Maybe it would have made me feel more secure, like you weren't going to be snatched away at any moment."

I was puzzled. "No one's going to snatch me away from you. I've never had even a passing interest in sharing my life with anyone else."

He nodded. "I just want us to be forever."

"I put my hand on his cheek and we kissed with a tenderness and passion we hadn't allowed ourselves in years. "As long as I exist, I'll love you."

"Ditto," he said.

I laughed. "Ditto? That's not the acme of romance, is it?"

He smiled. "I do what I can."

Geney 218 was breathing easier and stabilized by the time we got back to the cave. Tuwa had worked some real magic for the young woman. It was getting late. All the CAT members grabbed a bedroll except Dave and Todd, who were sleeping on the nearby bus. The four set up camp near the cave's entrance, checking their weapons before cuddling up with them to sleep.

The asymmetry of the leftover bedrolls obsessed Freeman Fred, who had been stacking and restacking them for nearly an hour. Ira approached him, watching Freeman Fred tidy up the sleeping bags, carefully setting them in a line and then repositioning them. La Donna saw me watching and whispered into my ear, "He hasn't said a word to 218. I suspect this behavior is a manifestation of his guilt."

I nodded and was about to go to him to try to get him to talk, but Ira intervened instead. Ira put a hand on Freeman Fred's shoulder and asked quietly, "You OK?"

Freeman Fred didn't answer; he just kept stacking and restacking.

"218 is going to be OK."

"Why I OK? Why her hurt?" Freeman Fred's voice was loud and angry.

Ira whispered, "Let's go outside and talk. Everything's OK in here right now."

Ira gently guided Freeman Fred toward the small mouth of the cave. Outside in the cold desert air they walked west to a set of small boulders and sat. It was far enough away to have some privacy, but close enough to get back to the cave safely if Environ security were on patrol.

In the cold, Freeman Fred moved a bit more slowly. He stared into the distance. His football-shaped eyes, which were swallowed by the black of his dilated irises, finally met Ira's and he said, "Why I luck one?"

"That's a dangerous question, one that can lead you straight into the dark pit of existential crisis."

Freeman Fred crinkled the skin around the small mound of his nose and tilted his head in confusion. "No understand."

"We all wonder why me, and there just aren't any good answers. It's why religion and astrology were invented, I guess." Ira took a deep breath and stared up at the stars for a moment. "I asked Tuwa a question close to that once."

"What say she?"

"Life is a classroom - we're all here to learn different things at different times. And pain is the greatest teacher we have while we're on Earth."

Freeman Fred chewed on this bit of wisdom. "And dead – what she say?"

Ira had gotten used to Freeman Fred's strange shorthand language. What he wanted to know was what happened after death, if Earth were a teaching tool. "In her religion, people's souls get recycled into new bodies until they ascend to the next level. The people of the Environ believe they go to a place called heaven. My parents believed someday they'd be resurrected into a paradise. Some people believe they just rot in the ground and become part of the Earth again. Everyone has different ideas."

"What think you?"

"I don't believe in waste. To me, Tuwa's ideas make the most sense: We're on a journey of individuation, and we keep growing and learning and coming back. Maybe we are reborn on other planets later on and learn stuff there. I don't know. But I can't imagine all of this being an accident," Ira said, gesturing toward the stars. "The universe is just too well designed."

Freeman Fred always got stuck here, at the place where the Creator made everything. Freeman Fred could never really get past the idea that if it weren't for human intervention he would never have existed. In essence, man was his God, and he wondered that if this were true, where did his people fit into the grand scheme of God's will? Tuwa had told him many times, in many different ways, that God programmed the universe and it was God who created his people, not man, and many species had been born due to other animals' interactions, all of which was God's will.

But Freeman Fred always felt a bit ripped off by this answer, and when he expressed his disbelief or frustration with Tuwa's answers she would try a different way to explain. "People make babies with their bodies, but they don't, really," she had said. "God has programmed their bodies to create new life, and in this way man's mind was programmed to make the Geney." He hoped these explanations would be good enough for the other Geney because he found himself more in the camp of agreeing with me than with the rest of the Collective.

He wanted to fit in just as I did, but he couldn't fake belief or understanding. His mixed feelings about humankind confused his ability to find his connection to God. He found tracing his connection to the source meant going through the evil human beings who had enslaved him and his people, and as hard as he tried to find gratitude for the life they had given the Geney, he couldn't find enough joy to get past the darkness that surrounded the birth of his race. Why would God allow people such tremendous greed and selfishness? And reward that greed and selfishness with the ability to make slaves?

Freeman Fred tried to shake all these confusing and contradictory feelings from his mind. He had to remain positive and thankful for the people of the Collective, for as evil as the people of the Environ were, the Collective had been its opposite in goodness, and perhaps God's plan for the Geney could now be activated. Perhaps now the Geney could learn and individuate in the way Tuwa had told him they needed, perhaps now they could find their own individual purpose and help fulfill the destiny God had in mind for them.

Ira patted Freeman Fred on the back. "You OK?" Freeman Fred nodded. "We should probably get back, then." They walked silently back, both taking in the quiet peace of the night and its cool, gentle breeze.

By the morning, after a full eight hours of mostly sound sleep, 218 was doing better and was able to sit up, drink a cup of herbal tea and take oral antibiotics.

The crew put on their UV suits to do some local scouting and program landmarks and notes into their wristcoms. Freeman Fred and I volunteered to watch the Geney woman to give Tuwa a break from being in the cave.

Freeman Fred dabbed the Geney woman's forehead with a cool rag. She opened her eyes and stared at him. "Who you are?"

"Call Geney 199," Freeman Fred replied. "Who you are?"

"I Geney 218. But 199 dead."

"No, I leave go better place."

Geney 218 stared at me for a moment and asked him, "How be with them? Smooth skins you friend now?"

"Yes. They help me same they help you. They no from big beast." Freeman Fred handed her a cup of water and motioned for her to drink from it.

"But if no come from big beast where from?"

"I walk long time then only trees. Hear noise and follow, many days no food, hungry can no think. Walk to white clothes over tree, call sca-rims. Over there maybe food. Smooth skin see me first, I scared, but not know what to do. But they not smooth skin from beast. They good. They help and teach many things."

"Why they hang white clothes?"

"They can no sun, it burn them. Same as smooth skin from beast, but not same."

"How you know? Maybe they make work and beat same as here."

Freeman Fred cast his gold eyes to the cup she still hadn't drunk from and said, "You drink. Good for you. Make heal." He waited for her to finish. "I live in Collective for thousand days. No mines. They help more than I help. Psyche friend. Ira friend. Tuwa friend. La Donna friend. They come to help our people because my friend."

"People?"

Freeman Fred nodded.

She stared at him with suspicion for a moment and said, "You talk, too good for Geney, like wrangler."

"New friend teach. They teach you, too."

"How? Taser make you smart?"

"No. They kind, no taser in Free Land."

"But we lizard creature. Geneco. Geney we not people."

"Yes. We like them. Collective do tests. Some lizard but most people."

Geney 218 put the cup down next to her and stared at him. He had the same gold eyes as she did, the same scaled skin, thin lips and long face, but the more she gazed at him the more he seemed different from her.

"Why you look at me with dark eyes?" he asked.

"Tell truth for you but I can no believe. Smooth skin mean. These they make me better so they make me work. Heal and beat again."

"You know not same as other smooth skin. What smooth skin give medicine? Say prayer to Great Spirit for healing?"

Although her face didn't change in anyway an ordinary person could have read, it did to Freeman Fred. Her eyes dilated and the slits of her nostrils widened. She was confused and she asked him, "What Great Spirit?"

"It make us. It make everything."

She shook her head. Now she knew he had lost his mind. "Smooth skin make us. Smooth skin make everything."

"No." He paused for a moment to collect his thoughts, reminding himself that he, too, had once thought this and sometimes still did. It was a struggle to stay calm and away from the anger he had welling up, not at her, but at the lies the people of the Environ had propagated. He was afraid his feelings would spill out onto her and so he thought of Tuwa's spirit song and waited until the feelings abated.

She pointed to her head. "You full of falling thoughts."

"You pain. I know pain. But story we hear at bunks of other place where Geney free and food to eat and kindness. It true. I live there."

She was softening a little. Her eyes readjusted. "Free Land real?"

He nodded. "I take you. Must believe. My friends are here to take all Geney to Free Land."

She remembered the stories she had heard since childhood in the nursing cave, of a place were the Geney could talk without worry, eat until their bellies were full and rest when they were tired from working. Where no smooth skin beat anyone. But Free Land also had never included smooth skins at all. It was supposed to be a paradise, and this was where her mind glitched.

It was impossible for Freeman Fred to explain that Free Land was a mythic place, but it was real in a metaphorical way, like the stories he had heard around the Circle campfire, of Eden or paradise. Collective members had shared their previous religious beliefs. But it had taken him a long time to understand what 218 needed to see in a matter of hours, and his only hope was to play on her imagination and her trust in him. It was all he had, and he knew it.

"How you explain smooth skin? There no smooth skin in Free Land."

He used the mythology to coax her into believing. "They are Special Ones. Remember story?" It felt strange to mislead someone, to manipulate the truth. He had never lied before, but he told himself it was not so much a lie as a greater truth he was revealing.

She nodded. "One Geney come back from dead." She stared at him, the slits for nostrils turning round as marbles. It was starting to sink in. The prophecy, although their word for it was "telling," was coming true.

Once he was sure she was getting the serendipitous connection, he nodded for her to continue and she did. "Five Special Ones come from each finger on horizon to bring Geney to Free Land."

It was a vague-enough idea to fit almost anything, and it was on the short list of stories he had heard repeated more than once, along with the dead Geney coming back to life. At first he was resistant and didn't understand why he should bother with the assignment of trying to remember stories, but Tuwa had urged him to reexamine his "culture," and this had inspired him to look back with different eyes. With them, he saw in the stories and imaginings bits of philosophy sprouting that could be used to seed an identity and a "culture," as Tuwa had called it. Thinking about the Geney this way had made him feel human, and proud, for the first time.

Free Land was a story he had heard in childhood, and when he reflected on it in the mines, he had cast it aside as a small kindness of his mothers because they couldn't bear to have the children taken away. But as he was writing the story down, he rethought it as the mothers' coping mechanism for the guilt of having to give up the children to a life of slavery and cruelty. A way for them to have hope that allowed them to nurture the next batch of hatchlings.

Now he wondered if Tuwa hadn't set up the mission by the story's parameters to make conversion of the Geney easier. "There are five," he said. "Ira, Psyche, Tuwa, La Donna and Aine, they are the Special Ones here to bring us to Free Land."

He could see her eyes relax and cloud over into the world of imagination. Her jaw slackened and she went silent. Knowing it would take a while for all of it to sink in and change her view, he got up and poured some water into the pan and set it on the stove to boil with the herbs Tuwa had left. Once he was finished making the tincture, he brought her a cup.

After she drank it down she said softly, "So it true. I knew it true sometime, but pain so bad I no believe anymore."

He nodded. "It true. You sleep. Heal for journey."

She lay down. He covered her with the sleeping bag. Tuwa came back into the cave to relieve me of duty.

Before I tucked into my sleeping bag next to Ira, I pulled Freeman Fred aside. I was worried. A life of slavery was all the Geney had ever known. Change was never easy for human beings.

"Is there someone the others have always looked up to? A leader of sorts?" I asked him.

He shook his head and said, "When we in cave some tell stories. They called the story makers but mostly the story makers are the Geney mamas and they live separate in the nursery."

"You have to make them understand all have to leave or none of them can. Otherwise, they'll be slaughtered."

Freeman Fred nodded. "They know. Punished this way now."

Outside, Ira, Aine, La Donna and the CAT members were spying on the wranglers from different locations beyond the mines. The desert was unbelievably hot during the day, especially in UV suits, and the built-in cooling systems were too loud to use. I followed Ira's trail on my wristcom.

In the daylight, the Environ was an even more horrifying sight, shaped like a gelatinous slug – black veins snaked under its slimy, gray skin, and trailing behind was thick, black, viscous goo. After a few hours of observation we realized the black trail was foul, toxic excrement. The Environ was alive and sucking up whatever was left of the desert, leaving only black death in its wake.

At sunset we watched the Geney march back into their cave. It looked like something from an old movie, hundreds of slaves herded from work on the great pyramids. Their clothing soiled and full of holes, ripped from lashings. Except for the White Shirts who yelled things like, "Hurry, hurry. Quick, quick."

Some of us watched the wranglers to get a sense of what we were up against, others plotted the Geneys' escape route.

East of the Geney caves I found Ira. This place was where the truth of the Environ's politics, religion and spiritual beliefs were laid bare, like the stacks of dead Geney and their scattered bones. This was a killing field, the way I imagined Cambodia must have been during the last century, or Auschwitz, or Dachau, or Darfur, or Rwanda. The grotesque stench of evil baking in the sun – death and rotting flesh. The inhumanity was a noxious sulfur, a penetrating, sickening, confounding, desensitizing and numbing spiritual poison.

A white metal cross inside a circle loomed over the area like a sadistic centerpiece. An altar for human sacrifice, equipped with restraints and splattered with blood. It was flanked with the dead. It looked vaguely scientific, but it was as barbaric as a medieval torture device. I inspected its lumpy seams and welding marks and noticed a brand name, Gymco, a manufacturer of exercise equipment in the early '20s. Someone had gone to the trouble of modifying a once-benign machine into an executioner's toy.

We weren't there long before the sound of a wrangler's voice drew near. Ira grabbed my hand and pulled me to an alcove near the Geney cave, which he must have sussed out while I examined the circle cross. Once their noises subsided, we made our way back to our hiding spot.

"No recent dead," Ira said after we settled in.

I stepped on a jagged rock and twisted my foot: Ira caught me just before I hit the ground and potentially ripped my suit.

"Let's take a break," he said.

I nodded. There was a little alcove and he took my hand and walked me over to it. I tugged at the fabric and plastic helmet, trying to adjust it to let more air in. "More than anything, I just feel like ripping this suit off."

Ira watched me for a moment. "You know, we look like astronauts. These suits remind me of the pictures I saw of the Mars Insomnia mission back in 2030."

"That's where this technology comes from."

He nodded. "I guess so. Hadn't really thought about it. It's pretty sad."

"What's that?"

"We're aliens on our own planet."

I took his hand, and for a brief moment we were able to connect in the way we did before the Collective, when we were just struggling to survive the old world, before life and death was our responsibility - when we could share a bag of rice treats and laugh at some stupid Bill Surnow movie. Or take a walk and just be together, or have a bite to eat at some greasy D.C. hang where we could spot the occasional politician ordering a guilty plate of home fries.

"I miss getting out of bed in the morning, making breakfast and feeding the cat before work. I regret taking that simple life for granted," I said.

He nodded. His eyes looked weary and dark; there was so much pain in them. Pain I had never allowed myself to see until that moment. "I miss that, too."

I wanted to reach out and comfort him in some grand, warm gesture, but I didn't know how and instead came up with, "Maybe we should get going."

Past the Geney cave was the series of circle crosses; surrounding them were scattered bones and skulls. A few hundred feet away, closer to the mines, were piles of decaying Geney bodies. The smell intensified.

We walked for another mile before the canyon started to open up and the mountain terrain changed from mostly uninterrupted walls of hard, brown clay with patches of limestone to outcroppings of large boulders.

I pinched a sample of the soil into a baggie to take back to the Collective for later testing, in case it might be needed. It had been very quiet for a while now, and I was just about to suggest we turn our UV-suit fans on for a moment when I heard the unmistakable sound of a gas-fueled engine and bounce of an old Army jeep echo through the canyon. It was distant, but it was racing very quickly toward us.

We flattened ourselves inside the cracks of boulder outcropping, hoping not to be seen. The noise got loud – tires squealed, kicking rock and dust. I grabbed Ira's hand. The hoarse thrum of the engine was something I hadn't heard since I was 10 years old at the anniversary parade in New York City, in a memorial for the Third World War. Whatever these people were driving, it had to be antique, not a solar-fueled hovercraft like our fleet.

My heart stopped when the engine cut. Ira squeezed my hand. The door slammed and we could hear a group of men talking in the distance. I could have sworn I heard one mention "footsteps in the dirt."

I looked at Ira. He knew what I was thinking – they were on our trail and would find us, but he shook his head. After a few minutes of hushed, serious-sounding conversation, a few men laughed.

Ira looked at his watch and wrote with his finger in the dirt: lunch break. I had an overwhelming urge to turn around and peek at them. Their conversation became looser and then lulled. A few moments later the doors to their vehicle slammed shut and the engine revved.

We watched them through a small crack. It had, indeed, been a Jeep manufactured for WWIII, painted desert-camouflage. Through its small windows there was a blur of bright-orange UV suits. They turned past the Geney cave and we lost visual contact. Both of us let out a sigh of relief.

"Let's stay put and eat some lunch. Maybe we should run our coolant while the coast is clear," I said.

"Not me. I've gotten used to the heat," he replied.

"Well, I haven't," I said turning mine on. It wasn't too loud, but Ira wasn't happy and made a sour face.

Not much stayed in edible shape with the intense heat of the desert. I took out some crude peanut butter, flatbread and jam and made sandwiches. We ate them slowly, with lots of water. They were surprisingly tasty. Ira's head bopped while he ate his. It made me happy; any sliver of pleasure made the sacrifices more bearable.

While I was putting away the jars, Ira frantically tapped me on the shoulder and made a cutting motion. I turned off the coolant system. At first we couldn't tell where the sound was coming from or exactly what it was. And then it came into focus.

One of the White Shirts was driving a converted golf cart full of mining equipment; riding shotgun was one of the wranglers. Ira and I looked at each other. I whispered, "What are they doing this far away from the mines?"

Ira shook his head. "Can't be good."

The White Shirt and wrangler got out of the cart and walked toward us. We crawled deeper into the shadows of a recess in the mountain's face. Their voices got loud enough for us to hear, but they didn't come any closer. We listened vigilantly.

"...They come Freeland."

"That's just a story. I still don't understand what you're trying to tell me."

"Secret. Say no tell. Take us Freeland."

"Who are they?"

"Smooth skin.'

In the silence, it seemed the wrangler decided not to put much stock in the White Shirt's words. A few moments later we heard footsteps and the wrangler said, "Don't think there's much I can do." The cart's engine started up again and its noise drifted into the distance.

Tuwa and La Donna walked eastward on the trail behind the mountains until they came to an alcove that overlooked the mines. La Donna videographed the activity while Tuwa used binoculars to monitor the mines. They took turns recording activity and counting the Geneys, then made maps of the area.

Ira and I went through the canyon to the outskirts of the Geney cave. We hid among rocks; from there it was possible to monitor activity coming from the Environ. I took readings on its motion, digestion and waste cycles. A few hovercrafts departed just after noon, most likely a shift change, but other than that not much happened.

"It's moving approximately 4½ feet per hour," I said, running the calculations on my wristcom. "Do you think it can reproduce?"

"Let's hope not," Ira said.

From where La Donna and Tuwa were, they could overhear the electronic voice emitters of the wranglers when the wind blew just right. It came in bits and pieces of conversation, snippets of paragraphs or sentences.

Through her binoculars, La Donna spotted three large circles of aluminum dotted with dark splashes and what looked like leather straps attached to them. Behind them was a pile of decaying Geney bodies. She didn't want to focus on them. She knew what they were. She pulled the binoculars away to force herself to stop looking. The scene was wicked, morbid and making her upset. She was fascinated and angry with herself and the people of the Environ all at once. She didn't like the feelings coming up – they made her feel dirty, as if she were somehow responsible. "Look." She pointed. "The rock. I didn't think there would be more than one."

Tuwa followed La Donna's finger, but quickly averted her eyes when she realized what she was doing. She had glanced over there, too, but couldn't bring herself to fully take the bodies in, nor did she want to. Instead, she kept her binoculars limited to the wrangler's tent and the area directly in front of the entrance to the mines.

At the shift change, several wranglers huddled together and La Donna said, "That doesn't seem normal."

Tuwa nodded. "It has an inauspicious feeling about it."

A hovercraft glided to the southeastern perimeter of the mines and a series of men exited the vehicle in UV gear, but these UV suits were different – light blue instead of the orange uniforms the wranglers wore. Tuwa studied the patches on their suits with her binoculars.

"Can you make out an emblem?" La Donna asked, trying to focus.

Tuwa took the binoculars from her eyes and turned to La Donna. "Double helix. It's the double helix."

"Shit!" La Donna gathered up her supplies and stuffed them into her backpack. Tuwa did the same. "How are we going to warn them in time? We can't use the transmitters from here."

"We'll have to find them," Tuwa replied.
They took off running down the trail.

Freeman Fred took a gulp of air, wiggling his tongue like a
fan. Before he lost his nerve. He ran out from behind and dashed the
same path. It was a few hundred yards, but every foot seemed like the
home stretch in a marathon. His heart felt like it moved sideways,
revving like a hydro engine in anticipation.

He rounded the gate and headed toward the Geney cave
entrance. A hovercraft in the distance pushed closer. He turned to
see a small, white speck floating out from behind the Environ. It was
not a wrangler's craft. It was the wrong color for that. He hid in the
shadows and watched it speed toward the mines. When it came close
enough for him to be spotted, he ducked inside. There was a strange
symbol on its side. He had only seen it once before, but couldn't
remember where – two serpents intertwined around a disc.

He rushed through the long, dark corridor toward the
nursery; even in the day it was too dark for an ordinary human to see,
but Freeman Fred's eyes dilated like a cat's, gathering the red,
ambient light leaking from the Egg Cave entrance halfway between
the entrance and the nursery.

The Geney were all out working in the mines, all except the
mothers and the little ones. He didn't want to scare them – most of
the little ones had never seen a grown man, and he worried they
would cause enough of a fuss to attract a wandering patrol guard.
They usually checked the Egg Caves several times a day, and there
was no telling when they would show up.

If there has been a door he would have knocked first, but
only a threadbare bed sheet separated the nursery from invaders. He
pushed the sheet to one side and announced himself: "Hello,
mothers."

Freeman Fred bowed to the women and now the children
who stared at him. There was no emotion readable by human
standards. They had the same small dark eyes and unmoving snout-
like jaws, but Freeman Fred knew there was a mixture of shock and
fear in the women, curiosity in the children. He wondered for a brief
moment if the Collective members would ever be able to understand
the Geney since they didn't show their feelings with as much drama
as ordinary humans did; their faces were not capable of it. The key to
reading was in the subtle muscular movements and swishing tongues,

and either the lack of or succession of blinking. These skills of detection were innate in the Geney, but would have to be learned by those unfamiliar.

Being there in the nursery was both reassuring and melancholic. He had almost forgotten how much he had missed his people, especially the mothers. It had been many years since he had been reared inside those cave walls, and he hadn't seen the room since. A word he had learned in the Collective came to mind – sacred. Even more than being in the Collective, this had been the happiest time he could recall. But it was bittersweet, too.

"I 199 want make sure you come tonight, no be scared."

A woman holding a child on her hip shook her head. "You ghost. You ghost. Why you come haunt us?"

"I no ghost in bad dream. Not dead come to make suffer the Geney. I here for real," he said, inching closer. "Touch me. I no hurt you."

A young woman and new mother slipped in behind Freeman Fred. She had come from the Egg Caves to trade places with her counterpart.

One of the women nursing a newborn near the wall said, "You tell us why human? We know human. Human give pain. Make us work. Why help? To kill, yes?"

"I will tell long story about how world has been made. How Geney made. More out in world than caves or great beast or mines. This I know now, and come to you. Just believe what I tell and know I come help."

"What about eggs? Help them?" the young woman asked. "They break if touch."

Freeman Fred's eyes dilated and the women knew the answer before he said it. "No can bring."

"I no go," said the young woman.

"No go, too," said the young woman's counterpart, on her way toward the threadbare bed sheet. "We mothers. We go, eggs dead." She exited to start her shift at the Egg Cave.

The Environ was a gray, gelatinous monster, like a giant slug sliming its way across the desert; through the telephoto lens I could see its black veins pulsate beneath the sheen of slime. I was taking pictures, at the urging of Robert, for tactical purposes. A concession I had agreed to after insisting we stay and save Geney 218. He wanted pictures of a doorway, but I was having trouble finding anything except varying slimy shades of gray flesh, from the black of its thick veins to the off-white of the sun's reflection. The only thing slightly reminiscent of an entrance were door-like discolorations in a few places. It was a truly monstrous beast.

I heard footsteps approach, and then another set. Before I could set the camera down I felt a hand on my back. My blood went cold.

"It's OK," La Donna said. She was with Tuwa. In the distance I saw Ira's UV suit moving behind an outcropping of rocks where he, too, was taking pictures.

"What's going on?"

"Paul Lamont and his men are at the mines," Tuwa replied.

"Did you tell Robert?"

La Donna nodded. "We found them on our way here. It's not safe to be out here. We need to lay low."

I nodded and gathered my equipment and Tuwa went to get Ira.

THIRTY-EIGHT

Geney 218 was in good enough shape to be transported. She had slept most of the day with Freeman Fred watching her, except for his short stint at the Geney caves. Tuwa had checked on her status throughout the day, refreshing her poultice and making sure Freeman Fred was giving her antibiotics.

Luckily, we had prepared for the worst, and there was plenty of food for a big meal. We waited in the encampment, until the sun was down for two hours, just to be safe. We had listened to the sounds of patrol jeeps until they had disappeared for their cursory check.

The buses were completely invisible, but Todd's memory was amazing and he led us a few miles north, to an indistinguishable outcropping of rocks that hid our fleet. How he was able to recall them from the hundred or so similar spots was remarkable. He had a map but I didn't see him reference it once.

The fleet was tightly packed inside. It took almost an hour to negotiate the rocks and get them all out safely. I took my place in the line and once La Donna finally got her bus straightened we followed Todd back to the Geney caves.

On the trip back, Tuwa suggested the use of CAT members as drivers. She said it would give them a feeling of control and power, and lessen trouble with the Geney. She worried Robert's aggressive attitude toward the mission had contaminated his men. I agreed; the men had become very distant over the past 24 hours. Robert had kept them segregated and there was no way to tell how they would interact with a group of scared Geney who already lacked trust in smooth skins. If we appeared too harsh or militaristic it would damage our burgeoning relationship with them. We decided to divide up council members as envoys on the buses and give the mothers and children extra support by putting Freeman Fred with them.

Ira, Freeman Fred and Tuwa had gone to the Geney cave to get them ready for the trip while we grabbed the buses, but when we pulled up to the docking location, no one was there. It was not a good sign. My heart sank. I parked and went to Robert's bus.

"Keep the line. I'll check to see what the holdup is." He snarled at me. I rushed to the Geney cave.

At the mouth, Tuwa waited with a line of Geney behind her, but she looked distraught. "What's wrong?"

"Three of the White Shirts and two of the mothers don't want to come, the two who tend the eggs. Freeman Fred is talking to them."

"Where's Ira?"

"With the mothers and children who are coming with us. Some of the eggs started to hatch today and the women taking care of them say they can't leave them to die."

I nodded. "And the White Shirts have very misplaced loyalties - betrayers of their own kind."

Tuwa frowned at me.

"Let's start loading the people we have."

Tuwa nodded.

The line moved and the first 50 Geney climbed on board Robert's bus, the next 50 onto Todd's. Still, there was no sign of Freeman Fred or the handful of Geney who refused to come with us. I made my way through the darkness of the cave, listening for the sound of Freeman Fred's voice.

They were gathered in the sleeping quarters. The three White Shirts were sitting on worn bedrolls made of rags. The two mothers stood together near Freeman Fred; they seemed more unsure than the male White Shirts, whose minds seemed made up.

"Who take care of egg?" one of the women asked just before I stepped inside.

"The scientists from the Environ will. Unfortunately for these Geney, they'll live to repopulate the clan here," I said. "But if you come with us, someday you can come back and rescue them."

One of the women's eyes trained on me, her nostrils flared. "How know you?"

"I'm a scientist, too. I know how they think."

Freeman Fred shook his head at me. "But she not same." I was blowing it for him.

"No, I'm not the same at all, but I know how they think. And I know if you stay here you will suffer and lose your chance to help your people." It was clear Freeman Fred wanted me to leave. I nodded at him and said, "Sorry to interrupt but the buses are getting ready to leave. I'll give you another 10 minutes; after that I'll insist you come with me."

Freeman Fred nodded and I left.

Kevin's bus was last in line. I watched it fill with what was left of the Geney. Ira and La Donna were making the rounds, trying to calm those who were afraid, explaining what being in the bus would feel like, telling them about their new home. I waited by the mouth of the Geney cave, anxious to see Freeman Fred walk out with the rest of his people. It seemed like I was waiting forever, certainly more than 10 minutes. La Donna finally came to me and said, "Honey, it's getting late. We need to get out of here before the night guards lock the caves. That's less than an hour."

"I know, just give him another minute."

La Donna shook her head. "One minute."

But before she got to her bus near the front of the line, Freeman Fred exited the cave with the two mothers. I was relieved and disappointed the three White Shirts weren't with him, but the mothers were more important to the morale of the group and I tried to be positive – at least we had saved them. I helped Freeman Fred corral them onto the bus and then pulled him aside to ask what happened.

"Mothers no want to go but what you say make them think it OK for baby. White Shirt call mothers name wranglers use. They no can live with them."

"What name?"

"Call nest brothel – mother, whore. They laugh, very funny but mothers no like. I no like."

I shook my head. "Thank you, Freeman Fred." I gave him an awkward hug that turned very tender. Despite all the torture and pain he had gone through, no one could break his humanity. He was a truly great man. "You did a wonderful job."

"Wish White Shirt come."

"Maybe it's for the best," I said, walking him to the bus. He got on and I walked back to board the one Kevin was captaining. Of all the CAT members, Kevin was the easiest to relate to, even-tempered and likable. His wife was one of out lab techs. The two were always affable but somewhat distant.

On my bus there was a mix of men and women. Most no longer looked scared, just resigned; some even seemed happy. Kevin pulled away from the loading area. Behind us, the rest of the buses followed.

I had finished explaining the temporary shelter and was telling the Geney about our plans to build an adjacent sister community for them, with their input, when one of the Geney who had been staring out the window pointed to the horizon and yelled, "Look!"

I went to the window and cupped it for better visibility. "Shit." I rushed to Kevin's side and grabbed the radio. "Todd, everyone pick up the pace, approaching from the southeast is an Environ security jeep."

"No worries, they're no match for us," Kevin said, smirking. "Those things are fossil-fuel monsters from the last century. They can only go 100, max."

"Everyone," I said addressing the Geney. "Make sure your safety belts are fastened." I sat down in front and strapped myself in. I had a queer feeling in my stomach. Moments later our speed had gone from a comfortable 125 to 300 miles per hour. Going that fast made my stomach turn; twigs and rocks rushed past so quickly they were just a blur. But we left the security jeep in the dust, and once we had cleared the last mountain range on our way to the 5, we slowed back down to our comfort zone.

But even though we had lost the security jeep, they had seen us. We had left our scent all over the scene, and there was going to be hell to pay.

THIRTY-NINE

The Geney settled into their temporary home in the labs. After a few weeks, the rains ravaged the land. Small lakes and ponds surrounded us. Water rushed underneath the walkways and between the buildings. CAT members had worked for more than a week, throughout the day and night, to secure the hillsides.

But despite the terrible weather, spirits were high. Everyone seemed OK – except Tuwa and me. I was suffering with terrible stomach pain. Something told me that when the rains stopped, so would out safety. Tuwa wasn't making me feel much better, although she was trying. She had insisted on teaching me more prayer songs, and day after day she insisted I meditate with her for hours at a time. It felt like we were trying to rewrite the inevitable. We both knew the Environ would not tolerate the miracle we had pulled off. The bad weather had been a security blanket. Every day that it poured was another safe day.

There was very little we could do during the deluge except tend to things indoors. The animals were put in an elevated shed the techs had built. It constantly leaked, but they were safe from the worst of the savage rains and occasional golf ball-sized hail that pounded against the aluminum, which drove some to kick down their stalls. The edible garden had been transplanted to a sturdy acrylic hothouse, and nearly all the plants survived.

Unfortunately, when the sun reappeared in patchy waves a month later, so did something far worse. The thirteen of us were in a strategy meeting in the communal hall while the rest of the Collective was crammed into the biology labs, watching an old film. The lab had temporarily been converted into a recreation room and most members spent the day there, playing games and picking through books left out to be shared. Even if no word was ever uttered, everyone on the council knew a day of reckoning would come. But they'd been lulled into a false sense of security.

The pictures taken at the Environ were being passed around. Naomi was paging through them admiringly. She said, "You've got to admit – it is impressive."

"So were the Nazis, but I don't admire them," I said. "Without a greater good as the central core of science, humanity uses it as a tool of destruction."

"I'm sorry. I'm a scientist. I can't help but admire innovation."

"We're all scientists." I said trying to wipe the snarl from my face. "Don't forget the scientists who didn't consider what their work was used for. Thanks to them, the lofty ambition of saving the plutocrats of the Environ came to be, and they perished."

Naomi leaned against the table and stared blankly at me. "It's not as if they are personally responsible for the demise of the entire world. You can't blame it all on Reginald Strauch and Paul Lamont."

"They were in power. They knew the truth. Instead of warning people, they suppressed information and sold room in the Environ to the privileged few who could afford it. And then used the Wrath of God Inc., to control their populists with fear."

"Living in the belly of the beast, like Jonah and the whale. But in their case, they aren't getting out," La Donna said.

I was still angry with Naomi. "They committed genocide for profit – turned America into a hollow corporation and sold it to the masses as a theocracy. They wielded Evangelism like a gun – turned America into a perverted, greed-based empire masquerading as capitalism, with the rules unfairly slanted so the rich could suck the marrow out of the poor until there was nothing left."

Naomi ignored me and consulted a sheet of calculations. "Well, we have to make peace with it at some point – it's moving north and will hit the border of Oregon in..."

"Approximately 50 years," I said. "Another 25 and it will get to the heart of the Collective. I know, and we can't let that happen."

"What do you propose? We start a fucking war?" Ira said.

"Maybe a treaty," Naomi offered.

Ira shook his head. "Do you really think they'd do that, especially since we liberated the Geney?"

"You're right. We've stolen their property," Naomi said.

I felt fire explode in my gut. A kind of rage I hadn't felt since my mother's death. "It's hard to believe you're a Jew. You bring shame to the memory of all who died in the Holocaust."

"Hey, settle down, Psyche," Ira interrupted.

But I was on my feet, inches from Naomi's face, screaming, "According to your logic, our people rightfully belonged to the Egyptians and the Africans belonged to the Englishmen who captured them! Isn't that right? Traitor!"

She stared blankly back at me, more shocked than anything else. No one had seen me so angry or threatening; even Ira looked frightened. And the rest of my twelve colleagues stared blankly, mouths agape. "Right?" I screamed at Naomi. "Right? Answer the question, traitor!"

The room was as still and quiet as a crypt. "No…" It looked like she wanted to qualify her statement or expand on her answer, but thought better of it. I took myself to the water cooler and poured myself a drink to calm down. I was shaking. No one spoke for a few minutes, and then it was just light conversation about the architectural plans for the Geney buildings and talk of materials to be used.

The Geney were involved in the design and wanted the buildings to be round and open inside, much like the caves they had come from, but as most of our staff were not that skilled in building, we were having some trouble accommodating their wishes. We had a few carpenters, and of course the crew who had built the compound for us, but our buildings were very simple and functional rectangles with square rooms. I sat back down at the table, rejoining the meeting like a mouse trying to steal cheese from a trap. I wanted to melt into the floor and said nothing for the remainder of it, just listened to the mundane concerns about the leaking roof in the garage and weather projections for the commencement of the Great Storm, as Tuwa had dubbed it.

Inside one of the science team's expedition hovercrafts, Paul Lamont and his companions, Sam Malone and Herb Jones, were traveling down the river that was once the old 5. Malone was too cocky a driver for Lamont's taste. He made the men switch, so the tentative Jones took over the wheel.

Lamont had chosen the men because of their personal

connections. The 270-something miles they had traveled together had given him time to wonder if he'd picked the right men for the job. They had both worn down his patience in their own unique ways. But Malone was good at navigating and, despite the sheeting rain, signs of the Collective appeared.

They turned down a frontage road. Their headlights reflected off an aluminum storage shed. They continued until they spotted the matrix of buildings half a mile away. They'd have to climb the muddy hill or risk forewarning the Collective.

The meeting was running longer than expected and Naomi had promised her only child, Steven, she would bring snacks to the kids during the break between films. "I'll be back in a few minutes," she said to her colleagues just before ducking out.

On her way to the kitchen, Naomi heard a strange digital noise at the front door, as if the alarm system were having a nervous breakdown. She inched closer to examine it. And although she had never possessed a strong sense of intuition, the hair on the back of her neck stood straight. The numbers on the keypad were swirling, morphing into one another. Something was very wrong. Her mind went through all logical explanations. Only the most bizarre and irrational thoughts made any sense: some kind of evil lurked on the other side – perhaps the Circle had stirred a spirit in the woods and now it had come to get them. She shook herself – that was crazy. Slowly she grazed the door handle. It was burning hot.

There was a small peephole Robert installed in the door after the Geney had arrived, for fear of repercussions from the Environ. Naomi had almost forgotten about it. Gingerly, she positioned her eye and saw a group of three men in foreign UV suits fumbling around. There was something familiar about the middle one. A tuft of salt-and-pepper hair showed through his clear plastic visor and she waited for him to turn and face the door – it was an aged Paul Lamont. His eyes met hers through the peephole. She gasped. Who could forget his icy, cool blue eyes? Abruptly the door flew open and she was knocked against the wall.

They rushed inside. Paul noticed Naomi on the ground and offered a hand up. She took it.

"What are you doing here, Paul?" As much as she hated what he had done to her, she couldn't help but love him.

Lamont nodded. "I'm not here to talk about the past, Naomi. I'm here to save you and the future of the Collective." Naomi crossed her arms. "I didn't know you cared."

"How else could the Collective have survived so long? Strauch certainly wasn't rooting for you." Lamont paused and stared into her eyes. "I'm sorry. I should have told you from the beginning I was married."

"Did Tricia ever find out?"

"No." Paul paused for to compose himself. "I need to talk to Psyche. Where is she?"

"This way." Naomi started down the hall toward the meeting room. Lamont and his men followed.

Naomi opened the door. Lamont, Jones and Malone followed her inside. The room went silent.

Lamont displayed his palms to them, showing he had no weapon. Malone and Jones did the same. "We're here to stop a potential war. We know you have the Geneco."

"Sit down," I said, grabbing a chair. "It's good to see you Herb," I said.

He nodded. "You, too."

"Malone," Ira said, introducing us.

"We finally meet," I said, shaking his hand.

We made room for them at our table. Before Naomi left to finish with the children's snacks, she brought us some water from the kitchen.

Lamont took a sip and said, "Believe it or not, I've been fighting this day from the inception of the Collective. Strauch wasn't keen on letting you and your people live."

All of us were a bit shocked by the statement, even though we shouldn't have been, knowing the type of person he was. Lamont continued, "But I explained it was in the Environ's best interest for the Collective to try and reverse global warming for our future generations. He didn't much care about it, too abstract for him, until I pointed out that your work might save his son one day. He called off his dogs with one caveat."

"And that was?" I asked.

"The Collective couldn't cause any problems for him. I assured him you wouldn't. But I'm no idiot, I realized the day would come when you would find out about the Geneco and feel it your duty to help them."

"How did you know that?" Ira asked.

"I have extensive records, psychological reports, spending habits, political affiliations, work histories, criminal histories, searches you did on the internet, virtual games you played. You name it, I know everything about everyone here – except what you dream at night." He stared at us. "And it was clear from all my research you're a bunch of bleeding-heart liberals."

I noticed Tuwa wasn't saying a word. She stared at Lamont with her hawk-eyes and shivered. "Are you OK?" I asked from across the table. She nodded. La Donna wrapped her sweater around Tuwa and felt her head.

"You're burning up," La Donna said.

Tuwa didn't look at her. She continued to stare hard at Lamont. "Stop trying to ingratiate yourself and tell us why you are here."

Lamont stiffened.

"You make yourself sound like some kind of hero, but what you really want is a sacrifice, isn't it? You came to demand blood, to feed the hungry demon you serve, Reginald Strauch."

It wasn't like Tuwa to be negative and angry. And I realized it was her rage and anger making her physically ill. "Perhaps this negotiation is too upsetting for you, Tuwa. Maybe you should go to your sacred space and cleanse yourself."

"Tell her," Tuwa spat at Lamont. "Tell her."

Lamont squirmed in his chair and averted her gaze. "She's right, a sacrifice will have to be made to avoid war. Strauch wanted blood after you took the Geneco. It was everything I could do to keep him from bombing your encampment that night. I convinced him to just punish one person, make it seem to our people this was a random mutant wandering the desert. I told him if he started a war with you, our people would find out about the existence of the Collective and they would no longer trust him or, worse, they would rebel. But Reginald is not a logical man. He still wanted blood. I went to his wife, Camille. She sided with me, and after twelve hours of intense discussion he agreed to a compromise, which is what I came to present to you."

"And what is that?" I asked.

"He wants to execute you back at the Environ."

"No way!" Ira shouted. "That's not a compromise."

"He has access to a nuclear weapon."

"Why weren't they destroyed?" La Donna asked.

"I did my best to orchestrate their demise, but he managed to get one of his military advisors to put one in a bunker somewhere in case he ever had problems with you. I found out about it after the Geneco disappeared. But I suspected as much."

"What choice do I have?" I asked.

"Wait a second. What proof is there of this bomb?" Ira asked.

"We've seen it, me, Lamont and Herb. One of his top aides took us in the middle of the night and gave us a camera so we could show you pictures," Malone said.

Ira took the pictures from Malone and studied them. "How do you know it works?"

"Believe me, it works. The place was on fire with radioactivity. And I checked the electronics – it was wired and ready to go," Malone replied.

"Why didn't you hack into it and make it malfunction?" Ira asked.

"I tried, but there was no way. We were blindfolded on the ride to the location, and the computer running it isn't linked to anything in the Environ."

"Strauch is not as dumb as he looks," Aine said.

"No, he's dumb," Lamont said. "He's just clever and devious. He thinks like a predator, not a human being."

"He is a psychopath, unbound by morality. Everything he does is ego-driven for gratification of his lowest desires," said Tuwa. "He is an evil trickster."

"That he is," Lamont said. "But as I said earlier, I expected you to emancipate the Geneco at some point, and I've been working on a plan."

"We aren't going to let you die," Herb said to me. "We just have to make it look like you do."

"Can you guarantee that?" Ira asked.

Lamont paused, and with a somber look on his face, said, "No. But we have a plan to give her a fighting chance."

FORTY

Lamont and Malone went over the plan dozens of times with me on our way to the Environ. Malone had given access codes to Ira and an extensive map of where to find my "body" after the execution.

But I knew my chances of survival were extremely remote, and all the preparation in the world was futile. Lamont had warned me there would be torture involved; of course, he hadn't told me until I was on the way to the Environ with him, but it wouldn't have made any difference. I would gladly lay down my life for the Geney and my people. There was no greater reason to die than to protect those you loved. At least my death would have meaning, stand for something. Most didn't get such an opportunity.

But the reality of what was happening didn't really hit me viscerally until I saw the slimy, gray slug on the horizon, glistening in the late-afternoon gloom. It was floating in a small lake that had once been a dry desert basin. The great storm had changed the area so much I would never have recognized it.

We traversed three quarters of the beast's circumference before arriving at the proper discoloration that opened into an orifice. The holding area flooded when we entered. Herb cut the engine and the gray flesh healed behind us. We waited until the beast digested the water and docked the hovercraft onto a platform. Lamont punched in a set of numbers on a mounted keypad near another skin discoloration and it opened for us. We entered next to a garbage shoot in the back of a lovely garden and walked through the bowels of the beast to the prison.

It was past primetime viewing hours when I arrived at cell one. Lamont contacted Ellis Rush and Surnow and told them to set up the studio. This was big news to be vigorously exploited, an opportunity to keep "the fear of God," as Strauch put it, in the Environ population.

The Applegates were already conspiring with Strauch and Camille about how to best manipulate the situation and which angle to play. Now that they had a Grade-A Environ-hating heretic, the theatrics were to be blown into an enormous spectacle.

The timing was fantastic for Camille, who felt the workers' fear waning. She noted that after the public execution of Kaitlin, productivity and subordination had been at an all-time high. She wanted to keep it that way.

An ebullient Rush and Surnow anticipated ratings that would outperform all other executions and hungered for a protracted drama. Strauch and Camille agreed. "Why not make the most of it?" Camille said, huddled around the Strauch bar with her cohorts, drinking the special bourbon she hoarded for such occasions.

"What's the longest possible death?" she asked.

"Tasering could take hours if we do it slowly, but still..." Rush said. "It's not very dramatic."

"Bleeding to death could take a while if it's done properly," Jessie said. "I know of one famous case where it took days."

Sandy smirked. "Oh, yes – you are a genius, honeybuns!"

The Environ itself was profoundly disturbing. It had a musty foulness. The soles of my shoes were engulfed if I stood too long in one place. The squishing sound the floor made when walking, sitting or leaning made me nauseous. The way it absorbed waste through its skin was particularly disgusting.

If there were a Hell, then this was it.

For the first time in my life, I was truly afraid. It wasn't just my impending death – it was being inside the gray beast. Everything about it was foul, from its perverted inception as a secret escape-hatch for the rich and greedy to its very real stench of human waste and stomach acid. I was in a world created by people I would never understand. They were as alien to me as extraterrestrials. I had never felt so alone.

A hundred years ago, no one would have believed this future. People would have laughed if someone said, "Democracy will be replaced by corporate interests and right-wing fanatics. Our government will treat citizens who differ ideologically with a death sentence."

All the beautiful concepts and ideals that had made America a shining beacon of hope, inspiration, morality and goodness would be brought down by greed, corruption and insanity. And all those along the way – all the good people who were too good to believe it was possible by remaining naïve – they unknowingly let it happen. All those too afraid to fight the powerful and greedy became silent accomplices.

But who could blame them? They, like everyone before and after, believed in the goodness of man's soul, only to find good and evil inextricably married inside each of us, some more bad than good, more selfish than selfless.

It's too easy to believe we are all alike. And unless there's a rational reason, or at least an emotional one, the decent person cannot understand evil because he or she would never willingly engage it. But for the sociopath, the person without the ability for empathy or love or anything except lower-limbic feelings, destruction is the only means of abolishing the emptiness inside. For a brief moment, he can feel something – excitement. The desert inside his soul can be momentarily satiated in the most minuscule, fleeting and insignificant way. But to him, this small relief is all he has and is worth any destruction – even the death of our planet. He is incapable of thinking or feeling past the nanosecond he lives in. What normal human being could imagine such a thing?

Unfortunately, things don't have to make sense to be true. The Strauchs were a dynasty made up of psychopaths and sociopaths, from the great-great-great-great grandfather entangled with Hitler to the present monster, Reginald – a long line of criminals too powerful to stop, too scary to fight.

The work I had done with Tuwa had changed me. But I hadn't felt it until I was in the Environ. My heart hurt with the pain and fear the people living inside the gray beast felt. The air itself seemed laced with anxiety and repression, all natural joy squeezed out – their freedom crushed. It was what I imagined a Jew in Nazi Germany would have felt. The knowledge that at any moment your life could be snatched away; living in constant terror of crossing the wrong person; ever-vigilant to appear the good citizen; afraid to look cross-eyed at anyone in authority.

It felt like hours had passed in the gray darkness. One lone bulb swung overhead, providing just enough light to accommodate a trip to the waste area. I smoothed the tattered blanket over the shelf of flesh I was to sleep on, so I wouldn't feel the wetness of the beast.

My mind raced to Ira, Tuwa, La Donna and Freeman Fred. I hoped for one last chance to see them.

I still didn't know if there was anything after this life, but it didn't really matter either way. A part of me was glad to rest from the struggle of this world. If I was a snuffed candle, I would never know it. And if there were a God, I had lived a life of compassion. If that wasn't good enough and He truly was the model the Applegates sold, then I didn't want to join Him in their Heaven because that Heaven would be Hell.

During Circle I had felt the Great Spirit's presence embrace me tenderly in a gentle, pink cloud. And the day before the mission, when Tuwa had prayed with me, I felt it again, only deeper, as if my cells had been infused with an overpowering ecstasy. I can only compare the sensation to the heart-stirring feeling of witnessing tremendous beauty and heroic bravery beyond self-preservation. From that day to this, the seed of those experiences had taken root and I felt the first blooms opening inside me. If I concentrated hard enough, I could sense the peace from its bouquet.

And then a strange thing happened. It had to be supernatural, because I was alone in the windowless cell with only a dark spot where a door should have been. The room filled with the scent of star lilies. The smell was so overpowering it was as if I had been transported into a hothouse.

I stayed in my meditation for a while and heard Tuwa's voice. She said, "Be still in heart and mind. Follow the stillness into the void. There you will find all time, truth, understanding and knowing. All knowledge is available if you connect to the Great One. Pluck what you need like a book from a library."

I knelt on the squishy gray flesh of the Environ and grabbed onto Tuwa's song. Singing in unison with the memory of her voice, I visualized the Circle of the Great Spirit around me and smelled the sweetgrass burning, heard La Donna playing the drum, saw Freeman Fred's smile and felt Ira's ardent kiss.

I saw Mom smiling on the stairs of the brownstone, in her striped knit cap and scarf. She smelled of patchouli and sandalwood. Her thick curly hair, painted with streaks of white. An afternoon came back to me, when I had been in middle school. A boy at recess had teased me about my name. After school I found Mom working on a research paper at the kitchen table and asked her, "How come you named me Psyche?"

She put down her pen and smiled as if she had been waiting to answer that question. "There was a great scientist named Sigmund Freud. I named you after one of his concepts; to him, the word signified the seat of consciousness. He borrowed the name from ancient Greek mythology. Psyche was a goddess who represented the human soul. She was married to the god Eros. But because of a trick, she faced a series of trials before being reunited with her husband in the afterlife, where she bore two children, Love and Delight."

"Why couldn't you just name me Sarah or Elizabeth or Janet, something normal?"

"I quite like it. It's a wonderful allegory, something you'll appreciate when you're older," and with that she went back to work. Now I wished I could tell her she had been right. Even if it hadn't been my mother's intention, my name was a gift of faith in something greater, a soul, an afterlife. I had never seen this before; the main focus of the memory had always been its preface about Freud, the other an afterthought, a clarification about the origin of scientific idea. All my years I had been so fixated on science, as I had presumed my mother was, but within my own name was a key to something bigger, discarded by me as irrelevant. Empirical knowledge had been my mother's godhead; science was the church through which she worshiped. I had kept this tradition alive for her sake and had resisted the Circle for what seemed like nothing but a child's misinterpretation.

Mom had known Psyche's mythological connection to the soul. Maybe she, too, had wrestled with mixed feelings. Perhaps she hadn't been an atheist. Maybe she just had no time for theology. Just because she rejected Judaism didn't mean she rejected the notion of a greater intelligence. Even if the choice of my name had been subconscious, Freud himself had said there were no accidents.

I held back tears. All these years I had clung to a child's black-and-white world. Believing this had been my mother's legacy. Perhaps my mom had simply put off these questions out of fear, like I had. Did she pray the day the hurricane came, or had it happened too fast to contemplate? How ironic it seemed, that in trying to honor her I had missed out on knowing her subtlety.

I found myself shaking in fearful anticipation of the torture to come. My logical mind wasn't scared. I would go into shock and feel nothing after the initial pain, but the irrational side wrestled with the nothingness and fear of feeling the cold, hard earth of the grave.

Death was inevitable for everyone, I told myself. It's natural, nothing to be afraid of.

What if there really were nothing else?

But time was not linear, so by virtue of that fact, there had to be something – if I could theoretically occupy more than one place in time. By that logic I would live forever in at least one of times' streams. Somehow that round of logic didn't make me feel much better.

A faint ribbon of patchouli and sandalwood drifted by. I heard my name called in the melodious tone Mother used when reading me to sleep as a girl. A brilliant white light broke the dark, putrid air and with it came a warm halting peace so profound I evanesced into it, away from the pain of this world. My mother's arms surrounded me. Everything was going to be all right – there was another side. I was touching it.

I heard a pop and felt a jolt. Every detail of the room became sharp – the subtle blue-gray veins in the walls, the bare light bulb, the discoloration where the beast's flesh opened – everything was perfectly clear in every direction, as if I were seeing in 360 degrees. I looked down at the shell of my body still kneeling on the Environ's flesh and noticed a silver cord connecting me to it. I told my body to get up and lie on the tattered blanket; it obeyed as if by remote control.

There would be no pain.

I was free.

FORTY-ONE

Freeman Fred begged to go on the rescue mission, but there was no way to bring him along. Inside the Environ he would stand out and blow the mission. Instead, Ira gave him the task of organizing the Geney into training groups. According to Hyunae, the water would continue to recede and soon they would be able to start building the Geney encampment.

Freeman Fred was to gather all knowledgeable people in the building trades to have them teach Geney volunteers. It wasn't really necessary because most of their training would be on-the-job, but Ira knew Freeman Fred had to have a focus or he would be thrust into despair about my circumstances.

Freeman Fred was already plagued with guilt and remorse, and no matter what I said before I was taken by Lamont, he was against my going. He had pleaded with Lamont to take him, instead, but there was no way around my fate.

La Donna and Tuwa felt their involvement in my rescue from the Environ was absolutely necessary. Ira didn't argue. No one wanted to deal with Robert, but he was head of CAT and insisted on being included. Ira picked Todd and Kevin because of their demeanors and familiarity with the area.

Lamont had left pictures of the symbols on the Environ's hovercrafts. Safia stayed up all night tweaking the colors to match the scans exactly, blowing them up and printing out stickers. Early that morning, before the sun rose, the techs applied them to a carefully selected matching model in our fleet.

The team was to arrive at the docking station at exactly 6:30, just after sundown. They took all the medical supplies they could for the trip home, hoping I would still be alive for the equipment to be useful.

Ira didn't want a lot of fanfare, so only a handful of people saw them off at the docking station. Naomi was one of them. Ira noticed how distraught she looked. Her skin was ashen. Dark circles hung beneath her eyes. She didn't seem herself. And her son, who was usually glued to her when she wasn't working, wasn't there.

Ira put Naomi out of his mind. They had four hours to get to the Environ, plenty of time, but there was still a lot to go over on the way.

Robert insisted on driving, being the control freak he was, and everyone was all too happy to have him preoccupied. Robert took it slow, pacing the ride so they would get there on time and not a minute earlier.

As they approached the gray beast, Ira handed out the science uniforms Lamont had left behind. La Donna held one up and said, "You call this a uniform?" She shook her head. "How am I supposed to fit into this?" She raised an eyebrow. "Even if I strip naked I'm not sure I'll fit into this puppy."

Ira looked through the tags and found Kevin's extra-large was a hair too big for him. He traded it for La Donna's large. Kevin complained it was a bit tight in the crotch, but La Donna was satisfied and the matter was settled.

They found their way around the back of the Environ to the orifice on the elaborate map Lamont had given them. Robert hit it right on the nose, exactly 6:30. As soon as they got into position, the orifice opened. They did as instructed, entering quickly and shutting down the engine. The orifice closed behind them.

Malone and Herb met them at the next orifice opening and quickly led them to Lamont's office, where monitoring devices had been pulled out after the first week of living in the Environ. At the time, he just wanted his privacy; now he was thankful he had a place to hide the Collective members.

Lamont was waiting for them. He had prepared the room with everything they would need for the next few hours – food, water, chairs and a monitor on which to watch the execution, if they were so inclined.

Ira had insisted on being at the execution as moral support for me. Lamont protested, "She won't know you're there. It will just upset you – possibly make it harder for you to do your job."

"She will know I'm there. It's important to me. I can't let her go through this alone," Ira replied.

"Hey," Malone piped up. "A friend of mine from maintenance died a few weeks ago. The CFO gave me his effects after looking over his will. I have his old uniform. It might be a little big, but…"

"Perfect," Ira replied.

"Wear a cap, don't let anyone see your eyes, and whatever you do, don't look directly at any of the cameras! Keep your eyes obscured at all times," Lamont said.

Ira nodded. "Promise."

FORTY-TWO

"Almost ready," Ellis Rush said to Jessie Applegate. "Get some powder on his nose!"

Sandy came out from behind the red velvet curtains in a dress that looked like it was spun out of cotton candy and speckled with glazed sugar. She stood next to Jesse, waiting for the makeup woman to finish her business with his nose before standing on her mark.

Rush raised his arm and counted, "1, 2, 3... and go!"

"A heretic is among us," Jessie roared. "A woman whose soul purpose was to destroy our civilization! Take our property and ruin our way of life... She is a Godless woman. A scientist from a small group of MUTANTS who had managed to live by a PACT with SATAN!"

"These people were an abomination!" Sandy screamed. "They had no good Christian values. She's the only one left of these bandits who lived like animals, drinking the blood of the dead in the decaying cities and marauding from city to city, feeding on what was left of the old world like VAMPIRES!"

Jessie stepped forward to stare into camera one with a look of supreme authority. "These were a truly wicked people – the devil's concubines, whores and minions of Lucifer. We knew about them, but we assumed they were all dead. Not until this lone madwoman came here did they pose a threat. But I will leave the rest of the explaining to our honorable CEO, Reginald Strauch, and his lovely wife, Camille Pamela."

The studio lights came down and Strauch and Camille took their places behind the curtains. A spotlight shone and the velvet curtains parted. They walked out. Camera two zoomed in on their faces.

"Psyche Hershenbaum is an evildoer. I know, because she worked for Digibio before the Environ was complete. She was never considered for entrance into our world due to her Marxist, Godless upbringing and her association with the criminal hacker Ira Rubenstein, who she lived with in sin," Strauch said.

Camille put on her best husky baby-girl voice and said, "But her madness goes far beyond this. The scoundrel group of scientists she had assembled pillaged the old cities, as Sandy has told you. All of these scientists are now dead, praise Jesus. But somehow she alone managed to survive and in her UV-demented mind she saw the Geneco as her only hope of salvation – by stealing them she hoped to build a new civilization where she could reign as their queen."

The curtains came up, revealing the same torture device on which Kaitlin had been murdered. It was a large aluminum circle with four black-leather straps spread to Psyche's approximate measurements. Strauch cleared his throat and then spoke. "She has committed the highest act of treason, and for this, she will be executed. For her evil act we will make her suffer a long, painful and slow death."

"Let this be a lesson to those who do not believe in God and the ways of the righteous. Bring her out!" Camille shrieked, stomping her high heel into the squishy gray flesh of the Environ.

Two overweight guards muscled me in from the side of the stage. I watched my body from above. My arms and ankles were shackled to a chain around my neck, which one of the guards tugged to get me to hit my mark. I was tired, hungry, thirsty and lonely. It showed on my wan face, but the fire in my eyes still blazed with their injustice and I looked angry enough to be crazy. My eyes met Camille's, and instinctively Camille pushed off her mark. Rush motioned her to step forward again, but it took a few seconds before she noticed and found her spot.

"Take her to the post," Strauch said. The guards pulled my chain, ripped open the back of my shirt and strapped my body into the belts of the aluminum circle. "Give her the standard 30 lashes the Geneco get when they step out of line. She's an animal – treat her like one."

I watched my body brace itself, eyes squeezed shut. Above me I heard praying and Tuwa's voice filling the air with song as my body felt the sting of the first lashing, the second, and then as the third was raining down, my body hummed along to the song only I could hear. With each strike my voice grew louder and the light in the room grew stronger. The stinging pain and warm, sticky blood were kept away from me in a hazy cloud.

The other side was opening in its full glory.

Strauch was horrified. He jumped protocol and ran to Rush. "What is she doing? Get her to stop that!"

"She's crazy. What can I do about it?" Rush replied.

"You have to do something!"

Rush just shrugged. Strauch was so incensed he stole the whip from the guard and stuck my back, screaming, "Harder, like this!" But I continued to sing, to rant, and the noises frightened him. "Harder!" I watched my back split open, exposing the red, stringy sinew of muscles. Camille rushed toward the side stage and made cutting motions, but Strauch was worked into a frenzy and hadn't noticed his bloodlust showing, threatening their "moral" empire.

Camille finally stepped in front of him, pulled his arm back and, smiling into the camera, said, "Now that will do, Reginald. I think you've contributed enough to the saving of her soul. It's time for the next phase."

Strauch was still in an altered state, like a shark in a feeding frenzy, his eyes dilated into black orbs. She smiled at him and repeated herself. He turned slowly toward the camera and said in a stiff voice, "Now the Applegates will explain the next... phase. Phase 2."

"That's right, Reginald, Phase 2," Camille repeated.

Jessie Applegate took the spotlight, puffing like a rooster who had just won a cockfight. The camera tightened on him and his pompadour. "We will transform this heathen and make a believer out of her! For yea, she hath spit in the eye of Christ. Even if we can't save her body, we shall save her immortal soul. Yea, shall she seek Thine glory in God almighty, Yahweh. Psyche Hershenbaum shall walk the walk our Holy Father's only Son doth took. He who sacrificed his life, at his Father's command, to purify us of our original sin. I speak of none other than Jesus Christ our Lord and Savior. It is in his name we give her this gift of ultimate redemption. Her flesh may burn, but her soul shall be saved. It is only through seeing the pain of Our Savior and the sacrifice Our Lord made for all of us sinners that she shall be received into the kingdom of Heaven, knowing the love of Jesus Christ, amen." He turned to face me. I was still strapped into the aluminum circle and he said, "I pray for your sins and ask you to repent! May God have mercy on your soul!"

Sandy Applegate bounded to his side and exclaimed, "An eye for an eye, the Bible commands. Psyche Hershenbaum would sacrifice our way of life and so it is now her life which must be sacrificed."

"Amen!" Jesse commanded.

"OK and CUT!" Rush yelled from the booth. "Do we have the corridor set up for the transition shot yet?"

Surnow nodded. "We sure do."

"Camera three rolling."

My eyes squinted from the blinding-hot lights of the camera crew. The executioner loaded two large wooden planks onto my back and secured them around my waist with rope.

I thought of Ira. One last, sweet kiss on his lips, the scrub of his beard against my cheek. One more look at his small, handsome brown eyes or the coarse skin on his hands. That was all I wanted. Yes. I wanted to see Freeman Fred's strange, faint smile welcoming his old friends into the Collective. I wanted to hear Tuwa's song loud and clear above all others chanting in the Circle of the Great Spirit. I wanted to feel the wind against my face and the way the sun beat down before it became a laser. I wanted all of these things, but they were beyond my grasp and felt like worn memories from someone else's life – everything except Ira.

If I could have held his hand it would have been enough. Had I told him how much I loved him? Or how much having children with him would have been a gift, if the world and circumstances had been different?

The executioner yanked on the chain pinching my neck and I stumbled a little; the wood planks rattled and pushed into the Environ's fleshy floor.

I longed to go back 15 years, to the time Ira had picked out a ring and asked me to marry him. I should have said yes instead of giving him a diatribe about the sordid history of the institution. The truth was, I had been scared to be dependent on him – to love him too much. I wished I hadn't been so pig-headed. Marriage didn't seem so bad now. It seemed like a promise to see him again. I wished I had made it.

FORTY-THREE

Tuwa was holding hands with La Donna in Lamont's office. Both had their eyes closed and heads bowed, singing a sacred song. I could feel their prayers and hear them echoing through the viscous walls of the gray beast. And in the distance I could hear Freeman Fred, Naomi, Aine, Marina, Fayza, Hyunae, Safia, Xin-Yi, Eva, Kimi and Zoe and so many others singing their prayer songs, some together, others individually.

Ira was in the hallway, pushing desperately through the crowd to get to me. I couldn't see him yet, but I could sense him.

One of the guards refastened the planks to my back with a tightly cinched rope. The wood dug into my wounds. I heard Strauch's voice, like a bee buzzing behind me, and felt the hot lights follow as the guard pulled the metal chain around my neck. Walking was difficult, having lost so much blood from the lashings. I was dizzy and dipping in and out of my body.

There were people behind me screaming and throwing things as we headed down the corridor. It was a maze. My head spun and I dropped to my knees. My neck jerked back as the guard grabbed my hair, pushing me forward.

"Get on your feet!" he screamed.

I fumbled my way upward, my mind racing. *Nature made chaos, but man made evil. I will die for the sin of greed. I will die for the sin of murder. I will die for the sin of denial. I will die for the greatest sin — squandering this world the Great Spirit gave us to protect. Just as they murdered the world, they are murdering me. Great Spirit guide me. Great Spirit stay with me.* Those words repeated in my head and brought me temporary peace by snapping me back out of body again.

There was a light so bright I wished I could put my hands in front of my face to shield it. It was the beast opening its belly and expelling us into the garden. Artificial lights had been strung all around, and as soon as we entered, a cameraman had shone a blinding spotlight into my eyes. The mob was still behind me, screaming different things that had become a wash of nothingness. I saw the pelting, heard the stones hit me, but felt nothing. It didn't matter now. I felt the other world opening as if ready to swallow me. And in the brilliant light I saw the garden open up. I saw beyond the sea of adversarial faces.

A voice whispered from above, "See how the world should have been?"

Something grabbed my hand – an angel? A brilliant being made of crystal-white light and pop: the Environ disappeared, replaced by a lush, green valley teeming with life of all kinds. Children played in front of round-shaped houses made of a strange, dark material I'd never seen.

We went higher, toward the hills. There the earth was covered in vegetation; deer grazed by a stream while frogs hopped by and butterflies flew overhead. It was the most beautiful thing I had ever seen, like the Eden my mother had told me about – a place that no longer existed during my time on Earth. I felt tears streaming down my face, and a sudden crash.

And I was hovering back over myself, watching my legs stiffly move across the squishy soil. The angel or great being, whatever it was, had shown me a stream of time we had not chosen. My heart ached for the world we had destroyed through sheer greed and shortsightedness. If we had faced it, we would have developed technology to change it, but the few who had money and power had protected their personal empires instead of putting the greater good first. And what did they gain? A few short years on Earth, full of wealth and privilege at the expense of all life to come?

It was beyond comprehension for anyone with a drop of empathy or kindness in their soul. Even for those who made the choice to deny the reality of climate change, what would it have hurt to embrace the possibility if it meant saving the world? It was ironic that the people who claimed to be the most pious had inadvertently protected the wicked, greedy, destructive plutocrats out of ignorance and fear. But what can one expect from a religion based on fear and ignorance except to create more fear and ignorance? What a masquerade the masses had been sold. So much perversion of morality for the self-interest of the so-called elite.

I heard a strange humming all around, like Tuwa's singing, at the periphery of the horizon. It was washing closer. I trod toward the center of the gardens, where a circle stood. A once benign turn-of-the-century exercise machine turned into a gruesome torture device. The guard stopped. Strauch came forward. "Unshackle her."

The guard obeyed. Another guard came forward to nail the planks together. They fastened the cross to a circle. Once secured, the guard tied my arms to the cross and bound my feet together with rope, cinching them around the bottom plank. Two men came forward with stakes and hammers. Sandy gave them the signal.

One man hammered a stake through my right palm and then another through my left. Below, I heard my body screaming and writhing in pain. But through the grace of the Great Spirit, my consciousness felt nothing except a deep sadness at man's cruel inhumanity.

The prayer songs grew louder, surrounding me, protecting me. As dark as the Environ society was, people were good when given a chance. The people who lived under Strauch's rule weren't evil, they were simply mislead. Human beings want to trust their leaders just as a parent is trusted, believing that those in charge have their flocks' best interests at heart.

A decent, normal person has no ability to reconcile the unimaginable mind of a sociopath. How could a kind, empathic person conceive of joyfully annihilating another human being? Projecting one's own motivations onto others is natural, which is why serial killers blend in and dictators often murder millions before the truth of their atrocities are accepted.

But no matter how hard people willfully denied the psychopathy of the Strauch regime, and no matter what church the Strauchs attended, their deeds were clear. If one removed the glamour of their wealth and power, clarity came, but it wasn't so easy for those in the Environ – their very lives depended on believing a lie.

I watched the hateful faces jeering at my body and felt pity. These people were not bad. Their sin was seeing themselves as small and powerless. They didn't understand the gifts of the Great Spirit. Logic, feelings, empathy and compassion had been replaced by fear and survival. Their limitless potential had been stolen. They were held captive by a devil formed from fear.

"Great Spirit, keep her safe, keep her whole," Ira whispered. My eyes were drawn through the sea of faces. Ira had pushed and bullied his way through the crowd and was at my feet. My body was too weak to show recognition no matter how hard I tried to steer my lips to smile at him.

A guard got up on a ladder with a garland of gnarled, mutated, cactus thorns and placed it on my head. He nailed a sign above it: Queen of the Geneco. Before he got down, Ira handed him a wet cloth. The guard wrung it over my head. It was cool and mixed with my blood. Liquid streamed down my face. The guard patted my forehead down. I watched as my body gave way, hanging limp, eyes opened – staring into nothingness.

There I hung above the angry mob.

Strauch spoke into a microphone, his voice booming, "Let this be a lesson to all of you. No traitor left behind!" He laughed.

"But seriously," he continued over the PA. "We need to wrap this up, the UV levels are too high in this area to stay more than an hour without severe burns. Hope you all wore your sunscreen!"

There was a big, "Hell yeah!" from the crowd.

"Well, good. The only goose that'll get cooked, then, is the Queen here." He sniggered and the crowd burst into uproarious laughter.

But the louder that the cruel laughter got, so did the humming prayers of my people. I felt my spirit turning toward them as they lifted me upward. Their prayers joined a new sound bursting forth everywhere. A sound so beautiful and ethereal only one word could describe it – angelic.

I was floating, ascending into a beam of brilliant, golden light pouring through the clouds. Tuwa's prayers and Ira's love warmed my soul. I felt the pulse of the earth and sky, and the loud booming song of the Great Spirit singing me into the next world.

FORTY-FOUR

"Die, bitch, die!" Ira heard one man scream. He wanted to throttle the man, but couldn't. Everyone around him was screaming. He hoped I saw him, and felt his love. I was speaking, but he couldn't make out words over the din of hatred. He wondered, *how could people be so cruel? She had never wanted anything more than to save all of them. Didn't they see that?* The voice in his head stopped when he began to hear my singing rise over the crowd. He couldn't take it anymore and jumped protocol, grabbing the poison cloth from its bucket and handing it to the guard, commanding him to use it on Lamont's orders.

Almost instantly the singing stopped. My head hung limp, eyes open and vacant.

He wanted to rush over and hold me in his arms but he watched the maintenance crew breaking into groups. He had to leave now before he was found out.

Psyche is dead. She's dead. He felt nothing. His body went numb. His legs moved. His arms pushed the crowd out of his way. And he made it back to Lamont's office, not remembering how he got there.

FORTY-FIVE

Josephine was left to tend Jacob, Elijah and Jezebel in corporate daycare, with a dozen other nannies and 200 of the most privileged children in the Environ; their parents were deacons in the church or lead scientists, like Lamont's son, Bryan.

Elijah's diaper had been wet, and while Josephine was changing it, Jezebel started screaming and Jacob wandered out of the room. She called a young woman over and handed Jezebel to her. "Her formula is in the fridge," Josephine said. The nanny nodded and took the baby to the kitchen. Josephine put Elijah in his private playpen and went looking for Jacob.

The playroom was crowded with infants, toddlers and children from three to 12 years old. She tapped one child after the next, but Jacob was nowhere to be found. Her heart raced. The daycare was in lockdown. He couldn't get out without the code. He had to be somewhere. She took a deep breath and walked down the hallway toward one of the private napping rooms. She could hear the faint sound of a man's voice coming from a room three doors down. She rushed to it and burst open the door.

There, in the dark, Bryan Lamont and Jacob were sitting, mesmerized by the crucifixion playing out on the monitor. Bryan had found a way to jerry-rig the monitor into receiving mode. Josephine went to grab Jacob's hand, but something about the woman being murdered stopped her. It was as if a brilliant white light swirled around the figure. Josephine wondered if something was wrong with her eyes or the monitor, and paused.

"Do you see the light around her?" asked Bryan.

"You're not supposed to be watching that, turn it off," Josephine responded.

Bryan studied her. Josephine was obviously shaken. "That's not normal, is it?"

"Turn it off."

"What is she singing? It's another language, isn't it?"

Josephine grabbed both Bryan's and Jacob's hands and pushed them out of the room. She shut the orifice, putting in a lock code so it couldn't be open by any of the children, and rushed the boys into the playroom.

Josephine ran to her old friend Shirley's office. Shirley was Herb's wife and had started as a nanny, but after they lost their child to the plague, Shirley retreated to caring for paperwork instead of babies.

"What is it?" Shirley asked.

"Turn on the execution," Josephine said.

"You know how I feel about that."

"No. There's something strange going on. Something different. As a devout Christian woman, you need to see it."

"Turn the other cheek, Christ said."

"I know. I know," Josephine said, hitting the on button on Shirley's monitor. "Look at her." Shirley turned to see the screen behind her. "Do you see the light all around her?"

"Some kind of spotlight, I'm sure."

Josephine shook her head. "I need to go. I need to be there."

"We need you here."

"Open your heart, Shirley. This woman... this woman is not just a woman. A miracle is happening right in front of you."

Shirley stared at the monitor and an overwhelming feeling of peace overtook her. Was it that woman's voice or an angel's? Herb had sworn her to secrecy and then told her all about Psyche heading another civilization. It was a secret Shirley had sworn she would take to the grave. Herb had warned her that he would be the next one crucified if anyone found out. Was it possible a woman could be the Second Coming? Shirley watched the light around Psyche's body spiral and grow. Or was this some kind of camera trick? But why would they do that?

"She may be the one we've been waiting for," Josephine said.

"Go. I'll cover for you. Hurry before it's too late."

Josephine nodded and ran out.

The halls were empty until she got to the garden orifice, where the crowd spilled out. Josephine pushed her way through the mob, mumbling "please excuse me" and "pardon me." She managed to get to a flat concrete bench about 100 meters from the crucifixion site and squeeze her way on top of it.

It wasn't a trick of the camera. All around the woman was a yellow glow, and around the crown of her head, like the ancients had painted around saints. White lights danced around her, swirling and blowing out into supernovas in spiraling vortexes upward toward the heavens.

Josephine heard the jeering and looked around. In the sea of contorted faces full of vile hatred, some stood out – their eyes wide with rapture, faces placid like the beatific. Through this woman, God was separating the True Believers from the sinners. Judgment day had come. It hadn't been the day of the Environ occupation – no. Judgment was here and now.

And they were killing God again.

FORTY-SIX

After I was gone, Strauch, Camille and the Applegates left. When the last stragglers headed back into the main body of the Environ, Rush yelled to his cameraman, "And cut. That's a wrap."

Surnow asked, "So are we going to shoot the disposal?"

"We'll make a montage of the highlights of today. I'll have you do the voiceover tonight, then in the morning we'll go to the disposal site and get an update. She should pretty well be digested by then. Probably just get her outline through the wall, or maybe her legs or head or something sticking out. That will be more than enough to make the point. We'll see how the ratings go. If there's interest, we'll do another update at noon."

"Sounds good," Surnow said.

"OK, everybody pack it up. We're out of here," Rush said to his crew.

FORTY-SEVEN

Lamont had been careful, locking the Collective members in his office until the time was right. He watched them on surveillance from his wristcom in Malone's office after he was sure Malone had jammed all the camera signals. He had been meticulous in every way, thought out 10 steps ahead.

Ira was extremely upset about the lockdown. He was screaming at the cameras, but it was for his own good. Lamont understood why he was so upset; my body was in very bad shape, the lashings and wounds becoming obscured by the severe UV burns as I lay limp on the circle cross, waiting for the disposal team to take my body to the dump site just a few hundred meters away. But it would do no good for me to have my team found out and murdered alongside me. Ira was being irrational, which was to be expected.

The disposal team took me off the cross. Lamont had positioned Herb to be their leader, under the guise that the science team wanted pictures of the wounds and scans for documentation purposes. Really it was to make sure no more damage was done to my body. Herb made sure they were very careful and no more tearing was done to my palms when I was released from the planks – Lamont's biggest worry.

They carried me to the disposal orifice and laid me down in front of it. But this was no ordinary orifice. It had hundreds of tentacle-like sensors under its dark-gray spot. As soon as they set me inside the yellow box at its mouth, the sensors wiggled and swayed. Herb took pictures of my wounds. "It's OK, guys. I've got it from here," he said. The disposal team dispersed.

Inside Herb's camera Malone had rigged a signal interference device, which first taped me lying in front of the orifice and looped it, projecting these images back to the security cameras. But there wasn't much time before security would get suspicious. The tongue usually took anywhere from 20 to 30 minutes to come out. It would slowly pull my body in for digestion.

Herb made sure the coast was clear and pushed the direct line to Lamont on his wristcom. "Ready."

"The team will be dispatched," Lamont's voice came back. Herb stayed with me, pretending to take pictures while talking to my body. "You're going to be all right, just hang in there, Psyche. You're gonna make it. You'll be fine."

But, of course, I wasn't fine.

Hours of Tuwa's and La Donna's prayers had gone by. La Donna's voice was hoarse from singing, but Tuwa's was as clear and committed as it had been hours earlier.

Lamont had given all of them disposal uniforms to change into while Ira was tracking me. He had been happy to see all of them prepared when he arrived, but he was starting to worry. It had been over an hour; surely the disposal team would be done by now. Ira had rushed Robert through the rescue, thinking Lamont would be back for them any minute. But Ira was getting antsy – something was wrong. He searched for a camera to scream into, but after turning the place over, he gave up and began pacing.

"You're making this more difficult. Just sit down and wait like everybody else," Robert commanded, but Ira ignored him.

Moments later, the orifice opened and Lamont motioned everyone out. Ira wanted to kill him: *None of this would have happened to her if it hadn't been for Lamont.* "We were caged in there for an ungodly amount of time. Every second counts for Psyche right now."

Lamont didn't respond; he simply walked in a fast clip, followed by Robert and his men. *Getting angry now isn't going to do any good.* Ira took a moment to breathe and caught up to them.

My body appeared to dead, but technically, it wasn't. It had created a sort of false apoplectic state. My heart was beating imperceptibly. I still had brain-wave activity. The wet handkerchief that had been applied to my forehead during the crucifixion was infused with Zombutal, a little-known drug developed for surgical procedures for patients allergic to anesthesia. The first company Lamont bought into had developed a chemically engineered version of the herbal compound. It had been used by Haitian sorcerers to make zombies as well as an antidote to the drug.

The product and company had caught Lamont's interest after he had nearly died under anesthesia during an appendectomy in his

20s. The drug was rarely used, only on patients who were deathly allergic to conventional anesthesia. But Lamont had brought stockpiles of it to be used in case of emergency for himself or his child.

The orifice had opened and inside was the enormous tongue. The tentacles had pulled my body closer to the orifice while coating it with a gelatinous saliva. It was strange, hovering over my body, unsure whether it would survive. I saw Tuwa's prayers washing over my body in strange, vibrant colors. Colors too vivid and beautiful for the human eye to see.

During the crucifixion, when I asked to go into the light, I had heard a woman's voice whisper from above, "Not yet, not yet." Now the great light remained open above me. I heard voices moving closer to my body. My soul was in a suspended state while the heavens remained ready to receive me.

The tongue was wiggling, slowly feeling its way toward my discarded shell. I wanted it to hurry. The light was so warm and inviting I hungered to dissolve into it and feel the oneness with creation I could now taste but not savor.

The sun had gone down, but I had second- and third-degree burns on every inch of exposed skin. Ira ran ahead of the team to my body, pulling it away from the grasp of the tongue on my midsection. He rocked my body gingerly. "You're going to be OK," he whispered into my ear, and softly kissed my forehead.

Lamont, Robert, Kevin, Todd, Herb and Tuwa arrived next, followed by an out-of-breath La Donna. Tuwa was still singing, although her mouth was not moving. Ira was holding me, crying. Everyone froze and waited for him to pull himself together.

"What have you people done to her?" Ira wailed at Lamont.

"We need to clean her off," Lamont responded, nodding at Robert and his men. Ira stepped away as they rolled my shell onto what looked like a white sheet and carried me a dozen meters to an open plot of soil. Lamont grabbed the garden hose and showered me as gently as he could. He handed Todd a bottle of homemade-looking cleanser. He and Kevin applied it thoroughly to both sides, with Ira keeping careful watch so they didn't miss anything.

My shell was wrapped in an enormous, thick cotton blanket. Tuwa put her hands on me while singing and rocking in a trance.

Lamont gave Malone a signal via wristcom to jam the surveillance cameras on the way to the orifice. "C-section," he said. He watched his wristcom for a few moments and then nodded to the men. They carried my shell quickly through the soggy garden and toward the garage orifice where the hovercrafts were docked. The garage was now dry. The Environ had absorbed all the floodwater.

The men carefully laid my shell into an awaiting cot and covered me with blankets. Tuwa stayed by my side, holding my dead hand and singing, vibrant colors shimmering from her mouth and penetrating my broken flesh. Lamont took out the mechanized injector. It was much bigger than anything I'd ever seen. He opened the buttons of my shirt, placed the flat nub under my sternum and pushed the button. Tuwa's voice grew piercingly loud. A fiber-thin needle punctured my skin and went directly into my heart.

I felt a thud and then... the pain, oh, God the pain! Every inch of my skin was on fire and my insides felt as if they had been steamrollered. I wanted to jump out of my body, but couldn't. I was stuck in the excruciating pain. It was like being stuffed into a nail-lined shoebox.

Ira yelled, "Give her something for the pain!" Lamont pressed the morphine gun to my skin and everything went numb and fuzzy.

I saw Herb hand something to Ira and mumble, "Use this to keep in contact. We want to know her progress. Malone and I, well, we're both so sorry and..."

I blacked out.

FORTY-EIGHT

"Well, she couldn't have just disappeared," Strauch screamed at Lamont. "She was fuckin' crucified! Last I heard she was dead, for fuck's sake. And dead folks don't just get up and go for midnight strolls, now do they? These people are superstitious – they'll think we killed the fuckin' Second Coming!"

Lamont had been careful to cover every step, to plan for every possibility except one. After reviewing the crucifixion footage, Surnow decided to cover his bases by sending his crew to the disposal platform. Executions like Psyche's didn't come around every day. They were big ratings. He had made a spur-of-the-moment decision to do a documentary which he could air a few months down the road, when Strauch would need something to dissuade the "restless" population from ideas of sinning. But when the crew got to the platform, the body was gone. According to all calculations, the Environ should have been in the middle of its digestion cycle.

"I checked the digestion cycle. It ran fast that night: According to our records, the Environ had been starved for almost a week, so it's really not a surprise." Of course, this was utter bullshit, and Lamont had gotten Malone to override and falsify all evidence to the contrary. Lamont had been scrambling since Herb caught the camera crew on the monitor.

But Strauch continued to rage. "We need that fucking body. Rush and Surnow had set up their goddamned camera crew this mornin' and went there to report what they called the missin' body. Fuck, they'll do anything for motherfuckin' ratings. How are we gonna keep this secret? This is just what I fuckin' need! Smarmy fuckin' has-been Hollywood weasels startin' shit! We need her body!"

"That's impossible. Her body has been pulverized and digested by the Environ. There's nothing left."

Strauch was pacing, sweating, in a terrible panic. "Can you prove that?"

Lamont nodded casually. "Of course." He threw a stack of papers onto Strauch's desk. "The enzyme breakdowns and digestion calculations are all in here."

"No one's gonna understand that horseshit. I need a skull or somethin', somethin' people can see with their own two eyes."

"Well, we won't be able to change whatever they broadcast. I'm sure if you explain what happened to the people they'll understand."

"Don't be so fucking smug," Strauch said. Lamont shrugged. "This is a fuckin' mess."

Strauch stopped mid-pace, his eyes suddenly glimmering with glee. "We can pin it on one of the Geneco, like they came in to try and save her.... And fuck, I don't know, feed the fucker to a pack of wild dogs."

"There are no wild dogs left," Lamont quipped.

"No shit. I know that... It's a fuckin'..." Strauch lunged close to Lamont and shouted, "Just fuckin' find me someone to blame."

"I'll do my best," Lamont said.

"No. You'll find someone or I'll pick one of your scientist bitches, one that gives you a hard on, and use her dead body as a replacement. Got it?"

Lamont was cool, not a hint of emotion on his face. "Do what you have to, and as I said, I'll do my best."

FORTY-NINE

My body had been carried to the top of the mountain named Sage Peak. The CAT members had built a basic shelter inside one of the storage caves they had found on a training exercise. It had been used for their cache of pillaged weapons from the ghost cities. They considered the area top-secret; only they and the team leaders were privy to it. Robert feared bringing me back into the Collective as a wretched, half-dead, bloodied mess would incite war with the Environ. When the team leaders saw the broadcast of me from the hoverbus, they agreed.

Dr. Harold Candell had done everything medically possible upon my arrival, but there were limits. After he had given me all he could, he handed me over to Tuwa and joined the rest of the Collective in praying for a miracle, the sort only a holy person like her could deliver.

Ira had been ceaselessly at my side despite La Donna's urgings for him to get some rest. Only when Tuwa insisted on his removal did he take transport back to the Nest, where he took short, fitful catnaps.

It amazed Tuwa how alert I was. I was able sit up when eating or drinking, even crawl a little. Most of my day was spent sleeping, but when I was awake I was different and this scared her, although she tried not to show it.

Tuwa was also worried about Ira. He had not made peace with fate, as I had. Sometimes he would pace back and forth outside the tent, cursing and vowing revenge. At other moments he would coo to me about all the projects we had yet to finish in the year ahead. The worst was when he broke into inconsolable crying, cursing everyone from Lamont to Naomi for letting him in that day, and even cursing himself for not being brave enough to offer himself up as the sacrifice – even though he had.

Tuwa wondered if he was the reason I was hanging on. I appeared ready to pass, but it wasn't that simple.

On Friday, each of the team leaders was allowed a visit. Tuwa agreed I seemed well enough. Ira took this as a sure sign I was on the road to recovery. Eva, Fayza, Aine, Marina, Kimi, Xin-Yi, Safia, Hyunae all came and stayed a few minutes in succession and then left, gently saying goodbye with hopeful masks for faces. But Naomi didn't show until much later, and instead of walking right in, as the others had, she stayed at the doorway, looking terrified and ashamed. I said, "I look that bad?" But she didn't laugh at my joke.

"No, no…. you look very good." She walked in and sat stiffly in a nearby chair. "I'm sorry, I…"

"Don't worry, Naomi, everything will be fine. It's all as it is supposed to be."

She looked stunned, repentant and humiliated. She stared down at the backs of her hands folded on her lap. "I don't know what to believe anymore." She paused, took a deep breath and looked at me. "I trusted Paul. I never thought he was the kind of person who could purposefully hurt anyone."

"What do you mean?"

She looked away. "We were lovers. It was a very long time ago. I was a graduate student and I worked on a project for his company." Her eyes met mine and she must have read judgment in them because she defensively said, "I didn't know he was married."

"It's OK."

"No, it's not OK. Nothing about this is OK, not what he did to you, not what he did to his wife, not what he did to me."

It hit me. "You were still in love with him?"

She nodded. "Stupid, huh?"

Wow. I could see it now, all of her bizarre comments about the Geney made sense. They were Lamont's creation – a part of him, his property. She had been twisting reality around this strange, confused love, trying to mollify his monstrous acts into some lesser version of what they were. But seeing me, she could no longer do that. And now she was broken.

I grabbed her hand and held it. "I'm sorry."

Her eyes reddened and she choked back tears. "Please, no, I'm the one. Please, don't apologize to me. I'm the one." She got up, kissed my cheek and ran out.

Tuwa rushed in. "Everything alright?"

I nodded.

Naomi ran into Ira on her way into the Nest and told him it looked like I was doing much better. It gave him hope and he decided to make a transmission to Malone on the strange little button device hooked up to stay in contact. He spoke at the box. "It looks like she's going to make it. It's a miracle. She's speaking and eating."

Malone's voice came back, small and tinny, "That is a miracle! I'll pass along the good news."

"Thanks for all your help."

"My pleasure, man. My pleasure."

Freeman Fred heard I was conscious and stole away from the newly assimilating Geneco to see me. He knelt beside my broken body reverently and took my hand in his, his eyes dilated, nostrils flared in what I had learned was an expression of abject pain and remorse.

"I not know peace or love, only pain my whole life 'til you."

I smiled at him and touched his cheek.

His expression became focused, his mouth bowed into a small circle. "But greatest gift is hope, not just for one man." He pointed to himself. "But all man. You able to give one self to save many selves."

Freeman Fred kissed my forehead. "You are the way, the true-eth. Love too small word for you." He got up to exit.

"Wait," I said as loudly as I could. Freeman Fred turned to me. "You must promise me one thing."

"Any thing want," he said bending close so I wouldn't strain myself.

"Never let it be about me. You must promise. Don't let anyone make the mistake of believing there is one path - the Great Spirit is everywhere, in every person, animal and thing. I am no more a part of It than anyone else. There can be no one true path because the road to the Creator is inward and different for each. Don't let them say I am the one true way. Anyone whose heart is open would have made the choices I made – the only difference was, I was given the opportunity." Freeman Fred looked quizzically at me. I grabbed his hand. "Don't let them make a martyr out of me."

Freeman Fred nodded gravely. "Promise."

"The lesson isn't in my death, it's in you and your people's life."

That night Ira hovered around me while I slept, stroking my head until Tuwa reminded him he might infect some of the blisters on my scalp. He whispered softly into my ear how much he loved me, over and over, until he fell sleep at my side.

FIFTY

Malone couldn't believe the transmission. He really hadn't expected the good news. In fact, he'd spent a sleepless night worried – perhaps the only time Malone remembered being worried enough about anything to keep him awake since his first big hacking job. And weirder still was the odd twinge in his gut, something he'd never felt before – guilt.

Malone had done many unsavory things in his life, committed many crimes, but he'd never looked back, never once felt a bit of shame or sorrow or remorse. He'd come to believe he was a sociopath doing whatever needed to be done to survive. But seeing me tortured to save a group of strangers - and not just strangers but the Geney, a people not even their own creators had cared about -it moved him. He realized in that moment that he could feel for others – he'd just witnessed too much pain, death and selfishness throughout his childhood. He'd cut his feelings off, hadn't allowed himself the joy of love or the pain of remorse, sadness and guilt – nothing. He had turned himself into a big zero, a big nothing, an empty pit. But everything felt different now.

It wasn't just Malone who had been touched by my suffering. Herb, too, was moved into a kind of religious fervor, which was exacerbated by his wife Shirley and her friend, Josephine. Josephine claimed she, several children and one other childcare worker had seen an unnatural light around me while I was strapped to the circle cross, just before I was given the toxin.

Malone wasn't convinced. For him the lesson of my death wasn't about salvation and the afterlife, it was about saving yourself in this life, the here and now, reclaiming the ability to feel and have empathy and a full inner life – something he'd lost by the time he was five years old, when his parents died of plague. Suddenly, he didn't have to steal something or break into a defense-department computer or rob someone to feel a rush; now he felt a tsunami. My crucifixion had been the earthquake in his subconscious, awakening all the emotion he had spent years burying.

In order to spread the good news, Malone had called a meeting in his small office. Minutes later it was jammed with a dozen people. They were Josephine's people. She had a network of True Believers, people who followed the word, walked its talk, and had been waiting for the savior to return. They, too, had seen the lights around me, heard the angelic music, and upon hearing of my survival were convinced I, Psyche Hershenbaum, was not of this world.

"She's alive?" Herb asked for the third time with the same awe he had shown the previous two.

Malone nodded.

"You see," Josephine said. "We witnessed a miracle."

One of the believers, a young woman named Lisa who worked in food preparation, said, "Why couldn't God have sent us a Daughter? It makes sense. We wouldn't be expecting it. It would be a great test for the True Believers. His only Son and now His only Daughter. It's so clear."

"Yes," Josephine added. "There are so many wicked among us. He had to send Her to sort out the unworthy before his final judgment."

Herb nodded. "Right. And if it weren't for Psyche, the Environ would never have been - without her research, Lamont said the Environ would have taken another 10 to 20 years to complete, and by then we all would have been dust."

"Now wait a second…" Malone said. "There is something special about her, I'll give you that. But she's not God. God doesn't exist."

The faithful stared at him as if he had just murdered one of them. Josephine said, "Then how do you explain Psyche waking from the dead when you know better than anyone that no human being could survive what she endured?"

Malone stared back at Josephine's pious, watchful eyes; there was innocence and goodness in them. What could it hurt to let these desperate people believe there was something more? Perhaps they were right to have faith, if believing gave purpose to their lives and allowed them the strength to endure their pain. Who was he to take that away from them?

FIFTY-ONE

Strauch was desperate for proof of my death, and Lamont had spent the past 48 hours trying to figure a way to keep Strauch from taking another life. Lamont had considered sending one off his men to the boneyard; chances were that if they braved the rain and dug into the sludgy waters they'd find a few skulls and bone fragments to choose from, but even a casual observer of the Geneco would know one of their skulls from that of an ordinary human. Lamont racked his brain. There had to be a medical skeleton in an old closet somewhere, but where? If he asked one of the medical crew, later, when Psyche's remains were found in the excrement trail, they'd be suspicious. The only two men he could trust now were Malone and Herb.

He rushed to get dressed and exit his comfortable cell, his son still asleep. He couldn't call one of the corporate nannies - it was four in the morning and this would sound an alarm. He told himself he'd just be gone a minute.

"Computer," he whispered toward the dialing system. "Get Malone for me."

It rang only once before Malone abruptly answered, "Hello."

"You're awake?"

"Who is that?" Lisa sat up in bed and whispered discreetly into Malone's ear.

"I'll pretend I didn't hear that. Meet me at the lab."

"When?"

"Now."

"Give me five minutes." Malone gave Lisa a kiss on the cheek; for a True Believer, she was one hell of a lover. He mouthed the words, "I won't be long - stay here."

She smiled and nodded back, mouthing, "I'll make breakfast."

"See you there." Lamont aimed his voice at the computer and said, "Disengage."

"Disengaged."

"I thought I programmed it not to talk back," he mumbled to himself. He popped his head in on Bryan. The boy was sound asleep. His mother would be coming to pick him up later that afternoon, but since the day had officially been declared a day of celebration, Bryan would most likely sleep in until nine. But to be safe, Lamont would have to hurry. Bryan had been having terrible nightmares since the execution. And if Lamont were caught AWOL, Tricia would never agree to let Bryan stay over again. Half an hour at most, Lamont told himself as he walked through the orifice.

Malone was still buttoning his shirt when he came through the lab orifice. Lamont was right behind him. "Thanks for being prompt," Lamont said.

"What choice did I have?" Malone countered. "I owe my life to you."

Lamont nodded. "I don't have much time. I need you to dig up an old medical skeleton for me."

"Just give me a shovel."

"Problem is, I don't know where one is. I don't want to go to medical because they'll get suspicious. Strauch is asking for evidence that Psyche was digested."

"Won't the waste-cycle people know the timing is off?"

"I'm going to distress it and put it in the trail at the right time."

"Risky," Malone said. "It won't look natural. Some people might not believe it."

"Enough of them will. Besides, I'm not worried about them. I'm worried about Strauch going on another murderous rampage."

Malone nodded. "I'll get on it. Shouldn't take me long. I'll have something in your office by noon."

"Fine. That will give me 12 hours to manufacture its digestion. We'll set it out on the trail at midnight."

Malone nodded.

Lamont hurried back to his cell. Bryan was screaming. He rushed in and held his terrified boy. "It's OK. I'm here. Shhh," he said, rocking Bryan back and forth.

It took minutes for Malone to locate an out-of-use, broken-down teaching skeleton. And all the better, it was female. Lisa would not believe what he was being made to do. He called his cell. It took a while for her to answer; she was probably afraid of getting caught.

"Hello?" she said in a strange, fake-masculine voice.

"It's me."

"I thought it was, but…"

"It's OK. I won't be able to make it to breakfast. You'll never believe what I've been ordered to do."

"What?"

"Suffice it to say Strauch himself doesn't believe Psyche died. That's all I can say. You'll figure out the rest by tomorrow."

Lisa glowed. It was true – now there would be proof to use for converting the lost. Psyche had been the second coming so many had waited for - judgment day was just around the corner. Soon she would be reunited with her beloved mother, father, three sisters and brother. Every person she had ever loved; now she would get to hold them in her arms again, hold their hands, hear their laughter and voices, speak to them again. For Lisa, the saddest part of losing her family to the Skeleton Plague wasn't their deaths, because she knew their spirits survived and were with God – it was seeing her mother in a dream and not being able to speak to her. Over time, the sound of her families' voices had been silenced by memory, and now all of them were but mute ghosts she could only hope to catch a glimpse of in the background of a dream.

It was just quarter to five in the morning. Shirley and Herb would still be home, although they might be sleeping. But Lisa was sure they'd want to hear the good news.

"Computer, Give me Mr. and Mrs. Herb Jones in section 2-A, cell number 3, please."

"Dialing… Dialing… Dialing…"

"Hello?" Josephine's voice croaked.

"I'm sorry to wake you but I have some big news," Lisa said.

"What is it?" Josephine said nervously, sitting up in bed.

"It's not bad. It's fantastic! So good I don't want to spoil it by telling you over the phone. We need to gather the devoted together and take our vows tonight."

"She's alive?"

"Yes."

"Praise be to God!" Josephine said so loudly that Herb woke with a start.

"What's going on?" he asked. Josephine waved him away for the moment and he settled back on his pillow.

"We need a place to…"

"No worries, we can use our cell for the meeting."

"It has to be late," Lisa said.

"Yes. When everyone's gone to bed. Midnight should do."

"Great. I'll get everything together."

"Come by in an hour."

"Will do," Lisa said, disengaging the computer.

FIFTY-TWO

Ira prepared the juniper and sage detoxifying tea just as Tuwa had instructed. Both of them had cots brought into the tent hidden inside the cave so they wouldn't have to leave to sleep. They took care of me in shifts, although Ira had yet to take advantage of the new arrangement. My progress had gotten him so excited he had spent the eight hours he should have rested talking to me about everything that crossed his mind. It was as if he felt I couldn't die while he was speaking.

Ira handed me the tea. It was bitter and unpleasant to the palate. I wrinkled my nose during the first sip. "Is this really necessary?" I asked.

"Yes," he said, sitting down next to me. I put the cup to my mouth and couldn't help souring my face at the smell of it. "Drink it."

"It's disgusting. Almost as bad as that 'wine' you used to make out of old, decayed grapes back in DC."

He smiled. "I can't believe I'm actually happy you're teasing me about that."

"I know. It used to make you so mad."

"I never said a thing about it."

"But your face did," I said, gulping down the rest of the concoction as fast as I could. "Could I have something to wash down the taste?" Ira handed me a cup of freshly squeezed apple juice. I took a sip. "Ahh, that's more like it." He smiled quizzically at me. "I've changed, that's what you're thinking, isn't it?"

He nodded. "But it's not bad... it's good."

I took hold of his hand and smiled. "I want you to know I've never felt happier or more at peace. And I know things now. I understand."

He stared at me. "What kind of things?"

"Anything I want to. I can feel it. Everything's different. I don't have to wonder about why the world is the way it is; why the galaxy revolves around a black hole; how space-time is curved by giant celestial bodies; or ponder what it really means for time to be a dimension. I know. I feel all of it as if I've been plugged into the Source of All and my cells are glowing."

Ira watched me with a blank look on his face. I could tell he was scared. I wasn't the same Psyche - either I'd gone nuts or I was on my deathbed. I gently rubbed the flap of skin between his thumb and fingers and said, "Don't be afraid. No matter what happens, just know there is no such thing as death, just as there is no such thing as time." But he continued to stare blankly. "Everything and everyone is eternal, you see?"

He shook his head. "You had an experience while you were..."

"Dead? Yes. How long was I technically gone for?"

"The poison Lamont concocted did more than just reduce your vital signs to indictable levels."

"So, how long was I gone?"

"We think the poison alone would have worked, but with all the other injuries, it was too much."

"And again, how long?"

"It took a couple hours before we could get to you."

"Shouldn't I have brain damage?"

"Ira nodded. It was a miracle the antidote got your heart going again."

"If I were truly dead, it wouldn't have worked."

Ira stared hard at me.

"It was Tuwa, wasn't it."

He nodded. "Paul pulled me aside just before we left and told me the antidote shouldn't have worked."

Tuwa awoke and put a kettle on. She came over with some sweet tea and handed it to me. "You'll like it," she said, and then turned to Ira. "You look exhausted. Go to sleep."

"But it's not time."

"I'll be fine," she said.

Ira kissed my cheek and climbed into the sleeping bag on the nearby cot. "I'll be right here. Don't worry about waking me."

Tuwa and I nodded. The moment his head hit the pillow he was snoring. "You will teach the path of the Great Spirit to the Geney, won't you?" I asked.

"Of course. You need your energy. You should get some sleep."

I handed her back my tea and sunk into my pillow. "I am tired."

It was a cold, windy night. She stroked the crown of my head softly and sang a prayer song. She turned the lights off, leaving one just outside the tent, near the portable toilet, and slipped back under the blankets on her cot. She hadn't intended to fall back to sleep, just rest a moment, but her body was fatigued and asleep she fell.

A few hours later, I was awoken by a brilliant white light. It was burning hot and I was covered in sweat. My eyes were open, but I couldn't see anything except white, so I closed them and through my lids I saw the cave perfectly. A few moments later the light dimmed enough for me to open my eyes again and there, standing in front of me, was a tall, luminescent woman. I wasn't sure if she was an angel, or maybe a goddess, but she beckoned me forward, holding out a hand to help me up.

I threw back the covers. The being unwrapped my bandages and said, "You won't need these anymore." It felt good to be released from the tight restriction of my wounds. She grabbed my hand.

It felt as though we were speeding through the cave faster than light. We were already somewhere deep inside, and I felt weary from the journey through the twists and curves. I couldn't understand how we had gotten there or where we were going or how far we had come. I looked down and realized I was naked except for my underwear. But how had it happened? I couldn't remember taking anything off. Water was rushing up ahead from an underground river and the being stopped once we reached its edge.

"The water is cool. Let it take away your pain," she said. "It is time to be released. Time to go home." She put her hand on my forehead and I saw my body peel off my underwear and walk into the river. I stayed with the being, watching my shell float downstream. "Time for the flesh to be returned to the Mother," she said.

The angel put her arms around me in a sheltering gesture. I heard the ancient prayer songs Tuwa had sung, getting louder and stronger, until the cave went blinding white again. My spirit became light and the pain disappeared. I was cleansed of all my earthly chains and felt the warm, all-encompassing love again and heard my mother's laughter bleeding through from the other side. And into the tunnel of pure, radiant white light, we dissolved.

FIFTY-THREE

It was midnight. Malone and Herb waited at the docks in wetsuits. A few minutes later Lamont walked in with a large suitcase; inside was the fermented skeleton. It looked good, but there was no way it would stand up to testing; of course, Lamont had fixed that end of things.

They got on the hoverboat. Malone opened the orifice and the trio braved the stormy night and choppy seas. "Engage the infrared searchlight," Lamont said.

"Engaged," Malone responded.

Lightning cracked the sky and the rain turned from sprinkles into sheets. The little hoverboat pitched and dipped in tandem with the ripples underneath. Herb, who was using the infrared monitor to look for the tox stream under the current, called out, "Stop! We're right on top of it."

Lamont strapped Malone into the harness. "You really think this will work?" asked Malone.

"A boat is coming out here tomorrow morning at daybreak to look for her remains," Lamont replied while he unrolled the twin set of steel cords and hooked them onto Malone's harness. Herb strapped the oxygen tank on Malone and then got into a harness on his own.

"Ready?"

"As soon as I see Herb prepared to save my ass, if need be." Malone put on his helmet and turned on the oxygen.

Herb strapped on his tank and hooked himself to the other set of dive reels and gave Malone a thumbs-up.

Malone shook his head. "Uh-uh, not until you put on the helmet. It's a fucking nightmare out there."

Herb secured his helmet. Malone walked onto the deck while Lamont waited for his signal.

Malone took a deep breath, nodded and closed his eyes, jumping into the stormy abyss with the suitcase. Lamont hit the red button in front of the reels and the cord engaged, giving Malone more than enough slack to reach the bottom.

The trail was worn down by the water, except for the 600-or-so meters from the Environ waste orifice. Malone swam to within a meter of it and popped open the suitcase. The skeleton wanted to float away. It was a struggle to get it to lie still in the toxic goo. He had to pile it over all of the body, leaving only the top of the skull to pop through enough to be obvious to the diving team in the morning. The gunk burned through the rubber gloves he was wearing. He'd have to get back on the boat and do a scrub-down before it burned through his skin. He yanked on the line.

FIFTY-FOUR

Ira's wristcom went off. It was pitch black in the cave; the light Tuwa had left on had burned out while they were sleeping, and he couldn't see an inch in front of himself. He turned on his flashlight, but it was still too dark. He fumbled his way toward one of the other lights near my cot. As soon as the light came on, he saw a small pile of bandages near my cot and gasped.

"She's not here! Wake up, Tuwa. She's gone!" he yelled.

"I'll check outside," Tuwa said. "You look in the cave, maybe she woke up and got confused."

He wondered, *what kind of crazy fever dream or delusion had she had to take off the bandages?* He couldn't understand. He pulled out a head lantern and put it on. Immediately, he saw signs that I had gone through the cave. He found a bloody shirt I had discarded a few yards in. He called out, "Psyche? Psyche!" But no answer came. He figured I must have sleep-walked or gotten mixed up. Before he continued, he went to find Tuwa.

Tuwa was walking back inside when he found her. "She went through the corridor. I found her T-shirt."

Tuwa grabbed her head lantern and followed him with a cup of herbs to sprinkle as they went through the maze. It would be impossible to find a way out without markers. She thought it was likely I had gotten lost in the labyrinth. They yelled my name periodically. When they came to a fork, Tuwa filled Ira's pocket with juniper berries before they split up.

FIFTY-FIVE

No one was allowed to examine the bones, once the divers had found them - except through the lens of Bill Surnow's live documentary, broadcast throughout the Environ with only a 30-minute delay just in case disaster struck and some emergency editing was necessary. To the naked eye, there was nothing unusual about the striations on the skeletal remains, or the pattern of fecal cover.

Lamont and his men had been waiting on the hoverboat for the evidence, and as soon as the divers emerged from the water with the sludgy remains, Malone swaddled the bones in a special "holy blanket" and quickly ushered them into a small safe, followed by bright lights and the watchful eye of the camera. The remains were then shepherded to the church altar, with Surnow's crew in tow. They were wrapped at the altar, where the remains would stay until the mandatory-attendance ceremony at eight that evening.

Josephine was holding court back at her cell, with Lisa and the other True Believers. They watched the monitor like archeologists examining new fossil evidence of an ancient queen.

"They did a good job," Josephine said. "There's no way anyone could tell."

Lisa nearly jumped out of her skin. It was as if someone had stuck a hot poker into her back. She narrowed her eyes at Josephine. "Are you stupid? Or do you want me dead?"

"It's OK," Josephine cooed. "They have all taken an oath, and they know the repercussions of breaking it."

Lisa snapped back, "And what are the repercussions?"

"Permanent exile from the group and, if need be... exile from the Environ."

Lisa's expression went from repugnance to shock. "You may as well kill them."

Josephine shook her head. "Perhaps for some, but others would survive - and some might even find their way to the colony of Psyche."

"That's absurd."

"If they stayed here they would surely be murdered. We all would. At least they would have a chance."

Lamont arrived early at the church, something he never did, but he was anxious to make sure everything went smoothly. Before the doors opened, Surnow and Rush surveyed the altar to find the best angles for the broadcast, which would be viewed as a reminder the following day. And, of course, Rush and Surnow hoped the footage would be traipsed out, cut and re-packaged on the anniversary in some variation for the next 100 years; this might very well be their legacy.

Lamont watched them scramble around, yelling to their crew as if every little thing were the next cure for cancer. He couldn't help smirking. Malone walked in and snuck up on him. "Are you actually smiling?" Malone asked.

"Just look at them. If you squint hard enough, it almost looks like they're wearing berets." Lamont chuckled at his own joke.

Malone pretended to squint. "I just see two guys with tiny dicks."

A quick, hard belly laugh escaped Lamont before he had the chance to rein it in. The crew stopped to look at him, and Surnow turned around with a smile on his face. "I think that's the first time I've ever heard you laugh. What did I miss?"

Lamont shifted his weight and crossed his arms. "Nothing."

Malone chimed in, "I just recited the daily limerick."

Surnow's face soured and he went back to sorting out camera angles and script problems. "You're pretty quick on your feet," Lamont said to Malone.

"That's why you hired me."

The stagehands motioned Lamont and Malone off the altar. Shortly after they moved, down came the crucifixion scrim. Lamont hated this particular backdrop; it was an unnecessarily gory depiction of Christ's final moments, blood streaming out of the wounds on his hands and feet. And instead of the clean line of the spear's entrance point, God's guts spilled as if he had been eviscerated instead of stabbed.

At the stage manager's request, Lamont and Malone moved behind the ghastly scrim. The bright, white stage lights gave the illusion it was solid in front, yet it was completely transparent from the back. It was as if Lamont and Malone were standing on stage, something neither would have relished under normal circumstances, but this perspective would give them a heads-up if anything went wrong.

Rush made a motion and the camera's light turned on. Surnow patted his hair and tugged on the sleeves of his formal jacket. "One, two and… action," Rush said.

Surnow's face contorted into his signature look of false concern. "Reporting live from the Church Room, this is Bill Surnow." He paused for effect.

"Tonight, the final conclusion to our nation's saga, the remains of the crazed mutant woman who poisoned to death all but a handful of Geneco. Tonight we will witness an even greater punishment than her death itself. For as the Lord God himself said in the book of Nahum, 'The LORD is a jealous God, filled with vengeance and wrath. He takes revenge on all who oppose him and furiously destroys his enemies!' "

Surnow sobered his expression even more and said, "Indeed. Indeed…. This has been Bill Surnow, reporting live. Services start at 8 p.m. sharp, formalwear is required."

"And, cut!" Rush yelled. "That's a wrap." Rush hurried to Surnow's side and patted him on the back. "Great work, Bill, such intensity!"

"You really think so?" Surnow replied.

The men's voices became too faint to hear as they walked toward the exit orifice. Once they were out of earshot, Malone said to Lamont, "You don't think they really believe that shit, do you?"

"They'll believe anything if it makes them special."

The stage lights dimmed and Jessie and Sandy Applegate got in place, one behind each curtain, stage left and right. Both had more makeup on than Queen Elizabeth I. Lamont whispered, "It always amazes me how a little bit of fame and a hell of a lot of vanity can castrate and humiliate a man without his knowledge."

Malone snickered.

Moments later the orifice opened and the room filled with all manner of people, from the lowliest commoners - in simple jobs such as housekeeping, education, gardening and childrearing - to the grandest Environ citizens – leaders in banking, accounting and government. The lower classes of women wore simple, gray button-down dresses, just past their knees, and half-moon bonnets. The men wore gray suits. The upper classes dressed in garish colors, dripping in whatever gems, gold and platinum they could afford. The more

they were adorned, the greater their status. It was a vile new custom –
one that offended Lamont's sense of propriety.

The scientists trickled in last, sitting mostly in the back rows
or wedged between people who had stupidly left a seat open between
their party and the next. They came in specially adorned with badges
or metals on their dress lab coats, according to their rank of
importance - much like the ancients dressed the military for special
services. Strauch had decided it would be easier to keep track of them
at church, and this way there could be no sneaking out; and if there
were, the public would believe it was for a legitimate reason.

The role of scientist had taken a strange turn in the Environ –
they were both revered and hated. The Wrath of God Inc., preached
that science was wicked, yet it was science that had saved them and
kept them alive. Despite these obvious facts, there was a growing
movement among zealous church members to downgrade the
importance of science and publicly revile it. The upper classes
pretended to agree, but secretly bribed genetic specialists and
chemists to allow them live longer and provide beauty treatments.

Strauch himself was conflicted on the issue - not because he
truly believed the horseshit fed to the lower classes, but because the
scientists posed the only real threat to his regime. He had been
careful not to let anyone into the Environ unless they had shown
absolute devotion to him and his family. Almost everyone picked,
except the scientists, had familial friendships with the Strauch gang
that spanned generations - even among the lower classes, or "worker
bees," as he referred to them. They had been chosen through the
Strauch network of friends, and friends of friends, or because they
were huge Applegate devotees. After all other posts had been filled
by the highly connected, they were squeezed in for menial tasks. A
few were warned to fake their IQ test scores so they could get in,
Josephine and Lisa chief among them.

The lights in the audience went dim. The stage lights came
up. From stage right, Jessie Applegate bounded like a spry 15-year-
old boy, straight to the center. Behind the altar was the safe
containing Psyche's supposed remains. And the circus began. For
most of it, Lamont stayed focused on the crowd, watching their
reactions to Jessie's and Sandy's overly dramatic presentation.

Sandy was particularly opulent and confident. Her lavender
hair had been deepened to a royal purple and raised in a curly cone
nearly three feet high. Her dress was designed to look modest but

hugged her curves inappropriately. No one had to tell her sex sold; she had figured that out on her own, at the tender age of thirteen.

Lamont couldn't bear to listen to the sermon. Instead, he thought about getting custody of Bryan. The boy's brilliant mind was in danger of being spoiled by his mother's and stepfather's blind faith. It was essential someone carry on Lamont's work and keep the passion for science alive in this forsaken place. It would surely degrade into nothing within a few generations if Strauch and the Applegates had their way.

Jessie struggled to open the safe. He couldn't seem to dial in the right combination on the lock. The energy in the room was fading and he was starting to sweat. He glanced at the scrim and seconds later Malone swaggered out. "Ah, I see God has sent me a helper," Jessie joked to the audience.

Malone nodded his head and in seconds had the safe open, then promptly went back to stand by Lamont's side behind the scrim. Lamont was so locked in on how to win custody of his son he barely noticed Malone had gone until he was back. Lamont could make Tricia look as though she had a drug problem, but that might get her killed. Forget about setting up Dick; the church would protect him, as they had so many times before. No, he had to make them want to give Bryan to him.

The sound of an enormous mallet crunching bones and cracking wood broke Lamont out of his daydream. The site of Jessie smashing the remains of what the audience though was Psyche was so gruesome it would have caused him to vomit, had he not known she was safe at the Collective. Even still, it was nauseating and he focused on the row of people he could study in front. Some looked excited, some cheered, but there were those whose faces had turned green and looked like it was taking everything they could to hold in the contents of their stomachs. Seeing it gave Paul hope for the Environ.

Of course, that was it, he thought. He would convince Tricia and Dick through education and privilege. If Bryan stayed with them, he wouldn't get the same access to the scientific community. He would barter an apprenticeship for his boy with them. If they allowed Bryan to live with him, he would promise to train him to take over the science department. There was no higher position than his, except Strauch's and perhaps the Applegates'. And this would guarantee a higher class of marriage partner. Staying with them would relegate Bryan to the middle ministry class.

Lamont would appeal to Tricia's ambition and Dick's need to be the center of the universe. With Bryan out of their lives, Dick would be her soul focus. It was foolproof. Why hadn't he thought of it before? Lamont wondered, knowing perfectly well it was because he hadn't had a chance to think about any of it until then.

From that point on, Lamont watched the ceremony with a glee he hadn't felt since Bryan's birth. Finally, his boy would come home to him. He had found a way to take back what Tricia had stolen.

Josephine watched the pulverizing of the bones with malice. She and her followers knew the truth, and the absurd and vile spectacle of Jessie Applegate taking a mallet to a batch of digested remains and smashing it to bits - yelling, "Hallelujah!" between breaths and expecting the congregation to parrot him and his sick enthusiasm - twisted her heart to revenge.

She had never intended to let the truth go beyond the True Believers, but now she felt she had to answer God's calling to expand the new religion. Of course, it would have to stay secret and underground. But what good did living do if it meant being complicit in this perverse new world? It was a prison, not a community. The truth had set her free. Let it set all those called to it free. God would be the judge. She would take whatever mortal punishment was meted out by the government. If God wanted to make a martyr out of her, then so be it.

The ceremony didn't last long, and when it was over, victory parties erupted all over the Environ, in the bars and communal areas, privately in people's cells. It was a good excuse to get drunk – a sanctioned excuse, the first communal celebration and holiday where they'd been encouraged to show glee. The bars ran out of their allotments quickly and citizens broke into their private reserves, sharing them with near strangers. The entire Environ was drunk, everyone except for the True Believers who met at Josephine and Herb's cell and quietly meditated on how to grow their movement slowly and without being noticed by the ruling class.

FIFTY-SIX

Ira looked at his wristcom, only half an hour left before he had to meet Tuwa back at the pass, but he was on the right path. He had found more of my discarded clothing and heard rushing water up ahead. The corridor narrowed and he had to crawl through to a ledge that went down onto the bank of an underground stream. There he saw the last item, my underwear, and picked it up. But I was nowhere.

There was no place to go but into the water. He had to face it. I had probably gone into the river, and the current was strong. If I had, my body would have been swept too far downstream by now to ever be recovered. He put a finger in. It was freezing cold. I would have died of hypothermia within the hour. There was no hope I was alive.

It was too late.

He broke down at the water's edge, calling my name. "Psyche!" then, softly, "Psyche." He was helpless. He lost track of time and stayed there, waiting. Other miracles had happened. He prayed I would reappear somehow. They had been so close to saving me. His strength had gone.

About an hour later, he heard a woman's voice calling his name. He sprang up hopeful, filled with joy. "Psyche! Psyche, I'm over here."

Tuwa followed Ira's call for me. She slipped under a series of stalactites and squeezed through the narrow opening that led to the underground river.

Ira's heart sank when Tuwa entered and said, "It's only me." She felt the stabbing pain in his heart as if it were her own. "I'm sorry."

Ira put his hands to his face and bawled. Tuwa held him.

FIFTY-SEVEN

The Environ was quiet again. Things had returned to normal. The only whispering of miracles were those at secret gatherings of the True Believers. They had collected all the transmissions between Malone and Ira and had transcribed them, reading them daily to each other like a book of psalms.

Lamont's plan had gone off without a hitch, as far as the Strauchs and Applegates knew. He worried the True Believers would be found out by trying to convert the wrong person, or would be overheard in conversation about their radical beliefs and turned into one of the bishops. They were on their own now. He couldn't protect them, and he told them so, but he also couldn't stop them.

Tricia and Dick put up a fight to keep Bryan, but gave up when they found out she was pregnant and in danger of losing the baby due to all the stress. Bryan, they agreed for everyone's sake, would be better off with Lamont. Just being in his custody would elevate his status and give him a better chance in life. He had shown no signs of the spiritually devoted and no talent for public speaking, but he did have the same brilliant and questioning mind as his father.

In the end, Tricia let him decide, and he wanted to be with Lamont. It broke her heart, but freed her at the same time – strange, mixed feelings she could never admit to anyone. She and Dick relinquished the fight to stay involved, and when baby Joshua was born, weekend visits dwindled to an end. Bryan, over the years, became so like Lamont that he had no tolerance for his mother's superstitions and his stepfather's manipulations. Besides, they had another son to dote on, and they preferred him, anyhow.

FIFTY-EIGHT

Naomi could feel their eyes on her everywhere she went, and there were whispers, too. When she came into the lab, her workers turned their backs on her, pretending to be working on something too important to talk to her. Worse was when she addressed them and they wouldn't look at her, answering only in monosyllabic grunts. She could feel their hatred. *They blame me for Psyche's death*, that's what she thought.

Ira had stopped attending committee meetings. His excuse was his devotion to teaching the Geney, so that when the cycle of rains stopped they could help with the building of their community. But Naomi knew the real reason; it was to avoid seeing her. Ira had made no secret of his anger toward her or toward Lamont. Early on, after my crossing, he had lashed out at Naomi, calling her a murderess - but he hadn't meant it. In his grief he had yelled at her for opening the door that fateful day, called her Pandora, likened her to Delilah and to Eve, to every known villainess in history. But it wasn't him. It was his pain talking; in his heart of hearts he blamed only himself for not being able to save me.

Naomi had been having terrible nightmares since my murder. In many they started out with a happy reunion with Paul, embracing him and going into a private room to make love - only to find midway through he would get rougher and rougher until his face distorted into that of a demon, horns on his head, claws for hands ripping her flesh apart. She would wake in a cold sweat, heart racing, afraid to go back to sleep. It became impossible to rest, and when she could no longer keep herself awake, if it wasn't the nightmares about Paul there were the other ones of my suffering, her imagination far worse than anything I ever suffered.

And then one day, Steven came home from school and asked her, "Why did you open the door that day?" She had no answer. She had thought about it over and over, but how could she explain to a 10-year-old boy the complicated feelings of a woman's love for a man? Or the trust that comes with loving someone enough to want to be bound forever with him through the legacy of a child? How could a child understand what she herself could not? There was no reason she should have loved Paul the way she had, no good reason. He had done nothing to deserve it. But she had loved him more than perhaps anyone should. All he had given her was heartache, broken promises, lies and empty gestures that went nowhere. When she saw him that day, all the love she had came back and overtook her as it had all those other foolish times. She was a rational woman, and it endlessly vexed her that she had allowed a part of herself to be out of control. Yet she had. She stood wanting to explain all of this to Steven, but couldn't.

"Roger's dad said CAT would have stopped them if you hadn't let them in. That if they hadn't had the element of surprise, we could have taken the Environ people hostage." Naomi stood stunned, dumbly watching Steven. "He said it was all your fault."

Before she knew what happened, her hand made contact with his tiny face. And the slap was so hard it made his ears ring. His cheek swelled to a hand-shaped candy-apple red. His betrayed expression mirrored how she felt. He ran out of their tiny room to hide in the kitchen larder, where he cried himself to sleep among the preserved food.

Naomi stared at her red hand. She had never hit anyone, not even as a child, and never Steven, not so much as a tap. She couldn't believe her own strength, her own anger so beyond her ability to control it, like so many things now. She had made a fool of herself loving and trusting Paul, and now she had wounded the one person in the world whom she loved more than anything. The one person she would have laid her life down for. "What have I become?" she whispered to herself, feeling her grip on sanity ebbing away.

She wanted to go look for Steven but was afraid to see the pain in his eyes reflected back at her. It wasn't just she who had suffered for her mistake. Steven had lost friends because of her. He had come to hate her as everyone else had. And there was nothing worse than seeing hatred in your own child's eyes when all you ever wanted from them was love.

What good was her life now, except to ruin Steven's? If she stayed to be a reminder of Psyche's death, Steven would take on his mother's sins. It was already happening. He was teased at school, had been caught fighting with another boy. Up until Psyche's death he had never had a cross word with another child, as far as she knew.

He had been the model student; now he seemed filled with rage and shame. But if he could have a fresh start, if he could be associated with someone else before anger and shame distorted him, he would have a chance. He was young enough that he might even forget about his real mother. And over time, if he had the right person to raise him, someone like Tuwa, he could blossom.

Naomi reached under her bed and pulled out her personal storage box; inside was a diary she had kept since she had found out about her pregnancy. She resisted the urge to read her past. It was full of too much hope and possibilities that never materialized. She considered burying it so no one would find it, but there wasn't anything scandalous in it and she decided Steven could come to know her through it. Maybe he would even understand one day, forgive her ignorance in love and shameful, foolish belief in promises.

Naomi paged through the small leather book until she found the place where the ink stopped and a clean, yellowed page began. She wrote:

Dearest Steven,

I loved your father, Samuel, very much, and for many years I believed you were very much like him. But as you've grown, I've seen you blossom into a very different young man and realize now what a mistake I made by keeping secrets for so many years. If you have read this far into the journal, by now you know that I had a romantic relationship with Paul Lamont before you were born, during one of the darkest times of my life. Your father had cancer, and in my pain I turned to Paul.

I believed he was a good man and that he would leave his wife. We didn't expect your father to live much longer, but things worked out very differently. Paul decided to stay with Tricia and your father lived through the cancer. I know it wasn't right to betray Samuel when he most needed me, but I was not strong enough, our marriage was still new, and I suppose I felt vulnerable and angry at him for getting sick and leaving me, even if it was through death.

I can't really explain why I did what I did. I have lived alone with the guilt and the shame of it all these years. Your father never found out, for which I was forever thankful, because I never meant to hurt him. The very thought of betraying him now turns my stomach, and I can't believe I could have ever done such a thing to a man as kind as he was. Worse still, I truly loved both your father and Paul Lamont. And I believed both men truly loved me. Paul and I parted out of respect and love for our partners, or so I thought at the time, and not because we didn't love one another. It's very complicated and hard to understand, even for me after all these years of thinking about it.

After seeing Paul again, I realized, you were not Samuel's son but Paul's. I was never sure, -and I guess I wanted to believe you were Samuel's. The timing of my pregnancy always made me suspect it couldn't have been his - your father was going through intensive electric and concentrated radiation treatments, which often have a sterilizing effect. Which is why you have no siblings.
Please don't hate Paul Lamont or blame him for any of this. It wasn't his fault. He is a part of you, and you are a remarkable and wonderful young man. You have his great intellect and even demeanor; you should be proud to be his son.

Understand I love you more than anything, and none of this was your fault. Sometimes circumstances arise and we are like a canoe in a hurricane, struggling to find our bearings and stay on course - but nature will not allow it. Sometimes things happen that are nobody's responsibility - they are just the necessary conclusion to a series of events, and no one can stop them. This was one of those times.

We can't help who we love, no matter how hard we try. I'm sorry for the shame I've caused you and for the heartache I've brought to so many. Please find it in your heart to forgive me. I will always love you.

Naomi shut the journal and left it on her pillow. She went to look for Steven. One of the chefs had discovered the boy in the larder, shortly after he had cried himself to sleep, and had carried him to the daycare room. Naomi found him tucked away from a group of half a dozen teenaged boys who no longer wanted to stay in the family bunkrooms. Naomi kissed his cheek gently and slipped a copy of her most recent will in his shirt pocket.

There was rope in the equipment closet just down the hall. She remembered seeing it there when she had put away the sweeper a few days before. Gingerly, she crept down the empty hallway. It had to be near three in the morning; everyone was asleep and she didn't want to wake them.

The closet was in disarray. The rope was buried behind a toolbox and a year's supply of masking tape. It had been pushed into the deepest dark on the bottom shelf, where she soundlessly cleared a path to it.

It was misty outside, something she hadn't seen since they had first come to Oregon, but mostly she remembered the fog from her girlhood in Massachusetts. She was sure there had been fog in all the other places she had lived, but somehow only the childhood memory was clear.

The cool, wet blanket of mist caressed her skin as if with gentle encouragement. It both comforted her and steeled her resolve. A bright, full Strawberry Moon hung low in the sky. She caught glimpses of it between the thin, swirling gloom. Its light bounced off the white air, giving the night a magical luminescence.

As Naomi journeyed into the forest beyond the scrims, an aberrant intoxication overtook her. The feeling was a surprise. She had expected a heavy inundation of guilt to paralyze her and erase the pain, perhaps even amend her macabre decision.

The construction crew had left a pile of supplies near the pathway to the forthcoming Geney Village. Naomi scavenged around, contemplating a small footstool made of metal, but decided it was too heavy. She grabbed a head lantern and with its light found a plastic bucket full of tools. After emptying it onto the ground, she carried the bucket with her.

Just off the lab's path, some 300 meters from the scrims, was a senescent red alder. Its branches looked hearty enough to hold her without snapping. She tossed the rope around a low-hanging limb and, before she could chicken out, she tied a figure-eight knot - a skill learned from sailing with Paul - and secured the noose around her neck.

Standing on the bucket, she anticipated her impending freedom. She had never been a particularly spiritual or religious woman, preferring to deal with the known world rather than faith.

It had only been in the Collective that she had felt the stirrings of a spiritual side – even still, she had never been convinced of life after death. A part of her hoped there was nothing that she could simply cease to exist and sink into the deep abyss. But if there were a life after this one, she wondered about going to a hell or evil place for what she had to do. Would God or the Great Spirit be able to see her intentions and forgive her weaknesses? Naomi prayed the Creator was the one Tuwa spoke of and not the angry, jealous and spiteful God of her ancestors.

Naomi took up the slack in the rope.

The Collective would be better off. Her death would provide them closure and perhaps a modicum of justice. She had been the citizen of Troy and had opened the door for the wooden horse. And poor Steven would finally have a worthy mother, a woman who could love him with all the strength of her divinity and grace.

She kicked the bucket – her body dropped hard, snapping her neck.

Her vision went white, into a sea of darkness and pop. She was out.

I was waiting near the pathway to the Geney village. At first, she was confused and stood, watching her body swing gently from the branch.

"Naomi," I called. She turned but looked frightened. "Everything is OK. Let me help you."

A powdery shadow clouded her features. "I'm sorry… I'm sorry…" she mumbled again and again.

"Don't be."

"Please forgive me."

I drifted closer and realized it was her guilt and sorrow creating the shadow-play. I grabbed her hand. "All is forgiven." The darkness dissipated. I stared into her clear, bright, brown eyes and said, "Now, come with me. I want to make sure you don't get lost."

She nodded.

We glided through the forest toward a bright, golden light. It appeared whiter and more brilliant the closer we got. I motioned her to it. "But what about you?" she asked.

"I'll be there soon. But right now I have work to do."

Coming from inside the light, a muddle of jubilant male and female voices called, "Naomi!"

I waved goodbye.

She smiled and stepped into the light, where her spirit dissolved into the next world.

FIFTY-NINE

Ira awoke before daybreak, the same time he had every morning since heading the construction crew for the Geney Village. He didn't bother trying to fall back to sleep anymore – it was a waste of time. He threw on jeans and a T-shirt, put on his work boots and went to the utility closet to grab a UV suit. The crew wouldn't be on the job for another two hours. Normally he would eat breakfast and leisurely map out daily assignments, but since the living structure was basically done, he decided to survey the burgeoning village.

Outside, the fog was perched closed to the earth and the sky glowed behind the tree-lined mountains to the east. The UV suits were claustrophobic and he decided to wait until after leaving the scrims to put it on. The air was cool and still unusually fresh. The month-long rains had revitalized the forest and charged the air.

Ira tried to focus on how beautiful the morning was and on his new mission instead of on me. But it was hard when he wasn't surrounded by distractions, either the construction site or the barrage of people who kept a watchful eye on him. Sometimes he pretended I was still alive, just to get through the days; and some late nights he would wander outside, feeling his deep aloneness. By himself, he could weep without worrying someone would try to cheer him up.

The sun popped up behind the mountains. Ira reached the scrims' edge and began putting on his UV suit. But before he could finish, from the corner of his eye he caught a swinging movement coming from the ancient red alder.

At first he thought it was a dummy, or some kind of trick of light. But as he crept toward the tree, he recognized the pale-blue shirt Naomi had worn to dinner the night before. And even though her dark, curly hair should have confirmed it, the sight of a dead body was such a violent shock after so many years outside the ghost cities that his mind played tricks on him.

He grabbed hold of Naomi's midsection and pulled her head out of the noose. Her body was stiff, in rigor mortis, and its surprising weight made him stumble forward and lose control of her.

She slipped to the ground, skull thudding against the soft earth. Her hair tangled under her, giving the illusion of a crown similar to statuary he'd seen of the Goddess Shakti wearing a headdress.

Naomi's face was gruesomely contorted into a twisted snarl. She didn't look real. The sun broke through the trees and he worried she would become severely disfigured from burns if he didn't move her to the scrims soon. He could already feel the hot itch on his own skin, and he didn't want her son to be any more traumatized than he would be after discovering her suicide. He couldn't let Steven's last memory of his mother be like Ira's was of me. With every ounce of strength he had, he dragged her body under the scrims and quickly made his way to the Nest.

The first trickle of breakfasters lined the dining tables. After searching their faces for CAT members, he made his way to Tuwa's bunking room and found her heading out. One look and she knew what had happened.

"Get Robert and a couple of his men to help you move her body to the medical freezers. I'll tell Steven. We can have a service for her in the next few days, once a casket has been built or taken from one of the ghost cities."

Ira was astonished. "How did you know?"

"I saw it last night with spirit eyes. I hoped it was a premonition and I could talk to her today, maybe stop her. But the Great Spirit abided, so it must have been her time to go home."

SIXTY

When the word got out, people mourned Naomi more than she would have ever believed - and no one except Steven grieved more for her loss than the Geney. They understood her guilt because they had shared her burden. They were, however, confounded by the idea of self-annihilation; none had ever heard of such a thing, and it triggered a host of complicated questions Tuwa would field for years to come.

The Geney's notions of an afterlife were still forming, and several stories had competed for potential doctrine. Chief among them was Mountaintop – an Edenic place on the acme of Mount Free. It had been the highest mountain among all the ranges near the mines and was occasionally capped with snow, giving it a mystical quality. They had never seen snow up close. In that legend, no smooth skins existed on Mount Free. There, the Geney played like children while paste (a sort of slop the wranglers fed them monthly) and water ran in plentiful streams.

But now that the Geney were acclimating to freedom and their new home, the myths had been abandoned for the stories and wisdom Tuwa imparted. They made hungry students and learned remarkably quickly. In the short time they had been with the Collective, most had learned the written alphabet; some had learned to read and do simple arithmetic; and all had a basic understanding of mechanical engineering and construction. Ira wondered if their intellectual voraciousness was due to the human mind's need for structure coupled with their utter deprivation of any ideological framework. Whatever it was, he knew they would do fine. Perhaps within as few as five years they could have their own government and become independent from the Collective, if they wished.

It seemed ironic to Ira that the Geney had insisted on scouting a burial location for Naomi's body and demanded to do the hard labor of making a path from the Collective to a clearing they had found approximately two kilometers west. They had wanted to find an area big enough to become a cemetery in years to come.

Freeman Fred had told Ira, "No one must alone forever. When we die, want to keep company."

And indeed, when Ira went to survey the clearing, it was big enough for several generations to be buried there – from what he could tell, a forest fire had burned a hole over a kilometer wide and three kilometers long. Ira figured it must have happened early during the last storm, with a lighting strike before the rains came to snuff it out.

Kevin and Dave volunteered to scavenge one of the ghost cities for a coffin, and it was decided Coos Bay was closest and would do fine. They set off in the morning, took a cherry-wood casket lined with pink satin from the Williams Brothers' Funeral Home, and returned just before lunch was served.

There had been no funeral for me, partly because no body had been found, but mostly because the grisly nature of my murder had been too heart-wrenching for even the most stoic Collective members to publicly mourn. Tuwa had decided to wait and meditate on the proper time and ritual to celebrate my passing. She had given me prayer passage to the next world each time she felt my presence. Each time, the light would come, and I would have to let it pass by because I was not yet ready.

But now that the Collective prepared for Naomi's burial and ceremony, naturally it set off a firestorm of discussion of what to do about me. Among those who hadn't seen my state after coming back from the Environ, there was a small hope I had wandered into the forest and would return. Search parties had spent weeks looking for me, despite Tuwa's insistence that I wasn't lost. She knew. Ira knew. But the people's belief in me gave Ira a minute, irrational glimmer of hope that he clung to in his darkest hours. Tuwa couldn't bear to rip it from him. But now it had been two months, and that tiny flicker of hope had slowly been snuffed, like a candle flame in a covered glass jar. It was time to say goodbye.

Tuwa had found the note written to Steven and a copy of a will, witnessed by a tech just days before Naomi's suicide. It was a simple document, leaving her personal possessions to Steven and Steven's care to Tuwa. And in the event Tuwa didn't want to take guardianship, La Donna was second choice and Fayza third. It was a shock to Tuwa, and she read it several times before it hit her. She wondered why her guides had not told her in spirit vision about

Naomi's wishes, and decided they did not want to influence her
personal decision.

Tuwa had been called to what old-timers referred to as the
Medicine Path before she was old enough to understand its
consequences. There were sacrifices – a husband and children were
some of them. Only once, when she was a young woman, had she
been tempted to stray and marry a man with whom she had
accidentally fallen deeply in love. But fate had stepped in to make her
decision.

After years of unemployment, her fiancé was offered a
research job in Washington D.C. at Digibio, and just before Tuwa
joined him, he contracted Skeleton Plague. It was the first wave of
the disease, and very little was known about it. He was exiled to a
secret research facility. She went to extraordinary lengths to find him,
but wasn't able to get to him before he passed. He died in quarantine,
along with her dreams of a family.

Tuwa spent all day in her meditation room, fasting and
praying and seeking answers from the Great Spirit. Her guides
dictated the service, which she dutifully wrote down and later
committed to memory. But no answer came about Steven. It was as if
both possibilities were on either side of a page - and both were
empty. She couldn't read either future.

It wasn't like the old world, where the rearing of a child was
done in isolation by two parents or, more often, a single mother –
raising a child that way would have been impossible for her. And
Steven was old enough to mostly take care of himself; all he really
needed was someone to love him, guide him.

Tuwa's room wasn't equipped with an extra bed, but she
could have Steven's moved in. It might be strange for him or her to
sleep in the same room as a non-relative. If it was, he could bunk
with the other teenaged boys in the daycare center, or perhaps with
one of the families big enough to have kids in an adjoined room.

And then she realized that if she were going over the
mundane details of where to put Steven's bed, she wanted to be his
parent. She had idealized her own mother, and had always wanted
children from as early as she could remember. Now was her chance.
She suddenly felt a surge of happiness and thanked the Great Spirit
for the gift.

She had planned to grab everything she would need for the ceremony and set up in the Circle Tent, but she was too excited to focus on anything except straightening out Steven's guardianship.

La Donna was coming out of a session with a client when Tuwa found her in the Medical Building. "I'm going to take him."

"You sure?"

"Positive. I've weighed all of it, down to the smallest detail."

"OK, then."

"I'm going to put his bed in my room until he's old enough to complain."

La Donna looked at her watch. "Shouldn't you be getting ready for the ceremony?"

Tuwa nodded. "But I need to get Steven set up."

"I'll take care of it. Samuel and his friends can move the bed. Is there anything else?"

"No."

"OK, then we'd better get it together. Tonight's a big night; people are going to be expecting you to pull out all the stops. Too many people in denial around here – you've got to get them to understand that Psyche is really gone. We need to jumpstart the mourning process so healing can begin."

"I know… Thanks for your help, La Donna."

As Tuwa walked away La Donna shouted after her, "No problem." La Donna mumbled to herself, "I think that's the first time she's let me do her a favor. She's making progress."

It was dusk, and procession was about to begin. All the outside lights were turned on in tribute to the newly dead. Collective members began gathering on the deck, wearing head lanterns and dressed in their finest clothes. The casket was at the entrance of the path and strapped to a cart Ira had jerry-rigged. Robert, Max, Todd, Jack, Dave and Kevin surrounded it. Robert motioned to Max and he began to unstrap it.

"No, hold on," Ira said. "It's perfectly weighted the way it is."

"We're going to carry it," Robert replied.

La Donna stepped onto the deck in a red dress while her husband, Charles, wore a three-piece suit, their kids mirroring their parents in coordinating outfits. As La Donna was brushing lint from Harriet's dress, she spotted Ira and Robert getting into it at the start of the path. "Here, help your brother. I'll be right back." La Donna nudged her way through the crowd.

"The site is two kilometers away. Someone will hurt themselves," Ira said.

"We can handle it."

Ira looked at Kevin. "Does everyone agree with him?"

"It's tradition," Robert spat back.

"Yeah, for the pallbearers to put the casket in the hearse and take it out again at the site. Not to walk it all the way down to the cemetery."

La Donna arrived, out of breath. "OK, everyone put your swords away."

Ira and Robert ignored her completely. "Max, go back to work," Robert commanded.

"No, Max. I'm in charge, and I say no."

"Boys, this is no time for a cockfight," La Donna screeched. "It's a damn funeral! Now get yourselves together and act right."

Ira nodded at her. If they wanted to be macho assholes, then so be it. He turned to the men. "Do whatever you want. They're you're muscles to pull. Why should I care?"

Max finished unstrapping the casket from the cart. The six men took their places at each side and lifted it. Ira forcefully shoved the cart into the dirt. It toppled over and smacked into the mud. Everyone followed the casket except Ira. He marched, away from the crowd. La Donna followed him.

"It's OK to be angry. We all are," La Donna said.

"Sometimes, in the middle of the night, I wake up and reach for her before I remember, oh, yeah she's gone. I needed to pretend she got lost in the forest, but I knew it wasn't true. I knew it. I saw her clothes and the water and still I believed she'd be back. I really did."

"It's all very normal, Ira – everyone goes through denial."

"Each morning I get up early so I don't have to see anyone else and get that look from them."

"What look?" La Donna asked.

"The 'I'm sorry, poor guy,' look. I can't take it. It makes it real and it can't be. I'm afraid I'll end up like Naomi if I take it all in."

"You're not her – you won't."

"How can you be sure?"

"I'm a psychologist. I used to get paid pretty well for those kinds of opinions."

"Seeing Naomi swinging from that tree, it made me so mad. For days I've just wanted to punch someone. And it was going to be Robert, in about three seconds, if you hadn't come along."

The line of mourners was disappearing behind the trees. "We should go," she said. Ira nodded. "But before we do, promise you'll come see me?"

"I will."

They started toward the procession. La Donna said, "I know you've been using the Geney Village as a way to remember Psyche, but it's time to go deeper." La Donna slipped her arm into his. "You're going to be OK. I'll make sure of it."

Several dozen votive candles horseshoed the grave. Tuwa stood behind them and said a prayer:, "Back to the Mother the body goes, up to the Father your spirit soars. Peace will be the land you occupy and love the song of your heart. Great Spirit, bless Naomi's journey to your kingdom." She nodded to the pallbearers.

In unison they answered with a slow and steady walk to the grave, lowering the casket with grace and control only the strongest of men could accomplish. Tuwa went to Steven and said, "Hold open your hands."

She freed one of the medicine bags from around her neck and emptied its contents into his cupped hands. She nodded to Steven and he knelt beside the grave and released the sage, lavender and sweetgrass; by the light of his head lantern, he watched the herbs float in slow motion to the casket six feet below.

Tuwa pulled Steven away. The men threw dirt in leaden rhythm. The sound of it became a stream of softer and weaker thuds until the earth's wound was healed again and Naomi's body was swallowed by the Mother.

The Circle Tent had been erected a few weeks earlier to accommodate the new Geney attendance. The afternoon before the funeral, Tuwa had gone inside and set candles at each direction and replenished the supply of sweetgrass and sage at the altar. The crate of noisemakers and musical supplies had been delivered and left near the main opening. She went through and picked out maracas, shakers, small hand and djembe drums, a couple of flutes, ocarinas and a guitar.

The mourners had stayed behind at the gravesite until the earth burial was complete. But Tuwa had left a little early to ready the Circle Tent. She lit the candles and fired up her wand of sage and sweetgrass. Tuwa walked in a spiraling motion, careful to smudge every inch. When she was satisfied, she laid the wand in a small cast-iron cauldron and sat in the center of the room. She sang a purifying song and a blessing song until she heard voices approaching.

The mourners filed in, each taking an instrument from the pile - except Ira, who grabbed the guitar from its stand. He had been permanently relegated to playing it at Circle after confessing he knew how.

Tuwa pointed and La Donna pounded the same big drum she always did at Circle. Following La Donna came a chorus of djembe drums and small hand drums, shakers and ocarinas. Layered on top of it was Tuwa's clear, strong voice, which climbed to delirious heights.

Tuwa danced clockwise around the center pole, pulling children along with her, and soon parents, CAT members, Geney, techs and anyone so inclined. After nearly an hour of repetitive chanting and impassioned movement, Tuwa pushed harder, encouraging La Donna to speed up the drumbeat. Members followed her frenetic movement to a fevered pitch and into a state of mind where time stood still and the lines between life and death blurred.

This is what I had been waiting for. It was time. I concentrated all my power. "Wind, blow!" I commanded. A gust of air blew the tent flap open. A few people noticed but soon ignored the phenomena.

"Wind, blow!" I shouted.

An enormous gust of cold air shook the tent and swept the members so hard it stopped the ritual. The room went silent and Steven pointed to me. And in concert, Fayza shook herself as if trying to wake from a dream; Marina tilted her head and squinted; Kimi smiled; Hyunae fell to her knees; Xin-Yi gasped; Safia's eyes went wide; Eva took a step backwards; Fayza grabbed Robert's hand; Aine laughed; Zoe covered her mouth; La Donna stared in awe; Ira wept.

"Don't be afraid. Death is not the end. It's just a new beginning," I said. I didn't know if they could hear me. But I did know they were seeing me and I was OK.

My mission was complete.

Tuwa sang a sweet and ancient song in an unfamiliar language. But I knew its meaning. It was prayer passage, a guiding song between the worlds. A bright golden light appeared above me. A collective gasp came from the Circle and I knew they were still watching me.

Instead of avoiding the light, as I had so many times before, I stepped in and all at once a thousand colors burst in every direction...

... Into blinding white light.

I melted into the warmness and love of the All One and rose to the roof of the tent. I was allowed one last glimpse of the people I loved so dearly. Their faces turned upward toward me.

I smiled and let go into the light.

51739699R00171

Made in the USA
San Bernardino, CA
31 July 2017